DETROIT PUBLIC LIBRARY
3 5674 00580315 1

W9-BXM-697

A LIFE IN ORDER

Also by Arthur Hadley

FICTION

Do I Make Myself Clear?

The Joy Wagon

NONFICTION

The Nation's Safety and Arms Control

Power's Human Face

Crisis Now, *as collaborator for General James M. Gavin*

PRODUCED PLAYS

Winterkill

The Four Minute Mile

ARTHUR HADLEY

A Life in Order

NEW YORK THE VIKING PRESS

First published in 1971 by The Viking Press, Inc.

625 Madison Avenue, New York, N.Y. 10022

Published simultaneously in Canada by

The Macmillan Company of Canada Limited

SBN 670-42787-x

Library of Congress catalog card number: 71:146598

Printed in U.S.A. by Vail-Ballou Press, Inc.

Any resemblance of characters in this book to actual persons, living or dead, is unintended and accidental. It is true that some of the places and institutions mentioned, such as New York City, the Congress, etc., do exist—in spite of evidence that they don't. But they are backdrops. The characters are fictional.

For my friends who kept saying, "Write. You can," when "survive" seemed my total.

Especially:

Jane Danish
George Keathley
Adam Kennedy
Nancy and Theodore White
Patricia Zipprodt

Thank you.

If at times my eyes are lenses
through which the brain explores
constellations of feeling
my ears yielding like swinging doors
admit princes to the corridors
into the mind, do not envy me.
I have a beast on my back.

—KEITH DOUGLAS, 1944

A LIFE IN ORDER

Congressman is induced by family tragedy, a love affair, and the unresolved conflicts of his past to abandon politics for painting, while gradually sinking into the abyss of madness.

one

His alarm wrist watch rasped.

"I hate to stop you good people; but I've only fifteen minutes to make my plane."

He pushed back his desk chair; pumped the hands before him; headed for his door. An assistant held out his briefcase. Dent checked its contents as he moved through his outer office. Five constituents still waited there, the last of the forty-seven who had dropped in that day. "I'm sorry I have to run. I'm sure Mr. Davis here, my assistant, can help you." He automatically flashed his smile at them. Often he was told, "It's a great gift to love people the way you do." Most people bored him.

He strode down the marbled corridors of the new House Office Building with brisk purposefulness. A man and a woman approached.

"Aren't you . . . ?" they asked.

"Congressman George Dent. Good to see you people." Handshake. Backslap. Break. The door of the elevator was open, Joyce Farad holding it for him.

"See you Monday, Joyce."

"Have a good weekend, sir."

The door slid shut.

"Goddamn it, George, why do we have to wait for you?" It was Congressman Phil Trout of Maine, known as "speckled Trout," since he had freckles, to distinguish him from Congressman Bob Trout of Georgia, known as "Steelhead." "Steelhead" told friends he got his nickname because of his fighting qualities. That wasn't the reason.

"Ah never mind seeing that secretary." Jack Forman of Tennessee whistled. Dent smiled. Though senior to him, neither of them was important. If they'd been important Joyce, who knew her stuff, would have let the elevator go.

They reached the ground floor. His stomach churned a little and his neck cords tightened as he waited for Trout and Forman to leave the car. They stopped in the door, jawing. Dent pushed through, giving them a wave and a smile as he ducked out the C Street entrance, and into a waiting Air Force car.

Congressman Forman watched him dive through the revolving door. "Our boy Dent's always shoving."

"I do believe there's a New York Senate seat open in sixty."

"How old is he?"

"About thirty-five, maybe forty."

"Too young."

At 4:48 on Thursday the drive to the Washington Airport across the traffic-crammed Potomac River bridges would have taken Dent close to forty minutes. So he didn't go that way. The Air Force car took him to the Potomac yacht basin in four minutes. There a Navy launch waited to pick him up. The launch ferried him across the river in five minutes and nosed into a grassy bank at the north end of the Airport. Dent scrambled up the bank, waved good-by to the launch, jumped into a Federal Aviation Agency car, which raced across the runways to the New York shuttle. He uncoiled from the car, shook the driver's hand, the ramp agent's hand, waved to a couple of porters, took the stairs into the plane two at a time. He'd made it in twelve minutes, thirty seconds; two minutes thirty seconds to spare.

"Welcome aboard, Congressman, we've saved your usual seat in the rear."

"Thank you." Smile again. He settled into his seat and relaxed.

Since Dent was on the Armed Services Committee either the Air Force or the Navy would have been glad to fly him to New York in one of their jets. His Republican predecessor, whom Dent had defeated five and a half years before, had commuted by Air Force jet. Dent had won, in part, because of those flights, tagging his opponent with spending the taxpayers' dollars to fly home to politick. So he paid his own air fare. The cars and the launch were invisible, as was his bypassing the waiting line.

Up front in the cockpit, in the left-hand seat, the command chair of Eastern 667, the 5:00 p.m. shuttle to New York, Captain Arthur McTurk checked the door-closed light, and fired up the inboard starboard engine. McTurk was chief pilot of the airline. He made it his business to fly at least once a year every route of the line and every type of plane they owned, serving his triune God: precision, planning, safety.

Today's route was New York–Washington. At precisely 5:00 p.m. he taxied the Constellation from the gate and lined up behind three other planes at the runway's end, all waiting take-off clearance. Ordinarily there would have been many more planes, but today's foul weather had caused most flights to cancel. McTurk set the parking brake, and began the take-off check. Arthur Rossen, his young copilot, read the check list off to him. McTurk knew the list by heart as he knew by heart the list of every one of the seventeen types of aircraft the company flew. Still he used the list rather than memory. "Planes fly, pilots plan," was McTurk's motto.

A stationary occluded front stretched from Lewiston, Maine, to just south of Washington, with secondary storms running like waves along it. McTurk would be in cold fog, flying on his instruments from four hundred feet above the runway at Washington until LaGuardia. It seemed quite probable to McTurk that before he reached LaGuardia the weather would close that airport. If so he would try Newark, then proceed to Harrisburg, his alternate—no problem.

Twenty-three minutes later the tower released him. "Eastern 667 cleared for take-off."

McTurk was moving before the transmission was finished. The plane started slowly, the propellers biting the fog thick air to hurl whirlpools of water rearward, then the speed grew and they were airborne. At three hundred feet the wingtips became invisible. McTurk shifted frequencies from Tower to Departure Control. Departure vectored McTurk zero eight zero to intercept his course. At four thousand feet Departure changed the vector to zero nine zero and handed McTurk to Center. Seven minutes thirty-two seconds later McTurk hit his first electronic checkpoint on course, on schedule, in place.

Over Pittsburgh at twenty-three thousand feet in the ice-blue upper air, Consolidated 4, jet service from Los Angeles to Idlewild (now Kennedy), began its inbound descent. Below the plane at twelve thousand feet stretched a solid layer of cloud that had been there since the Rockies. Like McTurk in his fog, Captain Dan Parker of Consolidated 4 could locate himself only by the spider web of electronic radio beacons crisscrossing the sky. At present he was watching his right omnirange indicator where a needle slowly traveled from left to right. When that needle reached dead center Parker would be at a pinpoint of sky called Murphysberg intersection; from there he would turn southwest toward Solberg, which he was already tracking on his left omni. After Solberg came Idlewild.

At that instant the right omni needle swung suddenly to the center of the dial and a little red "OFF" flag flashed on the dial's face.

"Shit." His right omni was gone. No danger; he still had the left omni, and if that failed a radio low-range compass and radar vectors from the ground. Still he was going to be a lot busier than he liked, switching his one remaining omni hastily from station to station to get crossbearings and fix himself in the sky. Parker told his copilot to report the omni failure to Traffic Control and Company Headquarters, and began resetting the dial on his remaining omni to identify Murphysberg. Here came the intersection. No sweat. "I love to fly and I love my girl," Dan Parker hummed to himself.

Five days before in the Consolidated hangars at Omaha, Carl Stransky had lain on his back twining upward off the floor where Captain Parker now rested his feet, to replace the right omnirange finder. His hands raised above him into the sharp narrow space behind the instrument panel were tightening the four Allen screws that secured the delicate instrument. His Allen wrench kept slipping. That was because he was using a number seven wrench for number eight screws. Carl knew he should be using an eight; but he couldn't find the sucker. That wrench, about the size of a bent toothpick, was in his left rear pocket, where he'd put it to be sure and remember it.

A bunch of crap taking these things out every thousand hours to check them, Carl thought, just so some white-coated bastard with a college education can collect a soft three hundred a week for brushing off the serial numbers with a little broom. One day I'm gonna bounce one of these fucking omni units off the hangar floor before puttin' it on the inspection truck. Prove those dumb bastards never looked at nothin'. The wrench slipped again. He swore.

Man, he and the boys had really showed those sacks from traffic how to bowl last night. Eight games to two. Hell, three hangar might win the company cup this year. Did he have a head. A blowtorch-full right on top of his neck bone. Yet last night walking home he'd been cold sober. He could sure as shit hold the stuff. It was Alice caused his hangover; not feedin' him any breakfast this morning; just because he'd done a little celebratin' last night. He'd wrap that skillet around his wife's goddamn ears some day.

"Hey, Carl, I got your coffee. You want I should bring it up?" It was Pop, his helper. A nice old guy, just stupid. Still he didn't mind cleanin' up; and he didn't ask questions all day like these wise-ass kids that were always bullshittin' about changing the seniority system.

"Naw, Pop, I'm through." The wrench slipped again, skinning his fingers. Fuck it, that omni was in solid. He rolled out from beneath the instrument panel.

Three other great jets stood in the hangar beside the one on which he was working, looking strangely vulnerable with unaccustomed parts of their bodies removed for human handling. Stransky sat down on the steps leading up to the plane and Pop handed him his container of coffee.

"Jesus!" He started up, spilling his coffee. Something had pricked him in the ass. It was the number eight wrench. "I was lookin' all over for this little sucker up there."

"You get through?"

"Yeah. Roll up my work light will you, Pop."

In her one-room apartment in what legend refers to as New York's swinging East Fifties Sonia Oliphant, Dan Parker's girl, sat in her bath and soaped her twenty-five-year-old softness. She was using a large; real sponge to lather her bath oil; much too expensive she thought, but it felt so wonderful. She considered again the black sheath dress she was going to wear. Dan hadn't seen it yet. Dan had three days and nights in New York. She had no flights for three days. They'd be together. Her breath caught. There's beer in the icebox, and chicken breasts and tomatoes, if we just go to bed and don't get to dinner. She laughed because that idea was still a little frightening. You're becoming a woman, Sonia, she thought.

She and Captain Parker had been going together for eight months. Four weeks ago they'd become engaged. They were both from Toledo. They both flew with Consolidated. They were looking for a house in the Los Angeles suburbs, and they'd decided on three children.

George Dent sat in the rear row of plane seats because accident reports showed those near the tail had the greatest chance of survival. He'd put a pillow and a magazine between himself and his seat belt to widen his belt area and lessen possible damage to his kidneys. He didn't expect trouble, but this was a rough stinking flight. Already several passengers near him in the rear, where the motion was most acute, had vomited. And they looked like seasoned travelers, men and a few women on a schedule like his own, who flew in any weather.

Dent amused himself, as he often did in spare moments, by sketching. It gave him a pleasant feeling of successful cheating. His briefcase carried a mass of mail and a report on the Lower Manhattan Expressway he ought to read. But he liked to draw; particularly caricatures of people. God forbid some of his colleagues should see how he'd rendered them. Right now he was transforming the businessman studying reports three rows ahead into a timidly rapacious mole.

Dent put down his notebook and rechecked his watch. They were already half an hour late. Maybe the pilot could radio a message. No, he thought, my delay's not that important. Besides, they might not even be able to land at LaGuardia.

McTurk, waiting for the planes ahead of him to attempt landings, held flight 667 in its precise segment of sky, a rectangle with a base one minute long at an altitude of six thousand feet. The rectangle's northeastern tip was the intersection of two omnirange beams, one from Colts Neck, the other from LaGuardia, labeled on aeronautical charts as Red Bank. To McTurk, Red Bank was far more than an abstract electronic intersection; it was a definite piece of sky nine miles southwest of LaGuardia, twelve miles west of Idlewild, and ten miles east of Newark. Level, turn, level, turn, level, turn, account for turbulence and crosswind; his two omni needles recentered as he arrived precisely back at his beginning, then turned outbound again.

Descending over eastern New Jersey, Consolidated 4 received the next command to move it towards safe touchdown at Idlewild.

"Consolidated 4, Idlewild approach." Parker readied himself to receive a command. "Proceed direct Bansonville; hold there at six thousand. Expect further clearance at 2432."

"Consolidated 4," replied Parker, acknowledging the command. Only Parker hadn't heard "Bansonville." He'd heard ". . . anson" and then static. But he knew what that was. He smiled. "That was Ansonia." He'd held there before, familiar electronic country. He smiled again and thought of his girl, Sonia, as he reset the one omni, banked the airplane, checked his map, adjusted four throttles, noted the compass heading, and switched the omni again.

Parker was meant to repeat back the order. Control was supposed to make him. But they were both rushed. Consolidated 4 descended to six thousand feet and headed for Ansonia.

Tonight no other planes held at Ansonia. For the extreme northwest portion of the one-minute square around Ansonia slightly overlapped the southeast corner of the one-minute square around Red Bank. McTurk still held at Red Bank at six thousand feet.

If you flip a dime long enough.

There was a great deal of air around the two planes. To meet they had to occupy at precisely the same time and altitude an identical point in a field of fog four hundred square miles wide. Three times the two blind planes turned toward each other in the murk and closed at their combined speeds of seven hundred miles an hour. They never came close. They wheeled around each other and turned away; McTurk back to Red Bank, Parker to Ansonia. At any moment Idlewild Approach Control's radar would see Parker off course; question him, and set him right. At any moment LaGuardia's radar would note another blip on its screen converging on McTurk; investigate it, and warn him. Bucking and skidding, the two planes turned toward each other again; danced around each other; and parted.

McTurk held Eastern 667 on course with automatic gentleness. "Great planes, these Connies," he yelled at Rossen. Rossen nodded. He wanted to fly jets. Over McTurk's earphones came the rapid sound of his world in order, other pilots performing their complex minuets of survival.

"American 502, outer marker."

"United 27, holding Riverhead, five thousand, at two zero."

"Consolidated 42, cleared direct Cobra."

"Cessna 679, left turn, zero-four-zero, maintain three."

"Clipper 86, Center now: one-twenty-one point five."

McTurk began another right turn.

Parker began another right turn. Damn the wind drift and the one omni, he was about two miles south of where he should be. LaGuardia Approach noticed the two blips coming together; and decided to check with Idlewild. But he didn't hurry. He figured the other blip for a jet at high altitude. He knew no planes could be close to McTurk because regulations said they would not be.

Suddenly the night flamed red around McTurk.

The Constellation staggered. Lurched down. Flopped over on its back like a child's toy thrown in anger. The port wing had nicked the jet's tail. The last ten feet were in shreds. The outer port engine fell. The inner one windmilled wildly: kicking, knocking, rocking, tearing the plane apart.

Explosion of gas.

Fall.

Fire.

End.

Hung from his seat belt upside down; right left; left right; down up; in solid black; on fire; crippled; falling; McTurk remained certain of his plane, his location, himself. No time lost checking instruments that might no longer work, trying desperately, this altitude, that throttle setting, adjusting, experimenting. Instead, his left hand and feet forced ailerons, elevators, and rudder into the marginally possible ritual that might just check the falling plane. His right stabbed through the dark again and again, a furious cobra, to hit in precise order fire switches, fuel boosters, throttles, pitch control, trim tabs, tank switches.

Consolidated 4 hit the Jersey marshes. Exploded. All dead. Sonia's father had wanted to call her Alice.

With the last ten feet of its left wing gone, the outer left engine fallen, the inner one dead and on fire, the two right at full power, Eastern 667 steadied, the nose came up. McTurk's left thumb pressed the control column mike button.

"Mayday. Mayday. Eastern 667. Hit by jet. Both left engines gone. Am proceeding LaGuardia at two thousand feet." His voice could be asking for a ham sandwich.

McTurk's equation was blindingly simple. If with each mile he flew he dropped eighty feet, he would die. If with each mile he flew he dropped seventy feet he would live. This was true only if he was precisely where he believed and on the exact course. To have to turn would kill him.

The plane gave him his chance. For American airplanes are not like American cars, yet, constructed of cost accounting, consumer surveys, advertising, feather-bedding, and tinsel to draw envy from the neighbors and kill the driver. Now the extra metal in the wing held, the extra lines in the fire extinguisher functioned; the backup booster pumps caught, the fire died, the starboard engines performed. Two engines doing the work of four, pawing up the night, flaming, roaring, kicking, exploding, shaking, delivering.

LaGuardia Approach confirmed McTurk's position. Cleared the sky for him.

Come on horses, McTurk thought, buy me the moon: another hundred yards before I fall a foot. Come on horses, buy me the sun: another thousand yards before I fall ten feet. Come on horses, buy me the stars: three thousand yards before I fall fifty feet. Come on horses!

Eastern 667 clawed toward LaGuardia with the aerodynamic grace of a heaved brick. Crippled. Staggering. On one side the overpowering engine roar. On the other the frightful silence. LaGuardia reported the ceiling two hundred feet, the visibility one-quarter mile. Rossen looked out his window. Nothing but black.

In the plane's rear George Dent leaned forward against the back of the chair in front of him, his head cradled in his arms.

The nearest emergency exit was two rows up on his right. He mentally ran through the instructions: rip off the cover; pull out the handle; and turn it left—remember, left. His necktie he'd already yanked off. Now he reached down and unlaced his shoes, they might hit the water. He began to curse himself: Idiot to fly in this weather, stupid, blind idiot, to kill yourself for something you don't care about. Outside his window he saw a flash of light. An Esso station. Christ they were low. Recradling his head in his arms, he braced himself.

McTurk saw the Esso station, beyond it should be a parking lot, then an H-shaped building. They came up in that order. He was within a hundred feet of where he supposed. His altimeter read 230 feet. He didn't have 230 feet. He had closer to 190. He wasn't home yet.

Here came the approach lights. About a mile and he had eighty feet. Next, the parkway and beyond a small hill. A quarter mile and thirty feet. The boundary fence. Would he?

His right hand struck again, cutting the two remaining engines. The plane settled on its belly, screeched across a concrete runway in a shower of sparks, hit the mud between two runways, pivoted, caught, spun around, hit another stretch of concrete, tearing, sparking, slowing. McTurk could see the flashing lights of the fire trucks converging on them. Silence. The plane stopped.

"Rossen, get back there and get that back door open."

His copilot pushed out of his chair, opened the cockpit door, and passed into the cabin. "You go help him," said McTurk to the flight engineer. He shut the cabin door after them. He wanted to be alone. In a few instants, the fire trucks would be alongside to smother them with foam. A small boy's smile suddenly transformed him from exhausted pilot to prankish elf. Were his radios still working? He pushed his mike switch.

"Eastern 667 is on the ground."

Silence. Then from the listening air, breaking every Federal regulation, a personal question: "That you, Turkey?"

McTurk recognized the voice: Red Bill Wooster with United. They'd barnstormed together with a wing-walking act in the twenties.

"Yeough," he answered.

Then the white CO_2 foam from the fire engines seethed over the plane which lay beneath it broken, an amputated leg in a bubble bath.

Now on the ground small, scared men began to shovel dirt over the truth to protect themselves and their kingdoms. The radar operators at LaGuardia and Idlewild realized their future depended on their plane having held at the right place. Wrenching their memories to protect their skins, they marshaled subordinates and friends to swear that Eastern 667 had been at Red Bank (true) and that Consolidated 4 had been at Bansonville (false). Pete McNab, head of the pilots' union, hearing of the crash on his radio, was already rehearsing a speech denouncing the airlines for carelessness and demanding more money for his "brave knights of the sky."

Both Eastern and Consolidated ordered squads of lawyers and public relations men to get the hell out to LaGuardia and Idlewild and stick the other guy with the crash. In Washington the Chief of the Federal Aviation Agency wondered if he dared point to Congress as the cause, for cutting his funds, or if his agency would get the blame.

Sonia Oliphant, her hair carefully protected by a bandanna, was dressing when the radio music stopped and the bulletin came on. Hands raised, trapped in the dark of her new dress, she heard. Automatically she kept dressing. Then she sat on her bed and looked at the cracked white wall of her apartment. The building was only two years old but built cheap and quick to grab rents fast. Already it was crumbling. The next bulletin came on, mentioning Parker by name. She got into bed; pulled the covers over her head; and shook. Why him, oh God, she sobbed over and over, why him?

Dent had the door open. The instant the plane stopped he jackknifed for the exit, grabbing two other men to help provide more muscle. By the time Rossen could work his way back to the door, Dent was handing people onto the firemen's ladders that had been raised against the plane.

"Take it easy; don't worry; there's plenty of time." If fire broke out he was well positioned to leap himself.

Rossen came over to help him.

"Why don't you take one stewardess," said Dent, "and open up one of the emergency exits. Help people out there."

"Good idea," said Rossen. That couldn't be the pilot, thought Dent. He's too shaken to have brought us in.

Several firemen entered to carry out three badly hurt passengers. Then Dent was alone in the cabin with Rossen. He looked around. The plane appeared a little messier than normal, as if the passengers had thrown a drunken farewell party, otherwise all was as usual. Now that the danger was over Dent began to tremble. He smiled as he went back to recover his briefcase. That was the way he had been in combat, afraid after the action was over.

The door of the pilot's compartment opened and a gray-haired, weathered man swung out. Dent went up the aisle to meet him.

"Congressman George Dent," he said. "Thank you, Captain."

"Yeah," McTurk lowered his eyes, embarrassed. What with the press, boards, reports, and investigations he probably wouldn't get in any solid flying for three months.

"Do you know what happened?"

"We got hit," said McTurk.

"The other plane?"

McTurk hunched up and shrugged, then politely indicated the exit. Dent recognized the silence. The hostility of those in the action toward those who tried to horn in. He started out of the plane; then paused and turned back.

"Not to interfere, but a lot of passengers climbed out so fast they left all this luggage." He waved his hand around the plane. "My admiration for our brave fire fighters is limitless, but I'd leave somebody in here."

"You're right," said McTurk. "There's always a son-of-a-bitch. Rossen, stay aboard till a company agent gets here." McTurk stuck out his hand to Dent. "Arthur McTurk," he said.

In the terminal Dent stood a bit apart, watching his fellow passengers explain to everyone present, or those they were telephoning, garbled details of the greatest event since the flood, their survival.

"It was the hand of God," a man said to Dent, "the hand of God."

"Which hand?" asked Dent. The man backed off.

Dent looked at his watch. He had to get moving. He could still make the end of the Citywide Reform Democrats Dinner; and look in at the Kips Bay Democratic Club meeting. Sarah would have to handle her fund-raising party for the Galesville Home for Boys without him. But first he needed to know more about the accident. He'd be interviewed about the crash, in fact he'd make certain he was; and he couldn't sound like just another dopey bystander.

Dent turned, pushed through the crowd, and buttonholed a company lawyer.

"I'm Congressman George Dent. Could you take me someplace where I could learn what happened in this accident?"

"What alleged accident would your question be in reference to, sir?" Dent restrained his impulse to bust the young man in his Wall Street-shined teeth.

"What's your name?" he asked.

The young lawyer heard the tone and paused. Someone had just threatened him personally.

"Frederick Martin, sir."

"All right, Fred, let's find your boss."

Dent soon arrived at a layer of officialdom where the danger to the airline of a hostile Congressman was immediately recognized. He was escorted into a conference room beneath the tower.

There were a great many people in the room, dictating to secretaries, talking on phones, arguing, staring at a large map. Dent saw McTurk sitting at the far side of the room, totally immobile except for his hands, which kept playing with his flight bag. He was flanked by a soft phalanx of lawyers. Is truth so dangerous and difficult in America, Dent wondered, that there must always be a team of lawyers around to soften and interpret?

McTurk was furious. Company officers had wanted him to dictate an immediate statement. He wanted to call his younger sister, who lived alone in New York City. He'd called his sister.

Now, his statement finished, he was looking for a chance to duck out. Would the Congressman slow things down or speed them up?

Dent was introduced to some official whose name and title he didn't catch.

"What happened to the other plane?" he asked.

"It's down in the Jersey marshes, Congressman, seven miles northeast of Newark. I'm afraid there're no survivors."

Jesus, thought Dent, once again, Dent, you are here and they are there. All those people on the ground in the absurd broken-marionette positions of the dead.

"Poor bastards." He saw shock on the faces around him at the look of a taboo word about the dead. "Do we know why?"

"That may take days, sir. We believe Captain McTurk was in his assigned airspace. But Idlewild claims their ship was on course too."

"Can't you figure that out from where the jet fell?"

"We believe so. And we believe the evidence indicates the jet was off course. But that's a highly tentative conclusion. However, our flight recorder is intact and that should indicate exactly where our flight was. Can we do anything more for you, sir?"

Dent realized he was being told that while he could stick around if he wanted, he was in the way. He appreciated the politeness. He was on a level where he could deal.

"No. No, if that's all you know, that's ample for me."

"Also Congressman, and by the way I understand that you

were the one who opened the rear door and began helping out the passengers, we appreciate that, I believe you met your pilot. Arthur McTurk is our senior pilot. He was flying your route today as part of his company responsibility. He has a rather awesome record, for precision."

That's why I'm alive, thought Dent. I'd like to talk to that man, but he's probably tired.

Across the room, McTurk gazed at Dent out of two eyes of pure blue. The Congressman didn't seem such a bad guy. He was more concerned with the other plane than himself. Suppose he left with the Congressman? Got free of these people that way? And the Congressman could answer the reporters' questions.

McTurk rose and went toward Dent.

"Thanks for helping the passengers out, Congressman."

"You're thanking the wrong man, Captain McTurk. Say, there are a lot of press outside. How about going out there with me? Fielding the questions together? I'd like your help."

"I was hoping you'd answer them. I don't like . . ." McTurk left the rest unsaid.

"A shy pilot and a shy Congressman. Don't tell anybody." Dent turned to the group. "Well, thank you all. —If there's one suggestion I might make. I'd get any tapes and records you have of the event under lock and key, sealed, so no one can claim tampering. And I'd have Idlewild do the same. Not that anyone would." He smiled reassurance. "But it looks better later." He hauled a white file card out of his right pocket and a pen from his jacket. "Now if you'd give me a name and number I could call for information tomorrow, I'll get out of your hair."

They did. He and McTurk went out to face the press, followed by a clutch of nervous PR men and lawyers.

The press closed in around them. What had caused the collision? McTurk repeated he didn't know. He was certain he had been in his assigned air space. But probably the other fellow thought so too. Maybe they both were. His left wing had hit another plane. He had brought his ship in. —Had it been close? —It wasn't routine. McTurk clammed up.

The press switched to Dent, who maneuvered himself slightly forward to where the TV cameras had an unobstructed view. He began by praising McTurk's great skill in bringing in the stricken plane. He stressed it was impossible to pinpoint the cause of the collision this soon; and pledged himself to stick with the investigation until all the facts were known; and the air safer for everyone. He closed by recalling the dead on the other plane: they were the real tragedy.

That satisfied the press and he and McTurk were able to thread their way past the notebooks and TV cameras. Again he pulled a file card from his pocket to write himself a note. Perhaps he could get the Speaker of the House to form a select committee on air safety with himself on it. There'd be good press mileage in that. As he made the note he gritted his teeth at the necessity of trading on the dead. Suddenly he turned to McTurk.

"McTurk, let me buy you dinner. I know it sounds crazy. Believe me, I don't want to pump you with questions or hero worship. But I've got a lot of places to go tonight and I suddenly don't want to go. If I eat alone it will look funny. You're my excuse. Besides I'd like to talk to you."

McTurk nodded. "I'd like to, Congressman; but I can't. I called my sister and she's already on her way out to Long Island to see me. Besides, I'm bushed."

"I understand." Unconsciously Dent drew in his breath and got his set smile back in place. "I'll just have to listen to all that stuff about fate and the hand of God. So long."

"Come out to my place," said McTurk. Dent started to protest. "I don't have to ask. I've got some great steaks in the freezer that a friend flies in from Kansas City."

Dent hesitated another instant. Would he be intruding?

"I'd love to. —I get called Dent."

"Turkey."

They shook hands again. Then both looked at their watches.

"My God, my wife." Dent smote himself on the forehead with the palm of his right hand. "How could I forget her? She may have heard something on the radio, or someone may have phoned, and she'll be worried sick. —I'll be right back." He sprinted off toward a phone booth.

Sarah was at the table in the middle of her dinner party. The maid from the catering service didn't recognize his name or who he was, and he had a hard time getting through. He was quite high from the excitement of being alive and about to play hookey. Sarah came on with normal voice.

"Love-dove, I'm right in the middle of dinner. I hope it's important. Are you on your way up? The Van Devenders are here. And the Hughes who contributed two thousand five hundred to your last campaign, and . . ."

"Sarah, I'm calling because I've been in an air crash."

"A what?"

"An air crash. But I'm all right. Not hurt a bit. So don't worry. But I'm going to be late, because I want to stay around and find out what happened."

"Where are you?"

"At LaGuardia."

"You're going to miss the Citywide Reform Democrats Dinner!"

"Yes."

"They're awfully important."

"I know, conscience, and thank you; but I ought to stay here and talk to the pilot; and other things. I'll see you later. Don't wait for me. Have a good dinner."

"Thank you for calling, love-dove. I'm sure everyone will be glad to know you're safe. Was it a bad crash? Will you be on television? Can I call the Dinner for you and make your apologies?"

"That would be wonderful, Sarah. I made a statement on camera. I don't know if it will be aired."

"We'll all watch the ten-o'clock news. You take too many chances, love-dove."

"Good-by, Sarah."

"You're missing a good dinner."

"I know. Good-by."

two

The fog was lower now, shedding rain. Trapped beneath the oily stratus the industrial stink of Long Island slithered over McTurk's sports car. The two men drove in silence; both turned inward replaying mental tapes of the crash.

Almost my end, thought Dent. Once again so close. He could feel the lurch of the plane, the slam of his body against the seat belt, hear the total change in sound, his being suddenly levered open by the frightful knowledge: I am going to die.

Then he had felt the plane check and began to hope. He had not known with absolute certainty he would die. Not like the time before. Then too he'd been upside down, floating through the air beside his fragmenting jeep. He had passed so far outside his body that he could view himself twisting through the air in slow motion with the rest of the world almost still, coming toward him from incredibly far away, as if seen through the wrong end of a telescope. Bits of torn jeep and landmine that should be moving too fast to see glided and tumbled about him with slow liquid grace, outlined in a pulsing blue haze.

He flopped, broken, through the air down a long tube of time. He knew when he hit the end there would be nothing. He would be dead. He was so absolutely sure of this that when he finally woke into a streaky red-white light his first incredible thought was not: "I am alive"; but: "I'm dead and this is what it's like."

Then the fog about him began to shred and the knowledge he was alive seeped in.

He was on his back. He wanted to sit up and see how badly he was hurt; but could not move. He gathered his will and managed to raise his neck and part of his trunk. He looked down along his body and saw his right leg. It was twisted up beside him, the back of his tank-boot heel touching the front of his knee cap. My leg's off, he thought. Bemused, he inched up a bit further and reached forward with his right hand to throw the useless leg away. He expected it to come apart at the knee. He grabbed the boot, noticing it was completely undamaged, and weakly tugged. His leg moved but stayed attached to himself somewhere inside his pants. Try two hands, he ordered himself. His left arm would not move. It looked normal, but it wouldn't move, not even the fingers.

Pain had not hit him yet, the effect of shock still all numbing. Exhausted, he collapsed back on the dirt.

Sprawled there he saw the remains of his jeep. Blended into the scrambled metal was Triculo, his driver. —They'll come and finish you off, he thought in panic. They'll come and finish you off. Frantic, he worked his forty-five out of his shoulder holster. But he had no round in his pistol's chamber. With one hand he couldn't load it to fire. If they came, he was finished. And he was alone. He had been jeeping over to A company to see why they weren't moving faster. Taking his jeep and not his tank because he was in a hurry. The mine wouldn't have hurt him in his tank.

Then he noticed that the edges of the world in which he lay had started to turn gray.

Again he fought his trunk upright to inspect himself. About his twisted leg his combat pants showed the stain no words can describe. The wet grew as he watched. You're bleeding to death. Alone. Savaged. Bleeding to death.

"Oh, God," he called with all the strength of his inner shout. "O God, I don't want to die now. Not now. Not now. Save me."

They had crossed the Rhine. They were almost highballing toward the Elbe. The war was closing to its end. A late spring was coming, though it was still cold. "I don't want to die now, God. Not now."

The total truth exploded in him. God would have nothing to do with it. He had not believed in God before. He did not now. He would save himself or die. That thought was cold, deathly cold, but it triggered energy. He began to function.

To stop the bleeding he needed a tourniquet. His belt. His belt was on his pants. Over his pants was his sweater. Over his sweater was his British army leather vest. Over the vest were his combat pants, their tops came up to his chest and were held by suspenders. Over his combat pants was his outermost layer, his combat jacket. He had to unzip his combat jacket; unfasten his suspenders, lower his combat pants, raise the British leather vest, raise his sweater. Then he could unfasten his belt; take it off; and make a tourniquet. My, I'm thinking clearly, he thought, conscious that actually he was thinking very fuzzily, putting out thoughts with great effort from another world, probably too slowly to save his life.

He reached up his right hand and began to unzip his combat jacket. The zipper jammed. He burst into tears as he tugged. Useless. Whatever had damaged his left arm and shoulder had so shredded his combat jacket the zipper wouldn't move. Not from a jammed zipper, he thought. Not die from a jammed zipper. No.

Then he remembered his pocket knife. That was in his trouser pocket. There was a special opening in the right leg of his combat pants that let him reach into his right-hand trouser pocket where he kept his knife. With his knife he could cut open the combat jacket and cut the suspenders. But if you can get at your knife that way you can get at your belt that way. —What clarity of thought! But again he knew he should have thought of the opening in his combat pants long ago.

Panting, he reached for and zipped down the opening in the leg of his combat pants. He put his hand in, burrowed under his leather vest and sweater, and felt up the leg of his flannel pants toward his waist. He couldn't reach his belt. His arm, swollen by combat jacket and sweater, would not permit his hand to reach through the opening far enough.

I'm going to die, he whined, the tears starting down his face—I'm going to die because some goddamn fucking civilian hasn't made the opening big enough. Some civilian draft-dodging quartermaster bastard has killed me with a small pocket.

He remembered his knife again. He could still cut open the front of his combat jacket, get at his belt that way. As he started to worm his hand into his trouser pocket he saw his pistol lying beside him. It's getting dirty, he thought. Then, my shoulder holster! He could much easier slip the harness of his shoulder holster over his leg for a tourniquet. How clever, he thought, again knowing at the same moment that he should have remembered his holster first; that perhaps it was now too late.

He worked the shoulder holster down over his limp left arm, wondering again what was wrong with it. He could wriggle the fingers of it now; but it still wouldn't move. He tried to slip the loop of the holster over his lifeless foot; but he couldn't sit up far enough to do this one-handed. He put the holster on the ground beside him and tugged the bottom part of the leg around to where he could reach the sole of his boot. Then he was able to slip the loop of the holster around his foot and drag it under. His foot looked both funny and frightening, flopping around at the end of his pants without life.

Now the edges of his world were turning black behind the gray and compressing. He sank back on the ground to rest. After a few moments he worked back into his half-sitting position, got a grip on his forty-five, shoved it between the loop of his shoulder holster and his thigh; and began to twist to tighten the crude tourniquet. His breath came in great gasps of effort. The small world in which he yet lived narrowed frighteningly. The dark borders lunged in, then pulled back, then lunged in again; shrank him; squeezed him, a tiny point of light. His pistol as he tried to twist it came up and down at him floating on slow gray waves. Up; down. Then the black slammed over him. He crumpled. Drowned into dark.

Later he surfaced for a brief instant to hear one of his own medics say, "To hell with the morphine. He don't feel nothin'. Get him plasma."

When he came to again he was outside the safety of his own outfit, in an ambulance, in great pain. The medic in back with him and the driver were shouting over who would get his precious tank boots.

The lurch of the ambulance, the lurch of the plane, the sway of McTurk's sports car separated into different motions. Once again he had been saved. Why me? Why had he survived? In the immediate postwar years he had chewed that question over and over, recognizing the problem as meaningless, even stupidly romantic, yet unable to escape the question's burden.

"Just another four-tenths of a mile," McTurk said.

They pulled into McTurk's driveway and stopped before his garage. The front door yanked open and a slim figure rushed out into the light.

"Turkey, Turkey, you're all right. Oh, Turkey, love, you're all right." The woman threw her arms about McTurk and leaned her head against his—she was a bit taller than he—sobbing, with relief.

McTurk held her tenderly. "Now, Dee, it's okay."

"The risks you take, Turkey," she stopped, just holding him, then slowly dropped her arms, noticing Dent.

"Dee, this is Congressman George Dent. He had to go someplace where they'd ask him a lot of fool questions. So I brought him here to hide. The steak big enough for three?"

"Oh, yes. And I brought spaghetti and clams out with me."

"I get spoiled rotten," McTurk said happily.

George Dent stuck out his hand. "It's a pleasure to see a brother and sister who act like brother and sister."

"I don't have much else," said Dee, hugging McTurk again.

They entered the house and while Turkey made drinks Dent looked with delight around Turkey's den-library. How his son Jim would love the room. Models of planes, pictures of planes, and books on flying jammed the shelves. Hung anywhere they would fit were pictures of McTurk with the great and near great. Autographed greetings and thanks from President Eisenhower, Winston Churchill, Marilyn Monroe, Knute Rockne, Franklin D. Roosevelt, Will Rogers, John L. Lewis, General George C. Marshall, the New York Yankees, and a host of other makers and shakers.

But the places of honor, eye-level around the fireplace, or next to the models, were given to older, faded photographs. In these pictures McTurk was hard to single out: another freckle-faced, boyish grin among groups of young men poised before machines that were by now almost unrecognizable as airplanes. In one group of six before a patchwork biplane, two of the kids in flying helmets and goggles had no shoes. Was the towheaded boy in another photo propping Turkey's plane the "Lone Eagle" himself? McTurk's first pilot's license was also framed and hung. Dent looked closely. Signed by Orville Wright. Was America that young?

How profoundly different the faces in these pictures, thought Dent, from those around the first nuclear reactor beneath Stagg Field, or the men in the bunker at Los Alamos. Here rested the old simple world of heads or tails, guts or chicken, right or wrong—a boy and his oil can setting out to make his mark.

Over the fireplace hung a truly remarkable oil of McTurk. Dent had expected a better than average noble-aviator-peering-into-the-blue. But this hard-edged portrait, done in a modified pointillist technique, could hold its own in any modern gallery. And the artist had understood McTurk, the scramble of pilot, executive, and pixie. Dent knew a good deal about contemporary American art, indeed the protection and sponsorship of art and ideas was an important part of his political image. So he studied the picture closely. But the signature on the portrait—"D.M. '54."—meant nothing.

McTurk lit a fire and they relaxed, drinking slowly, Dent and Turkey their bourbon, Dee a martini on the rocks. McTurk began to unwind, describing the accident and the moments just before as he'd felt them, the big picture plus the fascinating small details. "All my flying life other pilots have laughed at me, and some of the young ones gotten mad, because I won't allow coffee in the cockpit during instrument weather. Suppose I'd had a cup of hot coffee in my face tonight."

He's lucky, thought Dent. The coffeeless years have been proved correct. But suppose the crash hadn't happened, or McTurk had been killed anyway, all he'd have would be a lifetime of something missed. He watched Dee deftly rise, make them another drink, glide into the kitchen and return. What was the emotion she showed toward Turkey? It wasn't quite love; certainly not just relief. He had it: hero worship, mature variety.

"Come on, you two men," said Dee. "It's late. Come with me into the kitchen while I finish cooking."

Dent followed them. He noticed that the first strong whiff of food brought instant hunger and that he wasn't tired any more. He'd been wise to come. To have to sit at a boring political dinner and swallow lumpy mashed potatoes while being properly humble about "a brush with death" would have made him explode.

He watched Dee move about the kitchen, place the steak in a preheated grill, give the salad to Turkey to toss, drain the spaghetti, taste and stir the clam sauce, check the steak, then flip it over with a satisfied smile. What did she do, Dent wondered? With that energy and organization she was probably some sort of executive: sales, advertising? But she didn't seem that lotioned, or tight; and her dress, black legs under a sort of chamois skirt and thin black sweater, seemed too casual. She certainly was having a ball cooking. And great legs. Sarah's were good; but these were timeless.

Dee shot him a quick glance and Dent shifted his eyes hastily. He'd been staring without realizing it and gotten caught. He sloshed the ice around in his glass, eyeing it intently, as if his drink's coldness were his world's most vital matter.

Carrying the dinner they went into the dining room. How pleasant it was to be able to just relax and listen, thought Dent, without having to watch for traps or make points. On the wall of the dining room was another great oil, obviously by the same artist, again the heavy but sharply distinct use of built-up color. This painting was of a man swimming, his outlines broken and diffuse, while the whole held a dark terror, as if the swimmer knew the waves had his number.

"Dee," said McTurk after a couple of mouthfuls, "This is wonderful. Thank you for coming out. How about it, Dent?"

"Perfect. A Washington lobbyist who served food like this could get anything passed."

"I was just relaxing at the end of a hard day, Turkey, puttering about my studio, about to take a shower and get the paint off myself. . . ."

—D.M., thought Dent. That's what she does. —

"When you called. I grabbed a package of spaghetti and some frozen clams to surprise you and rushed out. Bang, I remembered I had to rent a car, I was just in a smeared sweatshirt and jeans and those clerks judge by appearances. So I put on something else quick. Of course, if I'd known you were bringing a handsome man." She laughed and batted her dark lashes at Dent with intentional theatricality.

"You did those oils?" He was surprised. The paintings seemed so strong it had not occurred to him that they were by a woman. But that was sexual discrimination. He wasn't going to admit to that sticky charge.

"Didn't Turkey warn you I was Deirdre the struggling artist?"

"What do you call this man swimming?"

She turned herself off, going back to her eating. "*The Swimmer*. What would you call it?"

" 'I'm a strong swimmer, but I may not make it.' "

Dee stared at full intensity. "But that's my name for it, word for word. My own private name. I've never even told you, Turkey."

"Dee's a great painter," said McTurk.

"Well, you won't believe this," he said, "but up to the time I got out of law school, I thought I might be a painter. That I was just becoming a lawyer as backstop if I couldn't make it in painting."

Dee looked at him—executive, controlled; he'd even hesitated before admitting he painted. Still, there was all that energy, and he'd hit on the name of her painting.

"Which picture do you think came first?" she asked.

"The portrait. This is a much more complex painting; those gasps of color pulling it apart, yet the lines holding it together. Besides"—he grinned—"I'm a Congressman. I looked at the dates."

Dee let herself go in laughter and Dent happily watched her body ripple. She'd had a bad time with acne in adolescence, he noticed, some of the pock marks still showed. Dent had a close friend in Washington, Congressman Red Donner of Florida, as wild a bachelor vote-getter as ever straddled an issue or a girl, who maintained you could judge a woman's bed performance by the way she ate and sneezed. If she took small bites and gave a dainty "achoo" forget her. If Red could see this alive girl put away clams, spaghetti, and steak, and the way she laughs, thought Dent, he'd dispose with the sneeze test and start operating.

The phone rang; Turkey swore and excused himself.

"They should let him eat," Dee bristled.

"People like to feel close to a catastrophe; vicarious importance."

"Will Congress investigate this crash?"

"It might. Investigations are the in thing. The government has grown so complex we can't control it by legislation; so we investigate. That takes less work and brains and gets us more publicity. But to investigate an air crash is tough. Politicians make their big under-the-table money out of airline routes and TV franchises. Just as they made it out of railroad right of ways after the Civil War."

"I hadn't thought of that."

"Most Congressmen are good guys. But they protect each other."

McTurk got off the phone, they finished dinner, and went back around the fire.

"Tell me, Turkey," Dent asked, "were the 'good old days in flying when the air was free' as great as we nonflyers get told?"

"No. That's nonsense. We used to fly for short hops in good weather, waiting for the engine to quit, with one eye on the oil gauge, the other looking for a field to land when the roof fell in. Our planes spun in, if you took your hands off the stick to scratch your ear, they fell apart in the air, they caught fire, hell, termites and moths ate them. I haven't had to make an emergency landing before tonight in seventeen years. I had to make six the first year I flew. I couldn't afford a very good engine."

"Did the good old days exist for anybody?" Dee asked. "They talk about the art in ancient Greece. But Euripides was torn to pieces by wild dogs."

"Things don't get better or worse," said Dent, "they change. Deep freeze for the dinosaurs is a break in the heat wave for the mammals. People over forty look back to good days. The young think they'll live in them. They're both wrong."

"Do you really believe that?"

"Sometimes, Dee."

"So do I." She held him with a physical intensity he could feel working inside him from across the room.

A short while later he looked at his watch. Ten to twelve. His first appointment tomorrow was at 7:30. He'd played hookey long enough. He rose; and suggested they call him a cab.

After a brief flurry of ritual politenesses, they agreed that Dent and Dee would drive back to New York in Dee's rented car, which is what Dent had hoped would happen.

"I've had a great time," he said, shaking Turkey's hand. "You don't know how wonderful it is to meet people."

"You must meet hundreds of people a day."

"No, just voters and people who want something. I don't get much chance to be alone and talk."

Dent caught the final look of love that passed between McTurk and Dee as they embraced good night. He hoped such looks would pass between his children, Jane and Jim, when they were grown. And between his children and himself.

Dent offered to drive and Dee accepted. They started off, Dee guiding him expertly through the suburban lanes and on to the superhighway.

"You can't be much over thirty-five, Dent?" she said.

"Thirty-eight."

"It's the gray hair that doesn't fit."

"I know. The Army tried out a new 'miracle drug' on me in the hospital. It turned my hair gray. I used to hate it. Now it's an asset."

"All your hair?"

"Yeah, down there too." Dee laughed and moved a little closer in the car. He glanced quickly at her, feeling the sexual tension. "Your brother seems much older than you."

"He is."

"Has he ever been married?"

"No, no, he never found anyone good enough." The answer was so unexpected that Dent laughed. "What are you laughing at?" Dee sensed a slight against her brother. "Some people should stay single unless they find someone exceptional. He never has. He's happy. He has his work. Every stewardess with a father complex jumps at him. Why should he marry?"

"I wasn't laughing at him, Dee. Just your answer was so unexpected and honest. Does the same apply to you?"

"I've been married."

"Oh."

"It was some time ago. And you, Mr. Interlocutor?"

"I am married. It's close to a must for a Congressman over thirty."

The parkway, which would be jammed with commuters in the morning, was now deserted in the fog and rain, the real estate developments on both sides almost as dark as the potato fields they had replaced. Here and there they could see the light from a TV screen where some occupant, glazed by canned beer and blended whisky, numbly watched the Late Late Show.

Dent moved the speed up to seventy, as fast as he liked to drive in an unknown car on a wet night. Cops didn't like to give Congressmen traffic tickets, but when they did, the press ate it up. And supposing he got into an accident while driving with a strange woman. It was such reasonless little slips that zapped a man's political career.

"I can't get over, Dent, your naming my painting."

"I think it's a superior picture, Dee."

"I've had friends who were artists, friends, hell, lovers, who saw the despair in that canvas but not the fight. I was beginning to think I hadn't put the strength in."

"It's there. I'd like to see some more of your paintings."

"I'd love to show them to you."

"Dee, what's it like being an artist? I know that's a broad question; but when I thought of being an artist I never could see myself past thirty."

"I'm not sure I know what you want. I could use more money." She paused. "I still live in a crummy neighborhood; though I've got an all right studio and heat. I don't have to paint all bundled up in sweaters and live on cheese and pig's liver because it's cheap. My body doesn't move well, because of all those years of bad food and cold. I'd like to have more nice dresses and go out more. And now some of my friends are making it and some aren't, and either making it or not making it changes them and divides us. And suppose I don't sell; or get blocked. I get furious with myself for not being able to solve my problems, my artistic problems, faster. That all sounds negative. It's exciting too, sometimes." That's enough she thought. It's foolish to go into my flashes of rage over women who have children, men to take care of them, over what the world has forced me to go through to paint.

Dent listened, excited by her intensity and directness. The trouble with being a Congressman, he knew, was having to be so careful about going out with anybody because of gossip.

"Do you like being a Congressman?" she asked.

"Yes, I do, though I just drifted into it when nothing else

seemed to work. A lot of Congressmen get there that way, perhaps the majority outside of the South. But I like being ahead, Dee. I love to flip the dime; take a chance. I'm out in front of practically everyone my age now. And if I could make the Senate." He fell silent. The excitement of Dee had brought out a more honest answer than he intended.

The rain shifted from drizzle to downpour; the chatter of drops and the increased click of wipers made talk difficult inside their water-covered box. I see why Turkey liked him, she thought. I wonder what his wife's like? How they get on? How his house is furnished? He certainly hasn't rushed home. She noticed she'd moved closer to him and smiled.

They reached the city and had a brief, polite argument about whether Dee should drop Dent or Dent should help her return the car and then drop her. He insisted and pulled up beside an empty cab, lowered his window, yelled at the driver to follow them to the garage, handing across a five-dollar bill.

"That's an extravagance," said Dee.

"I don't want you to get wet."

"Thank you."

They checked in the car and entered the cab. Dent approached a moment that always made him slightly uneasy. He was about to make a request and he might get turned down.

"I'd like to see you again, Dee," he said. "As well as your pictures. How about dinner some night?"

"That would be fun. I'm in the phone book. Deirdre McTurk, lady of sorrows." She laughed.

They drove to Dee's studio, half a floor through on the top floor of an old law tenement on Paul Street, part of that amorphous area between Chelsea and the Village. He looked at his alarm watch: 2:03. If she asked him in for a drink he'd say no. They were both tired. He had that 7:30 breakfast; and he'd get wet finding another cab.

"I'd ask you up for a drink," she said, "but it's so late."

"You're right." He told the cab to wait; walked up the four flights with her to her door; had a brief glimpse into her studio;

stacked canvases, drawing board, some tall plants, two portraits on the wall, work in progress covered by cloth. They shook hands; said good nights; then he was back in the cab racing uptown.

Quite a night, he thought. You start out going to two political dinners and end up almost dead and meeting an artist you want to take to bed. Could he afford the risk and time? He was not a chaser. "Casual copulation," he told his friends, "is for the birds and the boys." Not for George Dent, a man with a mission. Since his marriage he'd really only had one affair and he'd been relieved when after two on-again off-again years France-Presse had saved him making the decision to end it by transferring Eugenia to London.

Now Red Donner would be sitting on the floor of the House waiting for a roll call when he would suddenly spy some lusciousness in the gallery. Dent had learned to recognize the I-have-just-made-the-most-important-discovery-of-my-life grin that split his friend's face at such moments. Red would rise from his seat, head for the gallery, drift back to the floor just in time to vote, and after that vanish. Where? How? Dent never knew whether to be envious or indignant. Anyway he wanted the Senate too much to accept such risks.

At the door of his apartment he paused and again looked at his watch. Two-thirty. Sarah would almost certainly be asleep. He flicked his keys over to get the proper one. It annoyed him to carry five keys: his New York office, his Washington office, his Georgetown house, the Easthampton House, and this New York apartment. Yet the one he left off was always the one suddenly needed. So he put up with the extra weight and had the tailor sew a double lining inside his right-hand pocket.

No light came from beneath the bedroom door. For an instant he felt annoyed at Sarah for not waiting up to learn what it was like to be almost killed. But then he hadn't raced home to tell her. He took off his shoes and tiptoed through the bedroom into the bathroom to undress without waking her. In passing he scooped up the alarm to set it for tomorrow. He hung up his clothes carefully—there was a hanger kept in the bathroom for that purpose—and stepped on the spring scale. One hundred and sixty-two, right on the button. My God, you didn't see many figures like that on thirty-eight-year-old men. And his mother and father used to worry because he was so skinny. He turned out the bathroom light, opened the door, and felt his way cautiously toward the bed. Sarah always half-woke briefly as he climbed into his side. Tonight was no exception.

"Is that you, Daddy?" She always asked that. Some years before he had replied.

"No, it's Jimmy." She had sat bolt upright in bed.

"What! Who?"

"Just me."

"Who did you say? You know I'm tired. Don't be so funny."

"I'm sorry. But your question always amuses me."

"I'm trying to say I miss you."

"I'm sorry." He'd lost that round all right.

So now he said as usual, "It's me, love."

"Are you all right?"

"Fine."

"The crash must have been awful."

"Not too bad. I'll tell you in the morning."

"Brave Daddy. You looked just fine on television."

"Thank you."

"Poor people in the other plane. Horrible. —Human error probably."

"I guess so," he smiled. Sarah liked to blame the world's ills on human error. "Good night, love."

"You haven't forgotten your Scout leaders' breakfast?"

"No, I've set the alarm."

"Good night, sweetness."

"Good night." He could hear her even breathing as she rolled back into sleep.

He stretched himself against the sheets, adjusting himself as always to the pleasure of being in bed, rather than in a sleeping bag in some wet hole in the ground. Clean sheets tonight: that soft, refreshing luxury; he wiggled his toes against them. He slept naked, hating the binding feeling of pajamas. Sarah preferred frilly nightgowns. He didn't like this bed much, too soft and its chintzes rustled as he turned. But then he didn't sleep in the New York apartment often.

As he lay there the bed began to buck and sway and the room rotate around him in the dark. He could feel the pressure of his seat-belt against his stomach, the feeling of impotent finality as the plane dropped. His stomach muscles hurt where he had slammed against his seat belt. They would be really sore if he hadn't positioned that magazine and pillow. If the plane had crashed, would such tiny preparations have possibly saved him?

If, if, if. If he had just lain on that German road and not tried to put a tourniquet about his leg. Had the struggle to stop the bleeding from his leg just made the wounds in his shoulder, about which he did not know, bleed faster? In the hospital he'd break out laughing at his silly efforts to save himself. But he was also proud of them. He'd acted and that action was the mark of his grace; meaningless, but constant.

In fantasy he held Dee McTurk close to him a few instants. He passed into sleep.

three

At 6:45 a.m. his bedroom and his wrist-watch alarm rang within ten seconds of each other. Dent struggled from his heavy cocoon of sleep and lurched, limping slightly, to the bathroom, where he automatically turned on his bath, relieved himself, and shaved. Then, pulling his schedule out of his briefcase, he settled into the hot bath water for a planning session.

Here in his hot bath, back on schedule, yesterday's events seemed nonactual. Would he ever take Dee McTurk out, he wondered? He'd send a telegram to the Speaker of the House about the crash; try and set the stage for a subcommittee on air safety with himself a member. He winced inwardly at this trading off the dead; but the crash was a public relations gift.

He picked up his schedule for today from the table beside the bath, reading:

7:30 New York City Scoutmasters Association Breakfast. Hotel Edison
8:45 West Side Hadassah, Spring Meeting, Breakfast. Hotel Wyoming
10:00 Mrs. Joel Smitkin, 310 West 68th Street. Kaffeeklatsch
10:45 Mrs. William Farbster, 200 West 62nd Street. Kaffeeklatsch
11:30 Mrs. Frank Boyd, 115 Central Park South. Kaffeeklatsch
12:15 Mrs. Frederick Donner, 309 East 40th Street. Sherry

12:45 Advertising Executives and Copywriters Association, Hotel Waldorf, Green Room
1:30 Office appointments
5:00 Mr. and Mrs. Lyman Blitzner, cocktails, 9 East 72nd
7:00 East Side Community Associations, dinner, Hotel Westford
9:00 Citizens Committee for Mayor Wagner, dinner, Hotel Taft
11:00 Chelsea West Reform Democratic Club—look in, drinks with leaders after

He could skip his afternoon office appointments, let his assistant, Sam Kleinman, take them, and use that time to gain publicity from the air crash. He ran through several imaginary scenarios, from press releases to inspecting the wreckage, finally deciding to charter a plane and refly the course on which the crash had occurred. That was clean, noncommittal, and scientific and should produce a picture in the *News* and *Tribune* as well as TV and radio coverage.

He flipped over to his Saturday schedule and began to figure his sleep time for the weekend. He'd just had four and one-half hours. He'd get through with the Chelsea West leaders by 1:30 or 2:00. Bed by 2:30 at the latest. His first Saturday breakfast was not till eight. At least four and a half hours' sleep tonight. Saturday he had another late political rally and then a Holy Name breakfast at 7:30 Sunday. Four hours tomorrow night. Sunday night he would be back in Washington with his children. He could sleep from 10:00 till 8:30 and still see Jim and Jane before they went to school. Ten and a half hours' sleep, plenty to start the week fresh.

By the time he had bathed he was fully awake. The Dent secret of starting the day: Don't take the extra half hour of sleep, get up slowly, baby the system awake. Only if he was really beat did he sleep to deadline.

He got out clean underwear, white; a clean shirt, white; and opened his closet to choose a suit. They were all dark gray or blue, colors that showed off his blue eyes, with almost invisible pinstripes, red, blue, or white, to give them life. He'd be talking to admen and women about serious topics and be photographed worrying about air safety. He selected a conservative dark-red pinstripe.

Sarah sat up with a shake and a yawn, and he went around to her side of the bed and kissed her.

"Oh, Daddy," she stretched and kissed him gently on the forehead, "I'm so glad you're alive."

"Just luck, Sarah. This great pilot, the chief pilot of the airline, McTurk, just happened to be flying us. He was good enough to save us. I went out with him afterward; a fabulous guy."

"It must have been hideous. You should have come home."

"It was like combat. It happened so fast I didn't feel much till afterward."

"You take such risks, Daddy."

"We should be from California; not have to campaign on weekends."

"I worry so about you."

Dent gave her a friendly pat. "I'll be careful."

He checked that the ends of his necktie were exactly even, tested the tension of his garters, and picked up a pair of well-shined shoes, inspecting the laces. "Why bother to shine them, if you don't like to?" his son, Jim, had asked last year. He'd used the question to explain to a five-year-old the importance and craziness of symbols. How if you'd been in a good fight you often didn't want to wash up. You wanted people to see the dirt on you and realize you'd been down before you won. Shined shoes were the same way, a symbol you were so important you didn't have to muddy your feet.

"I miss the children getting up in the morning," he said.

"I certainly miss them too. And I'm not the one who is campaigning."

"Yeah." Sarah was quick to anger before her morning coffee. "I'll meet you at the Blitzner cocktail party. I'll need you there. You lunching with your father?"

"Umm." Her lips were firm, jaw out. When Sarah began to flame it took time to bank the fires. Part of what makes her such a great campaigner, he thought.

"Ask him about Buffalo, will you. It's been two months since I've had a speaking invitation from there. And Sam hasn't heard anything. Something's up."

"All right."

"And you might ask him for ideas on how to get publicity from this crash without appearing ghoulish. See you darling." He kissed her briefly again, then headed for the kitchen and his ritual glass of orange juice. He loved fresh orange juice, the cold acid-sweet taste of it supplying the final jolt that shot him awake.

He found a small pitcher of fresh juice in the ice box—trust Sarah—and poured himself a large glass, then called Jean Aaron, his New York appointments secretary, another key person in his political life.

"Good morning, Jean."

"Oh, good morning Mr. Dent. Thank God you're alive."

"When I look at today's schedule, I'm not so sure about that thanks. How are you?"

"I'm fine, sir. Are you all right?"

"Sure. I can get through the Hadassah breakfast by myself. Can you meet me in the lobby of the Smitkins' building at ten? I may be five or ten minutes late."

"Are you sure you can handle Hadassah by yourself?"

"Certainly."

"Don't forget Pat Levy will be there."

"I'll know her. See you at the Smitkins'."

Jean Aaron was his memory. His own memory for people was a standard joke among his staff. At the start of his political career he'd even gone so far as to take a memory course that stressed mnemonic devices. After graduation he confidently called an important Harlem leader named Dodge, Mr. Pontiac all evening (medium-priced-car association). He introduced a labor leader named Plotz as Stone (slang-word-for-drunk association).

And finally one of his fund-raisers named Monroe he called Hayworth (sexy-actress association). Now he used Jean or Sam for names; and if they weren't there, just smiled a "hi-ya, friend."

He didn't like to call Sam this early, so he left a detailed message with his answering service for Sam to scrounge up a free plane from the Long Island charter operators whose license he'd had reinstated when their own Congressman had failed. He called weather next: clear and colder. That meant his heavy coat. He checked his pencil, notebook, watch, briefcase and wallet, put on his heavy overcoat, and set off to the Scoutmasters' Breakfast, the first dubious battle of today's political war.

He didn't have to campaign so hard so early this year just to stay in Congress. Barring acts of bizarre chance he was in good shape to win eight months from now in November. In '54 and again in '56 he'd had to go flat out every day. In '54 he had been an unknown lawyer leading a divided Democratic party against a Republican incumbent in a district that had gone Republican for eight years. The very chanciness of the district had allowed him to win a primary and run. No old pro had claimed the seat as his fief; nor had any moneyed reformer put it genteelly in his pocket. If '54 was bad, '56 looked like the end of Congressman Dent. He was a one-term Democratic Congressman in a Presidential election year, running against the vote-getting magic of Eisenhower.

Fortunately the Republicans were so convinced he was beatable they staged a Donnybrook of a primary for the privilege of wiping his ass. As so often happens the candidate that won, while strongest with registered Republicans, was weakest with Democrats and Independents. The Republicans never quite united after their bloody primary; and Dent had several secret strengths. Sam Kleinman had joined him and was weaving an uneasy but vote-productive alliance of old line and reform clubs. His war record helped with the Catholic voters and his support of liberal causes with the Jewish money. Various good-government groups and the *Times* endorsed him. For once the "Citizens for Dent," instead of fighting with his professional organization, worked to deliver votes. Sarah tallied with several key women's organizations. Exhausted, he squeaked through.

By the law of politics he could now rest in 1958.

But there was a Senate seat up in '60. Dent wanted not just to win but to win big. So the king-makers had to sit up and notice what he could do in a district that used to go Republican. Unfortunately the Senate seat, held by a genial but ineffective Republican called Chattleworth, was so obviously up for grabs that many more powerful men than he wanted it. The prize would be handed out at the Democratic State Convention two years from now. Among those who would control the convention he was at present the first choice of only a few. But he was the second choice of a good number. With a big win this time and luck and more exposure upstate and in the suburbs, he had a definite chance.

He took a cab part way to the Scout Breakfast, then got out to walk the last twelve blocks. He turned left on Madison toward Park Avenue, striding his usual block every forty-three seconds. On the corner the foundations were being dug for a new building. He could spare three minutes to watch.

He stopped by a huge yellow air compressor the size of a small bus, the second in a line of five, standing close enough to be warmed, but upwind, so the diesel fumes did not blow over him. The metal-banded air hoses, the thickness of pythons, writhed over his head into the excavation, carried on a corridor of four by fours above the sidewalk. The diesels and compressors blanketed him with sound, pleasant and warm, like a tank park in the early morning.

Dent looked closely at the construction crew. By God it was integrated. It wouldn't have been two years ago. You had a small part of the action, he thought proudly. He looked up Park Avenue and saw that the derrick and trailer truck carrying beams for the pile driver were blocking two and a half lanes of traffic. That was both totally illegal and absolutely necessary. The police precinct would be making a good thing off this job. Well, let them, he thought, they didn't get paid enough. Graft was part of the tribute society shelled out for rapid progress.

As Dent stood in the cold spring sunshine, the roar, the jolt of rough work, the dust blowing on him, the diesel fumes in his nose, the explosion of energy all about, human, machine, and fuel, combined and burst inside him with a thrill like that felt by an evangelic congregation hearing the first chords of "Rock of Ages." "Don't fence me in," he roared at the diesels. Hell, nobody could hear him over all the racket. A giant black tending the machines looked up and smiled. Dent grinned back. That man knew. You were part of building or you weren't. You liked power or you didn't. In or out.

He turned and walked toward the hotel and the Scoutmasters' Breakfast, depression flooding in behind his elation. For this corner was probably the last place in America that needed an old building torn down and a new one thrown up. The new structure would house no one, instead hold offices, speeding the rich in their flight to tax havens in the suburbs while increasing the daytime congestion. Uptown, some fifty blocks or two miles north—beyond effective tank action but well within artillery range—building was desperately needed. But there, where the deprived of Harlem were penned ten to a room, shucked of hope, no jackhammers rang or derricks swung. How could he ever harness human greed to help the needy rather than serve itself? "Help me move the fast buck to the slums, men." With what shocked silence the voters would receive those words.

The scoutmasters fed him orange juice (frozen), scrambled eggs, bacon, milk, and coffee (hotel, weak). The ministers of the three faiths said grace, the Protestant minister being black, as were about one-third of the audience. All of them up so early, Dent thought, to feel the pleasure of belonging to something bigger than themselves. Probably they'd first asked the Senator to speak, then maybe the Governor, next the Mayor—though hizhonordamayor was not much on the breakfast circuit; and finally ended with him, Old Second-Choice, Dent.

"What are you going to talk about, Congressman?" the president of the organization asked him.

"I thought I'd say a few words, and I mean a few only, on the peculiar problems we face here in this city."

"That's getting to be a popular subject," said the secretary on Dent's left.

What do you want, thought Dent, for weak coffee and tough scrambled eggs at 7:30 in the morning from the farm team — Camus? —He crinkled his sincerest smile. Actually he was going to tell the scoutmasters how great they were and while they were glowing from that, slip in a little something humble about how great he was. The core of his speech was his fond recollection about his old scoutmaster at school who had molded his life. In truth, Dent had joined the Boy Scouts at St. Luke's because they got an extra holiday and could remember nothing about the scoutmaster except that he had gravy stains on his vest.

But Dent's office had checked with St. Luke's, his old school. St. Luke's had searched their records and come up with the man's name. Dent had prepared a story of how this man, Patrick Hood, had helped a boy to find a place in the group. This would lead him into a story about a bull who couldn't find his place in the group. Then he'd swing into brotherhood, the impossibility of brotherhood in bad environments, run through his efforts to help the city, throw in a few statistics (Dent the educated Congressman), and close with an invitation that they bring their scouts to visit his office whenever they were in Washington.

The chairman rose and rapped against his water glass for silence.

"Our speaker this morning," the scoutmaster began, "quite literally had a brush with death on his way here to address us."

Damn it, thought Dent, he'd forgotten about that. He had to have a personal attitude toward yesterday. One that avoided that old vote-loser, religion.

He would talk about McTurk and the human factor. People ate that up in this machine age. What the hell was the name of his scoutmaster at St. Luke's? He glanced hastily at his file card.

The speech went off adequately. Several of the scoutmasters introduced themselves afterward and commented that they lived in his district. He got their names and addresses in his book. They'd get a follow-up letter. Communication was his critical need—the damn New York newspapers and TV programs were so full of what was happening in Paris, Moscow, Israel, or the jet set, about the only chance an area Congressman had to get a mention was to be caught stealing.

He glanced at his watch. Five minutes to the Hadassah breakfast. He'd be about ten minutes late.

He got his coat from a chair near the door, where he'd carefully left it. Another Dent rule: keep track of your own coat. You can waste fifteen minutes because the boob who says, "Help you with your coat, Congressman," loses it. He gripped the hands of the organization leaders, exchanged a few final platitudes and bolted.

Outside there were no taxis. Damn. To use a rented car and chauffeur this early in the campaign was too expensive and ostentatious. He couldn't be seen in a city car, because economy and good government were part of his image. So he was stuck with taxis. As his friend, Congressman Red Donner proclaimed, tongue-in-cheek, "Good government is my greatest challenge."

A cab pulled up ahead of him to drop its passengers in the middle of the block. Two women were standing on the corner in front of the taxi waiting and waving. Dent sprinted up from behind, opened the cab door as the driver started toward the women, and jumped in.

"Mac, I was goin'—" said the driver.

Dent looked at the driver's license: McGrath. "I'm the speaker at a Holy Name breakfast on West 67th Street. The boys will kill me if I'm late."

"You're da boss."

Dent hoped the women had not recognized him.

George Dent's six-year-old son, Jim, squatted on the iron front steps leading up to Dent's Washington house in Georgetown. Behind him sat his sister Jane, two years older. They were waiting for the mother who had the car pool that day to drive them to school. As usual, Jim hoped the car would be late. After he'd eaten his corn flakes, bacon, orange juice, and milk; been to the bathroom; and gotten his homework together, he always felt so good. He liked to sit on the steps in the sun and hug himself and think. That's what he called it to himself: "thinking." Actually he let the newness of the world seep through him and ferment into a golden brew.

Pushing up through the cracks in the iron steps were tiny slivers of dark green moss. He could scrape them off with his fingers and carry the wonderful odor of wet moss around with him all day beneath his nails. He let his friend, Rick, smell and Rick agreed it was wonderful. Jim bent down to look close.

You don't find moss like this on everybody's steps, he thought. The steps have to face just this way so the sun hits them in the morning. And no cold wind. There have to be cracks just the right size. Otherwise the moss comes up too fast and gets stepped on. Or the moss might not even come up at all because the crack would be too small for the moss dirt to live. —But he was lucky. His steps got just the right amount of sun and his cracks were just the right size so the moss dirt, which must have been blown there by the wind, the wind which blew (blew and blue converged in his mind so as he saw the wind as blue and the sky as blowing, both all suddenly cold) in the time before he was, the time when he wasn't, the time he didn't like to think about, that same wind had blown the moss dirt here, for him, to take the smell on his fingers to school.

Tomorrow, no there was no school tomorrow or the next day, Monday he would let his father smell the moss. Not just the bit on his finger, but the whole moss as it grew on his steps, in his crack, in his sun. Everything is beautiful. But it's even more beautiful when I show father who loves me. Jim hugged himself. Here came the today's mother. He quickly picked off a piece of moss and put it carefully between his finger and his nail so as not to squoosh it. The moss had never hurt him.

"Hurry up, Jim," called his sister.

Dent gave the cab driver an extra dollar, put on his I'm-glad-to-see-each-and-every-one-of-you smile, and entered the lobby of the Hadassah breakfast hotel. Oh joy, the efficient ladies of Hadassah all wore little name tags, he could read them without peering. He'd have an easy second breakfast. He advanced on the four ladies bearing down on him and stuck out his hand. The most important one would grab it.

Congressman Dent, sipping canned orange juice, looked out over the tables of earnest, munching faces packing away breakfast. Bang into his mind came a new angle for his canned brotherhood speech. How sisters were naturally more friendly and loving than brothers; and that one should talk not about the brotherhood of man but the sisterhood of people because women paved the way. That was the type of verbal nonsense audiences sucked up. He smiled inwardly.

He and fellow politicians might crack private jokes against organized women; but this society would die if women dropped their active part. Their men were out hustling items people often did not need, while their women tried to do something about bad housing, crippled children, poor schools, the lacks in their own lives. Their men had the same lacks, indeed the vacuum in the men led to the vacuum in the women; but the men, being busy, believed they were full. The women were conscious of loss. Part of his vote-getting success was his ability to fill this loss, tap the electricity in organized women.

He hated his ritual brotherhood speech he was about to deliver. What these ladies, what all Americans, desperately wanted to believe about brotherhood, what Dent would tell them, was summed up in the driveling sweetness of the song from *South Pacific:* "You have to be taught to hate." They found this belief: warm, gooey, cozy, and satisfying. It took the responsibility away from them and put in on society, parents, teachers, anyone who had corrupted their sweetness.

Privately Dent believed the exact opposite. He reasoned that in the jungle from which man had struggled, the stranger was feared and therefore hated. The Bible had been concerned that man should move beyond loving his family to loving his neighbor. Now survival required that men love, or at least respect, people vastly different from themselves: other countries, other races. That required teaching, time, restraint, politeness, tolerance, all the complex fabric of society.

Each generation had to relearn to expand its circle of love. People got bored with this effort and listened to any pied piper who told them they were naturally good and all that hatred inside them just came from society's corruption, was put there by the establishment. Nonsense. Men didn't have to be taught to hate, to crucify. They raced to be first to drive the nails.

His canned brotherhood speech went well. He could feel the return begin: the pulse of strength, the physical excitement, listener feeds back to speaker. That vital nourishment the politician draws from the people pool in which he swims. The women's approval caressed Dent, quickened him, aroused him, freshened his hackneyed words. "Remember, children have to be taught to hate," he told them. And they burst into loud applause; the circuits between them closed, their voltage up.

He finished, naturally, with a panegyric to Israel. This he found easy to do. He liked democracy and bravery and felt that small state had both. —Even if some kibbutzim he'd visited had reminded him of concentration camps minus gas chambers and with better chow.—

"As Churchill called England during the war against the Nazis 'an unsinkable aircraft carrier,' so we today can call Israel 'an unsinkable carrier of democracy.' As he ended the ladies rose and applauded him. Even when he sat down their applause continued. Once again, he thought, the old lies work.

Dent turned toward the president and smiled. He had not been paid for the speech. Time to throw the lance of quid pro quo. "You know, Mrs. Prinz, there's a request I'd like to make. As a Congressman in New York I have a real problem. A small-town Congressman can reach people through local newspapers, radio, and TV stations. Find out what the voters think that way. I can't. I have to put out my own newsletter about what's going on. But it's hard to find informed people to send it to. I admit there's a little politics in the letter; but mostly it's information about events in Congress; and questions about what people want me to do. I'd certainly appreciate it if I could send an assistant, Jean Aaron, round for a copy of your mailing list. Believe me, no solicitation or political material would be sent out. Just the newsletter."

The president paused. Dent kept the smile on his face and his blue eyes on her.

"It's against the rules. But you're a firm friend. I think an exception could be quietly arranged. Have your assistant ask for Mrs. Asher."

He stayed at the breakfast a few minutes more to be polite, and left.

Mrs. Joel Smitkin, his next target area, lived in a chic aluminum and glass tower on West 68th Street. The ladies at her kaffeeklatsch would be studiedly intellectual and intense; their questions serious, general, impersonal. "Why don't we recognize Red China?" "How long must we keep troops in Korea?" "Why don't we have a UN police force?" If they wanted a job for their son or special legislation passed, they would hire a lawyer who would come to him privately.

They thought they were sophisticated and that they wanted hard, precise, reasoned answers. In fact they wanted the same type of simplistic reassuring as the "ignorant" they so despised. Their problem was that they had tried the old certainties and either found them wanting or distrusted their continued belief in them for fear of being judged unsophisticated.

Mrs. Smitkin's ladies sat in their expensive people cartons, nervous, disturbed, playing cards, talking, discussing great books, watching television, trying to love, to cope with children, holding piano recitals, experimenting with pot, getting analyzed—while the city went to hell around them. Hourly they prostrated themselves before their latest golden calf: raw carrot juice, psychiatry, One Word, the total validity of love, natural childbirth, the inner me, equality. What they wanted desperately was certainty. To be reassured by Dent that their lives had meaning, that the world was basically good, they were doing fine.

Jean Aaron was waiting for him in the apartment lobby.

"How did the speech go, sir?" She always called him "sir" the first time she saw him each day.

"Beautifully. They were wearing name tags. I got a standing ovation and their mailing list."

"Their list? Gorgeous. You must have talked about Israel, you politician."

Jean handed him a small white typed card on which were three names. Below each name was what he called the person and a summary of what they had done for him. He called Mrs. Smitkin "Ann." She'd been building captain for four years. Jean pointed out that "Ann" had recently moved from 14F to 22C, an upward step; and he should exclaim over her new apartment. Of the other two names, one had done canvassing for him in the last election; the other contributed twenty dollars: the key figure that placed a name in his "active givers" file. There was a special file for those who had given five hundred dollars and over. Even Dent could remember most of the names on that file and why the generosity. The National Union of Confectioners, Sugarers, and Pastrymakers hadn't shelled out four thousand dollars to let him eat oatmeal.

Dent restrained himself and let Jean push the elevator button for the twenty-second floor. She had few satisfactions in life, poor freckled, tall woman; and aiding him seemed the greatest. She believed that he was absolutely helpless and that he should be the next President. How she managed to square these two disparate faiths Dent never understood.

"How's your mother?" he asked. Jean's latest trial with her ailing mother had scarce begun as they reached Mrs. Smitkin's door.

He greeted "Ann" effusively and remarked on the beauty of her new apartment, particularly the drapes. Another Dent political rule: always admire the drapes. The couch, a table, some chair, may have been given a woman by her husband, or even her mother-in-law, and she may hate it; the silverware may be rented; the carpet cut to fit from some other home; but a woman's drapes are her own. As he greeted Mrs. Smitkin, he heard Jean whisper.

"People are here I didn't realize." That always happened; that's why he brought Jean. "The blonde in beaded black is Mrs. Warner, husband in construction, thousand-dollar contribution. The little girl in the corner, Ann Wilder, was a typist in your temporary office last campaign. I think she's just gotten married. The cool job, there, with all the leg, sitting down, Mrs. Jason, wife of the building owner. There's Mary Fedders; she's one of the best poll-watchers we've got. I didn't know she'd moved here."

Ann Smitkin, wife of Public Relations Counselor Arnold Smitkin, guided him through the instant nonliving of her apartment, shoving him at acquaintances, pausing him before equals, and genuflecting for him before the more powerful, such as Mrs. Warner. He had been in a hundred thousand such apartments. The abstract paintings on the walls required no response except perhaps "how nice" or more likely "how much?" Two children in Fauntleroy clothes smiled from a filigreed silver picture frame on the minuscule piano, showing the *de rigueur* braces. The chairs and couch impossible to lounge on, or make love, or read. The heavy drapes continually drawn against outside eyes, the textured wallpaper, the crystal glasses at the bar, the pile rug. He knew just what to give the twenty-five or thirty women in this room, his omelet speech: Three minutes of what he was for, six minutes of what he was against, one minute of uplift. It was the six minutes of what he was against that popped their eyeballs.

Dent's friend "Wup-'em-tommorra' Wilson, the Wyomin' Wildcat," had introduced him to the magic power of the antivote. Dent had been grousing to Congressman Wilson about his chances of defeat in the Eisenhower election year of 1956.

"Now lookie here, Dent," said Wup-'em, "voters don't vote for you because they like what you stand for. They vote for you because they hate what you hate." Dent had begun to routinely acknowledge his friend's philosophy; but the Wildcat held up a hand and continued: "If you're just battlin' for what they like, they wonder why you ain't doing better. But if you're in there pastin' what they hate, they love you. At least that's the way it is in Wyomin'.

"Now we hate three things in Wyomin': Railroads, Wall Street, and Communists. Did you know that single-handed I'd stopped Wall Street from taking over the banks of Wyomin'?"

"That item of history had passed me by, Wup-'em."

"Well, I did. And believe me everybody in Wyomin' knows it. Now what do they hate in your district?"

Dent thought for a moment. "Arabs, violence on television, and bigots."

"Makes as much sense as what they hate in Wyomin'. Here's what I did. You know old Tar Heel Jones from Carolina. His district's so safe he don't care what he does. I got him to introduce a bill makin' it legal for Eastern banks to charter in Utah, Wyoming, and North and South Dakota without permission of the Federal Government. Then I made a major speech against that poor bill that was never goin' nowhere and mailed that speech to all my constituents. They don't know that thousands of bills are introduced every session for nothin'. That all I got goin' for me is wind. In their eyes old Wildcat Wilson single-handed stopped Wall Street from rapin' the prairies."

"What you have to do for Tar Heel?"

"Not vote on the Civil Rights Bill."

"I couldn't do that."

"I know that. But you're on the Armed Services Committee. Maybe he wants a little something for his district. Supposing he was to introduce a bill curtailing the Federal Communications

Commission so the big TV boys could run any kinds of programs they liked? How would that sit in your district?"

"The voters would rise as one woman and the men would follow."

"George, I see you as: 'Dent the guardian of the airwaves' "

"Even old Tar Heel wouldn't do something that crazy."

"He's a friendly guy. Depends how much he wants something. I'll take you round tomorrow. —Besides, he owes me one."

"Christ, Wup-'em, how do you work that? Everybody in Congress owes you one."

"I stand firm on my principles, old horse, so they never get in my way."

A month later Dent the guardian of the airwaves was receiving favorable mail on his courageous stand against TV violence from all over his district. Each writer received a personal note from Dent himself (run off on a battery of five electric typewriters hooked in sequence and fed by tape, his signature forged by a young college student working for three months in his office to gain insight into government). In the note their Congressman informed them that "there are compensations to the constant strains and frustrations of being a Congressman and one of them is to be able to lead the fight against such invidious legislation as the bill to cripple the FCC. This bill was a back-door sneak attack on the precious lives of our children." Tar Heel had been worried that two armories in his district might be closed.

Sometime later, Congressman Sneed of Mississippi had a friend whom the Pentagon quite rightly objected to promoting to brigadier general in the National Guard. After about three months of pressure, the Pentagon decided it really didn't care that much about one more crook in Guard uniform; and Sneed in return introduced a totally unnoticed bill to prohibit the United States from giving foreign aid to any nation not complying with decisions of the UN Security Council.

All of Congress rightly ignored this bill except for vigilant George Dent. He recognized it as a sinister plot by Southern bigots to deny aid to Israel. He placed a blistering speech in the

Congressional Record against: "This flagrant attack upon the freedom of our stanchest ally."

Instant, total success. Dent the lover of Israel had always got his goy share of invitations to Jewish affairs. But Dent the defender of Israel was overwhelmed by thanks. Indeed, a couple of Brooklyn Congressmen came to his office to complain at not having been cut in on the deal.

"Here I am getting letters wanting to know why I didn't attack this menace. How do you think I feel?" angrily complained Jack Rosen.

"Welcome to the act," said Dent.

"Goddamn it, nobody gets up early enough to be more of a friend to Israel than Jack Rosen."

"I get up at five a.m. What time do you get up, Jack?"

"All right, Dent, but let me in on the next one."

"Okay, if you do the same for me. You haven't before."

"It's a deal."

Wup-'em had been right. They loved him most for what he was against. As Sad Sam Kleinman remarked happily, "No one knows how close to the brink this blessed union has tottered till you sock 'em between the eyes with some of those laws you've blocked single-handed."

Dent placed himself in front of Mrs. Smitkin's drapes. Time to begin his omelet speech. After the speech came the dangerous part, questions, where a man could get killed by one wrong answer. His personality gleamed from the edges of his teeth as he leaned sincerely forward for questions.

"Who is your candidate for President?" one of the women asked.

Damn it, why did that question have to be first? His district was divided about two-thirds for Adlai Stevenson, one-third for John F. Kennedy, with a few vocal Hubert Humphreyites scattered here and there. These numbers dictated that he should support Stevenson. But the state political leaders preferred Kennedy as the stronger vote-getter; and he needed their support for his Senate drive. Personally, Dent preferred Kennedy. Stevenson, fun to have dinner with, was weak; Hubert talked too damn much; Kennedy alone had the courage, brains, and style to be President —if his back held up. The choice between Kennedy and Stevenson was going to be politically murderous for him in '60. He had no intention of getting hooked on the question in '58. The people before him, intellectual, older, wealthy, and fond of words, would probably all be for Stevenson.

"Well, as you know, Adlai is a close personal friend. But as a Democrat, I believe in direct primaries, in letting the people decide. I want to see how the people feel before I decide among the many excellent candidates available." He knew this answer, his standard one, made him no new friends in the Stevenson camp; but it didn't blow all his Kennedy support either.

Then came a long string of easy questions: Were we spending too much on space exploration? Where did he stand on pornography and censorship? Was he in favor of a nuclear-test-ban treaty? etc., etc., etc. He had routine answers for all these queries researched by experts, tested by pollsters; and above all based on his question-handling technique: Don't reason with the questioner, come up with a unique fact. To take the known facts and out-reason the asker was to show up the asker for a fool, lose a vote. To produce an unknown fact took the questioner off the hook: "That Dent, he's no brighter than I am; but he's done his homework."

Are we spending too much on space? "Last year the people of America spent three times as much on deodorants as on the space program." Pornography and censorship? "There are sixty-three hundred and fifty-seven different titles of comic books on the newsstands. Control of these presents a problem." A nuclear-test-ban treaty? "Scientists tell us it will take thirty-two monitoring stations inside China and Russia to produce a workable treaty. I respect their judgment." With my answers, Dent often thought, Socrates would have drunk champagne, not hemlock.

The questions were running down. Time to cut the meeting off before someone asked about Federal aid to parochial schools, another Congressman-killer.

"Thank you for your questions," he said. "People often come up to me and say, 'Congressman, we disagree with your answer; but we admire the way you stand up and say it.'" (In point of fact this had never happened.) "That's really wonderful for me to hear. You are broadminded and challenging people to represent. I thank you for your help in the past; and for your efforts now to give me the opportunity to serve you longer."

He moved decisively toward the door, pumping hands, herding the people by him. This was always a dangerous moment. In every group might lurk at least one long-winded questioner, scheming to trap him privately. Jean Aaron came up beside him to assist his getaway.

Only three more stops till lunch. Another one hundred million and we're dead. And always fear knotting his stomach that at some one of them he would handle a question wrong, lose his temper, reveal himself, commit political suicide.

Lunch. Dent stepped out of the Waldorf's elevator to be sincerely handshaken by a mixed group of tailored white and striped shirts, expensive suits, and gleaming shoes that made up the Advertising and Copywriters Executives Association. What a handsome group of men they were: perfect teeth, jovial laughs, conspicuously displayed vitality. But how come so many wore glasses? Were bad eyes their status symbol? What had become of the archetypal American male who could spot a camouflaged Sioux sneaking through buffalo grass two miles away at night?

And how many votes could he gain in this room, he wondered? Most of these men probably lived in the suburbs, were members of their local "Citizens for Eisenhower Committee," voted comfortably Republican for Congressmen whose names they seldom knew. Yet they'd asked him to speak, his image of alert comer working for him even here.

He sat down at the head table next to J. Herbert Cary, President of the Association. "Herb the happy hustler," as he liked his subordinates to call him. "All one big family at this agency." — In private his underlings termed him "the shit-eating shark."

After duck, souffléed potatoes, and peas, instead of chicken, rice, and peas, to indicate the status of the organization, J. Herbert rose to introduce Dent. Dent noticed many of those in front of him had been continually drinking martinis with their luncheon. It wasn't going to make much difference what he told them.

"Fellow members of our distinguished association," began the president. "As you may remember last meeting, we here who travail on Madison Avenue arrived at the definite conclusion we should maintain a constant and close liaison with all sections of that important component of our increasingly diversified society, the Federal Government. Not only is this our duty; it is also to our advantage."

The speech punched on. Dent realized that Herb had got to be president of this organization by following the basic political rule, always remind your audience how great they are.

"We here in Madison Avenue know how to tackle big problems. That is the advantage of working in a highly competitive environment such as ours. We may refer to our shops as the old ulcer factory. But it is the old ulcer factory that permits America to enjoy her wealth and abundance! And we know it! You bet your bottom dollar, you bet your wife, hell you bet your mistress, we know it! And that's why criticism of us doesn't get under our skin!"

(Applause and tapping on martini glasses)

"The Congress, of which our guest this afternoon is a great captain, moves at a slower pace. Frankly, I know some of us think it's often too damn slow. But then they don't have our competition. And we are all humble enough to remember the hare and the tortoise. Though I doubt if either of those conversing quadrupeds had the old moxie to make it on our street, hey boys."

(Laughter)

"Our guest at lunch today, Congressman George Dent, is supremely equipped to tell us about Congress and its problems. For he is no ordinary Congressman. He is Madison Avenue's own. Part of our great street is included in his district. I could dwell at some length on his distinguished record; but I am certain that most of us know it; and besides you might think I was writing his material. So as the good salesman should reveal his product and not himself, let me without further word give you a man who can ably speak for himself and about his fascinating world of Washington and the Congress, the Honorable George Dent."

The admen received twenty-five minutes of Dent's off-the-record-shocking-details-about-current-politics speech which gave the listener a pleasant feeling of being on the inside without revealing any truths damaging either to Dent or the system. He tacked on a new ending asking the help of his audience in solving the problems of the city. There was nothing they could do about these problems; but the ploy served to keep him in touch with their organization. He would need their help when he ran for the Senate. Being a Congressman was much like being a small child, he thought. You searched for places to show off.

In his cab on the way to LaGuardia to refly yesterday's collision course, he reviewed his morning's work. He was running strong and well; but instead of feeling elated he felt grubby. He had another twelve hours to get through. Suppose he'd become an artist, he mused. He'd be through work by this time in the afternoon; nothing left to do but make love to Dee McTurk. He smiled spontaneously.

Connoisseurs such as his friends the Wollenbergs would have his pictures hanging on their walls, he'd be exhibited at the Museum of Modern Art, have parties thrown for him at the better galleries. If he was successful. That was the joker. In politics, in law, a man could measure himself, had some idea of how he was performing. In art a man never knew if he would succeed or fail, where he would be five years later.

How could he gauge his potential as an artist? He used to chew on that question right after the war. He remembered one decisive moment on his father's porch, after he'd been out of the hospital and the Army two months. It was Sunday, after lunch: rib roast of beef, Yorkshire pudding, lightly creamed spinach topped with hard-boiled egg slices, roast potatoes, Hospice de

Baune 1937, ice cream with a special caramel sauce brought in hot that hardened as it hit the cold pile on the dessert plate, demi-tasses, brandy, and cigars. (His father was down to his last few puffs. Dent, who smoked cigars seldom and slower, was only about two-thirds through.

Reclining in the pleasant torpor of that afternoon green beneath the maples, Long Island Sound shimmering at the foot of their Greenwich garden, feeling himself full, a bit sauced, alive, he should have been profoundly at peace. He wasn't. Physically his wounded shoulder jerked and twanged at his body. Psychologically he could not relax, admit he was safe; indeed he was often more full of dread now than he had been in battle.

His father turned in the deep cushions of his porch chair; and from that throne of peace and perfection inquired of his wracked subject George Dent, "What are you going to do now, George?"

Why the hell did his old man ask questions like that? His father had set the rules which still made honest answers taboo. Dent had rented a small studio in Houston Street. He was going to live there and (1) paint, (2) catch up, he hoped, on some of the screwing he'd missed during the war. He was more or less back with Helen, his girl from before the war whom his family had never liked. He was working besides on a zaftig little *Time* researcher for whom he had great plans.

"Father, I'm going to look around."

"The war, I take it, has not changed your feelings about architecture as a profession."

"No, sir."

"There are going to be some fascinating structures designed and built in the next few years, George. Technological and material breakthroughs. With your unique combination of talents . . ."

"Yes, sir." Pause. Dent contracted his shoulders, braced himself for battle.

"George," his father decisive now, cigar down, the hooded eyes suddenly up, full on him, "have you any idea what you want to do?"

Part of him, he believed the major part, wanted to paint. Financially, he could afford the risk. As a wounded veteran he did better than the GI Bill. He got Public Law 65, complete training from the ground up. He could go to the Art Students' League in the winter, someplace else in the summer, everything paid for, plus his retirement pay as a wounded captain, a hundred and twenty-five tax free bucks a month. And in five more years, at thirty, he came into twenty-five thousand dollars.

But . . . but . . . but . . . he'd been down to the Art Students' League to check it out. The people down there were so different from himself. Nice guys, friendly girls, he liked them all, but there were few in the bunch he'd trust with a tank section, much less a platoon. Did he really belong among these people, when he loved to lead, order, win? If they were artists, was he?

And if he found he couldn't paint he would have lost out to his friends and be stuck behind the eight ball ten years from now. At present he was way ahead of them. Did the fact he was facile at drawing, had got good marks in composition at Yale, say anything about Dent as an artist, numb before the canvas, attacking blank space day after day? Lots of guys who knew all the answers at the sand table couldn't even press their mike button, let alone move a platoon, when the hulls began to burn.

"Well, you know father, as I used to tell you before the war, I think I want to paint."

"That's always a possibility." Until he was about sixteen or seventeen his father had encouraged his painting; praised his pictures. Told his mother: "This is creative work our son is doing, dear." Later, when he wanted to be totally committed about painting, his father set up roadblocks. Dent wanted to go to art school. Father said Yale. The old man had been right there.

"I plan to try now."

"Oh, for how long?"

"Three or four years, sir."

"In most demanding professions, George, and art is certainly one of those, one scarcely gets started in three or four years."

"I know."

"Then why three or four years?"

"It will take me that long to find out if I'm fitted for it." He knew his father would try and wear him down. He'd been prepared all weekend.

"I have heard," his father continued, "and all the artists I know confirm this, that those who wish to paint, have any chance at all of being successful as artists, are certain from the beginning that that is how they must spend their lives."

"That's a problem."

"I have always assumed a major aspect of the profession that appeals to you is its bohemian way of life."

Dent smiled at his father's circumlocution. "Sex is not why I want to paint," he said.

"Are you sure?"

Silence. He'd gotten moments of full ecstacy, as total as leading men in combat, while executing some of his good paintings: *Birches over Ice, The Fishermen,* his huge *Red Nude* of Helen.

His father continued, "If to paint is what you want to do more than anything else in this world, George, you must do it. God knows you have earned your right to happiness, if any man has."

It always came as a shock that his father loved and was proud of him.

"George, could I make a suggestion?"

If his father had fought him, Dent's decision would probably have gone the other way. But his old man was too wise a bird for gun to gun. He maneuvered and hit you above the track from the flank. He suggested a "possible" compromise. Why didn't George go to art school in the summer and law school in the winter. Then if he found painting wasn't for him he'd have the law training to fall back on. He might even find he liked law—people did.

Dent said he'd think it over. The deal sounded reasonable. He could test art while he stayed up with his peers. He shoved his wounds, medals, and military record at Harvard Law School and got admitted for the fall.

Now he was here, Congressman George S. Dent, at thirty-eight well ahead of the pack; and with luck and a few more breaks like the air crash, he would lengthen his lead. He never had got to art school, instead had gone abroad with Helen, continuing to paint, of course, even turning out one or two good canvases, but not the full commitment. That he'd reserved for this, the real world. He realized he had ceased smiling. His mouth had hardened into its usual business line of grim determination, the left side of his lips pursed slightly down. He pulled a file card from his pocket and began to make notes on what to say to the press at the airport.

four

Sam had done his usual superb job hustling the press into believing that Dent was engaged in something important. Now, the press was here in force; anything he did would be reported as news and therefore considered important. He paid off the cab, relit his smile, and walked toward the two TV cameras and the knot of reporters. "Hi-ya, friends."

Dent answered the reporters' questions, stressing his interest not just in the causes of this crash but in increased air safety for all the nation. As he made his remarks he several times climbed in and out of the light twin-engine plane that waited for him. Another Dent rule: Always be on the move when you say anything. A politician while sitting in his office might deliver remarks worthy of Saint Paul's finest Epistles and the press would overlook them. Another while walking down a plane ramp would say, "The Reds are after us," and these words would be reported nationally as the greatest statement of American policy since the Monroe Doctrine.

Besides the press, both Eastern and Consolidated had public relations men present. Dent noted with appreciation the difference between the courteous treatment he got now and the fast shuffle they had begun to deal him last night. He had never met the representative from Eastern, but he had run into the Consolidated PR man in Washington. That airline must be gravely worried. This was no pat-you-on-the-back-give-you-a-free-ride-to-Miami-find-ya-a-blonde-and-pick-up-your-hotel-tab guy who bought the average Congressman; he was the real article, the well-tailored back-room operator with stock options, legal contracts for your firm, campaign contributions in five figures, service contracts for friends; and above all facts, facts, facts (as impressive as Dent's own selection), in which the name of Consolidated emerged pure and shining and bright, first cousin to the Savior of mankind.

"What do you hope to find out, Mr. Congressman?" the Consolidated man asked.

Dent answered him as he had the press, by quoting Marshal Foch: "Don't telephone; go see." He was going to look for himself; and he didn't want to prejudice the case by any speculations before he'd looked.

The press wanted to know if they could go along in the plane. Since with himself and the two PR men on board there would be only two places left and there were seven members of the press excluding TV technicians, Dent said sure; but they'd have to choose the two themselves. Ten minutes later with the two seats still empty the pilot fired up the engines. The reporters still stood arguing fiercely over the seats.

As Dent had suspected there was little knowledge to be gained from his flight. The air was blue and calm, the city and its suburbs stretched out below the plane glimmering prettily beneath the pollutants, a world totally different from yesterday. Though if the Consolidated flight was where it belonged and McTurk off course, the jet had flown a surprising long way before it hit the ground. Probably the Consolidated flight had been at fault and the line already knew it, hence the high-powered PR man. But why? He looked at the wreckage of the jet outlined in the Jersey swamp below him and suddenly felt small and helpless.

He got back on the ground in time to put in an hour at his New York office, three tacky rooms one flight up over a stationery store on Sixth Avenue. There for a time most Fridays and Saturdays, alternately fascinated or bored, he listened to the problems brought him by his voters; or else was threatened with political extinction, and sometimes bodily harm, by the compulsive right and left.

Those who came to his office for help, especially those on Saturday, were the strangers at the American feast. They had no powerful friends, or even slightly powerful acquaintances to make the opening phone call or write the introductory letter. So they sat before him, a few belligerently and schemingly but most shyly and beseechingly, with the numb look of lost hope.

Their problems seldom varied: help finding a job, immigration cases, Civil Service wrongs, military troubles, citizenship, and a host of complaints over items such as rent control that should have belonged to the city, but about which a groggy city did nothing.

Those who came to yell at him did so because he was the nearest part of the hated system they could insult. They blasted him for being either a fascist pig or a filthy Communist, depending on the beholder's eyes. To all the hostile Dent was polite. After all, he reasoned, they voted. Perhaps if he was nice they might find that at election time they hated the other guy worse.

Dent quit his office in ample time to get to the Blitzners' on schedule. They had helped raise over forty thousand dollars during his last campaign; and with that quality investment they had bought, at the very least, his promptness. They would also expect him to stay a reasonable length of time and delight their guests with inside information from Congress and the city, i.e., stuff they hadn't read in the *Times* or *Wall Street Journal.* The problem was not much was going on. Since his most recent heart attack, Eisenhower was acting like a pleasant retired general with a good job. Without any prod from the Executive the Congress, while huffing and puffing for the record, slept. There was a controversy over the division of the Air Force budget between missiles and bombers, and a major question about types of nuclear weapons, both of which interested Dent because of future applications to arms control and strategy. But he'd be thought militaristic if he tried to explain them.

City Hall was sitting on a dandy scandal involving kickbacks to the Fire Department from a sprinkler company. But Dent was as anxious to keep that quiet as any other scared Democrat. The Blitzner guests, munching canapés in the living room of an East Side town house from whose walls gleamed three Chagalls, two Rouaults, a blue-period Picasso, a Cézanne still life, and what Dent secretly considered a highly dubious Utrillo, weren't going to shout tallyhos over the battle between the Bronx and Brooklyn to chair the Board of Estimate, even though the outcome of that battle would have more effect on their lives than most of what went on in Congress. He'd probably stick to gossip on the changes for the test-ban treaty, a sure liberal latherer; and some stuff about the Southern Democrat–GOP coalition and its effects. Perhaps Sarah might have some ideas.

He was forced to abandon his coat in the Blitzner front hall to a formidable French maid who looked dubious about admitting anyone without a hat; and mounted the stairs toward the articulate, nonalcoholic noise. The party was for Democrats. Most of those present voted that way automatically, held in line by the waning charisma of Robert Wagner, Sr., Eleanor Roosevelt, and Herbert Lehman (a thin, ethnically balanced line of heroes). Though some would have disenfranchised themselves for tax purposes, or merely to avoid jury duty. Many present had contributed heavily to his campaigns and would come through generously again. What they wanted now was to make certain, things change so fast these days, that he was still the product they had bought: an independent liberal dependent on them.

Since they were bright and alert they would be thinking of the '60 Senate race. Was he a good candidate for their money? Against him would be his age, his lack of statewide exposure, and for some, the fact he was not Jewish, though that would cut two ways. For him would be his liberal record, his personality, and the fact that he was a winner.

Some time before the State Convention in '60, these people, in the empathetic communality of politics, would coalesce on one or two favorite candidates. And however they decided, the pros and the upstate conservatives would listen. The pols might not like or accept the man whom the money and the goo-goos put forward, but they would go through certain motions because they needed the liberals' cash, energy, and image.

Dent entered the living room, greeted his host and hostess with genuine warmth, and then excused himself from the first knot of people who converged on him.

"I haven't seen my wife since seven this morning; and I want to say 'Hullo.' "

Dent's public performance toward Sarah was far more than the standard genuflection the American politician had to make before home, wife, and family to expurgate the guilt of the voter over rising divorce rates and the preference of the American male for girls over women. Dent gladdened to see Sarah. Her energy, blond hair, and lithe figure sparked whatever part of the room she was in. She listened well, knew her facts, had a great memory for names and an instinctive knowledge of who pecked whom and how hard, though occasionally her temper led her to make mistakes. She was a vigorous and well-organized campaigner.

A friend, half joking, had once told him, "George, you made yourself Congressman with help from Sarah. But if you ever get to be Senator, Sarah will have made you one with help from you."

"That's true," he'd answered and told Sarah that night. They'd both laughed. They enjoyed their public life together. Sarah even liked to watch him on TV. He suspected, when he took time to look at his marriage, that Sarah believed in his mission more than he did. She thought he'd make the best Senator in the country. He wanted to win.

They kissed each other.

"You look well, love-dove," said Sarah. "You remember Mr. Honeywell, Mr. Darling, Mrs. Sullivan, and Mr. Finkenstadt."

He remembered Darling and Finkenstadt. He also noted an infinitesimal rise in register as Sarah pronounced the name of Mrs.

Sullivan. That placed her on a higher level of importance than the other three. Since Mr. Darling was a prominent liberal editor, who was she?

"George," Sarah continued, "has been flying over the scene of yesterday's crash and conferring with Federal officials involved. It was shocking, wasn't it? But then there's not much any of us can do about human error, unfortunately.

"We were discussing the test-ban treaty. Mr. Darling doubted that John Foster Dulles—"

(Had anyone, Dent wondered, even when Dulles was a little boy, undoubtedly wearing knickers, called him Johnny Dulles?)

"—was pressing actively for the treaty. Mrs. Sullivan wondered if anyone around Eisenhower was pressing for such a treaty. Pardon me while I slip off. I've a message for Mrs. Patterson, you know, George, over there, talking to Mrs. Banghorn and Mr. Walstein."

Dent followed Sarah's gaze and picked out the three people he was to remember. Sarah moved off. How skillfully she had thrown the play to him. With her he could be in two places at once. —And be a big-eyed blonde in one of them. He smiled at the three before him and picked up the ball.

Mrs. Blitzner's party, like her town house, was tasteful, expensive, and expertly organized. Cohostesses brought people over to meet "Mr. Dent." Old friends and supporters contented themselves with a smile across the room. He spotted Benjamin Wollenberg, of his father's generation yet one of his few close friends. Sarah brought over people she felt might feel slighted at either having to come over on their own or with a hostess. He also saw her in a corner with Mr. Jerrysild, the key party money man, who was patting her hand. Sarah beamed up at him, her baby-blue eyes on target.

With all this organization he didn't have to politick obviously. He stood slightly out of the room's center, sipping a tall Scotch and water, his least favorite drink, the one he drank the slowest. He was bent slightly forward, all attention, his thoughtful listening face pasted on. These informed people liked to lecture their

Congressman. That suited him fine—with his mouth shut he never trapped himself.

After about an hour and a quarter of such stylized informality, Mrs. Blitzner came over and inquired if he would like to speak. Dent said he doubted people were interested; but if they were, he'd be delighted. She thought they would, and clapped her manicured talons. Nothing had been said in the invitation or the follow-up phone calls about his speaking; but he'd guessed he'd have to.

At Mrs. Blitzner's signal the party congealed, except for two loud masculine voices in the hallway arguing about the market. Dent moved in front of the cream silk full-length window drapes and began.

"You don't know what a pleasure it is for me to meet so many old and loyal friends at a time when I'm asking you for neither money nor votes." He flattered them a little while longer and then proceeded as planned, opening with the Southern—GOP combination and test-ban outlook. He threw in a little gossip about Ike's health, some humorous scandal about French defeats in Indo-China, and inside intelligence on the latest Soviet satellites slipped him by his friend Colonel Oldenberry. He touched skillfully on banking legislation, produced some original ideas on Pentagon economy, and wept over the chances for Civil Rights Legislation and the prospect of meaningful financial relief for the cities. He closed with some more flattery.

Good applause. From the back, Wollenberg gave him a decisive thumbs up.

"You know," he said to Sarah when they were safely in a cab, "some day I'm going to meet an old friend and I won't know what to do with my face. I've smiled for so many strangers."

"You've made that observation before, love-dove."

"The thought returns."

"Many of those people are hardly strangers."

"True, but except for one or two like the Wollenbergs, they aren't friends. —It seemed to go well."

"I thought so. Oh, the Weintraubs are getting a divorce. You remember them. They contributed twelve hundred dollars. It was a mixed marriage."

"The girl with the big, soft figure?"

"You might call it that. I'd call it vulgar. He has the money."

"I remember them. I'm sorry."

"We hardly knew them. —Did you get who Mrs. Sullivan is?"

"No.—I heard a bell. But no saliva . . ."

"Really, George, you are the end. She is old Frank Sullivan's widow. She is adored in those circles; and controls millions."

"The millions I'll believe."

"Besides, her sister is Charlotte Drowser. Even you must remember what they gave. You knew about Darling, I hope?"

Dent did; but he let Sarah tell him.

Dent was not scheduled to speak at the East Side Community Association dinner, he merely had to put in an appearance with Sarah; greet the few old friends there; try and make new ones; identify himself with noble charity. The importance of the dinner was that most of the guests were Republicans; and Dent, like all politicians, spent too much of his time talking to faithful followers, the already convinced. Opportunities to persuade the opposition, or even to get them to listen, were precious.

"Glad to meet you, Congressman. Though I must admit I didn't vote for you last election." He would hear that often during these next two hours devoted to charity. Each time his smile would come on, his handshake firm up as he replied, "It's the people who don't vote for me keep me on my toes." Or, if they were slightly friendly, "Now that you've met me, I hope you'll at least consider a change." Maybe after he was old and gray and had sat for twenty-five terms he could afford to reply, "Good. The ignorant usually don't."

Sarah fielded the same remark with a bright smile and, "Now you know my husband, you can redeem yourself next November."

They sat down to dinner, and soon after, Dent, having been nice to everyone at the table, finished his fruit cup and, leaving

Sarah behind to cover for him, snuck out. He had more work: "The Citizens Committee for Mayor Wagner" dinner at the Taft.

Sarah watched him leave. George had really done quite well this evening, she thought. Too bad he wasn't going to speak to these people too. His little speech where he told some of the horrible things going on in Congress and then asked for more morality in Government. He certainly had nice shoulders, though he was moving his hands too much as he talked again. She would have to remind him not to.

It was too bad she couldn't go with George to the Mayor's dinner and help him there too. Still, there was work to do here. To split was best. She wished Daddy would appreciate more what she did for him, leaving the children, always on the go. He hadn't even asked her what her father had to say at lunch. He was probably still upset by the crash. She noticed that all the men at the table had been sneaking glances at her. She tilted her chin and looked up at the man next her. Really, he was talking absolute drivel. But as Vice President of the Association he was going to invite George to speak next year, though he didn't know it yet.

"My, you put that well," she said.

Dent hated dinners like the "Citizens Committee for Mayor Wagner." But he had to be seen there. The average politician lives in fear that he may be checking with Clancy when he ought to be clearing with Fred. In politics no one hands out keys to executive washrooms. The little guy picking his teeth in the front office may be running the show. Only at such party rituals as the large dinner can the anxiety-ridden practitioners gather some insight into who spits on whom.

Tomorrow the Mayor's dinner would be minutely analyzed by experts.

"Hey, Pete, I saw Al at the dinner last night."

"Me too."

"Did ya notice he was at Hermie's table?"

"No kiddin'. Hermie! Was Wenzel at the same table?"

"No. He was at annuder. A bit more to da side; but fudder forwud."

"How much fudder forwud?"

"Hard to say. Three to da left and maybe one-and-a-half up."

"Oh. You remember that guy that used to be in the Comptroller's Office, Hermie's friend?"

"Sherm?"

"Yeah. I didn't see him at the dinner."

"Me neither."

"Do ya suppose they're plannin' somethin' cute out in Queens?"

"You never know wid Al."

"I think we might take a readin' on dis one."

"Likewise."

"Be seein' ya."

Or closer to the heady stink of power—

"I had da opportunity of havin' a few woids wid hizoner last night about the little problem we been havin' wid da licensing boys. I think things are gonna begin to move now licensewise."

To be absent or unnoticed at the feast could kill—

"Bill, it's Artie, did Fitzarelli talk to you about his little problem last night?"

"Who?"

"Joe Fitzarelli, from the Thirty-second in Brooklyn."

"Artie, to the best of my knowledge and belief, I have no recollection of any such conversation."

"Oh, yeah, yeah—thanks Bill. Didn't mean to bother ya."

"Any time. Glad to see ya last night. That was a nice young kid, that Martin, you had with you."

"Yeah, he is Bill. A good kid. And smart too. Thanks a lot Bill. So long."

Exit Fitzarelli. Enter Martin.

George Dent pushed through the dining-room door, worried. There were booby traps all over the room. As a "reform" Democrat he was deeply suspect to the political barons of upstate, Brooklyn, and the Bronx, and their covert allies, the body-traders of big labor. To have a shot at the Senate he had to blunt this hostility—to become: "a guy we can live with." He didn't need the support of these men; that would be fatal. The reformers would desert him instantly, the Liberal Party, which always endorsed him, would have a public shit-hemorrhage, and the press turn naggingly hostile.

Though Dent agreed passionately with the reformers and usually felt one with them in spirit as well as label, he often found it easier to talk to the professionals. The pros might be devious and tricky; but at least they were pragmatic. Their word was untrustworthy; so was that of the reformers; but when the pros knifed him in the back, they didn't spend hours asking him to love them because they'd thrust in the name of higher morality.

The old-line politicians' problem was much simpler than reporters or sociologists had yet discovered; they weren't too bright. Failing to grasp that the city was moving from the age of personal contact to the age of symbol manipulation, the pros had fallen behind the times. Too slow to change, and arrogant about their old ways, they had allowed themselves to be intellectually muscled into the role of perpetual heavy.

This gradual passing of the professional "pol" was leaving a vacuum. For the reformers' expertise was in attacking symbols, not problems themselves. Liberals were profoundly ambivalent toward power. They sought it avidly, they advocated extension of Federal power as the cure-all for every evil; but when they held power themselves they felt their own use of it dirty. Basically they were a strange combination of bureaucrat and actor, more comfortable before the TV cameras or writing memos than around people. They got their kicks not from governing; but from the act of protest itself.

Dent had learned this lesson early, long before he became a Congressman, when he was on the Legal Committee of the Lenox Hill Reform Democratic Club.

Three half-block-size parks in the club's area were neglected and foul; and the club wanted the Board of Estimate to vote funds to repair them. Dent went down, saw one of the Board staff members; and got a commitment to have the parks fixed in return for some free legal work for a Board member's cousin. He'd been rather proud of the way he handled this. To his surprise, at the next club meeting he was loudly and thoroughly denounced for having failed as head of the Legal Committee. One Bernie Kuntz, head of the Legal Committee of the Kips Bay Reform Club, was held up as the *beau idéal.* Bernie had prepared an insulting fifty-page brief on the parks, with which he had harangued the Board of Estimate; infuriating them, wasting their time, and almost causing them to renege on their promise to Dent.

Dent made the mistake of trying to defend himself on the grounds that he had solved the park problem. This was greeted with hostile silence. Then several members took the floor to flay him further. He had made a "deal," the very thing the club was created to avoid. From then on Dent realized that goo-goos had no interest in parks; they never stopped talking long enough to sit in one. Nor did they care if blacks starved, if the fire department was decently paid, or city schools killed kids. They protested to feel good inside themselves. Their passion was assaulting the establishment with the flat of their rapidly flailing tongues.

Every time a member rose on the floor of the Lenox Hill Reform Club to denounce some new bungle or boondoggle on the part of the city—and God knew there were plenty of them to denounce—the speech always ended with the ringing battle cry of: "Are we going to let this happen?"—then came the giveaway as the gauntlet bounced on the floor—"without letting ourselves be heard?"

The audience would murmur a passionate, semiarticulate "No," the most superfluous answer ever returned a speaker. These fanatic liberals never let anything happen without making themselves heard. Even when they went to the bathroom they let their wives, husbands, children, friends, and unwary passers-by in at length on every detail. Then they paid some longsuffering analyst while they told it all over again. But talk was all. To work to make things better would spoil the purity of their feelings of impotence, the sense of powerlessness which excused them from responsibility in society, in marriage, in love, even in the rearing of their children. They were self-created sheep who in their need had invented their own wolves.

Dent was certain the most passionate liberals had begun to secretly hate him the day after his election. If he had failed, like Stevenson, he would have become a symbol they could identify with and love. In success he joined the establishment.

Dent went first to his table; checked its location and those seated with him to make certain no one had gotten cute and moved him toward the back of the room or placed him with a known Mafia Don. Then he forced his way toward the VIP cocktail party. His invitation was useless in getting through the door. Those with brass and strong elbows made it inside, others didn't.

Dent bucked toward the clutch of men about the Mayor. The Mayor broke slightly out of the group to greet him and inquired about the air crash. Dent assured him for once the city wasn't to blame, complimented him on the turnout, and reported his district was in good shape for '58. The Mayor opined the whole city was in good shape; they expressed optimism together; shook hands; danced away. Who gets the ring when the music stops, Dent wondered?

He maneuvered around several body-traders from big labor, greeted two fellow Congressmen, chatted with some of big money, avoided a female militant, got caught by a Brooklyn Assemblyman, mingled with two Harlem ministers, touched base with a district leader, and saw Tom Calahan, the patronage boss of the city. He had recently done Tom a favor. The son of one of Calahan's close friends, stationed in the Air Force in Japan, had planned to marry a Red Cross girl who was Jewish. The family, strict Catholics, were horrified. Tom said not to worry, he'd get the boy transferred before the marriage could take place. But the

Air Force refused; and both Irish and Jewish Congressmen were fearful of what could happen to them if pressure on their part became known. By the time Calahan called Dent he was desperate. Dent hadn't been too happy about the deal. But his friend Colonel Oldenberry had assured him he'd have the kid out of Japan and in Alaska within twenty-four hours; and he'd delivered. Now Dent was in the delightful position of "being owed one" by Calahan; and he owed Oldenberry.

Dent waved; Calahan waved back and turned toward Dent; Dent started toward Calahan. Experts pausing to observe the ritual whose every nuance was as stylized as classic ballet were surprised by the warmth of the greeting that followed. After backslaps, greetings, questions on the air crash, Dent lowered his voice and leaned toward Calahan.

"Tom, confidentially, I'm worried the Pentagon intends to close the Brooklyn Navy Base. I know the other members of the delegation aren't worried; and they're telling the Mayor not to worry. We've heard talk of closing the base before; but this time I think the Pentagon means it. It's outside of my district and I'm carrying the ball alone. I could use some help."

Calahan nodded. "Let me talk to a few people. And thanks again for that little matter."

"Forget it. Just stop sending me those high-school dropouts who want to be FBI men."

"I get some beauts from your district, George. Those beatniks who want to be Welfare Commissioners."

They laughed and parted. When I get to be Senator, thought Dent, I won't have to circulate like this. I can stand in a corner and they'll come to me. Now, though he didn't have to dance as fast as he used to, he was still among the marionettes even when they went in to dinner. One step forward and two steps back, wave, hop to the next table, return, grab a bite, shake, and hi-ya.

The ceremony was still at full blast, nor had the chief speaker of the evening begun his three-quarters-of-an-hour drone, when, at 11:30, Dent snuck out for his final appointment of the day: a look-in at the Chelsea West Reform Democratic Club's monthly meeting.

Chelsea West Reform was located three flights up over a laundry and Chinese restaurant, between Sixth and Seventh Avenues in the upper twenties. The side-street entrance with its flaked black lettering, heavy door that did not quite fit, and enormous double lock all shouted, "Look at us! Look! We're poor, but we're honest and will fight." As Dent tramped up the stairs, great breakers of gray cigarette smoke surged down, marking the gathering as liberal. In the chambers of conservatives the heavier blue burn-off of cigars would swirl about the lights.

The club room itself, once a long, low-ceilinged store room, was lined with beaten-up, fourth-hand filing cabinets and several nondescript desks with typewriters chained to them. Most of the file drawers were without labels, though a few bore signs that hinted at diligent labor in stony vineyards. "Major contributors, '48, semirevised." "Plans for Reform—Active—'49–'52." "Speakers unheard from, Dead File." "Resolutions pending, '51, A-D, partial."

The low length of room was crammed with folding metal chairs, the cheap kind whose sloping seats cramped the rump into spastic agony after fifteen wiggling minutes. Some one hundred and fifty people, mostly women, were impaled on these tortured thrones of local democracy. Dent believed the reason so many reform meetings were dominated by slightly fat female nuts was that only they had the physical padding and mental estrangement to take long hours on such chairs. Before the phalanx of chairs was a table, seated behind which the club's president, vice president, and secretary warily and wearily surveyed their co-equal charges.

At the back of the room milled knots of members, resting their tails, gossiping, arguing, dating, making long-distance phone calls over the club phones, whose locks, installed to discourage such a practice, were always broken. The buzz of noise in the back caused those who claimed the floor in the center to continually raise their voices. Those in the back then raised theirs till everyone was shrieking at each other; finally the club president would once again call for order, ask everyone to please be seated, and restart the cycle at a lower pitch.

In his own cleared bit of space at the back, puffing voluptuously on a cigar to disinfect the cigarette poison around him, giving all who approached his genial bulk—never too close—a grand yet equal greeting, stood Dent's guide, conscience, and one-man board of strategy, Sad Sam Kleinman, half Job, half carnie pitchman.

"Hullo, Sam."

"Hullo, George. Sarah looked in about two hours ago. Did a good job. —Where's your bandage?"

"I didn't get hurt, Sam."

"So what are you? A banker or a politician? I told you this afternoon, get a big bandage on your head, so people remember."

"Not on the head, Sam. That's giving away points. How long you been here?"

"Two and a half to three hours." (Dent winced.) "How was the dinner?"

"I thought it went well. I think you should have gone, Sam. I hate those dinners. . . . What's with it here?"

"A resolution denouncing the House Un-American Activities Committee and a resolution against making Seventh and Eighth Avenues one way."

"But they were made one way a year ago. Every study shows it helps the area."

"So I have heard—many times."

"Then why are people against it?"

"Some have uncovered a plot by City Hall to slaughter their aged mothers crossing the street. Others see the sinister hand of the Teamsters Union in conjunction with old line politicians forcing small business to the wall."

"—And Sam, they blasted HUAC last month."

"But not in language strong enough to satisfy the conscience of an aroused people."

"Which is before the floor now?"

"Both."

"What?"

"This is a reform club. You don't want to stifle debate, George."

"Both at once?"

"Well, not precisely. Since ten o'clock we have been considering at some length which should be taken up first."

"On which side is the present speaker?"

"She is denouncing Chiang Kai-shek."

"One of those nights."

"The nuts are restless."

As Dent's presence became noticed, members drifted back to greet him. Chelsea West had been one of the first clubs to back his first primary campaign and he still knew many present. Others Sam, who Dent sometimes felt knew every voter in the district, would greet first in a loud whisper. The president, grasping at Dent's presence like a poisoned fish sucking for air, suggested winding up the meeting so that the Congressman, who had been good enough to drop by, could say a few words.

"Just what would he be speaking in reference to?" One of the female members surged to her feet, glaring at the president.

"I am sure we would all like to hear the latest word from Washington, Sylvia."

"No. It is we who should be telling Washington the word."

Off on the other side of the room a benign elder statesman with a pipe rose and pointed out that several items on the night's agenda that the meeting had not yet had time to take up owing to the debate, were carryovers from three meetings ago. One of these items—he removed pipe and glasses to look at the members with the air of a man who sees plots everywhere—involved the number of slots the club had been allocated on the Central Manhattan Committee of Reform Democrats; and it could well be that the voice of their club was being lost. Gasps of alarm surged around the room.

The chairman pointed out that it was well after midnight.

Another woman rose and began, "I have been quiet up to now, Mr. Chairman."

"Mabel, you've spoken three times. . . ."

"But not about what happened to my mother trying to cross Seventh Avenue. She was walking. . . ."

"I'm afraid I'll have to rule you out of order, Mabel."

"Is this a Democratic club or the headquarters of a Fascist cabal?" the woman screamed.

The chairman raised his voice and pressed on. "Could the secretary state the motion that is before this meeting?"

"It's a bit confused, Joe."

"I think I can phrase it. Resolved: that this club condemns the House Un-American Activities Committee. I think we should refer that motion to our Legal Committee to be placed in the strongest possible language and transmitted to our Congressmen."

"I'll be glad to receive it," said Dent.

"Not many clubs get service like that," said the chairman, quickly calling for ayes and nays and gaveling the motion into committee.

Shelving the one-way-street issue was tougher. The chairman first tried to refer the subject to the Community Affairs Committee. One of the strengths of the reform movement was that every active member could be on at least two committees; many were on four or five. So the faithful were able to pass their nights safe from human contact and rational thought in constant debate.

The chairman's strategy did not work. Springing to her feet, a lady with long stringy hair shouted at him, "While we are referring to committees the little shopkeepers of the district are starving." Dent recognized her. Twice at rallies in predominantly Catholic neighborhoods she had asked him where he stood on U.S.-Government-supported birth control for India.

"But are they starving?" the chairman made the mistake of asking.

"Would I be telling you if they were not?"

There was a loud "Yes" from the rear of the room. The woman whirled.

"I heard that, Bertie Osterwise, you toady for the reactionary forces of City Hall; and I want you to know, and those who think like you in this club to know, and they know who they are, and who I mean, that you are unworthy of the name of reform."

"It seems rather strange, Mr. Chairman," an unusually quiet voice addressed the chair from the front of the room, "that we should start out crusading for political reform and end up debating whether we should turn the one-way avenues back into two-way avenues."

"From little acorns come great endings, never forget!" someone yelled.

Never forget the squirrel vote, thought Dent.

The gallant president tried again. "In the interests of hearing the Congressman speak, I propose the issue of this club's stand on one-way avenues be carried over until our March meeting. . . ."

"Where it be placed first thing on the agenda," cried a voice from the floor.

"Its position on the agenda," the president continued inexorably, "to be determined by the Executive Committee in conjunction with the Committee on Agendas."

"There'll be a hot time in the old Executive Committee for the next three weeks," whispered Sam.

"I so move," cried a voice. "Second," came from various places in the room. The chairman put the aye and nays, gaveled down three women and one man who were on their feet shouting, and triumphantly introduced their own Congressman, the man reform elected, the Honorable George Dent.

Dent hadn't intended to speak. A short, snappy speech was out of the question. This audience would doubt the sincerity of anyone who, given a chance to speak, held himself back. That is why Hubert Humphrey was the secret god of so many present; they worshiped as heaven-inspired a man who could talk for four hours on the corn surplus, disarmament, or the need to solve the economic problems of the felt workers by having everyone purchase two hats, without saying a single constructive thing. So Dent came up with a fact.

"Mr. Chairman, I really have no speech to make. But I do have one item of news of importance to all of us in this club and in the district. You have asked me, officially and unofficially, about our policy in Southeast Asia, now that the Korean War has ended and the French appear in such trouble in Indo-China.

"I, of course, have been continually pressing the Pentagon and the State Department for more information for the public and especially for us here in the district, where we have a particularly vital interest in foreign affairs. I have now been able to pressure the State Department, or persuade the State Department if you want to be polite" (laughter and nods. They had a go-getting Congressman, they did) "to send us on the tenth of April, Ambassador Harper. Ambassador Harper, as many of you may remember, was the State Department representative at the Negotiations in Korea with the North Koreans. I know the Ambassador well. I can assure you he will give a fascinating evening. And there will be plenty of opportunities to ask questions when you all can make your voices heard." (Cheers) "Thank you, Mr. Chairman. It's a pleasure to see so many old friends here tonight and feel the continued energy in the reform movement. Thank you all."

"Thank you, Mr. Congressman." The chairman adjourned the meeting. Twitching off their chairs, a horde of professional question-askers swarmed toward Dent to make their views known.

Dent stood there fielding questions. He knew Sam would rescue him in about fifteen minutes, so he relaxed. Most of the questioners didn't want answers, they merely wanted to be heard. He was able to stand quietly nodding.

At the local bar he and Sam had a couple of beers with the president, vice president, and secretary of the club. This was part of the ritual too, that the leaders get better treatment than the followers. Since Chelsea West Reform was based on complete equality, the leaders' position had a highly schizophrenic quality.

"Boy," said Sam, "that was rough tonight—five hours."

"You handle them well, Jim," said Dent to the president.

"Those questions like one-way streets where you're actually meant to solve a problem are always tough. It was good to see your wife tonight."

Dent nodded. "I was talking with the Mayor at dinner"—the game was politics and he was a skilled player—"and I told him that as far as this district was concerned things didn't look 'just good' for the election this fall; they looked 'very good.' I'm right on that as far as your club's concerned, aren't I?"

"Yes sir."

"You're in solid, George."

Dent noticed the club president's use of his first name. Time for the next step.

"I wasn't just thinking about myself," Dent said, "but about our wing of the party. Personally I'm not too worried about this next election, though it gives Sam fits to hear me say that."

"When you're not scared you're not punching. And when you're not punching you get your face smashed in."

Sam and he had a great routine going. "I'm still not worried about winning, Sam. But I am scared, really scared, that we won't win big enough to give reform a voice in the Senate race two years from now. We need to win by at least thirty thousand more than last time, or we may get some old-line boss shoved down our throats. Then we're all dead."

The faces of the three club leaders got serious. They hadn't planned to work that hard this time.

"In politics," Dent continued, "you know this, the pros work all the time. We've got to work just as hard but with more efficiency and popular support. Our goal has got to be"—he paused to repeat himself—"our goal has got to be a position where no one can name the next Senatorial candidate without consulting us."

They weren't fooled. They knew he meant himself. But the ritual that no one in politics has ambition was being observed.

Even the crudest didn't gurgle: I want that soft job of Senator. They gassed about serving the state.

"Congressman," asked the secretary, "have you thought about trying for the Senate yourself?"

"Ask me that after we win by fifty thousand."

The three club officers sat at the Formica table—the bar was one of those places that made sipping Scotch almost like slurping an ice-cream soda—feeling the jolt of Dent's stimulant. Supposing they weren't just sitting with a Congressman; but with a Senator, talking to him like this, telling their friends afterward. There would be a knot of reporters at one of the booths so they would have to talk softly, autograph hunters, decisions affecting not just one election district but the whole state. And they would have done this, if they could put him over. They would have claims. Dent's shape changed a little as he sat before them.

"There's a great many of us think you'd make a great Senator," said the vice president.

"Right now, there're more aren't so sure. Many think Jim Donnegan would be better."

"Oh, no!" from all three. Dent had deliberately picked the most objectionable of the old-line possibilities, an inflated Albany dinosaur without a chance.

"Isn't that so, Sam?"

Kleinman removed his cigar and looked at it with the air of a man wondering how much of a vital secret to divulge."That's the word that's being passed out to the regular clubs and upstate. I got three phone calls on it this week already."

"It's unbelievable," said the president. It was, too. But it was part of the negotiations already under way. For his part, Sam and a few trusted whisper-buddies had begun to put out the word that the reform group thought the next breakthrough should be a woman Senator and that the likely liberal candidate was Alice Warbash, a harsh dynamo of a millionaire wild woman whose sole objection to Chou En-lai rested on the fact he wasn't black. The conservatives would react to Alice Warbash the way Dent's people were reacting to Jim Donnegan. Slowly the middle ground would be defined. But from which end of the middle would the candidate finally come?

Having made his pitch, Dent listened to the leaders for a while and answered their questions. He gave thoughtful, honest answers, they worked hard, they deserved that; but also answers slanted toward what they wanted to hear. By now it was 1:30. Time to grab a cab and head home. He warned them that Ambassador Harper was a dead beat, then wished them all good night, paid the check, headed for the door. Sam would give the three a final pep talk.

The club president watched him go, honestly conscious of his envy. There's a man, that George Dent, he thought, who handles life the way it should be lived. Handsome, with a cute blond wife who's loaded with dough and probably does tricks for him all night. He doesn't just sit around on his duff. And you can talk to him. If I had all that would I do anything but lie in the sun in Miami and diddle that broad?

When Dent got home Sarah was asleep. He remembered he'd forgotten to ask what her father had had to say. He'd do that tomorrow morning. That had been a great idea of hers to look in at Chelsea West on her way home. She didn't have to do that. He picked up the alarm clock and moved into the bathroom to undress.

When people asked him how he'd met Sarah, he had a reply he enjoyed giving. "The first time I met my wife, she was going rapidly downhill. —We were on the same ski slope."

He was twenty-seven then, a junior at Harvard Law, up for a ski weekend in New Hampshire. Old-fashioned, pre-resort skiing: no snow bunnies, just wooden skis, one lift, two narrow trails, and lots of deep snow. Dent's skiing had been none too good before the war and with mangled leg and shoulder he could barely handle the slope: also he hated the cold.

He was in New Hampshire for two reasons, both of which annoyed him. First, in spite of the self-knowledge he had gained during the war, he was still hooked on being part of the group, and his friends were skiing. Second, he was having problems with his girl, Helen. She liked neither law school nor many of his law-school friends. She thought he ought to be painting and said so. In the middle of last summer, in Oslo, they had called everything off. Though they were back together again, they fought often. Part of him was looking for someone else, so that if necessary he could phase out of Helen without a lonely period.

He had been resting at a twist in the trail, looking out at the thick snow beneath the pines; and wishing he was trudging through that blue-white loneliness by himself on snow shoes, when a sharp cry of "track" cracked into his thoughts. He pushed himself farther to the side of the trail. The last thing he wanted was to be rammed into by some drunken bruiser from Dartmouth. Instead a lithe, perfectly balanced blonde with blue parka, red headband, and goggles shot by with a quick christie and flash of smile. Behind, to be on hand when she reached the bottom, for trouble on the trail she was obviously not going to have, came six or seven professional type skiers booming down in full control.

Dent gave all of them the hidden glower he reserved for those who did what he was doing better than himself. Again he lashed himself because he was not back at Harvard studying; or at his studio in New York painting. Then he was furious because he'd thought about painting. Would he never decide that question? He turned down slope with difficulty, not having enough knee or ankle motion to kick-turn any more; and cautiously skied on down the mountain.

Chance arranged that he and the blonde were staying at the same ski lodge. Her name was Sarah Frost; and when Dent and some friends came back from having a few drinks someplace, she was seated before the fire in a blue sweater, dirndl skirt, bare legs, and slippers, surrounded by men bidding for her attention. Dent felt the need to take up the challenge. Only in part the challenge of Sarah, or even of sex; mostly that of place and effect: the cold, slim figure, the blond hair, the breasts beneath the blue sweater, the girl everyone wanted, the fire, the long room in which to move.

He had a drink, sat down on the far side of the room, watched Sarah, and deployed his forces. First he learned her name. Then that she worked on *Time,* was considered hot stuff, had a father who owned a string of newspapers in Connecticut and upstate New York, and was loaded. She was engaged—the challenge inside Dent intensified—to a hot-shot young lawyer in New York who had been a legal officer in the Navy. Dent let a few friends in on his intentions, then started slowly across the room.

Though giving no indication she noticed, Sarah saw him coming, walking across the wide rectangle of the ski lodge. She was way ahead of him. She'd seen him adjusting his ski bindings that morning and had asked who he was. On learning, she took a brief angry stare. One of her closest friends on *Time,* a really lovely girl, had for months talked of no one but George Dent. And that man had suddenly thrown over her friend with no word. A typical unfeeling male. (Her friend, without knowing it, had hit one of Dent's sudden and complete recommitments to Helen; and Dent had been too shy and afraid of a scene to meet and explain.)

Later Sarah found an excuse to ask a friend from Harvard Law School about Dent. The answer confirmed her belief. "He's a cold bastard. All for one and one for all and all for George Dent." When Dent remade himself in his imagined self-image, he burnished the statue daily. —Now he eased his six-foot-one outside of the group, sipped his drink, rubbed the little finger of his right hand with the thumb and index finger of the left and listened. Another Dent rule: Look and listen before the attack; don't just pretend, seeing and hearing only your own hope and fear, think like the enemy.

He felt that part of the enemy, this girl Sarah, though he did not know her, was issuing him a hostile challenge.

Sarah was aware of her masked anger. This was the man who had hurt her friend. Women existed to protect one another, to love the right man, and to be revenged on stinkers. There on the outskirts sat a stinker; not saying anything, completely sure the world would swing his way.

Dent could not think of anything bright to say. The talk of skiing bored him. He knew he was slow on repartee; that he could lose this battle and get laughed at. He stuck his hand through the conversation at Sarah. "George Dent. I'd like to meet you."

Sarah waited an instant and then looked at him. She hadn't expected so direct an approach. "I'm Sarah Frost. I've heard of you." Damn, she didn't want to put it that way. That sounded like a compliment. "Do you know these people?"

"No."

He sat down and left a hole in the conversation. She'd have to introduce him to the circle now, he believed, because she was polite. She did. Several men claimed to have met him before. Had they, or were they just having him on? Sarah saved fiancé till last. Her voice challenged with ancient trumpets as she brought him forward. "My fiancé, Schuyler Burnside; he's with Reed, Rogers."

Dent bit off inside himself the reply: "Must have had a short war." No point in opening fire at too great a range. They were undoubtedly sleeping together off and on. That's what a fiancé was about in polite society. First there was one guy who initiated you to sex. You dropped him after a couple of months because of guilt. Then came the guy you lived with for about six months, became engaged to, and married. Young Schuyler didn't exactly perk with sexual vitality. Sarah did, though. He let the gap in the conversation after Schuyler's introduction broaden. First tank to move often buys it.

"I didn't see you on the slopes much today, George." One of the group, a superb skier from Dartmouth, took the first kick at his balls.

"I'm too shot up to ski well any more. I sure miss it."

"There's a guy back at college skis beautifully on one leg."

"I'll try that next war." The hole in the conversation widened. Dent chose his ground. "Tell me, Schuyler, you know, as we sit in law school thinking about landing a job, we wonder what sort of place we'd like to work. Now in that downtown law factory where you practice, what percentage of the law clerks are for Truman? And what for Dewey?"

"I don't think you'd find many for Truman."

"Ten per cent?"

"I would doubt that."

"Five?"

"I don't know."

"Oh come on, you're not advising a wealthy old lady client now, you can take a risk."

"I am trying to be accurate."

"I wouldn't think in a place where intelligent people congregate more than five per cent would be blindly voting Democratic. Look at the two candidates." Sarah, impatient with her man, charged into battle. Dent's plan had worked; he had cut the rest out, shifted the subject off skiing, and was challenging Sarah, who he'd be certain would be for Dewey. One on one now.

"Haplessly Harry the harried haberdasher," someone remarked and laughed.

"In a contest," said Dent, "between the tailor and the tailor's dummy the tailor is going to win every time. Particularly as this tailor will probably rank with that broke rail-splitter, Lincoln, and that brawling racetrack tout, Jackson, as one of the three or four great Presidents of the United States." Whoops of laughter all around. Dent had crossed the line of departure and attacked.

The battle raged from politics, through legal ethics, to journalistic standards—Dent castigating reporters as licensed peeping toms—and on to female and male morals. Several times he found one of his friends at his side while some lunkhead threatened to push his face in.

Next morning at breakfast Sarah sat down beside him to continue the battle. That was better than he'd expected.

"I'm surprised to see you up this early," she said, fixing him with her baby blues.

She'd gone to a lot of trouble with lipstick and eye shadow just for the snow's benefit. She didn't look relaxed enough to have spent the night fucking.

"I love the early morning," he said, "especially with fresh snow like today. No one in the lift lines, the colors. Also I've got to leave early. I've work for tonight."

"I like the morning sun best too."

"If you hurry with those pancakes, I'll ride up with you."

"I don't want them all anyway." She pushed away her plate.

Riding the lift, Dent explained that another reason he liked to ski early was that his wounds made him stiff in the morning and he was embarrassed at the way he kept falling down.

"That shouldn't bother you," said Sarah.

"I know it shouldn't. But you get sensitive after a time. I was very fond of a girl once, and the first time she saw me without clothes, she left."

"I doubt that was the reason."

"Don't be too hard on her. About the bravest man I ever knew always ran when he saw a bee."

Sometimes I'm embarrassed for my sex, thought Sarah. A woman shouldn't run from a man because he's scarred. She should nourish him.

There was no such girl. Dent was merely introducing his wound strategy early. Usually he saved it till the very end. Then breaking off a kiss he'd say: "There's one thing I must warn you about. If and when I should take off my clothes, the left side of my body is badly scarred." (Pause for honesty.) "It looks quite awful." If a girl were in the middle of the usual yes or no debate, this gave her a psychological shove toward yes. She couldn't turn down a man for wounds. Though unfortunately some could.

Later that afternoon he paused briefly by Sarah in the lift line and asked if she was coming up next weekend.

"You've met my fiancé," she said.

"So."

"I'm engaged."

"I don't get you."

"It's been announced in the papers, and I honor commitments. I don't suppose that means anything to you."

"I assure you, Sarah," eyes fixed at her, sincerity full on, "I always honor commitments. Because I've committed me, not because of a newspaper announcement."

Sarah accepted that and told him they were coming up next weekend. Were they really? Or had she just decided?

The next weekend saw them all back at the same ski lodge. "You watch," Dent boasted to a friend, "within three weeks I'll have this made. I'll even be borrowing dough from her old man."

Well, he'd got that part right, both about the time and the money. Old Mr. Frost, even though a Republican, had turned out a very generous contributor to Dent's campaigns. The trouble was Mr. Frost felt that his special position as father-in-law, plus the handouts, entitled him to part ownership of the product. However, other contributors made the same mistake on less cash and no family ties. He grimaced as he set the alarm for 6:30 a.m. Another crunch of a day ahead.

Instead of going into the bedroom he suddenly sat down on the edge of the bathtub and opened his briefcase. He took out Saturday's schedule and looked at it. With a pencil he drew a hard line through the appointments and meetings after three o'clock. He also put a savage cross through the Sunday morning schedule. He was Congressman George Dent. He'd just been through an air crash. He was going home tomorrow and see his children.

five

April in Washington toys with perfection: warm soft days, light nights, summer's damp heat still off stage. Cherries, dogwood, apples, pears, rhododendrons, and azaleas explode against eyes and nose. Even the sluggish Potomac responds to the season, stops for a while smelling like the open sewer Congressional neglect has made it, to return to its old odor of sea and tide flats, where oysters multiply and ducks sweep, in liquid echelons of call and wing-beat. On Dent's Georgetown street the thin, new tree leaves glowed a sheer green to tint the houses.

Jim Dent woke early, bubbling out of a full night's sleep. He looked at the electric clock on his wall, the second hand marching round and round. I like to watch clocks, he thought. Several years ago, when he was little, he had been the first in his class to learn to tell time, even before any girl. Remembering the knowledge that he had been first, that he really had been able to figure it out, and wasn't fibbing, he felt warm inside.

His room seemed awfully green this morning. Staring at his window he noticed that the ivy which every summer tried to climb over his window screens, already partly covered their lower third. Small heart-shaped leaves about the size of his fingernails were waving in the morning shift of breeze. Other strings of ivy were swinging down from the top, a bug on them would get a pretty good ride. Pretty soon, Pop would notice and say, "Wow, we'd better get to that ivy, before we can't open the screen."

Sometimes the screen did stick and they had to go down to the cellar and get the blowtorch and blow flame at old ivy until its suckers let go. I'm scared of that blowtorch, he thought. It's heavy and dark and goes on with a roar that could set the whole house on fire, maybe the world, like A-bombs, if you didn't know.

To get the shoots climbing the wall, Pop held him out the window by his feet, the shears tied to his waist with string so they wouldn't drop by mistake. He once told Pop that he thought Pop could cut further down the wall than he could, even hanging by his feet. "Maybe," answered Pop. "But it's your ivy and your windows and you should have some of the fun of outwitting the ivy."

Mom said they should get a man with a ladder who would come and fix the ivy, fix the ivy "professionally." Pop said it was silly to pay a man to do something it was fun to do yourself. Mom said it was silly to waste time. Pop said, "Jim and I will take care of the ivy." Jim smiled again and nodded in his bed.

Would they have to use the blowtorch this year? If we do, maybe after Pop starts it I can hold it a bit. I think I can do that. Lighting is the bad part because the flame suddenly goes boom all around your fingers like from a dragon's nose. —There are no dragons. There are no dragons. —Their mothers took baby dragons to volcanoes to light their noses, he guessed. Otherwise the flames would burn the mother's tummy when the baby dragon was inside.

He decided to get dressed and go out and climb before breakfast. It's before I'm allowed up, but if I'm quiet I can sneak out. And I'll take Small Bear with me, because he likes it up in trees. I won't climb the cherry or the pear tree though. If I shake their branches the blossoms will fall on the ground and die because of me.

If Jim had clomped downstairs in his regular fashion Dent would probably never have heard him. But his son's unusual noise, small and clandestine, woke ex-tanker Dent instantly. What was that? Oh, Jim trying to sneak downstairs. He smiled and looked at his watch, six-forty-five, Jim was up three-quarters of an hour early. No harm there. Probably going out to climb a tree. —If you're ever up a tree, why call on me, Jim, because underneath are the everlasting arms. —The soft air massaged Dent, and the odor from the new grass in his back yard nourished him like fresh-baked bread.

He rolled over and looked at Sarah beside him. In sleep her features always melted into those of a little girl. He had seen other men and women asleep. With their muscles relaxed their present merely slacked; this quality of reverse growth which left as its residue a child's face was peculiar to Sarah. Perhaps he had the same trait, a deep psychological ambience they both shared. He'd never know. By the time he'd stumbled to the mirror to look at himself, the child, if there, would have fled back into the man.

He studied his wife, the blond hair, the deep, wide mouth, the almost sheet-white skin. His prick began to stiffen. He'd best get up or think about something unpleasant. Sarah did not like sex in the morning. "I shall not be poked awake to be the receptacle for your sperm."

If he shaved and dressed quickly he could beat their cook to the kitchen and make breakfast for Jim and himself. Jim always ate scrambled eggs when he cooked them "cowboy style," meaning very loose. Sarah had trained the cook to make scrambled eggs light and fluffy in a double boiler. He couldn't eat those dry things himself with any pleasure. They'd be so early that he and Jim could take the streetcar to school. Jane could go with the mother of the day as usual. He'd be about fifteen minutes late to his office; but what the hell, the sudden unexpected bits of time he could spend with Jane or Jim gave him such joy.

He and Jim were leaving as Sarah came downstairs.

"Where are you two going? It's breakfast time."

"We made our own breakfast."

"We pay someone in the kitchen good money to do that." Silence. Dent and Jim stood there smiling at her. "You certainly can upset things, Daddy."

"It's a lovely spring morning."

"Yes, isn't it." She came downstairs and he pecked her cheek. "We're going to take the streetcar to school. By-by."

"Good-by, Mummy."

Sarah watched them go. At the bottom of the steps they took one another's hand. They were cute; but really George was irresponsible in the way he broke discipline and schedules. Did he want her son to grow up to be some sort of tramp?

"It looks as if the men have left us to eat alone," she said to Jane. Jane nodded glumly. Luck just didn't come to her. She got up early and people got mad. Jim got up early and Pop took him to school as a treat.

The male Dents walked away up the street, laughing, catching the falling cherry blossoms in their hands and blowing them at each other.

Dent's meager seniority did not entitle him to an office in the more spacious fourteen-foot-ceilinged Old House Office Building. He existed, crammed in along with eight secretaries and four assistants, in two rooms of the new. Across his inner room a wooden partition had been thrown, which together with a line of head-high filing cabinets made a small third space where his two senior assistants worked. (That marbled triumph to American bad taste, the new, New House Office Building or Rayburn Building, the most expensive office building in the world, where every senior Congressman had his own sauna bath, was still a gleam in the grafters' eye.)

Dent had tried to get paintings on loan from New York museums to hang on his office walls; but insurance problems blocked that. So he had settled for some stunning air color shots of the city. He had fought clear of the world's largest oyster shell, or the world's smokiest stack, or the world's fattest peanut or other such prideful symbols of a district's excellence that adorned the walls of most of his colleagues. There was on his desk a small four-inch glass rectangle with nothing inside, labeled "Content of a 'one pound' package of detergent before the Dent Fair Label Law." That was boast rather than fact. The label law had died in the Senate; where the guardians of corporate privilege had quietly taken it for a ride in committee as part of some complex deal, dark even from Dent, involving permission to mine for uranium in certain Western national forests.

Along one wall he displayed lollipops for visitors: pictures of himself with the famous. Dent shaking hands with Mrs. Roosevelt for the liberals. Dent shaking hands with Cardinal Spellman for the conservatives. Dent in a double handshake with Ben-Gurion and Senator Lehman in a ten strike for the Jews. Dent with Jim Farley for the Irish regulars; Dent giving the big hello to Stevenson for the reformers; Dent with Robert Oppenheimer for the intellectuals. Two pictures of Dent romping with Jane and Jim and one kissing Sarah for the mothers.

On the wall were also several bare hooks. On these could hastily be hung appropriate pictures from his files. Dent with the Pope, with Gina Lollabrigida, with Carmine DeSapio for the Knights of Columbus. Dent with Senator Taft for the National Association of Manufacturers. Dent receiving the second Oak-Leaf Cluster to his Silver Star, and Dent peering at Communist bunkers in Korea with General Ridgway for the American Legion. These, combinations of these, and about thirty others, could be quickly arranged to produce the instant Dent the visitors wished to see.

At 9:32 by the electric corridor clock, Dent passed the mottled blue stone spittoon that tradition demanded must grace the door of his office. Why did other offices blink to life around ten o'clock while his phones were already ringing at nine? Four of his six secretaries, including Joyce Farad, his beautiful "wait-a-minute girl," were behind their desks nudging themselves into work with coffee. Dent passed the two mock orange trees kept slightly alive for him through the constant efforts of the Department of Agriculture and entered his inner office. The intercom buzzed. Congressman Wup-'em-tomorra' Wilson was on the phone.

"Hey boy, what ya doin' gettin' in so late? I already called ya once."

"Where are you, Wup-'em, home in bed?"

"Bed, shute. I'm at my desk on guard to protect the vital interest of every man, woman, and sheep in the sovereign state o' Wyomin'. Say, that subcommittee on air safety is makin' ya a lot of publicity. Ya get in any more crashes this weekend to improve your image?"

"I'm saving the next one till just before the election. What's on your mind?"

"Handball at twelve-thirty."

Dent looked at his desk calendar. Twelve-thirty to one, when he had a luncheon with CORE from New York, was open. He could be ten minutes late for the lunch.

"Okay."

His buzzer rang again immediately. The publisher of one of New York's major newspapers was on the line. He wanted to talk about the automation sections of the new labor bill. Dent made a luncheon date for a week from Friday in New York.

Now his office began to fill with people, twitch to the ring of phones and hump to the pounding of electric typewriters. The founding fathers, fearing that a Congressman would disappear on his horse into the wilderness, and while in Washington lose touch with the voters, had set his term of office at two years. But now the voters were in constant touch with Dent and all the urban Congressmen. They dialed them; they jetted in to see them. Soon they would yell at them over TV phones. A Congressman was never out of touch long enough to legislate for the common good. But any Congressman who proposed making their terms four years long was immediately branded as "scared to face the voters."

As his schedule exploded beneath the daily pressure of visitors and phoners, Joyce Farad came into her own. Before her desk were wedged three empty chairs. Dent would look out of his office, apologize to the important caller, and ask him to "Please wait a minute." With further apologies, the visitor would be seated in one of the chairs before Joyce's desk. If the visitor was male, the effect was predictable and instantaneous. Joyce would turn from her typing, give the man a smile bottled for him alone, and apologize that there was no comfortable place for him to wait. The man would wrench his eyes from Joyce's figure to her face, and reply he didn't mind. She would ask what he did. He would begin his life story suitably embellished. Fifteen, twenty minutes, or even an hour later, when Dent could sandwich in the visitor, the man would assure the Congressman he hadn't minded waiting, hadn't minded at all. Dent would always oblige with the spelling of Joyce's name, but not her phone number.

He himself would never risk being so publicly on the prowl. His desk calendar for tonight read: "District leaders meeting, New York." That was the truth; but not the whole truth. After the meeting with the leaders ended around seven, he was going to see Dee.

He had seen her twice for dinner since the accident, being casual about it; but creating the opportunity. He had taken her to one of the two restaurants he used when he wanted to be reasonably certain he wouldn't be interrupted; and just in case had developed a plausible cover story as to why he was with her. They had neither kissed nor embraced, not so much as a friendly peck good night.

However, Dent believed he sensed across their careful lack of physical contact an unspoken flow of energy charging them both. He was excited about tonight and apprehensive. To have an affair with someone as powerful as Dee would be both time consuming and a risk. Why couldn't he have met her in '57 when this next election was more than a year away? If this dinner turned out just another dinner, he would be wise to cut the contact.

In Dent's outer office Joyce Farad typed carefully, a shade

more slowly than usual. She teased herself that something must show, even though she knew she looked the same; and would continue to look the same when Colonel Catenberry walked through the door. Ever since she had first lied to her parents about whether she or her brother had stolen some candy, she had known that no matter what she felt, nothing showed.

Her brother had been spanked for stealing and sent to bed. There he still sobbed he hadn't done it and had been spanked again for stubborn wickedness. He lay in the bed next to her and cried and cried from hurt and injustice and she lied and lied to him until he was not certain whether he had or had not taken the candy. He even confessed to escape a third spanking. Three or four years later he asked her if she had taken the candy that day. She said no. He believed her.

She and Colonel Catenberry, Assistant Chief of Air Force Congressional Liaison, had spent the night in the Fourlough Missile Company suite at the Sheridan Hotel. Catenberry was big on missile production and the company let him stay there if the suite was free. Catenberry took his girls there. For the last two months that girl had been Joyce. The colonel told his wife he had to take all night duty at the Pentagon in case some junketeering Congressman got in trouble.

Joyce had longed for a man who would, as she once admitted to a girl friend, "put me in my place and keep me there." But all men before had deferred to her, either from greed or terror at her physical perfection. Catenberry held her, fucked her, filled her, used her. For the first time in her life, as if all the other men had been washed out by some new super-bleach, she was totally in love.

Colonel Francis Catenberry was driving toward the House Office Building with two majors assigned to his staff to aid him in keeping Congress informed about the Air Force. Across the left front of Catenberry's tunic, above his wings, appeared row on row of decorations.

Most decorations on pilots have little meaning. Air Force officers who go home to warm beds at night and leave combat after fifty missions suffer from deep unconscious self-doubts about their heroism, when measured against the infantry man, tanker, or Marine: men who in World War II and Korea fought twenty-four hours a day with no end in sight until they were hit. To hide its doubts about its pilots' courage the Air Force distributed its medals as automatically as social security and with a good deal less red tape.

Still, Catenberry's medals—two DSC's, a DFC, and three Silver Stars—were something even for the Air Force. Further, these decorations came not from service in bombers, the favored spot, or even from service in fighters escorting bombers, next in line, but from flying fighters in support of the infantry, a despised job for which the Air Force traditionally awarded few medals. Something, sometime, had fashioned a continuous and aggressive risk-taker out of a poor Oklahoma farm boy: a "hero" to some; a "fool" to others.

One of the majors was new and Catenberry was briefing him as they drove. The major was to be escort officer for three Congressmen and their wives on a week-long tour of Caribbean Air Force bases.

"Now you just got to watch that guy Congressman Rastles. He's worthless," Catenberry's voice was half drawl, half growl. "But he's on the Appropriations Committee; so anythin' he says or wants, agree with and get him. I know that's not what the policy says; but policy shit. I know him. I get on well with him 'cause I know he loves to quote the Bible 'afore he screws you. Do you know the Bible?"

"No, sir."

"Well, get yourself a book called Bartlett's *Familiar Quotations* and memorize a whole hunk of Bible sayings. I want you to know twenty of them by tomorrow morning. That's an order."

"Yes, sir."

"And see you have a Bible with ya where he can see it on this trip. That Rastles should have been in the service, he's the right age. I don't know what deal he pulled to stay out, though I'm tryin' to find out. It would sure help in handlin' that son-of-a-bitch. His family owns most all his part of Georgia, so I guess it wasn't difficult to fix. He'll want to get laid too. There's a Major Smithson at the tracking station at Eleuthera—get that name in your notebook—he always has some good pussy lined up for VIPs."

"Got it, sir."

"And when these guys you'll be escortin' make you sick, and they will, just keep askin' youself: what's the goddamn target? The target is more money for the Air Force and anything you've got to do to hit that—do it!"

The "do it" exploded out from Catenberry with the sudden crack of a sonic boom. Catenberry swiveled his head from the road and fastened his eyes on the two majors to make sure they both understood. They cowered their assent in the presence of his energy and legend. He continued.

"Now that Congressman Astland who'll be goin' with you, he'll make ya sick too. He's so old he pees all over hisself. You'll probably have to hold his prick for him, when he goes to the men's room. He'll be drunk most of the time. Drinks Scotch, Vat 69. Check the aircraft and make sure there are two cases of the stuff on board. Buy the cases out of the unvouchered funds if they're not.

"His wife does nothing but talk. At each base, order some handsome lieutenant to give her a little smooch-smoochie talk and she'll be happy. No Jew boys though. She don't like Jews. And don't tell no one what you're doing. This is the sort of trip the press loves to clobber; and then Congress turns around and clobbers us. If you get asked anything say it's a top-secret special investigation and that all answers have to come from Washington. Then shut up."

"Yes, sir."

Catenberry drove his car into the parking lot behind the New House Office Building; and parked in a spot that said: "Reserved for the Secretary of the Air Force." He'd put that sign up himself to have a place to park. The Secretary had a chauffeur-driven car and didn't need a place. He waited for the junior major to open the door for him. He hoped some Congressman saw. Congressmen bullshitted about democracy, but they loved that spit and polish stuff with everybody deferring, the way they wanted the voters to treat them.

Few men, Catenberry realized, saw the world with his own hawk eyes. They got blinded by the shit those on top put out to keep others away from the gravy. He'd been fooled once; but no longer. What counted everywhere was the invisible system: push, power, and connections. In Russia they told you you got ahead by being a good Communist; but you got ahead by backing Stalin and being from Georgia. In General Motors they said start at the bottom and cut costs. You made president by playing good golf and marrying the boss's daughter. In the Air Force they stuffed you full of bravery and seniority. Nuts. You got behind some weapon system that was coming, found a General who believed in that system, and let him pull you up.

Catenberry's insights had given him a mission; not a fanatic's dream, but a shrewdly calculated plan. The bomber's day was passing; that of the guided missile approached. Then the bomber pilots who now controlled the Air Force would be out and he and his fellow missile pioneers would get the promotions, while the bomber boys sucked red pond water. Among the secretly organized missile men Catenberry's job was to leak Top Secret Information on the vulnerability of bombers and the excellence of missiles to the Congress and press—information the Air Force high command kept carefully hidden.

Catenberry carried in his briefcase an illegally made photocopy of a Top Secret Air Force intelligence report on the growing ability of Russian antiaircraft missiles to shoot down American bombers. To have made such a copy, or even seen the document without signing the register, meant court-martial. An enlisted man or junior officer would have been imprisoned for such an act. Catenberry was planning to slip the copy to Congressman George Dent. The laws of the United States specifically made this illegal. The oaths of office of both of them forbade such traffic. But then, as all Washington knew, the ship of state moved forward by leaks and bounds.

Catenberry had been cultivating Dent because of the Congressman's independent interest in missiles and because Dent's combat record was impressive enough to enable him to stand up to the generals. He'd offered Dent a jet plane to take him to New York to campaign any time he wanted. The Congressman had been too shrewd to get hooked there. But he'd get something on Dent; of that Catenberry was certain. The Congressman was both impulsive and full of ideals: a vulnerable combination.

George Dent was saying good-by to a couple of voters as Catenberry came in.

"Hi, Frank."

"Good morning, Mr. Congressman. How are you?"

"Fine."

"Could I see you a moment, George?"

"Sure."

The two started toward Dent's inner office. Catenberry flashed a smile of greeting to Dent's staff as he went by. His eye scanned Joyce with the speed and warmth of a radar scope, identified her as a great target, one he'd hit twice already that morning. He planned to start off by telling Dent the latest story about Senator Mullholland and his drunken Far East inspection trip. Then while Dent was laughing at that, he'd bring out the Top Secret paper.

Dent read Catenberry's paper several times that morning between visitors, conferences, and phone calls. Then, canceling his last two appointments, he paced down the corridor and upstairs to Wup-'em's. Like Dent, the Wyomin' Wildcat lived in the New House Office Building. But he existed in tranquillity. In his outer office four secretaries and one legislative assistant gossiped. His inner office was his own. "It's too far to drive and we're too poor to call or fly. Ain't that a blessin'," Wup-'em would tell his envious cohorts.

On the wall of his outer office between the two windows hung a great American flag. "Fellah, when they get this far from home, I want folks to walk through this door and know they're still in America." Below the flag was a banner bearing the magic device: "Keep Wildcat in Congress and the Power Lobby out of Wyoming.—Their wampum can't buy our Wup-'em." Off to one side was a large picture of Wildcat himself, cowboy hat on, peering into some far dawn, resolute and defiant. "That's the way I look when I think about runnin' for the Senate in a few years and makin' me a big passel of dough like Lyndon Johnson."

Also on the walls were pictures of Wyoming, of Wup-'em in uniform; and the tail of a timber wolf said to have been killed by Wup-'em with a club when he was walking his daily nine miles to school at the age of seven. "Just 'cause I ain't got Madison Avenue in my corner don't mean I've got no image or no legend."

Beneath one window was a very small stuffed wildcat in a glass case, lying on its back, its rather scruffy paws stiffly in the air. Tacked to the case was a sign that said: "Wupped by Wilson."

"When they see that they call their wives over and laugh together and say: 'Washington ain't swelled our boy Wup-'em's head.' Then my secretary buzzes me and I come out and give them the big hullo. Then we go into my office for a little old Western talk: Whether there's going to be a job in the district's new electronics plant for Junior when he gets his Ph.D. from M.I.T. What a world."

Dent envied Wup-'em's quiet life as Congressman and the majorities he effortlessly piled up each election by running against the Eastern banks and the power lobby. Why hadn't he, Dent, ever been able to come up with a nickname like "Wup-'em tomorra', the Wyomin' Wildcat?"

Holding a road junction for the Fourth Infantry Division a few weeks after D-Day—the Fourth was another of the great outfits, just outside the magic circle of Dent's own and the First Infantry. Major William Wilson's battalion had taken a day-long beating. That night his company commanders and his staff wanted to use the darkness and pull back. Major Wilson had listened long, smoked several cigars, then remarked, "We got smeared today. We'll wup 'em tomorrow." A reporter heard this. The next day Wilson's battalion was brilliantly successful. "Wup-'em-Tomorra' Wilson the Wyomin' Wildcat" was born.

Of course in Normandy Dent had been only a first lieutenant and had said no memorable words. He had spent a great deal of time yelling, "Back up, driver, back up" when, having pushed ahead too fast, he would frantically order his tank reversed to get out of fire. "Back-up-driver-Dent-the-New-York-demon." That showed the commendable caution many voters wished in a Congressman, but was hardly a one-hundred-per-cent vote-getter.

By the time he crossed the Rhine he was a captain, still a bit junior for immortal words. Besides, as he stood in the turret of his tank, rolling over the pontoon bridge that spanned the Rhine, he had only two thoughts. Boy, the engineers did a great job of bridging. And, I hope I'm not getting the G.I. flu. While the first thought showed humility and the second revealed the type of small human foible beloved by voters and *Time* magazine, there was no visible landslide in either. Beyond the Rhine he had spent a great deal of time trying to move his tanks faster, continually asking over his radio: "What's the delay? What's the delay?" But where would "What's-the-delay-Dent" get him?

Now if he'd said: "Across the Rhine, men for Israel and the brotherhood of man," that might have done him some good. It wouldn't help much with the Irish though. And right after he'd said it they'd have hustled him to the rear diagnosed as combat fatigue.

"My start in politics was all luck, Dent, all luck," Wup-'em told him one day.

"I didn't say: 'Wup-'em tomorra'.' I said 'Wup-'em tonight.' The reporter fella changed it. Now where'd I be in politics as 'Wup-'em-tonight Wilson'? A long way short of dogcatcher, I'll betcha."

Wup-'em read the Top Secret paper (standing), then handed it back to Dent. He settled into one of the heavy black leather armchairs with which Congress furnishes to remind itself of ancient comforts, and asking for the paper again, reread it slowly.

"You're a lucky man, Dent. This leak is hot enough to be slipped to a Senator."

"Maybe we should just forget about this document, Wup-'em."

"I suppose a little rabbit brought it to ya in your garden. — Why forget it?"

"We're getting in pretty deep. We could be branded as helping Communists."

"Not Wup-'em."

"Besides it's so technical, who's going to understand it?"

"The guys that write newspapers."

"But the head could be: 'Congress Leaks New Figures.' Or 'Aid Given Reds.' Not 'New Figures Show Bomber Is Through.' "

"You figure that's the best we could do: 'New Figures Show Bomber Is Through.' "

"What else would you get?"

Wup-'em handed the three pages back to Dent. "I rather hoped for 'Wilson and Dent Save America,' at least in the *New York Times*. In the Wyomin' *Blade* I'd figured on 'Wup-'em Saves Wyomin'.' It's a simple head. They got it all put together so they can run it about once a month. They want my support in buying a TV station in Utah.

"Now there's another question we haven't considered. Bein' Congressmen there's no reason for us to consider it; but because it's you and me, we might. That is: Does this information help the Communists? Or better, does it help them more than it helps us? Us being you and me, naturally, not America. I don't want you to think I'm a simple-minded country boy with inflated ideas.

"I have considered that question and have reached this conclusion: Either the Russkies know how good their damn missiles are, in which case there's no harm in us tellin' 'em; or they don't know how good their missiles are, in which case we sure as hell don't, so there's no harm in us confusin' 'em. Havin' disposed of the question of national security, let us now play a little handball and consider how the hell to use this thing. Would you like to bet a dollar on the game?"

"You're sure we should use this?"

Wup-'em dropped his grin, and watched Dent. Another Western Congressman had once asked the Wildcat why he liked George Dent. "Ah don't know," Wildcat had replied. "He's from the East, he's too goddamn ambitious, he's got money, he's a lawyer, all them things that go to make an objectionable loudmouth. But instead he's a guy you can go to the well with."

Now Wup-'em rising from his chair, asked, "What's worrying you boy?"

"Wup-'em, I don't really know. I'm getting some flak from labor on this missile thing. We've got several bomber plants in New York. The United Aircraft Workers and the Steelworkers, plus the Machinists, all want me to lay off."

Wup-'em nodded.

"But that's not what really bothers me," Dent continued. "I just get the feeling that this is one of those decisions that's much bigger than it looks."

"You mean like tellin' your best girl you're going in the Army so she'll love ya. And she tells her mother. And her mother tells the neighbors. And the next thing you know you're chicken or a soldier."

"Cluck, cluck."

"Then let's not use it."

"That's silly too, Wup-'em."

"Come on, Dent, let's play handball."

Wup-'em rolled out of his office and he and Dent headed down the marbled corridor toward the stairs. When the two of them walked together a passerby would notice they limped. Alone, neither's awkwardness was discernible; but together the slightest check in the stride of each resonated in the eye like feedback in a circuit, as if they were both welded to a series of eccentric cams.

"George," said Wup-'em as they walked, "what I'm about to

say is the sort of thing they could hold against ya in this town, if they thought you believed it. But one of the reasons I got into this missile hassle with you was because I thought bombers were obsolete; missiles were better, and safer; and the right thing for the country."

Bless you, Wup-'em, thought Dent, you can even make patriotism sound decent when uttered in the House Office Building. And Wup-'em had made the key point. The paper was classified, Top Secret; but the secrecy was being used not to help the country but to protect the powerful. Dent felt his anger, which had started when he first read the paper, start up again. He checked his rage by stern inner command, without noticing that he had bent the wall stop of the House gymnasium doors as he slammed through.

"We'll use it, Wup-'em, goddamn it." Dent headed for his locker. "I'll think of a way."

The smell of the House gym, liniment, sweat, and damp towels, always reminded him of St. Luke's, where he had gone to boarding school for six years. There too he had often been in conflict with authority. Now accepting, now challenging that cold, isolated world colored everywhere brown. Brown mud and brown leaves on the walks and playing fields, brown wood on the schoolroom walls and desks and floors, brown flaked brick on the old buildings, brown light in the dim chapel, brown footballs and brown football pants. There must have been gorgeous autumn colors on the New England trees that hemmed in the school. But as a twelve-year-old "new kid" he did not have the height to see the foliage, nor did the school give him time as it chased him from place to place after brown subjects: Sacred Studies, Egyptian history, Latin. Through this sullen world, his world, trudged two hundred boys in white shirts and blue suits.

Almost immediately his problems with the system began. The rules of St. Luke's said clearly: "Thou shalt not haze." The unwritten commandments of the boys said vaguely: "Thou shalt not haze too much." Or perhaps: "You may break in the new kids but not maim them." Centered in the beaten zone where the two rules converged, crouched into himself behind a bush, the small figure of Benjamin W. Wollenberg II, wept into his broken glasses; while the rotten apples and, remember truthfully, Dent, you were throwing an occasional stone—thudded down on him.

More boys arrived all the time to throw. "Come on! We're pooching Wollenberg." The word spread: "Great sport!"

Suddenly Dent did not think so. Wollenberg's pain and fear became his own. Not that he liked Wollenberg. Wollenberg was the unfortunate type of sheep that brings out the wolf even in his fellow sheep. He had never learned to hide his fear, to join or avoid the pack; instead he cringed if looked at, panicked if threatened, cried rather than fought.

By the end of this second month at school, Wollenberg had begun to smell. He no longer dared to take a bath or shower for fear his clothes would be taken from him and soaked, ripped, or tied in knots. When he assayed the toilet, boys lobbed water bombs over the stall, or tried to lasso his feet and drag him off, or, if he used one without a door, shot paper clips at him. Always a bit shy about his bodily functions, Willenberg became constipated, headachy, full of fart and halitosis.

Masters noticing his smelly, unkempt form scurrying about put him down as "Not quite the right sort of boy for the school." Not that they were anti-Semitic. Good heavens, no. The masters were all Christian gentlemen; they just wanted to make certain that the Jews St. Luke's took in to prove the school's lack of anti-Semitism were the right sort. The Admissions Committee scraped up one of these about every six years. In Wollenberg, the rest of the faculty felt, Admissions had goofed.

Benjamin cried now, crouched behind his bush, not so much from physical pain or humiliation as from terror of the future. How would he get the apple goo off himself since he could not take a bath? How would he explain his third pair of broken glasses to his father? If he wore his emergency pair tonight and they broke, he would be unable to study, his marks would drop, he'd be sent home a disgrace. And tomorrow Bush and Lothrop said they were going to throw him in the cesspool and put the lid on.

The clock in the school church tower struck six. The pelting stopped. The boys dispersed to race to their dormitories and change for supper: stiff collars, blue suits, patent leather shoes, badges of gentlemen. Benjamin would be unable to tidy himself up in time and would be late for supper and would be punished, another proof of his unfitness. He cowered behind, making for the relative safety of his dormitory through a sparse late fall of arcing rotten apples.

"Sir, could I see you a minute?" Dent stood in terror that night at the door of his dormitory master. He was about to cross the all-important line that separated boys from masters and he did not understand why. Already to get to see "sir" alone he had had to lie, say he needed to go to the bathroom, get excused from study hall, go down to the cellar, sneak up a back stair.

"Come in, George."

He entered. What he was about to do was perilous; but after all, he was right.

Two days later his ordeal came.

All Dent had wanted was that the hazing of Wollenberg should stop. What he had not foreseen was that a crime having been done, the system required someone be punished. He had carefully skirted this area when questioned by the dormitory master.

"Who's responsible for this persecution of Wollenberg, George?"

"I don't know, sir."

"Someone must lead it." This was the area where the unwritten law ran strongest: peach-not.

"I think it's whoever gets the idea first. Whoever happens to see him."

"Who gets the idea most often?"

"I've never thought about that, sir."

"Well think about it now, Dent." Already the danger was

thickening, the trap of twin authorities closing. Besides, though Lothrop was a bully, he liked Bush.

"I don't know, sir."

Wollenberg, unwise, was not so careful. When summoned by the Rector, who ran the school in a loose grip of iron so that you were safe in the broad interior of his palm unless you ran into one of his fingers, Wollenberg committed the ultimate sin and named names: Bush and Lothrop.

Now faculty members, who hadn't liked Wollenberg anyway and were friends of countless Bushes and Lothrops, leaked it to the boys that Dent had reported the hazing and that he too had named names. Dent denied the names, and stuck by his guns on the reporting: "Wollenberg isn't tough enough to pick on."

Dent understood the signs. He hid important books such as his math and Latin texts which, if the pages were ripped from them, would cause him to flunk courses. He stashed two emergency suits in the room of a friend. He got up early to go to the bathroom; quit the playing fields first; spent his spare time in the library, which was always policed by a master. When attacked by packs small enough to give him a chance, he tried to turn collective slaughter into an individual fight. His gym locker was broken into and his clothing stolen. Ink was sprayed on his ties. He found ants in his bed, tacks on his chair. His books were knocked out from beneath his arms and he was kicked downstairs while picking them up. Twice masters, catching him fighting back, let his attackers go, but punished him severely for disturbing the peace of the school.

After five days of such pressure he began to doubt whether he had been right. That evening he was summoned out of study hall by the Rector.

As he walked down the bare wooden corridor toward the dark oaken door that guarded the Rector's study he looked at his watch—7:15. His ordeal with the school's head must last less than fifteen minutes. There was a recess at 7:30 and if he was not at his desk to guard his books they would be stolen and mutilated.

He knocked at the black door almost unable to clench his knuckles from fear.

"Come in, boy."

The Rector's voice echoed out of his bulk as from a subterranean grotto. Dent pulled open the heavy door and entered. It hissed shut behind him. The room was dark, even on a spring day the fresh sunlight retreated before the gloom of its interior. The Rector was writing at his desk by the light of one brass desk lamp with a green glass shade. The rays coming from below picked out the sagging, elderly power of the unforgiving face; while the round tube of the oversize clerical collar lengthened the shaft of neck on which the giant head was perched. Dent approached and in spite of his desire to stand still, fidgeted.

"I understand, Dent," the Rector began, his voice a challenge, "that you have seen a horrible occurrence at this school."

Was that what he'd seen?

"It's been a long time since we had any hazing at this school."

If he thinks that, Dent realized, it's useless to try and talk to him. Keep quiet and get out.

"You did see what you reported to Mr. ah, ah, ah."

"Hathaway, sir."

"I know who it was, boy. You did see it?"

"Yes, sir."

"Wollenberg says he has been most badly treated. I want that to stop."

Dent could almost see the arms about to bop Wollenberg arrested by the power of the Rector's wish. But he knew it wasn't so.

"And I want those responsible to realize I want it stopped. Who was responsible for this outrage, boy?"

Silence.

"Maybe you were one of the leaders?"

Deadlier silence.

"Silence is insolence, boy!"

Dent realized he was the real culprit for having reported the old man's dream empire to be less than perfect. The entire punishment might fall on him. At the bar before which he now stood, a twelve-year-old needed to be represented by the entire Supreme Court. He was alone. At that very moment Lothrop and Bush were probably scarring his books—someone had when he got back.

"You have ink on your tie, boy."

"Yes, sir. I spilled some on in study hall."

"We don't want messy boys at this school. Who was responsible for this?"

"I don't know, sir."

"What don't you know, boy?" The Rector shouted now.

"Who the leaders were, sir."

"Wollenberg says Bush and Lothrop were to blame."

"He should know, sir." Did that remark go too far? Was he now guilty of informing?

"Both those boys come from fine families. Lothrop's brother graduated from here. Played center for Harvard. So did Bush's father. He writes me on my birthday."

"Thank you, sir."

"Very good, Dent. But remember we want no boy here who uses a part of the truth to serve his own ends. You wouldn't do that." Not a question, an accusation.

"No, sir." In total anger Dent now had the message: Never tell the truth, until you knew who had written the old bastard on his birthday.

"You may go, boy."

He went.

Life did not improve.

Bush and Lothrop were put on probation but kept in school; which meant they were goaded into further action and left free to act. Dent got a lower front tooth broken, also a badly bruised left rib. The tooth showed. The rib he kept quiet about so boys didn't take socks at it. But with the rib he didn't sleep well; grew miserable; several times almost cried. He realized that as long as Wollenberg remained, jerking about the school with a frightened, Brownian movement, both of them would be picked on. Therefore

Wollenberg must do the unthinkable, run away. In the furor that would follow such an extraordinary action his own problems would fade.

He set out to persuade Wollenberg. One afternoon when they both should have been playing football, he took Benjamin down behind the boiler pipes in the gym basement. The place was hot and cramped; but secret enough to be safe.

"This is a good place to hide," said Wollenberg.

"Pretty good," said Dent. "But these hot pipes make it dangerous to fight. You could get grabbed and pushed against them."

Wollenberg drew in his breath and trembled, imagining himself tied to the pipes, naked, by his own necktie, with knots he couldn't untie, while they beat him.

How would he get off? Explain the scars to his mother?

"But it's okay for now," Dent added.

Wollenberg relaxed. Dent, his friend, was all-wise.

Dent measured Wollenberg. Did he have the guts to run away? "Benjamin, it's not going to be any better for you, is it?"

"I think so. I've found two new places to hide."

"They'll find you. —I've been thinking. You've got to get out of here and go home."

"Run away?" Benjamin's eyes swelled owl-like.

"Yes."

"My father wouldn't let me."

"Tell him what's been happening to you."

"I couldn't tell him."

"You couldn't?"

"No."

Dent understood perfectly. He couldn't tell his father. "Could you tell your mother?"

"That wouldn't do any good."

"I know. It wouldn't do me any good either."

"I've gotten you in trouble."

"Yes."

"I like you, George."

"Quiet. Let's think."

"You're tough."

No, you jerk, not tough, Dent almost exploded at Wollenberg, I've just learned to shut up and not show it. Instead he growled "Quiet" again.

Suddenly he knew how to persuade Wollenberg. Perhaps the inspiration came from something he'd read in the newspapers, from things said around his family dinner table, from the remarks of a schoolmaster, or his schoolmates. "If you ran away and told your father they were beating you up because you were Jewish, would he let you come home?"

"Is that why they're doing it?" That's what Wollenberg had secretly believed.

"No. They pooch you because you ask for it and won't fight. I've told you that. But when I can't tell my father something, I make up something simple he can understand."

"But that's a lie to your father."

"You want to stay here being beat up?"

"No. —Besides, I've got no money."

Dent saw they were over the hurdle. The question now was how.

On arriving at school the boys had been forced to turn in all their money but a dollar. Each Sunday they were issued twenty-five-cents allowance, five cents of which was kept back for church. Dent still had a dollar and forty cents saved out of allowances. Wollenberg had nothing. He had spent all his dollar and allowances on ice cream at the football games, being able to eat safely then, forgotten, while the rest of the school communed mystically with the giants on the field. One dollar and forty cents was certainly not going to get Wollenberg from Westfield, Mass., to New York City.

Could Wollenberg hitch-hike to New York? Dent doubted he could do this himself. He didn't know which road to stand on and night would fall in between. But Boston was only two hours away and possible. If Wollenberg had some friend he could go to in Boston while he called his father.

"Have you been in Boston, Benjamin?"

"No."

"Has your father ever?"

"Oh, yes, all the time, whenever a play he has money in opens there." The explanation was meaningless to Dent and unimportant.

"Do you know where he stays?"

"The Ritz. I remember because it has the same name as the hotel we stayed at in Paris."

Dent knew the Ritz. His mother and he had stayed there once when he had been forced to visit her Boston relatives.

"That's the best place."

Wollenberg beamed. His hero had not found his father wanting.

"Benjamin, you have it made. I'm going to get you home."

"You can?"

Dent's plan was simple. After lunch on Sunday Dent would lead Wollenberg through the woods out of the school grounds and on to the main road. There, with Dent watching from the bushes to give him support, Wollenberg would hitch to Boston. With luck the car that stopped for him would be going all the way. With bad luck he would have to hitch once or twice again. He would be marked late for supper but not definitely missed until study hall at 7:05. He would have time. Dent even made up for Benjamin a simple story to tell the car driver.

From the Ritz, Benjamin would phone his father. Wollenberg was sure he could find his father. His father and mother were almost always at home Sunday night. And if by chance they were out, his sister's nurse had their number. Wollenberg would recite what had happened to him and inform his father it had happened because he was Jewish. While his father was recovering from this, he would further tell his father he had to run away because they were going to throw him in the cesspool that Sunday. "And then he'll call up the hotel manager and the manager will give you a room. And your father will come and pick you up in Boston and he'll be proud of you."

"You think so?"

"I'm certain." He wasn't. But he knew Benjamin needed certainty.

"George, when I'm gone, will you look after my violin?"

"A violin!" Dent gasped at his final imbecility. "Why'd you bring that to school?"

"My mother thought the boys would like to hear me play."

"Jesus. She must have wanted to get you really killed." His own mother was dumb but not that stupid. "I like to paint, but I wouldn't bring my paint box. They'd smear paint all over me."

Wollenberg sighed. So much was inexplicable in the world. He missed his mother with choking pain; but he also hated her, feeling her in some way responsible for what had happened to him here.

"Is that why you're my friend? Because you like to paint?"

"I don't know."

"You must come and visit me. My family knows de Kooning, Beckman, and Kandinsky. We've some wonderful pictures." The names were merely sounds to Dent. His mother had taken him to the Metropolitan, but to no modern museum or galleries. "I wish I didn't have to run away. It's weak."

"You know, Benji, it's too bad you didn't go to camp. You'd have learned what it's all about before you came here. You'd have made it."

"You think so?"

"Sure."

Sunday came and Dent led Wollenberg through the woods. He had tried to help Wollenberg by getting the rules obeyed. Now here he was out of bounds, a crime punishable by a week on bread and water in a small room with only the Bible to read. Worse, he was helping a boy to run away, an offense so great as to be beyond the table of prescribed punishments. His rib hurt. So did his tooth. Right then he would have liked to beat up Wollenberg himself rather than help him. The idiot couldn't even walk through the bushes quietly. "When you get home don't tell anyone I helped you. Anyone. If the Rector learns, I'll be expelled."

"I'd like to tell my father you've been a friend."

"You'll kill me. Now, here's the road. Get out there and smile." Wollenberg managed to move the corners of his mouth up and display his teeth. "Forget the smile. Just get on the road. Good luck, Benji."

"You'll watch me in case no one stops."

"Yes."

"Here goes." Wollenberg planted himself by the roadside as if he expected the asphalt to jerk forward suddenly like a badly started commuter train and throw him to the ground.

The third car by picked him up.

Dent had expected Jean Aaron to meet him at LaGuardia when he arrived for the district leaders' meeting that afternoon. New York had been hamstrung by a taxi strike for two weeks, so he was being picked up. Instead, as he came out the Air Shuttle terminal he saw Sam.

He eased himself into the car. "What's up, Sam?"

"The Republicans picked their guy to run against you. It'll be in the morning papers. Paul Woodbridge."

"Jesus Christ."

"Him you'd have less trouble with in this district."

Dent had hoped the Republicans would put up someone attractive so his victory would have some meaning. But Paul Woodbridge was too attractive: a former assistant Secretary of Health, Education, and Welfare, head of his own management consulting firm, a go-getter a few years older than himself. Does Woodbridge actually believe he can beat me, Dent wondered? "Why is he running, Sam?"

"How can he lose?" said Sam. "He goes to some place in Rhode Island in the summer. That's solid Democratic so he can't move there. If he does better against you than that jerk they ran last time, he can say: 'See, I'm a vote-getter. I closed the gap.' If not he blames it on the off year, the market, or something. When he loses he's probably been promised a big job in Washington."

"He's got a big job."

"Not where they blow bugles at you and call you sir."

"That makes sense."

"And suppose you grab the brass ring and run for the Senate in sixty; or a Democratic President comes in and you take a big Washington job, who's sitting right here, with an organization, a prior claim, and known to the voters? Paul Woodbridge. He'd be tough to beat then. But this time you'll murder him."

"No. I'll win," Dent paused, frowning, "but I was counting on the Republicans behaving like Republicans, tearing themselves apart and then settling for a mediocrity."

"He wears a hat."

"He'll hire some bright public relations firm who'll have him take his hat off. Damn, in some ways his background is more democratic then mine. He's big on Medicaid and welfare reform. Now what am I going to say about his candidacy?"

Dee stepped back against the wall of her studio and scrutinized herself in the full-length mirror on her bathroom door. Her studio and living area were shaped like a dumbbell with the back end sliced in half. Inside the neck of the dumbbell was stuffed a tiny bathroom, toilet and shower, a small stove and oven, and a kitchen sink that doubled as a wash basin. The front, the large part, sixteen by twenty-four feet, was her studio work area with whitewashed brick walls, along one of which ran shelves for paints and brushes, and racks for finished canvases. Two folding canvas chairs, a kitchen table, a couch, easel, and a stool furnished this area.

In back, divided from the neck of the dumbbell by a stack of ceiling-high bookcases was where she lived, the small space bursting with a profusion of plants: green avocado branches across the windows, a palm tree between them, a rubber plant by the bed, African violets hanging from the walls, Japanese plants in a tiny rock garden in the corner by the built-in clothes closet. Beneath the bookcase, its head resting against the outer wall, was her monastically spare double bed, two unfinished doors bolted together and raised off the ground on nine wooden legs four inches high, the whole topped by a two-inch foam rubber mattress over which had been thrown a gay, brown-red, Mexican quilt.

Dee raised her arms, stretched, turned sidewise, looked at herself again. I got dressed faster, she thought, when I was married and had more clothes. This brown dress won't do; it just doesn't have enough life. Of course, if I wanted to say a definite "no" to George I'd wear that shirred blue number that zips under the arms; she laughed. That dress shouts "never." But I don't feel like that. Besides, at Harry Sandman's parties they'll be friends, and probably Bill, who'll look me over and wonder: How's Dee feeling these days? Who's feeling Dee?

And I'll be competing with those little broads that worked in galleries and didn't have a thing to do all day but plan a stunning wardrobe. No paint on their hands. They'll be in basic black with wild jewelry; so black's out. And maybe at the party there'll be one or two people in the market for a picture. That means I have to look sexy artist enough so Mr. Park Avenue thinks he might get a sexy artist with his picture; but not so sexy Mrs. Park Avenue thinks he might get the sexy artist. Shit, she thought, it's hell being a woman.

She parted the bamboo cords that covered her closet and considered her dresses again. There was nothing for it, she decided, but to wear the red Italian silk print she'd made herself out of the material Bill had brought her back from Rome. He'll remember the dress, so will others, but it's still about the best I've got. And Dent hasn't seen it. I'll wear my gold sandals and paint my toenails, I suppose.

Dent walked up the stairs of the loft building toward the noise on the third floor that represented Harry Sandman's party. He'd given his district leaders the latest Washington word, listened to how they felt he should vote, discussed the best ways to move against Woodbridge, joined them in the ritual after-discussion drink. He felt strangely lost, and suddenly realized it was because he practically never went to a party alone. There was always an aide beside him, people at the door to greet him, or a group of political friends involved in the same ritual. Here he'd probably know no one but Dee. This would be a Stevenson group, he'd better get those answers ready. He put on his particularly sincere smile, the one that crinkled up at the edges, and entered the loft.

As he suspected, he knew no one. A quick check over the room failed to turn up Dee; but there was another room beyond and he thought he heard the sudden crack of her laugh from there. Off to his right he spotted a small, slightly soiled, tense blonde with shoulder-length hair, a gash of scarlet mouth and an empire-waisted shift over what appeared to be a fabulous body. There's the first voter you want to meet, he thought, and began to edge toward her, noting automatically the bare left hand and the nervous way she shifted her feet as she talked to the two men, one black, one white, before her.

As he moved toward the blonde, keeping his eyes open for Dee or a drink, he was stopped by a thin, intense young man with a fringe of beard.

"Are you a picture buyer, man?" The youth jabbed a finger into him.

"No. Why?"

"You project the affluent air of a man looking over the producers of such merchandise as pictures and being slightly baffled, not to mention upset, by what befalls his eye."

"Well, I like the affluent part."

"Who said anything about affluent? You look like an underfed bum."

Dent had grown tired of this game while still in college. "Always a pleasure to hear from the loyal opposition," he said; and began to slide on toward the blonde. The man saw Dent glance at the girl.

"You're going to talk to June Farnsworth. Would you buy my pictures if I had tits and blew you?"

If I get into a fight here, thought Dent, I could be in big political trouble. He kept his smile fixed. "I'd have to see your paintings."

"June, get this son-of-a-bitch away from me before I waste him," yelled the man.

Dent kept moving. The blonde turned to him. "Do I know you?" she asked.

"Nope. And I don't know you. That gentleman seemed under the impression I'd been lured by your charms to buy your pictures."

"Do you buy pictures?" asked the black.

"Not often. I'm a Congressman." As he watched them, Dent could imagine the same look of disbelief and horror as it would flash across the face of an average Congressman faced with an artist. "George Dent," he said, putting out his hand.

"The Dent Amendment," said June Farnsworth.

"Sure," acknowledged the black.

The three introduced themselves. Dent had gotten quite a bit of mileage out of that particular Amendment, which had freed counterpart funds to buy pictures by living American artists to hang in USIA libraries overseas.

"You never select any of my pictures," said June.

"The State Department makes the selections." Dent flicked the buck sidewards. "You're J. Farnsworth, you did the dream animals eating each other. Come down and testify before Congress, June, and you might get a special appropriation."

"I never thought I'd meet a Congressman that looked at pictures," said the other man. Dent laughed politely. The trouble with stereotypes, he thought, is not just that they lead to prejudice, but that they force people to conform. The police officer barks, the plumber's a jerk, the businessman is conservative, the artist wears a beard, the politician a smile. So the dour politician, the educated plumber, the quiet officer, the radical businessman, the beardless artist become suspect.

Dent was still making conversation with June, when Dee put her head around the door of the inner room. She was worried that Dent, knowing no one, would be standing miserable in a corner of the room. She also hoped slightly he wasn't there yet. She was having a good time with old friends and didn't need an outsider under her wing. Her eye picked out Dent's tailored erectness. He seemed to be all right. He had a lovely sky-blue smile. Why hadn't he come to find her? Then she saw he was talking to June Farnsworth.

June Farnsworth! Goddamn all men, Dee thought. And goddamn that bitch who would do anything to sell a picture or pay the rent on that ridiculously expensive studio of hers. June had better keep her hands off George Dent and not go into her lost little girl routine. She waved at Dent and started toward him.

"Hullo, George; June dear."

"Dee, you're looking well. I've always loved that dress. Sold anything lately?"

"Hi, Dee. I just got here."

Dee shot him a glance.

"I should have guessed you two knew each other," said June. "Dee's always got some attractive man in tow. If you're not doing anything after this party my date and I are going to Fred Schwenger's. Why don't you come? It'll be wild."

"We might," said Dee. They made a little more conversation, then Dent and Dee edged off. "Do you want to meet some more of these people, Dent?"

"I spend my days meeting people, Dee. I'd rather leave with you now and go eat."

"Good." They found their host, a giant red-bearded man, who was unsticking a bag of ice cubes with a blowtorch, said their good-bys and left.

They reached the sidewalk and the evening began to work for them. An empty taxi cruised down the block; the restaurant proprietor recognized Dent and gave them a choice booth in a corner where they had quiet and room to talk. They both ordered light foods, Dent wondering if Dee did so for his reason: that sex is never good on a full stomach.

"Dee, I'd forgotten, or buried, how much I wanted to see you again."

"I too, Dent. I too."

They talked about why men led women into restaurants, what success meant in art and in politics, how they would know if they made it, the excellence of their food, good years for wine, good years for themselves, prices in New York, how each would change the tax laws, who would follow Ike as President, the meaning of Beckman's triptychs and Munch's *Frieze of Life,* why so much news about politics or art was wrong, if by magic they could live in the landscape painted by one artist, which they would choose. He chose Hobbema, because the soft, brown landscapes, so full of pleasant order, were the most peaceful world he knew. She chose Canaletto, because the hard bright light, the bustle, water, and people filled her with excitement.

"You should be in politics, Dee, and I should be the painter."

"We Irish have the talent; but I could never smile all day."

The proprietor brought them a free Armagnac. Looking around the room Dent suddenly realized it must be late, since only one other couple was still lingering over coffee. As they left the restaurant another empty cab came by. Dent gave the driver the address of Dee's studio. They settled back, close together but not touching. When the time came to pay off the cab, Dent was so excited he had trouble separating the dimes from the pennies and nickels in his palm. He followed Dee up the four flights of stairs, wrenching his eyes from the corkscrew of her hips so as not to be caught staring if she turned.

Dee took her keys from the small, red purse beneath her arm. Her lock was the police type, where a bar runs from the door frame down into the floor. "You never know, Dent. And it's not just being attacked. They broke into the studio of a friend of mine and destroyed three years of work." As Dent shut the door he could have turned and taken her in his arms. But the door is still unlocked, he thought, and our coats are on. He closed the door and reset the lock.

"Would you like a drink?" she asked.

"I'd love a light whisky and soda. I'll mix it. What would you like?"

"A gin and water, light, with lots of ice."

Dent started toward the kitchen alcove, then paused and took off his jacket and necktie.

"Never could mix a drink with a tie on." He finished that statement with a slight titter, hating the nervous sound of it. Seated on her canvas studio chair, Dee took a great feline stretch. Dent reached up on the shelf for a glass. Perhaps because his fingers were still wet from the ice cubes the glass slipped from him, bounced off the edge of the sink while Dent grabbed twice for it and missed, then hit the wooden floor, miraculously not breaking.

"Always buy from the five and ten," said Dee laughing. Dent concentrated on making the drinks and getting them across the room to her chair. He debated whether to bend down and kiss her as he handed her the drink; but with his own drink in his hand and in such an awkward position the moment was still all wrong. "We might go to the Schwengers' party," she said.

You might just end up there, Dent, you clown, he thought, if you don't pull yourself together. He wandered over to look at Dee's latest painting, a still life: a group of kitchen pans, two eggplants, some spices and spice jars on a warm marble table.

"Hey, that solid sunlight around this right hand corner is great."

She came over to him. "I'm glad you like it. I've never worked with light that way before." Their shoulders touched. Dent put his glass down carefully, put his arms around her, and kissed her. He had a kissing technique that he usually used, but this time he just held her and kissed. Like two suddenly aligned bar magnets they fused.

After a while he lowered his hands to her waist and pivoted her toward the back room of her studio. She moved a few steps, then stopped. He kissed her some more, then pivoted her again, moving her a few steps further. Get her on the bed, he thought, where the inevitable feminine "no" is easier to block.

"Where are we going?" she asked.

"We can't kiss standing up."

He sat her down on the bed's edge, sat down beside her, then kissed her as he fell backwards so that they lay together.

Men and the games they go through to get me to bed, Dee thought. I wish someone would just ask me sometime. But then I'm so conditioned I'd probably say "no."

"I don't do this, Dent," she said.

"I don't either."

They kept kissing. After a while he twisted away and took off his shirt. Sometimes when he did this the woman started to take off her dress also. Dee didn't. His scarred left shoulder was toward her.

"Is that the war?" she asked.

"Yes." He lay back down on the bed. "Does it bother you?"

She shook her head and kissed him. After a while he unzipped her dress down the back. She said no a few times but kept kissing him hard in between. He undid her bra, then after a while with her help he slid dress and bra down over her shoulders. Her breasts he saw, were elegant, firm, and tapered in the middle. They reminded him of summer squash or rifle grenades.

"Let me get my clothes off," she said.

Dent rolled away and sat up to untie his own shoes. The knot in the left one jammed and he yanked the shoe off his foot viciously with the laces still tied. He put his watch inside his shoe, its alarm already set for 4:30 a.m., and laid his pants on the floor where he could get at the condoms in his hip pocket, then held out his arms for Dee. They embraced while Dent carefully kept his crotch away from her so he wouldn't get excited too fast.

They stroked each other, Dent listening to her breathing grow shallow and fast, watching the slow reddening of her face. Then he quit observing, caught up in his own excitement.

He twisted from her. "I'll put something on," he gasped.

"You don't have to."

He stopped cold. As he had fondled her he had fingered inside and felt no diaphragm.

"I'm very regular; it's a safe day; unless you . . ."

The oldest trap in the world, he thought. But would this girl do it to you? Women can lie about this without knowing.

"All right; it's your body." He began to stroke the interruption aside.

Beneath her excitement Dee felt a deep surge of joy. He knows enough to notice when he's right on the edge, she thought, and he's willing to trust me.

Their first time was like most good first times, strange, new, exciting. He came a little too fast, but he realized they fit, with shared angles, shifts, and speeds. They lay side by side holding each other gently and kissing softly.

Soon they began again to press, explore, fondle. She has the magic for you, Dent, he thought. Already he was kindled stiff. The second time they were consciously slower, closer, deliberately withholding and meshing until the last uncontrollable rhythms. Again they rested, holding each other and whispering, then started to stroke each other.

This time she rolled on top of him to suit his measures to her ways. He was worried for a few moments that they weren't yet close enough, or that she didn't know enough, for them to be successful in this new position. As Dee pivoted, rocked, and twisted above him his fear drained. She was what he most loved in bed, his equal. Finally they came, grinding all sensation from each other, in a great, shuddering climax. He lay, eyes closed, limp and gasping on the bed. Dent, he thought after a while, you're lucky. You've found someone with whom in time, you'll be able to enter the whole, full glory of sex.

He brought his arms around Dee and, eyes still closed, still out of breath, held on.

six

"Where was everybody at the beach?" he asked Sarah.

"What do you mean, love-dove?" She was in her tennis clothes, seated at the glass-topped wrought-iron table on their Easthampton patio. How could she keep her sneakers and socks so white, he wondered, while his were always grubby?

"I was just swimming with the children. Jane is doing quite well."

"I know. The swimming pro is much better this year. The young boy the club had last summer spent all his time chasing girls."

"Well, anyway, there were lots of children and nurses at the beach but no adults."

"The Smiths and the Woodners both had swimming parties at their pools. I know you hate those things, so I said 'no.'

"Thank you. How'd the tennis go?"

"Mrs. Choat and I walloped them, six-three, six-two."

"Great!"

"Shall we enter the mixed doubles this year, Daddy?"

"I'd like to Sarah; but with the gubernatorial convention even if I'm here tournament week, I won't have time to practice before. I'm sorry."

"That's all right, love-dove. Not everyone's husband's a Congressman."

Inside he winced. His time problem came more from seeing Dee than from politics. "What's that you're doing?"

"Lists for the fall. We're going to be busy. I'll have to go to Washington for a few days and get the living room redone."

"Sarah, it's only June."

"If we're going to send the children to ski camp, the way we thought, so we can get some skiing by ourselves, we ought to make the reservations now. I wonder if we can get the Bradleys' cottage again at Stowe?" She paused. "Daddy, people keep asking me why you're for Kennedy and not Stevenson."

"Come on, Sari-dari, we've been round and round on that one." He hunched his shoulders. "The trouble with you ex-Republicans is that you're drawn to Stevenson because he's a secret Republican. He talks about problems, rather then solving them. He's the rich man's Hubert Humphrey."

"Most of the leaders in your district back Stevenson."

"I've superbly conditioned them to confuse words with action."

"You're not funny, you know."

"Part of my secret strength with the voter: absolute humorlessness. I'm going to shower the salt water off."

After a while she followed him upstairs. He looked at her after she's finished her shower, the tanned lithe roundness of her above the blue half slip, the neat fall of blond hair about her shoulders, the slender feminine legs. Really, she should try a bikini. He moved across the room to kiss her and then checked himself. Sarah sometimes got angry if fondled while dressing. Well, she couldn't object to being hugged. He held her closely, enjoying the supple feel of her nakedness muted through his clothes, then picking her off the floor swung her around and smiled.

"You ruin everything by leering," she snapped, wiggling down and away from him.

"I wasn't leering," anger flared him. "I was admiring."

"You were leering. And I was feeling so loving."

Let Sarah yell at you all she wants, he thought. You are getting great loving from Dee McTurk and are unreachable, behind a Gardol screen. He turned back to his neckties. He wished he didn't have to wear a tie this evening. He hated ties.

"You were leering." She had put on a blue silk blouse that opened deeply at the neck. What the hell did she look so attractive for if she didn't want sex?

"I'm sorry, Sari-dari; it must have happened without my knowing."

Sarah stared at him hostilely. Daddy always ruined her moods by being obscene. No, she thought, I'm being unfair to him. He doesn't always ruin them, just forgets sometimes. Besides I was running around naked so it was partly my fault. Men just can't help things like that. She looked down at the floor an instant, then back at Dent, smiling.

"You're forgiven, Daddy."

"Who's going to be at the party?" he asked. Ticking off names always had a soothing effect on Sarah.

The host back slapped him as he walked out on the lawn where the party was being held. "Good to see-ya, Georgie!" When he was younger he would hit people for calling him Georgie. "You spending all our money for us down there in Congress? Ha. Ha."

"Doing my best." His smile hurt as he said it.

The host introduced him. "Be careful what you say to this fella. He's a Congressman and a Democrat."

"Really?" She was all eyebrows. "How interesting. What do you do, Congressman?"

"I Congress."

"Now Daddy," he heard Sarah hiss as she moved off, "don't be hostile."

"Hey Dent, I've been looking all over for you. Wanted to talk to you about this migratory-bird thing." The man before him had kicked his elder brother off the executive ladder and watch him break without missing a swallow of his martini. Yet he became all fluttery in the presence of a robin. "The bird is disappearing from our blessed land and you fellows in Congress don't give a damn. Now our association has this 'For the Birds' bill that . . ."

"Congressman, how are you?"

"Fine, thank you, ma'am."

"I hoped you'd be here. I wanted to talk to you about Sizzle Bottom Park. I'm a member, as you've probably guessed"—Dent turned on what he hoped was his sphinxlike smile—"of the Weahokum Valley Association. We feel . . ."

"I was talking to Mr. Dent about the migratory bird."

"How nice. Now Sizzle Bottom . . ."

"Dent, hey. Just a second." Another captain of industry wove toward him. "I was having an argument over here with Nelson. You know he thinks he knows it all. And I said, 'There's Dent. He'll have the inside.' Isn't it true the Russians have a satellite big enough to lift an elephant?"

"Well, Fred," said Dent the diplomat, "that depends on the size of the elephant."

"I mean a regular-size elephant."

Trapped.

"Dent, I want you to meet Mrs. Darling and Mrs. Cooper, they both voted for you."

"Thank you both very much."

"Now, Dent, the birds."

"Sizzle Bottom Park is needed by the poor."

"We usually vote Republican. But we love you and your program."

When women looked at him and said they loved his program he always felt he should check his fly. Boy, if he ever told Sarah that. Dee would laugh.

"My house in Sizzle Bottom is valued at . . ."

"Couldn't they lift the elephant, Dent?"

"They could get the weight up, Fred. But the actual elephant. I mean with the hay and buckets for you know what." Always give yourself an out.

"Won't you come over and meet our husbands? They didn't vote for you." Giggles.

"Dent, old palo-mio."

"Hullo, Arthur." Before him stood Lothrop, Wollenberg's tormentor, a draft-dodger and a shit.

"I'll be in Washington next week on a little corporate matter. I'm going to drop by and see ya."

"Congress has adjourned, Arthur. Two weeks ago. Drop by my district office though."

"Adjourned. That's rich. You guys sure don't work very hard spending our dough."

Several people drifted up and remarked they missed him at this or that party. What the hell did they do, he flared inside. Keep a little book on where he went?

"George, why do you always vote to weaken our country?" He turned to greet the speaker warmly. He had not seen her for several years. They had shared a bed, briefly, his sophomore summer.

"Francie, hullo! How well you look." How old she had become: proper, gray, garden-club, hatted. People aged so suddenly. Did the dullness in their lives suddenly thicken their bodies, puff their chins, and dry out their faces?

"Oh, Mr. Dent, I want to talk to you about my son."—This woman barging in would have a draft problem. She did. She was interrupted by a man with a tax problem. So it went. How long did he have to stay here?

Sarah looked across the lawn and saw the group around him. She cased the rest of the party quickly. George's group was larger than anyone else's. One of the women talking to Dent looked across at Sarah with a small glance of envy she happened to catch. She smiled to herself, completely happy.

They went out to dinner with two other couples whose wives were friends of Sarah's. He knew them only slightly. They were handsome, well turned out, sun-tanned, and country-club conservative. He twisted and fidgeted in boredom, and his back began to hurt. But at least they didn't insult him, or carry on about their problems with government.

After dinner in their car in the restaurant parking lot Sarah began to kiss him. She did this energetically but never liked to use her tongue or have his tongue probe her. However, she used her fingers well, massaging his neck, reaming his ears, rubbing his crotch. Why Sarah should consider necking in a parked car the height of sexual fun he had never understood. He'd once suggested a motel instead. She'd been shocked.

"We've got a home for that, love-dove."

"In a motel we could take off our clothes and do it all."

"Aren't you feeling sporting?"

"Sporting." Why did Sarah use words like that? And why did she always play with him; but never permit herself to be played with? He felt himself getting angry and stopped thinking about the past. Sarah blew in his ear. He shuddered.

"Love-dove," she said, giggling, "let's drive down to the golf course."

He'd foreseen that. Well, he was already rather excited and he'd enjoy it even if he did feel a little silly. Besides a lot of guys would give their eye teeth to have a cute blonde like Sarah finger them off.

"Great idea, Sari-dari."

Sarah noticed one of the couples they'd been dining with pull out of the parking lot behind them. They'll see our car turn down the golf course road and be envious, she thought. She snuggled close to her husband and began to reach under his shirt.

Dent found a dark area on the golf course and parked. He kissed Sarah hard, fondled her breasts; he tried to be more passionate, but kept thinking intermittently of Dee.

"Ooo, Daddy," Sarah said after he'd come, "I like to make love like this."

Dent felt sticky, and a little silly.

"Jesus, Sam," Dent paced back and forth before Sam Kleinman's desk in his New York office late one hot July afternoon. "This fight over the Governorship, plus this Kennedy-Stevenson battle, is tearing us apart. Why can't we Democrats unite?"

"Dent, we've been in the wilderness eight long years," Kleinman took a puff on his cigar and shook his head sadly. "That turns even a sensitive statesman like myself into a ravenous wolf. Confidentially"—Sam lowered his voice and leaned forward—"I have in mind the Supreme Court for both myself and my wife. And I will loyally follow any distinguished candidate who pledges me those insignificant plums. But others are not so public spirited and selfless."

"Who are you for, Sam? And I don't mean who do you think I should be for."

"You mean in my heart of hearts where no man penetrates?"

"Yes."

"I don't look there very often, it's a violation of professional ethics. Besides I don't know. My people have been fighting Catholics for many years. And Kennedy kept silent on Joe McCarthy."

"And regrets it."

"So you tell me. Maybe he is different. That new Pope, John, there's a man any faith would be proud of. —Stevenson, his heart's in the right place. But has he got the chutzpah to stand in the White House and flip a dime against the world? Seriously, George, with most of your people and the money for Stevenson, you've got to keep ducking. You come out for Kennedy now and the goo-goos will scream traitor at you with all the strength of their overdeveloped larynxes. You getting much Kennedy pressure?"

"His brother is doing some arm-twisting. But that's his job. Sam, I'd like to come out for him. His only real problem is, will his back hold up? Christ, why can't I ever say what I think on this job!"

"Because nobody ever elected a loudmouth to anything."

"I trim my sails all the time. Look at the way I got off that subcommittee on air safety just to please Matchelder."

"That deal will never stick."

"That son-of-a-bitch. —Sam, growing up I used to be known as a loner. Now I'm so much of a team player I never take a shot myself."

"You know, Dent, we've also got to figure out who to support for Governor?"

Dent kept quiet. All around him were choices he didn't want to make. No right choice would guarantee the prize; but one wrong decision and his Senate chances were shot.

"You gotta choose sometime in the next two months," said Sam.

"Why can't I duck that one? Go to the convention with a block of uncommitted votes I can control and bargain with."

"It can't be done. George, I've said this before. Your trouble is you've got no rabbi. You're always out there pushing yourself. That makes waves. You need someone pulling ya up."

"Who do you have in mind, Sam?"

"That's why I asked you, who are you supporting for Governor?"

"Okay, Sam, who am I supporting?"

"What about Frank Zeigler?"

Dent considered Zeigler and his chances. Frank Zeigler was the Mayor of Rochester and except for the Syracuse area was reportedly pretty solid upstate. He was an organization man, which sat well with the regulars. He had cleaned up Rochester, which gave him some credence with the reformers, but also caused him hostility within the organization. Dent had always felt Zeigler to be an easygoing, affable guy, doomed usually to place second.

"Sam, he doesn't have a chance."

"If you could deliver a block of reform delegates, and guarantee some dough, he's got a chance. His big weakness is no one is pulling for him in the city."

"You think he can win?"

"He doesn't need to win. He just needs to wind up with enough strings in his hands to help you in two years. And besides, look at the other creeps running."

"Sam, you should have warned me. You've been thinking."

"Having been born with a losing personality, halitosis, slow reflexes, a paunch, and a weak heart, I have been forced to develop the only talent available to me. Does Zeigler make sense?"

"Let's get him on the phone."

"And let's hope Matchelder and the Jewacky forces aren't there first."

"Are you guessing?"

"The belief that the opposition is sittin' on its dead butt shooting tiddledywinks kills ya."

Mayor Zeigler was extremely friendly over the phone, which indicated that Dent and Sam were first. Dent made a date to fly to Syracuse for lunch on Tuesday; then he and Sam headed uptown for Dent's apartment and the monthly district leaders' meeting.

Normally June would have been the last leaders' meeting Dent had to inflict on himself. But with the nominating convention for Governor in September both he and they wanted to keep in touch. So Dent had invited them in once more for drinks and talk, talk, talk. This afternoon Jean Aaron would substitute for Sarah, who usually was hostess at the meetings, to charm the men and give the ladies a feeling of being in on something social. "Most of the leaders are out of town," Dent had lied to Sarah. "There's no point in your coming all the way in." Sarah had agreed. That gave him four whole nights with Dee.

In Dent's apartment all his district leaders had already gathered and were swapping lessons of political survival.

"Harry?"

"Yeah, Jack."

"You've been running your club nine years. How come you never have any trouble?"

"Maybe he doesn't have any social workers in his club."

"They're worse than housewives."

"Which one of you men is knocking housewives."

"See, Jack, you make enemies everywhere."

"I keep my club in line with the big-issue meeting. Every year we hold a dinner meeting to discuss some big issue. I put all the nuts and troublemakers on the committee to plan that: what will be the issue, the date, who'll speak, where, the menu; while I run the club. —Two years ago they fought so hard we never even had the meeting."

"I hear you got troubles, Jack."

"Mary, I face a real crisis. It's painting that center stripe on Fifth Avenue green on St. Patrick's day. There's a group in my club want the club to bring legal action to stop the Mayor from doing that. Violation of the separation of Church and State."

"You gotta stop that, Jack, that could kill us in an election year."

"Let Kleinman know tonight."

"The poor Congressman."

"You know our trouble. Since the Korean war ended and Eisenhower came out in favor of the nuclear test ban, the nuts have no place to coalesce so they pop up everywhere."

"You got an interesting philosophical point there. Do the nuts create the issue or the issues the nuts?"

"Issues come and go. The nuts are with you always."

"Here's the Congressman."

Dent went around his living room shaking hands, exchanging banter and greetings. He even managed a warm smile for a craggy newcomer Rosemary Firt, though she had fought him on a judgeship. Had he known she had just stuck her chewing gum underneath the chintz of the Louis XIV chair on which she sat, his smile would have been more genuine. He had never liked that chair. He glanced at his alarm wrist watch, 5:10. The alarm would go off at 7:30. Time to listen.

Toward the end of the two and a half hours Dent tested what would happen when he pushed the name Frank Zeigler for Governor. Miss Firt immediately wanted to know where Zeigler stood on aid to the Algerian rebels, free abortion clinics, and aid to parochial schools. Dent countered that it would certainly be interesting to know where all the candidates stood on such key issues. Gibbons of Upper West had some interesting information on what the fathers were saying about the candidates. Next they discussed the position of the Liberal Party; and what spot on the ticket would be reserved for New York City, if Zeigler led the slate. Since the Governor would probably control the delegation to the Presidential nominating convention two years away, where did the announced candidates stand on Kennedy versus Stevenson. That led them to question Dent, chipping away at his insistence that he would make no commitment until after the first few primaries.

Three of his leaders were definitely pro-Kennedy, three uncommitted or waiting craftily like himself, and six for Stevenson. Dent watched interested and amused as they went at each other. They might be home before their TV sets, he thought, getting bombed on beer, but they're here, arguing, exposing themselves; someone is going to lose. Why do any of us do it? He smiled across the room at Sam and Jean. He must remember to ask Jean how she felt privately on this issue.

The conversational ball was thrown to him and he ducked, again with a glance at his watch. Another nine minutes of this nonsense before his alarm went off. Why did he put up with such irritation? That question, he realized, was rather rhetorical. In part he enjoyed what he was doing. The major emotional returns of his life had come from leading. He remembered the first time he cleared twelve feet as a pole vaulter, and when the war canoe he captained won the camp's all-day race.

Then there was the day—in his boredom now he went back to the moment to refresh himself—the day the second platoon of Charlie Company had accepted Lieutenant Dent as its leader.

In England, before D-Day, he had watched his men, acutely conscious that he, the outsider with no combat experience, was meant to lead them, veteran tankers. And not just any veterans, but a platoon of "the Outfit," that charmed circle of efficient killers to which every gung-ho tank officer had hoped to be assigned. D-Day in France, the first combat for most of the American army, would find them already two invasions old, having spearheaded in Africa and Sicily. Patton had commanded them when a colonel. Wherever they went the nature of the war changed: became hotter, more efficient, professional. Eleven of his men had been wounded. His platoon sergeant, Costa, wore a Silver Star.

On a bright July day in Normandy, vicious wasps feeding on the rotting apples shelled down from the trees, Lieutenant Dent, now two combat weeks old, turned in the turret of the lead tank and saw the smoke. Further back in the same field Sergeant Costa's tank had been hit and burned.

Costa stood beside the tank.

"Run, Costa. Run!" Dent yelled. How ridiculous to yell. A man walking beside his tank could not have heard him and Costa was a hundred yards away.

"Run, Costa!"

Costa's tank continued to burn. The sergeant continued to stand beside it, dazed. On the far side of the tank the other four members of the crew scuttled for safety. They couldn't see Costa. His tank's going up, Dent thought, Costa's already dead. His tank, exploding like a mammoth bomb, will smear him over the field.

The book was quite explicit. Lieutenant Dent must abandon Costa. That was precise, definite, repeated over and over. To return for Costa would slow the attack, kill the momentum of the drive, give the enemy time to get set, make the fight for the objective more deadly. The book was law and that law bound Dent absolutely. Of his own free will he had accepted the covenant.

Reinforcing the book a thousandfold was a highly personal argument. Dent knew he was, at least at that instant, reasonably safe inside his own tank steel. To reach Costa he had to leave his cocoon; run naked across the open field toward thirty-two tons of gas and ammo. And whatever had hit Costa's tank could be tracking him now. He looked closely. No puffs of gray hung over the field between his tank and Costa's. He should be able to make it.

Heaving himself further up in the turret he checked what he saw against what little he knew of battle. To his right above the hedgerows, he could see the tops of aerials. That would be third platoon, still halted on the road. To his left he could just see one tank of first platoon. It fired away at something beyond his vision. His own tanks inched forward, hunting, wondering.

He bent down; switched his radio to intercom. "Driver halt. Gunner take command. I'm going back and get Costa."

Dent pushed out of the turret; swung his feet to the steel deck; leaped toward the ground. He had forgotten to take off his earphones. Halfway through his jump the cord went tight and he was checked in midair, to hang for an instant of agony by the plugs in his ears. Then they ripped out and he slammed backward against the tank side to fall stunned to the ground. The ground felt warm and soft, pleasant to lie on. The sun was shining. The smoking tank and Costa were miles away and tiny, as if viewed through the wrong end of a telescope. You can never reach them, he thought. To try is suicide. The book says . . . Fighting a paralyzing tiredness he rolled over, pushed himself up, and bending low as if socked in his stomach, began to dogtrot across the field. The ground seemed to be at a great distance from his feet, and uneven, tripping him.

"Costa!"

As he ran another figure came toward him from his right. Dent paused. The figure was screaming. Who was it? He didn't know. It wasn't one of his. The figure clutched a dangling, red half an arm. Dent hadn't time. He pointed violently toward the gap in the hedgerow that would take the wounded soldier toward the rear. The man didn't see and kept running toward the side.

Like a diver breaking back into sunlight. Dent's world snapped into focus. Off to his right a string of black noise burst. Some high-velocity stuff cracked by, way overhead. He was running well in the heat, toward a burning tank and a man. He might be doing his wind sprints for the pole vault.

He grabbed Costa by the arm and pulled him away.

"Run, Costa. Run!"

Costa staggered.

Dent grabbed Costa and steadied him. Together they broke

into a dog trot. Dent shoved and pushed his sergeant toward the far side of his number-two tank. They crouched there. With a roar Costa's tank exploded; its whole turret flying off. Chance. Blind chance. He put Costa inside number-two tank; sprinted back to his own. The battle was moving. He had to catch up.

That evening as his tanks coiled in a cherry orchard, Costa came to him.

"Lieutenant, how long did I stand there?"

"I don't know, Costa. Maybe two thousand years."

"I still don't remember."

"How do you feel?"

"No sweat. —Thanks, Lieutenant."

Costa walked away. Dent noticed his men now looked at him differently. He was light-headed, insensible with delight. He felt totally free and infinitely strong. They had accepted him.

Colonel Catenberry ran his eyes along the visual perfection of Joyce Farad and thought: boy, have I got what it takes. Girls like this were scarce as brick shit-houses in Georgia. That WAC, Major Fell, whom General Battenberg, the vice-chief of staff, was screwing, didn't come close to his live one here. He smiled contentedly: I fuck, fight, and fly better than anyone else in the world. He rolled toward Joyce and once again began to stroke her into excitement, his movements as precise and hard as when he jerked a jet fighter off a short runaway.

Joyce felt the abrupt confidence of his fingers and began to dissolve her thoughts, to remove everything between herself and Frank. She would have torn the skin off her body to place herself closer. She loved him. Not just for tonight and today; but for an endless succession of nights and days that stretched into what she dimly called forever. The moment she had put Catenberry and forever together she had known she meant marriage. The warm, soft place she belonged, with children to play with, a home and a husband other women envied.

She did not know that Catenberry's life plan called for a divorce from his present wife and remarriage to the daughter of some senior Air Force general or powerful Senator or business leader. She merely knew he had somewhere a wife about whom he said only, "Christ, that woman holds me back." Joyce believed her mission was simply to arrange that Frank leave his wife and marry her.

But how to make him change? There was her body, boys had wanted that since junior high, and her skill at, she never knew quite what to call it, well, at it. But would that switch Frank? She didn't cook well. Women who claimed they liked to cook must be liars; all that work and the dead oily feel when you touched meat. Because those women weren't beautiful like her and couldn't make real love, they had to pretend elsewhere. On one of their trips together she had made a play for someone else to get Frank jealous. He'd just beaten her and then forgotten about it. But she'd find a way.

Later, as he was dressing, Catenberry told her, "If you can get yourself up to New York tomorrow, hon, we can have a night out. I got to go up there and see your boy, George Dent."

"What about Frank?"

"A little deal I promoted." He smiled to himself. Some guys talked to their girls about such deals to prove how bright they were. He knew he was bright; he kept quiet.

With his interest in missiles, George Dent was becoming increasingly important to the missile officers in the Air Force. When Catenberry had learned that the Republicans had selected an attractive candidate to run against Dent, he'd put his underground to work. An Air Force security officer had checked with a buddy in the FBI and gotten hold of the raw data file on Paul Woodbridge. Woodbridge's firm had had to settle out of court for fraudulent tax deductions. When he gave the Congressman that secret information and Dent used it, he'd have a real hold over Dent.

Dee was out, taking some food to a close friend who had been mugged a few days before. Dent relaxed in her studio, thinking. He would have liked to run out and buy something to surprise her; but Dee was fierce about her independence. "I like flowers, Dent," she'd said, "and I'll keep this antique silver mirror you've given me because it's so lovely. But no more. You may not mean it; but I feel presents are a put-down."

He knew what he really wanted to do; but he was afraid. Finally he strode deliberately to the racks where Dee kept her materials, took out a large sketch pad, and tacked several sheets off it to her easel. Next, he went over to her pencils and with a knife worked the points of six into the shape he used to like.

If he was about to make his first serious sketch in eight or nine years what should he draw? Obviously it could have nothing to do with Dee. Women, female nudes came last. First you had to get rid of all that playboy pin-up shit. Then you had to outfox Madison Avenue. After that paint out of yourself all the other great visions of women, Modigliani back through Goya and Cranach. Then you could tackle your own feelings about women in general. And finally if you were great and blessed with luck you might be able to say something about a person you loved.

He had to start with the simple, the familiar. Perhaps get some fruit out of Dee's icebox and do a still life. But he never was any good at fruit. Try flowers then. Who do you think you are, he asked himself derisively, some sixteenth-century Dutchman? Give up the idea. You said you were never going to sketch again. He paused, strung up between choices.

His summer sports jacket hung from the back of a studio chair, with his briefcase beside it. He took his jacket and briefcase over to the table and folding the jacket, placed it on the table leaning the briefcase against it. He shuffled the two shapes around, added a bottle full of brushes, took these away, added some pencils, took these away. The shapes remained too cold and linear.

His face began to itch. He couldn't take forever just arranging these few shapes. He pushed and tugged at the jacket, letting a sleeve drape over the table. That was better. A nice human line that filled the lower right hand corner of the picture. As he worked he felt faint traces of forgotten excitement; also anger at how slowly he was progressing. Like walking, after lying in a hospital bed for months, you sweat and sweat and finally took four steps of a motion that everyone else did naturally all day.

From different parts of the studio he retrieved his socks, shirt, underpants, and shoes. He made a mental note to check his underpants for lipstick before going to Easthampton, then put them and the shirt on. His socks and shoes he added to the still life, balling up the socks to break up the left side of the picture. He took some papers from his briefcase and rested them against the shoes. There wasn't much there to sketch, but what the hell; he had some soft angles and some hard angles, some lights and some darks.

His first two attacks on the problem were dreadful. He crumpled up the paper and started afresh, this time on texture first. That didn't work either. Jacket, socks, shoes, briefcase, table, they all came out the same. He had thought that his fingers would be stiff that they wouldn't produce what he wanted. That wasn't his problem at all, he realized. He couldn't see. The hand remembered; the eye forgot.

He made little starts and experiments around the edges of his paper. They are all awful, he thought, because you haven't placed any sunlight on them, though it's there, scattered all across the table. He threw away another sheet. He'd remembered painting as fun. This was work, just like Congress.

Slowly he began to gain on the problem; not getting anywhere great; but at least moving. The sunbeams were solid; and where they hit and splattered on his still life, they left definite creases and scars. The dark mass of the objects on the table strained against the weight of light. Now the picture had some action and cohesion plus a limit. It wasn't going to be much of a sketch; but he'd got something. He shaded and erased; cursed at his inability to handle part of the perspective where the table turned a corner. He used to get so much more.

He remembered a canvas he'd done at St. Luke's when he was fifteen, in his fourth-form year; by which time he'd gained some control over his environment. He could take painting instead of

Greek; he could walk by himself in the winter if he took football and baseball in the fall and spring. He was trudging through the woods one glittery February afternoon. It must have been February; the day too light and intense for January but with snow too crisply bright for March. In the pocket of his parka were letters from his two best girls.

He felt grown-up and powerful because two beautiful subdebs were writing him. Morality and self-analysis required that he decide which one he liked best. His sketchbook contained a coded graph that plotted the standing of each of his girls month by month. He planned to seek out his favorite spot in the woods, study the letters from the two girls, and decide which was number one.

Dent, the school's only walker, had the woods to himself; especially the deep woods, beyond the places where other boys sneaked to smoke or jerk each other off. He headed directly for his favorite place, a large group of birches in whose center sat a pond slightly bigger than a good-sized mud puddle. There had been an ice storm during the night and the leafless branches of the trees—elms, maples, birches, shag-bark hickories, oaks, and locusts—were tightly gloved with ice. Glints of light foamed in the branches as he plunged through them. He walked lightly in order not to crack the crust of snow, but now and then broke through to sink in shin deep. His mind on his girl problem, he ducked and twisted his way into the center of the birch grove and, dusting off the snow with his mitten, sat down on a log beside his frozen pond.

The afternoon sun slanting down on the ice-covered birches set them afire and as the breeze moved their branches, rainbows shafted out. His trees had never been so beautiful: cold, winter-kissed, northern mermaids with glistening wet scales. Suddenly he realized that the clear cast of ice which formed the beauty of the trees was also their death-sentence. It dragged them down, rent, snapped, and chewed. His birches burned with total glory; and their glory would kill them.

Then the sun stopped, the world wheeled upside down, the

wind roared, the snow blazed black; and he exploded off his log into light-scratched darkness with the brutal cry of a man shot dead and knowing it.

He was inside a vision. Where the ice coated the branches the birches were red, fresh-cut blood red. And the branches were inside the spangled, silken sleeve of a beautiful woman. And where the branches met the trunk, this ice-woman of the sleeve tore the tree with garishly jeweled fingers and long nails. The branches were red, the tree trunks were purple, the snow was black, the tree roots writhed below ground like blood-red intestines. The sun was also purple and the shadows bled from the rent tree branches to splash against the snow in bursting gobs that shattered the edges of his picture.

He was dancing in the snow, yelling, in tears. Excitedly he grabbed at the two letters from his girls in his pocket. Wonderful girls, they had had too little to say to write on the backs. He grabbed a pencil from his suit coat and began to sketch. His pencil, touched by the magic, helped him, moving in unexpected ways. The power of his vision burst inside him, like a huge organ playing all stops out in a dungeon; and the more he drew, the more he saw.

He made notes about the colors, how they hit him. "Mad-dog-howl red." "Moon-cold dream-white teeth." "Costume-skate-dress glitter." "Throat-swallowed black." Finally he sketched in the lower boundaries of the picture, the black snow glinting like a beach of lava sand, the bursts of falling blood which smeared and froze over the ground.

His excitement began to ebb. The world around him simmered down to normal; flatter than normal. Though here and there a piece of the scene would erupt into its former glory. His pencil began to move in a more workaday way. He was exhausted. Also triumphant, taken apart, stretched. Inside himself, he realized, grew a self-sustaining feast. Walking back to school he recalled other times when he must have been close to such an experience but missed it.

The rest, while fun, was an anticlimax. He went back to the

school studio with his sketches. The studio was kept locked. To enter one made an appointment with the art master, after first checking with the senior master. St. Luke's wanted no loose, artistic living. Dent had a skeleton key and went in and painted. He sketched, painted, rubbed out, overpainted, sketched, and painted again for three weeks. He received a deadly series of forties and fifties in his classroom work while his entire purpose remained focused on his canvases. Finally he stopped. He could not get what he had seen. But the picture felt complete for the moment. Besides, from *Birches over Ice* had come a whole new series of ideas.

One afternoon, going through the art master's desk while illegally in the studio, he came across some entrance blanks from the New England Scholastic Art Exhibition. Pretending to have found them on the floor, he asked the art master if he could send a painting.

"I don't think so, Dent," replied the master. "We never have. Public schools enter the contest." The poor man lived in fear of getting the sack as an oddball artist; and tried as a result to be even more St. Lukian than the football coach, who taught beginning French with the aid of a trot.

Dent, who swung continually between rage at the school and total acceptance of it, kept back one of the blanks, filled it out, took *Birches over Ice* to the school shop, crated it, and shipped it off. He came in second. The school was notified and officially congratulated. Once again he was sent for by the Rector.

"Dent," he was known now, "what is this, ah, ah contest?"

Dent was scrubbed, his hair brushed, he had on a dark suit, white shirt, his shoes shined, and he was wearing a brand-new school tie.

"I am glad to have won it for St. Luke's, sir. The training you give here, sir, the training is really so good. It's not me that won, sir. It's the school." You couldn't just put the Rector off with a little bullshit as you did other masters; you had to spread it on with a dump truck and tractor. "The painting was of a Christian subject, sir. God's work in nature."

"You were refused permission to enter!"

"Permission, sir? The contest is sponsored by the Harvard Museum and the Boston Museum." This was partly true, since two of the forty sponsors had been the Boston Museum and a Harvard-affiliated gallery.

"Oh . . . the Harvard Museum . . . Mr. ah, ah, ah, who teaches art did not tell me that."

"We may have entered before, sir, and just not been fortunate enough to win."

"Boy, if we had entered before, we would have won. There is excellent training in art at this school."

"Yes, sir! . . . A friend of mind, a little older, from St. Paul's, got third last year." That was a lie out of whole cloth.

"St. Paul's . . . I'm glad we've beaten them. Well, Dent, since you've won, I cannot see the harm. I did not know about the Harvard Museum. But in future check with the senior master before entering contests."

"Yes, sir."

"And thank you, Dent, for the get-well card to my wife. That was most thoughtful."

After the conditioning he got at St. Luke's, the Army was easy: a benign, loving, rational structure, tolerant and permissive.

He once told Sam after a political rally at which he had successfully fielded several hot questions, "The great thing I learned at prep school was the successful lie."

"You got to be born lucky," said Sam, "to have the fifteen thousand dollars to spend to learn something the lower orders know by instinct."

Dent found himself laughing out loud at Sam's remark, as he plugged away at the sock circles, soft lines against the hard surface of his briefcase. In strengthening the sock circles, he realized, he was muddying the whole. He stopped; redid the socks as they were; tried the sleeve on the other side. No improvement there either. He'd gotten just about everything he could out of what was before him. He walked over to the stove to squeeze some oranges. He felt stiff and tired even, and after such a little sketch.

It had been a long time since he'd thought about *Birches over Ice*. The picture should still be in the family attic in Greenwich. He'd like to see it.

He was sitting in the studio chair, daydreaming about St. Luke's, when he heard Dee coming up the stairs. He opened the door for her, beaming like a child, unable to look at her because the sketch might be bad.

"I made you a house decoration," he said. He took the packages she was carrying from her and she walked over to the easel, then drew back. He knew by now she was a little far-sighted.

"My God, George."

"What's wrong?"

"Wrong? Nothing's wrong. You can draw. I heard you tell you could, but this is talent. —I don't sketch any better."

"Oh, come on."

He was both embarrassed and pleased and amazed that Dee could praise so freely in an area where her own success must be so vital to her.

"I mean it," she was still staring at the sketch. "Do you paint as well as you draw?"

"No. No. I get all fouled up in technique, too slick and mechanical."

"You can get around that; it just takes time." She tore at the jumble of beaverboards and canvases in her studio closet; finally yanked out two.

"Look, Dent, here's the way I painted for three years. Three goddamn years stuck here. I'd wake up in the morning and cry as I walked across the studio. Then one day," she took away the first canvas and pulled out the second, a powerful, bleak study of three faces. "Boom! I had it. Then after a few years this way dried up for me too. I had to change again. It happens to everyone, George."

"Only I didn't get through it."

To his complete surprise she came over and hugged him.

"Oh, George, how vulnerable you are. Sometimes my Congressman sounds like a little boy."

"You're wrong."

"No I'm not. I saw it at Turkey's." She turned from him, her mouth set.

"I sometimes feel I'm a Congressman by accident. If I hadn't been dissatisfied with the law. If there hadn't been a primary fight at that moment. —Oh well, I'm here."

seven

Dent watched the morning light streak through Dee's bead curtains to lie in long slants across the green of her plants. Though there was a heaviness about the air which promised a hot August day later, at this early hour the breeze was still cool and brought off the Hudson a faint sea smell which mixed with the odors of warming asphalt and oil to remind him that Manhattan was also an island.

He rolled over stealthily and picked his watch out of his shoe; the dial read 7:05. He hastily reset the hands so the alarm wouldn't go off. Dee hated his watch. He looked at Dee asleep beside him: the mole on the right side of the long neck, the soft oval of her face. He wanted to forget the day ahead and just lie here. But the morning's first appointment was already beginning to scrape at the soles of his feet. He had another meeting with Mayor Zeigler at the Rochester airport at nine. Which meant the 8:15 from LaGuardia. He eased himself out of bed.

Dee sensed his going and heard her shower turn on. She felt relaxed and warm, wanting to hold Dent and fuck him and then sleep some more. That's not good for my work, she thought, but that's what I want to do. He's getting awfully important to me. Reluctantly she got up to make Dent coffee.

"What breakfast is it this morning?" she yelled at him over the noise of the shower. "Or should I say breakfasts?"

"Breakfast on the plane," he called back. Did Dee realize what he was doing, he wondered? Something he hated, carefully washing all smell of her from himself. "I'm meeting Zeigler in Rochester at nine."

"Rochester. You didn't tell me."

"It upsets you so when I talk about leaving. I'll be back this afternoon, though. Then I've two late appointments downtown. I'll see you by 7:30 at the latest."

"Oh. And then the phone calls."

"It's less than a month before the convention."

"George, where are we going?"

He was out of the shower now, toweling himself. He deliberately avoided her last question. "I'm sorry about the calls last night."

"Where are we going?"

"How do you mean."

"We meet, we eat, we fuck, nothing more happens."

"That's not true."

"We never go anywhere."

"I have to be careful. In politics . . ."

"I've heard. There's a private showing this afternoon I very much want to take you to. Cancel your last appointment and come."

"I can't. It's with Matchelder."

"Matchelder. The lawyer who forced you to drop the air-crash investigation."

"Yes."

"Tell him some other time."

"I can't. He's lawyer for a lot of the big liberal money. He'll control a flock of votes in Albany. I explained about him. Would you risk a picture sale to come someplace with me?"

"Yes."

I lost that round, he thought.

"I told Turkey," Dee continued, "about your dropping the investigation."

"You shouldn't have done that."

"What cowardice."

"I didn't drop the investigation. I just got off the subcommittee." He was going to be late for his plane.

"That's right, look at that damn watch. Find out how you feel. Tick, tick, tick. —Don't give me that click-it-on click-it-off smile!"

"Dee, I've got to go."

"Go! Run! —Run, run, run. That's all you do. No wonder you stopped being a painter."

He started across the room to make a try at kissing her.

"Don't." She backed from him. "And I don't want a date tonight."

"As you wish." He pivoted quickly and went out the door deliberately closing it softly. He'd been lucky to get out before she started to cry. That really would have made him late. He hated fights.

Fortunately he found a cab quickly and just made his plane. The meeting with Zeigler went well; and this time Dent had some actual votes in the hand to show him. He returned to New York feeling better about the convention.

As he climbed out of the subway stairs at Wall Street on his way to see Matchelder, he noticed his left leg ached. There must be a storm coming, he thought. He looked about him at the crisp, white, white-shirted people in their dark suit uniforms: lawyers and bankers scurrying self-assured inside their keep of power. If he lost he'd never go back to practicing here. He'd be another Washington refugee, scratching out a living along the banks of the Potomac with the help of Sarah's cash. Suddenly the people passing ceased to be human and became crisp black tubes, shiny and angular, topped by white ovals. He smiled at the vision.

Matchelder kept Dent waiting for five minutes, which made Dent furious. There was another man in the lawyer's office when Dent was ushered in. Dent knew him slightly—Timothy Fiorello, Chairman of the New York and New Jersey district of the United Aircraft Workers' Union. Matchelder was seated in his leather rocker looking like an Egyptian mummy. He represented the Union and also several large aircraft manufacturers and airlines, hence his successful insistence that Dent drop the crash investigation or lose liberal support.

They shook hands all round, Matchelder did not rise. Dent noticed that both men had carefully manicured nails.

"Congressman," began Francis Matchelder, "Timothy Fiorello is an old friend of mine. . . ."

"And also a client, isn't he, Frank?"

"No, Dent," Matchelder hissed.

"But his union is."

"That's a different matter."

Dent turned to Fiorello with his warmest smile. "Some day I'm going to get a straight answer out of my old friend Frank; and I'll have to call the *New York Times*."

"Tim had a few things he wanted to say to you, Congressman, and asked me if I could arrange a meeting. After hearing his problem it seemed to me that there existed a thread of mutual interest, so I called you up."

Dent went cold inside. He began to guess what was coming and could see no way out.

"Mr. Dent." Timothy paced up and down as he spoke. He had the peculiar ass some fat men have that did not so much roll from side to side as snap back and forth like the tail feathers of a turkey. "I have supported you in the past, my union has gone all the way with you, because we regarded you as a true friend of labor and of America. And we've used our influence within the brotherhood of trade unions to support you. But now frankly, Mr. Dent, we're beginning to wonder."

"Look, Tim, if it's about the missile investigation could we drop the horseshit and talk jobs and contracts."

"Mr. Dent, I'm talking as an American."

"Tim always talks that way," said Matchelder.

"And so does our distinguished counsel," said Fiorello. "A former Secretary of the Navy."

"Mr. Dent, when we see you knocking the bomber program

which is the foundation of American democracy, and leaking top-secret figures against the bomber, lies which can only help the Russians . . ."

"Air Force figures," Dent interrupted.

"Congressman," Timothy jabbed his finger at Dent and Dent felt the power and anger in a man who was not used to being contradicted, a man with union sycophants and captains of industry to polish his ass daily. "General Eisenhower is a military man. He is for the bomber. He is our President and all loyal Americans should support him on military matters. That's the position of our union and the position we expect our friends to take."

"A reasonable position," said Matchelder.

"The fact that the Russians are making missiles and we're not doesn't bother you?" Dent asked.

"The Communists are probably just trying to trick us with dummy missiles. Get us to drop our guard."

Dent tried a few more arguments and received the same standard replies. "What I can't understand Timothy," he said, finally, "is what difference it makes to you, if I can get missile contracts instead of bomber contracts for this state?"

"Who wants missile contracts!" exploded Timothy.

"He doesn't feel such contracts to be in the best interests of the country," said Matchelder.

Dent got the message. Some other union might claim jurisdiction over missile production. There was silence in the office.

"I just wanted you to know where Mr. Fiorello stood," said Matchelder.

"And as his counsel you stand with him?"

"His position seems reasonable."

Dent nodded thoughtfully. "Are you still supporting Paul Jewacky at the convention, Frank?"

"What does that have to do with it?"

"Not a thing. I just wondered."

"I know of your efforts in Mayor Zeigler's behalf," Matchelder continued coldly. "I consider Mr. Jewacky more in keeping with the liberal traditions of our Democratic party."

They made a few minutes of small talk, promised to keep in touch; Dent said he'd carefully think over what they'd had to say, shook hands, and left.

"I think the whole thing is just a tactic with him, Sam," Dent reported to Kleinman later. "You and I have said it before, he wants to be Senator himself. Now I'm sure of it. He aims to kill off everybody else, particularly a younger man like me. He'll shaft me in the back with the money, liberals, labor, anyone he can, and all the while making a buck out of it. I was a fool to let him pressure me out of that air-crash investigation."

"I told you."

"You were right, Sam. But if his strategy is to split the party so he and the goo-goo money can pick up the pieces we're in for a tough time in Albany."

But Dent's first disaster came not from Matchelder, or the labor body traders, or the organization regulars, or the upstate conservatives, or the two-hundred-per-cent liberals; but from a small child. Sam Kleinman's eight-year-old nephew gave Sam the mumps three days before the Convention.

"Jesus, Sam," said Dent over the phone. "Hadn't you ever had them?"

"Only on one side," came the croak back.

"You got to be careful, Sam. It's bad if they go down."

"Quiet, quiet, they may hear."

So Dent had to face the convention without Sam.

Dent had rented a two-room office near the Albany Convention Hall for his Ziegler operation. With Sam gone Jean Aaron and his Washington assistant shared uneasy command of this headquarters and its five phones. Dent also worked out of his three room suite in the Rappahannock Hotel: an outer room in which droppers by and hangers on could swirl about, a first inner room for Sarah and another Washington assistant to see the people he had to see now while he was seeing the people he should have seen before in the second inner room. The second inner room was also where he and Sarah sat on the edge of the bed from time to time, looked at each other, laughed, and asked each other, "What in Christ's name is going on?"

The New York State Democratic Convention, like all state conventions, was far more chaotic than a national convention. No one had enough money to organize properly, many of the delegates stayed with friends or commuted from home and so were impossible to find; there were never enough telephones or operators; and without proper passes or credentials the mass of hangers on made it next to impossible for those rightfully there to conduct any business. Eight years before, a vital nomination had been obtained by the simple tactic of stalling the two elevators carrying the Putnam County Delegation between floors until the voting was over.

Of course, Sam would have been able to find more of the delegates, and having found them, told Dent how to talk to them. He would have known both how each delegate would vote on the convention floor, and also how he would vote if he stood alone before his God, whether that being was the Savior of Mankind, the distant image of Mrs. Roosevelt, or the Real Estate Lobby. And each vote counted. For Mayor Zeigler was agonizingly close to victory; but not quite.

The number of delegates to the New York State Gubernatorial Convention was 305. That made 153 the magic winning figure juggled by political expediency out of historical and legal confusion. One hundred fifty-three of the faithful would make the majority to decide the next candidate for Governor, perhaps even for President. By the day before the one on which they were to vote, Zeigler had 91 to 93 of the necessary votes. This put him an easy second behind Joseph Fratranelli of Brooklyn, the regular organization's candidate, who had 102 to 104 votes. Third, well behind Zeigler, came Paul Jewacky, the knight of the fanatic reformers and the creature of Matchelder's future ambition. Jewacky, who had no chance of winning, held 45 to 47 votes, which might have nominated Zeigler, but instead were thrown away on the altar of pure principle.

(Of Jewacky's 47 votes, six were secretly pledged to Zeigler. But Dent was saving these for a second-ballot switch, when Zeigler would have to show a gain to stay alive. And how many of his delegates, he wondered, had been reached by either Matchelder or the organization and were going to switch at the same time?)

Close behind Jewacky, in fourth place, panted Tim Bannon, the Bronx dinosaur. He had forty votes, composed, Dent believed, of superloyal party workers who distrusted Fratranelli because he could read. In last place, and here the smell of deals and cash was overpowering, grazed a genial fuddle-head from Erie called Trowbridge, holding down twenty upstate votes. Obviously these twenty sheep were soon to wander elsewhere to receive their highly lucrative earthly rewards. But where? And for how much? Merely to guess was no good. Dent had to know exactly in order to either leak the story to the press or make a better offer.

The Convention was almost set. After a few ballots the Bannon votes would go to Fratranelli under some complex Brooklyn-Queens-Bronx deal. Then a mere half of Trowbridge's votes would put Fratranelli over 153. The Fratranelli forces were already using bandwagon psychology.

But Zeigler had a chance. If Dent could persuade 40 of the Jewacky delegates to switch to Zeigler on the third ballot, on the grounds that Zeigler, while not a two-hundred-per-cent liberal, was certainly a liberal and could win, then Zeigler was home free. For Zeigler had a locked-in commitment from Congressman Humper of Queens, who would throw the 20 Fratranelli votes he controlled to Zeigler in return for Zeigler's support of his bid for the State Supreme Court. However, Humper would risk the organization's ire and switch only if his votes would be decisive. So the circle returned to Jewacky's hard core of compulsive liberals.

Dent called on Zeigler in the Mayor's suite at the Stanhope. Dent looked Zeigler's operation over and liked it; it seemed much like his own. The usual number of hangers on churned around in the outer room; but behind three card tables at the side sat some bright-looking young guys and girls with lists and phones. What's more, one of the professional politicians recognized Dent immediately, and he was taken into an inner room, where Mrs. Zeigler greeted him warmly.

"Sarah and I run our shop the same way," he told her. "About how far behind are you today?"

"Maybe three weeks and it's only ten-thirty."

Dent laughed. "I won't take long."

A few minutes later, he, Zeigler, and one of the Mayor's aides were sitting in Zeigler's bedroom.

"Frank," Dent began, "one of the things I've never learned in my brief years in politics is how to be a good politician. I'll come right to the point. I keep hearing rumors that it's not set yet who'll nominate you."

"Making that speech means a lot to you, Dent?"

"Statewide TV exposure means a great deal to me."

"I thought your interest was in getting me the spot."

Dent wished Sam were present. He could have defused the tension in the room with a quick joke and gained his point with a smile. "Frank, that's my purpose. And I'll keep working for you. But neither of us are in politics for our health."

"It's that Urban Affairs Bill you keep pushing. A lot of people upstate see that as a plot to rob them in favor of New York City."

"Frank, you know it favors Rochester, and Albany, and Syracuse just as much as New York City." The drawing up and sponsorship of a bill to create a Cabinet Department of Urban Affairs was in Dent's own mind one of his few real achievements as a Congressman.

"I know that," said Zeigler, "but I intend to vote for myself anyway. It's other people I'm worried about."

"You'd be surprised how many are concerned about that bill upstate," the Mayor's aide tallied.

"I get that from my father-in-law." The reminder of the press power Dent carried with him was not lost on the two men. "A lot of my people are upset because I'm supporting you and not Jewacky. I need that speech, Frank."

"Even if it hurts the Mayor?" asked the aide.

"I can use it to switch votes and hold my people. —I'm just a reformer at heart, you know. I'm in politics to feel good. Only what makes me feel good is getting ahead myself."

Zeigler laughed. "Dent, I see the team of Zeigler and Dent with a great future. Give me a couple of hours to touch some bases. I'll announce you as my proposer no later than one o'clock."

They shook hands. Dent exited to return to the thankless task of trying to hold his own forces together while prying loose Jewacky delegates. As he pummeled away at the delegates he recalled Sam's advice at a previous convention. "Remember every delegate is a livin' person with hopes and fears and human aspirations, a wife who spends too much, kids, a girl friend. He has a heart that beats like yours, full of pain, love, and sometimes truth. In short, delegates are human. Remember that. Because after you've dealt with those sons-of-bitches for more than an hour you won't believe it." —With the Jewacky delegates he didn't believe it after five minutes.

"No, Mr. Dent, no," the small intense woman yelled at him. "I will not embrace Mr. Zeigler. I think Mr. Jewacky would make the best Governor."

"He might well. But he has no chance."

"His record in Congress is superior to yours, Mr. Dent."

"He's never been in Congress, ma'am."

"His record if he had been. I will not kiss off a fighting candidate like Mr. Jewacky for a weak-knee like Zeigler. That would be bossism. Following wishes which aren't my own."

He called on another group of Jewacky delegates; began to reason with them. They berated him for "selling his soul to the bosses." They shoved beneath his nose their signs: a white club labeled "Clean Government" bisecting their slogan: "Let Jewacky Wack the GOP."

"Why aren't you with us?" they trumpeted. "Why aren't you with us?"

His temper exploded.

"Because of the deals you've made," he shouted back.

That rocked them silent. They looked at one another terrified. Had the pollution of politics come nigh them?

"Deals?" squeaked the leader.

"Don't take it from me," said Dent. "Go find a reporter from the *New York Times* and ask him. Go on. Go on." He herded them from his room. They limped out, banners at droop, a worried army. He was immediately furious at himself for losing his temper.

He rendezvoused with Zeigler again shortly after midnight.

"How are things going?" Zeigler asked.

"Only fair. I'm not having any luck breaking into the Jewacky strength. You doing any good with Trowbridge?"

"Not that you'd notice."

"Only fair" was an overstatement. In politics as in battle comes a moment when the winners can usually feel the invisible turn toward them. Dent had had no such feeling now.

"Yeah," Dent paused. "What I really get is the feeling something's going on I don't know about."

Zeigler nodded. "What does your assistant, Kleinman, think?"

"Didn't I tell you, he's got mumps."

"Mumps. Some days you can't win."

"I got an appointment with Calahan at the State Committee tomorrow at eleven. Himself sent word he wanted to see me. Maybe I'll learn something then. —This could be a long war, Frank."

"We'll hang in there."

The State Democratic Committee was crammed into a rabbit warren of ornate offices behind the Capitol. Dent often felt that the retainers in the outer rooms must be secretly in the pay of the Republicans. Why else did they contrive to look like minor villains on late late TV reruns, whispering out of the corner of their mouths to sinister, jowly cronies who chomped cigars? They might only be discussing the hour of their lunch break—indeed, when Dent had worked with them he discovered this to be the major topic—but they managed to ooze the impression that they were negotiating to buy at half price the quicklime for the shallow used-car-lot grave of some recalcitrant delegate from the outer marches of Queens, who had refused to sell his vote to the Mafia.

Dent, unrecognized as always by anyone in the reception room, went up to a large pear-shaped man who was chewing on a toothpick behind the reception desk.

"Good morning," he said, turning on his Congressional charm. "I have an eleven-o'clock appointment to see Calahan."

The toothpick shifted, the head snapped to the right and made a slight flick in Dent's direction. One of three cigar smokers on a corner bench folded his *National Enquirer,* eyed Dent up and down, rose, and slid out the back door.

"What would it be in reference about?" asked the toothpick. And this was the front office, where the average voter was meant to decide to entrust his future to the Democratic Party.

"I'm Congressman George Dent. We were just going to talk."

"What was dat name again?"

Dent reidentified himself. At the repetition of the word Congressman another figure on the bench lit the stub of his cigar and headed for the exit. From another door two new cigar-smokers entered to take the vacant places.

The pear-shaped man removed his toothpick and scratched his ear with it. "Hermie," he said to a figure leaning against the wall, "tell Lucy to tell Ed to let Marge know the Congressman is here." The figure against the wall shoved off. "I'd take ya in myself, Congressman; but I gotta watch things. You know how it is."

Dent allowed he did.

A tall gangly youth came in and stood before the toothpick, furtively shooting glances at Dent.

"It's okay," said the toothpick.

"Micky says 'yeah,' " mumbled the youth.

The toothpick reached into his side pocket, took out a roll of bills the size of a heavyweight's fist, quickly peeled off what looked to Dent like three twenties, and nodded. The youth took out a smaller roll of his own and added the three bills to it. He then turned, avoiding Dent's eyes, and beat it for the door.

"Hey, wait!" yelled the toothpick. With a gasp the youth jerked to a stop. One of the figures on the bench moved between the youth and the door. "Al will go wid ya"—the youth paled —"to help widda load." The toothpick then turned to Dent and smiled. "They're going for coffee, Congressman. Would you like a cup?"

"No, thanks," said Dent. Pushing party loyalty beyond all reason, Dent could just believe they'd return with coffee. But would the League of Women Voters ever buy it?

Dent was escorted back to Calahan through a bewildering series of rooms occupied by assistant licensing commissioners, Highway subdistrict supervisors, Liquor Authority inspectors, Sanitation under-department chiefs, and others such, whose promotions hinged on being known as "useful guys." Since no one could be quite certain how, by whom, or when this mighty title was confirmed, those who coveted it were forced to spend a great many waking hours just hanging about.

Calahan was talking to a group representing a local in the building trades when Dent came in. These fighters for the worker were urging the Democratic Convention to support a law making it illegal for a man to paint his own home without paying the union two hundred dollars first. "Paint It Yourself Is Communism" was their patriotic slogan of the moment. Calahan showed the unionists—all white—out, and Dent in. With Calahan was a Brooklyn State Senator famous for being "close" to the organization. After greetings and professions of neutrality from Calahan and the Senator—Dent recalled Red Donner's once describing an African nation he had visited as "violently neutral against us"—they got down to business.

"Dent, how deep are you in this Ziegler campaign?" asked Calahan.

"I don't get you." There was a pause.

"We mean," said Brooklyn filling the gap unwillingly, "are you with him all the way down the line?"

"Do you mean at some point will I throw in with Jewacky?" Dent paused. Was that what they were asking? Well, there was no harm in answering that question. "No."

"Dent," said Calahan, "you've always been a guy we could live with. I know you'd hate to see a deadlocked convention."

"You never know what happens in a deadlock." The Brooklyn Senator was more threatening. What were they trying to tell him?

"It might just be," Calahan leaned forward, "that twenty votes would put Fratranelli over the top. We'd remember that."

"There's no scandal connected with Joe." He of Brooklyn spoke up loyally for the native son. That was true. Fratranelli was honest when he understood the problem. Dent kept silent.

"Dent," Calahan was quiet now, letting his words carry his thrust, "why risk a deadlock, when your people can live with Fratranelli?"

"Your people can live with Zeigler, Jim. And remember Zeigler has a better chance of getting elected after he's nominated."

"I wouldn't say that," said the Brooklyn Congressman.

"Oh come on," said Dent, deliberately fast and tough. "If we're not going to tell each other the truth, there's no point in talking." They paused.

"What does Zeigler want?" asked Calahan.

"To be Governor or return to Rochester. He's not interested in second place on the ticket. —What does Fratranelli want?"

To his surprise they ducked that question. Instead Calahan answered, "Dent, we all gotta beware of deadlocks."

"If you both are hinting to me," Dent continued tough, "that if Zeigler doesn't withdraw in favor of Fratranelli the convention may pick someone worse, you're talking political suicide. You can't elect some old ward horse, like Tim Bannon, Governor." Dent had picked on Bannon only because he was technically a candidate. He saw both men stiffen. Had he insulted a friend of theirs? He added graciously, "Much as I like Tim, and he's a friend, we couldn't elect him."

"Tim's not so bad," said Calahan.

"Even in Brooklyn he has a good name."

"You'd support him, wouldn't you, Congressman?"

Jesus God, they couldn't be planning that!

"Tom"—Dent was quiet and level now—"when you start talking about Bannon like that you sound just like the Jewacky supporters." That rocked them. They thought the Jewacky supporters a bunch of nuts. "You're both so wrapped up in your own idea of politics, you'd rather lose the election than compromise. They believe in 'purity.' You believe in 'loyalty.' In them I can understand it. But you're meant to be professional politicians."

"Then why don't you bring your people over to Fratranelli and not risk a poor candidate?" Calahan was tough now.

"You bring your people to Zeigler. He's got the best chance of winning in November."

"Dent, we won't support Zeigler." Calahan paused, then continued. "If you got him nominated, which you can't, we'd support him. But not help him get nominated."

"Right," said Brooklyn.

That was it. They made polite talk a few moments. Dent left.

Looking down on the convention floor as the applause broke over him, Dent sensed that his nominating speech for Zeigler had gone over well. Friends and even enemies pressed round him on the floor as he made his way back to his seat to tell him what a great job he'd done. But he doubted he'd changed the minds of any delegates. Still, they hadn't been his target. His purpose had been to show the TV audience that the Democratic party held at least one live one.

For four hours, with an hour-and-a-half dinner break in the middle, the nominating speeches droned on. Finally the delegates shook off the leaden weight of countless "the man who bests" and began to vote, pawing each other at the smell of power.

Dent sat with the Manhattan delegation across the Armory

floor from Zeigler with the Rochester. Into his right ear was jammed the earphone of a pocket radio. The networks kept a faster, more accurate tally of each candidate's strength than anyone on the floor. No surprises turned up on the first ballot, though Bannon had about four more votes than Dent had anticipated. The count: Fratranelli 103, Zeigler 93, Jewacky 46 (seven of which they'd get on the next ballot), Bannon 41, Trowbridge 22. Okay, they'd felt each other out, now they'd fight.

Dent stood, waved to supporters, pounded a few backs, signaled Zeigler, checked some doubtfuls, watched the opposition, ordered subordinates. Oh, Zeigler, he almost yelled out loud, if there's a victory around I'll win it for you. He laughed inwardly at himself. What a hell of a place to be so happy, he thought, the grubby floor of a State Democratic Convention. Home is where the action is.

Right from the beginning the second ballot stank. First, the Bronx held solid for Bannon. Then where was Fratranelli going to pick up his strength? Next, Erie divided all wrong. Trowbridge lost delegates but both Fratranelli and Bannon gained; also Zeigler. He couldn't figure that bonus. By the time Queens balloted Dent realized all the city totals were wrong. Fratranelli hadn't gained as he should have. Maybe Zeigler had a chance of going over.

Dent broke from his place, shoved aside a sergeant-at-arms, and elbowed through the press of people to a prearranged pillar at the rear of the convention floor. Zeigler was there already, his patch cleared by two huge Rochester cops acting as alternate delegates.

"Those eight votes we got out of Erie are great," Dent yelled at Zeigler above the riot. They'd have to be quick. Already a reporter with a portable microphone was pushing toward them.

"They aren't ours, Dent. I know those guys. They'd never be for me."

"Then what the hell? And the city totals are crazy."

A group of raucous Fratranelli delegates forced Dent and Zeigler apart. Dent fought back through them. Someone offered to push his face in. Another yanked the ear phone from his ear. Dent grabbed it back, regained the pillar and the shelter of the two Rochester cops. Fortunately the crowd had carried the reporter away.

Suddenly Dent grabbed Zeigler by the shoulder, shaking him and shouting. "Goddamn it. Damn it. I see it. I see it. The organization is going for Bannon. That's what Calahan was trying to tell me. Fratranelli is their compromise. Either we put Fratranelli over the top, or they shove Bannon up our ass."

"That would kill the party."

"They're too dumb to see that."

"Christ, I think you're right. Bannon's already got more strength than I figured."

"Sure. And so have we. They slipped us some of his votes on this ballot, to take them from us on the next. All right. Do we hang on and fight or don't we? You're the candidate."

"They could be sucking us in. Getting us to panic and throw to Fratranelli."

"They could. But I don't think so."

"You're right. If they wanted him they could have elected him themselves. I hate to fold under pressure, Dent. But politics is politics. You can't move those Jewacky people? Even to stop Bannon?"

"No. They'll go down pure."

"We could live with Fratranelli. What do you think I should do, Dent?"

"Fight!" Even as he yelled it he doubted he was right.

Zeigler looked at him. That Dent was meant to be a politician. But here he looked as if he was ready to strangle people rather than compromise.

"Okay," said Zeigler. "We'll hold our delegates. Can you pick up any Jewacky strength?"

"I'll have another try."

Dent shoved across the convention floor to where Matchelder

sat with some of the other money in box seats above the crowd.

"Frank," Dent unwound at him, "the organization is going for Bannon."

"That possibility had occurred to me."

"That will kill the party. Stop it. Give us the votes to put Zeigler over the top."

"I don't control any votes." He had an aide with a two-way radio right behind him.

"That's not true."

Matchelder eyed Dent with complete hostility.

"You owe me one on the air-crash investigation."

Matchelder merely smiled.

"You can name the Lieutenant Governor." Zeigler would let him make such a deal, Dent thought.

"No."

"You're nominating Bannon; and we're going to lose."

"Mr. Dent, if we lose, they'll be someone around to pick up the pieces. Don't get so hungry so young."

"You shit." Dent went back to his seat so mad he could hardly talk. He swallowed hard and tried to make a small speech to a group of Jewacky delegates around him.

"No deals, no deals, no deals," they yelled, drowning him out.

"What the hell are you bastards in politics for?"

The third ballot began.

The end was rapid and unpleasant. On the third ballot both Fratranelli and Zeigler lost strength. Jewacky and Trowbridge held steady; Bannon gained. On the fourth ballot Bannon began to pull ahead of them all as Trowbridge folded. Suddenly there was a commotion in the Brooklyn delegation. The county leader mounted his chair and yelled for a microphone. One appeared in his hand and the sound cut swiftly to him. Good organization somewhere.

"Mr. Chaaaaiiiiirrrmaan," the county leader yelled. "It is my high honor and rare privilege to tell ya that Brooklyn's loyal son (cheers) Joseph Fratranelli (more cheers) recognizin' da wishes of da people releases his followers (pandemonium) and urges them to cast their votes for a fighting Irishman from the Bronx (cheers) who has never betrayed his party, Timothy Bannon (cheers and yells). Mr. Chairman, Brooklyn is solid for Bannon."

Everyone was on his feet screaming with joy, rage, relief, greed. Amid the pummel of sound the modulated radio voice in Dent's right ear correctly pointed out that Brooklyn's switch put Bannon over the top by fifteen votes.

Dent took the earphone from his ear. Through the chaos of the convention he saw a decision sweep down on him: black, dangerous as a squall line. Should he rise and move to make the vote unanimous for Bannon? He or Zeigler were the logical men. The organization would remember. He'd bank a credit he could cash later. The reformers would howl but he could placate them.

In fact he'd like to hear them howl, spit in their eye, show them how you worked the political system. He could pretend to be for that idiot Bannon now, get his rewards, if necessary switch later. He grabbed a floor mike, leaped on a chair, raised his hand.

"Mr. Chairman, Mr. Chairman." He heard his own voice boom back at himself over the amplifiers, saw the TV cameras swing. He was wired in. Members of his own delegation looked up at him, district leaders, personal friends.

"No. No. No." they were yelling.

"Mr. Chairman, I move the nomination be declared unanimous for Timothy Bannon."

Someone pushed him off his seat. Amid cheers, boos, and a few fist fights, the Chair ruled that it heard no objection and Timothy Bannon became, for the record, the unanimous choice of the New York Democratic party. The Convention adjourned for the night.

The next day the delegates were exhausted and listless. Bannon passed the word he wanted Trowbridge as Lieutenant Governor and Trowbridge received his brief reward. Dent, like many other delegates, did not even bother to go to the floor. Even the dull gray *New York Times* was moved by the Democratic maneuverings. "Bannon and Trowbridge," they editorialized, "a ticket to shudder over."

For Dent the day was hell. Delegates, friends, strangers, reporters fanged him for making Bannon's nomination unanimous. The attack began with Sarah as soon as he got to his hotel suite.

"I don't know why you did that, Daddy. I was right there in Father's box with my thumbs turned down. You should have looked at me."

"The people had decided. I did the right thing."

"The bosses had decided."

He was going to have to get a better answer than that. Or at least use longer words.

"Sarah, I'm exhausted. Turn off the phones and tell me in the morning."

"You wiped out all the good you'd done yourself with your speech."

By the next night Dent was too beaten down to endure listening to Bannon's acceptance speech from the floor of the Convention. Nor did he want to remain in his own hotel room at the mercy of the telephone. So he and Sarah joined a few of her father's top newspaper executives around their TV set. As Dent watched Bannon being helped through the crowd toward the podium, he noticed with horror in the entourage around Bannon one reasonably well-known hood. Fortunately the TV cameras didn't realize who they held briefly in their lens, and none of those with him in the room caught on; but would the editors of *Life* with a week to look be so dim-eyed? Or the Republicans?

Bannon grabbed the lectern, sweated for a few moments as if about to be electrocuted, and then started to speak in a low rolling monotone. He opened his speech in the classic style of political anesthesia by exact identification of where he was and to whom he was speaking.

"Fellow delegates here assembled in this historic Seventy-third Democratic, gubernatorial, nominating convention, held here in

Albany, capital of the great State of New York, the Empire State; alternate delegates, friends and families of the delegates and alternate delegates who are gathered here to witness this great event; distinguished members of our mighty party who have held high office in the past or hold high office at this present time, and others who work diligently and outstandingly in other endeavors of benefit to our great party, this great state and our mighty nation; friends of the Democratic Party, that great party of Jefferson, Jackson, Roosevelt and Truman; and you citizens of New York State, the greatest State in the Union, and the radio and television audience, it is with deep humility I stand before you in accordance with your wishes openly arrived at here on the floor of this Convention, as your candidate for Governor of the State of New York."

Dent realized with horror that in addition to the burdens of his material, Bannon was a compulsive pauser. The speech was festooned with sentences of infinite length, constructed like the opener. Bannon, as he wandered through them, gulped his oxygen as fancy struck him. In the thicket that began: ". . . distinguished members of our mighty party who have held high office in the past or hold high office at this present time and others who work . . ." Bannon halted after "work." This gave his opening words rather unexpected meaning.

As Dent winced over the disturbing questions raised by that first pause, Bannon struck again.

"I stand before you as your candidate for Governor without my hands." In the total silence that followed, Dent glanced hastily at the screen expecting the visible results of emergency surgery. But Bannon was waving two flabby globs of flesh that appeared to be hands. ". . . being tied in any way by deals, secret agreements, or understandings," the candidate continued.

Bannon next proceeded to punch his audience into submission with the historical record of the Democratic Party in New York State, beginning with the construction of the Erie Canal; undoubtedly shoveled into his speech by one of Trowbridge's alleged brain trust. From there he sloshed on doing his best to convince his public that in New York State God had been an organization Democrat.

Having bludgeoned his way through the past, Bannon swung into the future.

"Now as we turn to the future, my friends, I want to remind all of you of one important point paramount and above the rest: none of our programs exist." He beat the lectern as he gasped for breath after that one. Then went on. ". . . as just something we bring forth every four years just to mislead people. Oh no." Pause again.

Finally after half an hour, when Bannon pledged himself to "take everything whenever possible," Dent fled, before learning that this taking was confined to ". . . in the way of help and advice from all Americans without regard to race, creed, color, or country of national origin."

He did not run fast enough. As he and Sarah made their way through the lobby of their hotel, a reporter from the *News* stopped them.

"Congressman Dent, how do you feel about your support of Bannon?"

"He's our candidate."

"Yes, but how do you feel about the ticket?"

"Frankly there are other tickets I would have preferred. But he's our candidate."

"Will he help you in your district?"

"He's just been nominated."

It was going to be a long campaign.

After forty-eight hours Dent was convinced he'd been wrong to endorse Bannon; but he couldn't admit it publicly. That would leave him with the damage of the endorsement and cancel any benefits he might expect later from the organization.

Over the phone Sam was blunt.

"You should have shuffled your cards on that one, Dent."

"Sam, I thought I'd get in with the organization. And I was so mad at the Jewacky supporters."

"I've told ya before, Orthello would have died Dodge of Venice if he'd just mastered his glands. —You could have made them come to you."

"That's easy to see now, Sam."

"I'll be back in three days. Don't endorse the Ku Klux Klan till I get there."

His Club Presidents and District Leaders were split over three to one against him. Over and over again he heard: "You should never have endorsed him, Congressman. The voters of this district are independents, accustomed to thinking for themselves. They want a man who is the same way."

Only seldom was the same refrain played backward: "Don't worry, Congressman. The voters of this district are independents, accustomed to thinking for themselves, they'll understand why you endorsed Bannon."

Wup-'em, reached by long distance, was all sympathy, and asked him if he did much campaigning on horseback.

"None, Wup-'em."

"Tough. A really spooky hoss that'll bolt when they ask ya a tough question is a must out here." The Wildcat paused. "I don't know, Dent. Why my party runs a man that's no good, I try and duck. But if I've got to answer and I think he's a son-of-a-bitch, I call him a son-of-a-bitch. But then I never did think I have the future in politics you do."

"Thanks, Wup-'em."

Red Donner came down on the other side. "It's a mess, Dent. But remember: the voters have shorter memories than the organization. Much shorter. You've helped yourself."

"Thanks, Red."

On the run between two meetings he called Dee from a pay phone.

"Hullo, love, it's George Dent."

"I'm glad you added your full name. I've so many lovers who sound just like you. How are you?"

"Beat. I miss you, Dee."

"I miss you, George."

"I can get free Tuesday night."

"That would be lovely. I watched you on television. You were just fine. The only one there with life. —Did you have to endorse that man?"

"I don't know, Dee. I thought I did; to get my shot at the Senate. What would you have done?"

"Me. —I don't know. What is this, poll the voters? Seriously, George, I've had some pretty attractive men offer to pay the rent on this studio; and I was broke, too."

"I don't get the connection."

"Don't you? Being kept would have damaged me as a person."

"Oh."

After some verbal caressing he hung up. How like Dee to relate so personally to his decision. But politics didn't touch him that closely. He manipulated his political actions at a distance from himself, as if working inside a blast furnace through long mechanical arms.

And yet, he remembered, Abraham Lincoln had been one of six members of Congress to vote against President Polk's Mexican War. And been turned out of office for his act of conscience. He was no Lincoln, certainly; and Bannon was no Mexican War. Still.

He had a luncheon with one of his favorite oracles, Benjamin Wollenberg, Sr., about money.

"Money is going to be difficult, Dent. Quite a few of us have been talking amongst ourselves. What is the objectionable name you politicians have for us?"

"The goo-goo money?"

"Yes. The goo-goo money has decided for the Democrats this year no money, no names, no committees, no talent, nothing."

"Oh, Come on, some of you want to be judges."

"Those that do know this ticket won't win."

Dent grunted, stabbing at his veal scaloppine. Mr. Wollenberg's club served food too good to waste on a political luncheon.

"But for yourself, there will be funds, naturally, though it will be tougher. What happened between you and Matchelder?"

"He made a deal with me he backed out on."

"That doesn't surprise me; but you should have handled him better. A lot of people listen to him."

"He wants the Senate himself."

"Possibly. Is that why you moved Bannon's nomination? You wanted the Senate that badly?"

"Yes."

"That was not worthy of you, George."

"Don't sound like my father."

There was a long silence between them. Dent's stomach had concrete lumps inside.

"Some days, Benjamin, everywhere I look, the gap between the world I believe in and what I have to do gets greater."

"You think that will change if you make the Senate?"

"I hope so. —Maybe I'm not a politician."

"I never thought you were, George. That's what's made you such a good one."

Another pause. Wollenberg held his cigarette way down in the crevice between his index and third finger, and put his hand completely over his face to puff. Dent smiled, recognizing the ritual: Wollenberg was about to say something that made him shy. "Remember when I came to see you in the hospital, George?"

"To tell me Benjamin had left me that Beckman."

"Yes and no. That was my excuse for coming. I really wanted to see you, George. My son was dead. You had been his close friend. I felt that by seeing you I could touch him in some way."

Poor, lonely Benji, thought Dent, I guess I was his close friend. And in the end, to prove he was as tough as anyone, he volunteered into the Marines; and the Marines, who use people instead of brains or artillery, killed him; with an assist from the Japanese and St. Luke's.

Dent looked across the table and realized the man was close to tears. He looked away to give Wollenberg privacy. His own father would never show grief like that, perhaps not even permit himself to feel it. After a few masked puffs at his cigarette Wollenberg continued. Dent caught the forced evenness of his tone.

"I had prepared myself, of course. But unconsciously I had visualized your ward as a vast room in which everybody was getting better. I had forgotten there would be bodies there who would never get better. Who would suffer more and then die. And that boy with the head wound, who just wandered and giggled."

"Chuckles, I'd forgotten him."

"I came toward your bed, George, your leg was attached to a cage with weights at the end. Your arm was forced back over your head in steel and plaster. You were trying to wiggle your toes. Because they had told you that if you managed to wiggle your toes, some day you might move your foot."

Dent nodded. He felt the agony come back. The pain in the pinned leg that only left with the morning and evening morphine shot. Those terrifying shits on the bedpan month after month: messy, stinking, impotent. And that miracle day, electrodes taped to his lower leg, drenched in sweat from the pain, he had seen a twitch of self-willed motion in his toes.

"I opened my mouth to say some words about how well you looked," Mr. Wollenberg continued. "Words I'd rehearsed. But before I could force them out you said: 'Sir. I have learned one thing from this war. The best men die, sir.' I had come to give you comfort; and you were trying to help me. All those sirs. That's what made me cry, though I'd promised my wife I wouldn't.

"I knew right then, George, how much I respected you. Though frankly I have never seen you as a Congressman, or Senator. Like Benjamin, I thought you should be an artist. —However, you wanted the other, I helped, and I'll continue to help."

"Thank you."

They escaped from memory and doubt and back into politics and personalities.

As they were leaving Wollenberg's club, Dent asked, "What ever became of Helen Freid?"

"She's married to a broker. They live in Larchmont."

"Larchmont!"

"She was married to a sculptor for about two years. That didn't work."

"She was a great person."

They parted.

Dent walked slowly up the sidewalk, thinking. Benji had wanted him to marry Helen. Benji had done his best, beginning with the blind date he arranged. It was Dent's junior year at Yale. He was still carrying one painting course but that was more for show than anything else. His serious output had dropped to about zero. Art took so much time. He had made the track team, might even become its captain; gained the fraternity he wanted; he had a date every weekend. So he shifted his minor from art to French. He was good at languages, he and his sister had had French governesses, St. Luke's had trained him well, honors in French were a snap. The gentleman was set. Who among his Yale friends were going to be painters in 1938?

He had no idea what he would end up doing; but by graduation he'd line up something.

Against this background he went up to Cambridge in the fall of his junior year to pole vault against Harvard. He dropped Wollenberg, now a junior at Harvard, a note that he was coming.

Just what Benjamin had told his father as they held each other sobbing in a bedroom at the Ritz, Dent was never certain. But obviously, to make sure he was not forced back to St. Luke's, Benji must have at least polished the truth. The Wollenbergs always made Dent incredibly welcome. Walking home from the theater once—no one else ever took him to the theater—Mrs. Wollenberg had grabbed his arm so hard it hurt and said, "That you were there, George, to save my son, I thank God."

Dent adored Mrs. Wollenberg, the most beautiful woman he had ever met, so different from his family's friends. In his top-secret adolescent sex fantasies she showed her gratitude to him by taking him to bed and teaching him fantastic mysteries of love with which he became invincible over girls his own age. And he hoped that some day through Benjamin he would find, reduced in age, size, and power to manageable proportions, a Mrs. Wollenberg just for him. Therefore when Benjamin replied that he and another guy shared a secret apartment in Boston and asked him to come to a party there after the meet, Dent had arranged for someone else to take over his date and gone.

He arrived at Benjamin's Boston hideaway just after eleven: boys and girls talking, smoking, necking, and drinking beer. Mostly talking and drinking beer. Wollenberg rose from the floor, greeted him, and introduced him to a Radcliffe girl seated on the floor, back resting against a wall.

"This is Helen," said Benjamin. "I've been keeping the wolves away from her all evening. Saving her for you. So she can save you."

"Save me from what?"

"Becoming a Yale man."

Dent didn't think that was funny.

"He said, "Hullo." Helen on the floor said, "Hi." He looked her over quickly as he lowered himself beside her.

Benjamin, he thought, if you believe this is my Cinderella, you've goofed. Helen was too big. Not fat, but long: long jaw, long neck, long trunk proportioned like a locust tree, no hips, incredibly narrow thighs that merged into long legs in which the bulge of the gastrocnemius was nonexistent. Though at least her feet were small a counterpoint to the rest of her size.

"Benji tells me"—her voice was deep—"you've just run against Harvard."

"Pole vaulted."

"Same thing."

"No. One goes up and down. The other lengthwise."

She shrugged that off and with a hostile challenge held out her bottle of beer.

"Does coach let you drink?" Usually he didn't drink during track season. But next Saturday's meet was a week away. A beer was only a beer and a big sassy girl was a big sassy girl. He took the bottle.

"And I can go with girls till Saturday at midnight, when I turn into a pumpkin."

"Some life."

Silence. He looked around the room, then at her; and decided not to play who-do-you-know. Except for Benjamin they probably had no friends in common. That left what-do-you-study. They played that listlessly. She was taking English because she wanted to be a writer. Her courses were a bore. She'd read all the books years ago. She had a swell German course though: Literature of the Weimar Republic. No contact there. He was taking Medieval French Literature and European History from the Fall of Rome to Charlemagne.

"Why?"

"They meet at convenient times, and a lot of the reading's the same."

That ended that. They had met and not met. Bored, he began to search for some other girl. Helen again attacked his pole vaulting.

"So you spend your college time getting ready to jump higher than other boys on weekends. I thought that went out in high school."

Dent looked at her hostilely. She's a social protest type, he thought. They were the worst.

"Have you ever seen a pole vault?"

"No, and I'm not about to."

"Right." Dent almost hit her. "Like every other opinionated college type so sure of the truth you don't need to learn anything. It's either your world or wrong."

Helen looked at him. His total anger surprised her. This man was serious about track and Benjamin liked him.

"All right, convince me."

In a room he had just entered, with a strange girl he didn't like, tripped over from time to time by people getting beer, he broke one of his basic rules: Never reveal yourself to anyone, because they use it to trap you.

"Well, first, I pole vault because I love to. You know that lift you get when you've solved a hard problem or seen something for the first time in a painting? I get that from a good vault. These meets you joke about, they just exist to pit me against myself. Like seeing a Cézanne still life makes me grapple harder with my own canvas.

"Second, and this may sound funny, but the vaulters and the high jumpers are unique because we never win. By the rules, after we clear the bar at one height, the bar goes up another three inches. I may beat everyone else, but all that means is I have to keep jumping out there alone, in front of everybody, until I don't make it. Don't make it three times in a row. The pole vaulter always quits the field a loser. Oh, if I've beaten everyone and am just jumping against myself, I can call it off and refuse to jump any higher. You can guess how that feels. Or how the crowd responds.

"Also, Helen, I'm not naturally a good jumper. Next week I'll be going against Wislocki of Michigan. He's Olympic caliber, he runs faster than I do, and his shoulders are out to here. Vaulting is a lot of parts that have to fit together: the sprint, the placement of the pole, the grip, the hand position, the half somersault in the air, a head tuck, a scissor as the pole straightens, and finally a handstand on the pole. I'm a classy jumper, I do these things right; I work out on the weights, I admit it; to build up what strength I have. When I get over fourteen feet, I'm giving myself a gift, the reward of a great deal of labor which no one can argue with."

She was silent, looking at him; he guessed he'd gone too far.

"Me and my big mouth," she said. "I apologize." She held out her hand. "Benji told me you were a great guy; but I, well . . . I just never met anyone who gets such a return from physical action—that isn't sex. Maybe I'm jealous I don't have anything like it. Can I watch you vault?"

He could remember his total surprise at her answer. First, there was her open apology. He never apologized. If proved wrong he cunningly changed the subject, hoping his lapse would soon be forgotten. Then there was the flat mention of "sex," not added for shock value or a giggle, just as a fact. No other girl he knew did that—or boy. Then she had compared herself to him and found herself wanting. He would never so expose himself. And finally came the request for a date; something no girl was meant to do, straight out, after only twenty minutes.

He had a date for the Michigan meet already. He said, "The Michigan meet is at New Haven. Come next weekend. You'll love watching Wislocki. He's great."

"I'll watch him, George, but I'll come to see you." He felt wildly elated at this simple feminine flattery.

He got Helen a room for the weekend at the MacLean. Of New Haven's good hotels the MacLean was whispered to be the most relaxed about letting collegiate-looking types upstairs with girls. He dug out four of his better paintings, rushed them to a frame shop, and hung them in his single study. Then he thought and thought about Helen. What would they do Saturday night after the meet? Sunday morning? Sunday afternoon before her train? Whom should she meet? Where would they eat? Would she be put off by his fraternity? Would the hotel let him upstairs to her room to neck? Would she? His instinct told him the answer to that last question was yes, though back at Cambridge they had had nothing more than a good-night swipe before her dorm. But she was so different from other girls that he was certain of nothing.

Dent vaulted well against Wislocki. His problem was that each time Wislocki took off, Dent could see Wislocki's hands, they were a good six inches further up the pole than his own. He didn't have the leap in his legs to place his hands back so far.

He and Wislocki and the number-two Michigan man cleared fourteen feet. Wislocki cleared fourteen feet three inches on his first vault. Dent cleared fourteen feet three inches, on his second try. The number-two Michigan man failed three times. Fourteen-six: Wislocki missed the first jump. Dent missed the first jump. Wislocki got over on his second. Dent missed his second; got over on his third. Fourteen-nine. Wislocki and Dent missed their first jump again. Again Wislocki cleared the bar on his second jump. Dent missed on his second. Missed again on his third. Fifteen feet. Wislocki missed three times. They shook hands and walked off trailing their poles.

"How did it feel?" Helen asked him when he joined her in the stands.

That was the right question. Not how he did, but how he felt.

After two parties, at which they stuck close together, they went to the MacLean. Dent's feet felt like lead as he and Helen crossed in front of the desk clerk and got eyed by the bell captain. He got Helen into the room and hastily double-locked the door, the second fall of the tumbler resounding like a crack on his head. He had never been alone in a hotel room with a girl before. He started toward her to grab her and start kissing; but she had already turned from him to her suitcase. She pulled out a pint of Old Grand-Dad. Dent's student heart leaped to have a girl so wise and worldly. For someone under twenty-one to procure a bottle in Connecticut or Massachusetts was difficult.

"How'd you manage that, Helen?"

"I just waited outside a liquor store till I saw a man going in to get a bottle and asked him to get a pint for me."

They shared the bourbon out of the one glass in the bedroom and talked: about the meaning of college, Roosevelt's third term, Hitler, Woody Herman's jazz, blues, Kandinsky and Beckman, fraternities, radicalism. They could laugh together. Kissing began naturally. Dent was amazed. He hadn't had to put any of his strategies to work. They rolled back on the bed and necked. Dent, more thumbs than usual, twice tried to unzip her dress, at least far enough down so he could feel her breasts. Each time Helen grabbed his wrists firmly and put his hands someplace else. He accepted that boundary. In those days before the war there was a ritual about how far you could go each time. Already he was way beyond the limits established for a second meeting on a college weekend with no dance—even with a dance.

Three weeks later during the midwinter recess in her sister's apartment in New York they "went to bed"—his phrase—"had sex" was hers. After that they could seldom keep their hands off each other, getting together for as much time as two college students, one in New Haven the other in Cambridge, could possibly manage with a full schedule of classes and track meets.

"If we had guts, Dent, we'd quit college."

"No. Guts is walking forward one step at a time."

"What are we getting out of our studies?"

He began to paint seriously again, without conscious effort. Ideas for pictures just began to arrive. As he worked them out he was excited and happy, and aware how much his painting impressed Helen.

In New York she led him into a world about which he had read and heard but he regarded as hopelessly apart from his own. Men and women from his father's age to his own, often living in places he regarded as slums, sometimes without heat or furniture, some existing on relief or now-and-then jobs, not liking it that way but accepting it, as long as they could write or paint or dance.

As in all groups there were many dropouts, hearers of the word only. When he got to know them all better he felt close to very few of them. But then he got along well with only a few of his Yale classmates. And when he was with Helen and the few friends of hers who had become his also, he felt more relaxed than at any time in his life.

He discovered other things about himself: That he could sketch better than most professional painters. That, try as he might, and no matter how much it was justified by current philosophy, he did not respond to abstract art. That he enjoyed ballet, something he'd regarded before as only something for sissies. That when he was with Helen, while he still looked at other girls, he didn't feel the need to chase. That Bosch and Brueghel and Munch and Schiele and Beckman spoke a language he totally understood.

To get more time to paint he changed his minor back from French to drawing. This provoked a major scene between himself and his father. He could not change his schedule so late in the year without paying a twenty-five-dollar fine. His father had refused to fork up the money. Dent said he would pay it; and pivoted abruptly to leave his father's study.

His father called him back.

"George, I have a few words to say."

"Since I'm paying the fine myself, do I have to listen, sir?"

"How would you like to pay for your entire college education?" He'd stayed.

It appeared he was not living up to the fine potential he had inherited and sometimes shown. He was casting about without purpose. He was doing things that were wrong. He was wasting his time. Dent had heard this drill from the pulpit at St. Luke's —standard sinner number two, the wastrel. —Well, at least he'd avoided sinner number one: the vain man who denied God. Those were hopeless cases. Sinners number two, wastrels, could return as prodigals and get feasted; but number ones, blasphemers, were damned irrevocably.

"What are you smiling at George!"

"I'm not smiling, sir."

"I am not here for humor." His father was furious now. "I understand that you are living with a girl rather than attending to your classes. She accompanied you to the national meet at Annapolis." One of his classmates must be ratting. "Because of this you were disqualified as next year's captain by your peers." That hurt. "You are together in New York constantly. I trust nothing has occurred in our apartment."

"No sir."

They'd gone to bed in his family's apartment quite often. But his father, like the Rector at St. Luke's, bathed daily in revealed truth, and there was no point in reasoning with him.

The lecture ended with the foreseen peroration.

"I am telling you this, George, not because it gives me pleasure; but because what you are doing is bound in the end to make you unhappy. You are destined to lead your life in a better fashion. And the sooner you learn that the better for you."

"Yes sir."

His mother, demurely mounting the bandwagon, wrote him

several letters about the nice girl she had met in Greenwich who was just his age. All the girls his mother found for him were nice. Usually they were the daughters of her friends or college classmates. All of them, he knew, could eat corn on the cob without getting butter on their fingers.

That summer, the one before his senior year, he got a job teaching track and running a day camp at the White Spring Country Club on the North Shore of Long Island. The club was exclusive, luxurious, and gave him a cabin on the beach. Other clubs had offered him more money, for a pole-vault champion from Yale who just might sneak into the Olympics meant more children in day camp and added revenue to the club coffers; but the cabin had determined his choice. Helen had a summer job proofreading for a pulp magazine firm and writing occasional back-cover copy. "Chased upstairs by a fiend with six green eyes." She had a heavy reading load but short office hours. His campers didn't arrive till 9:30 a.m., and he had every weekend off. The whole summer spread fat before him: vault practice, painting, Helen.

As so often, a fly imbedded itself in Paradise. Shortly after Helen came to live in what they named his "shack-shack," and to spend the greater part of her days reading proofs by the club pool, Dent was approached by a grave senior member of the board. He was told Helen could not be on club property, even as his guest.

"Why not?" he asked, prepared to lie about the fact that they were living together.

"Certainly you understand, Dent. She's Jewish."

He had never considered the possibility of a club rule against Jews. He was about to say "I quit," when it occurred to him he had a bargaining position. If he left, either they would have to find a substitute in the middle of the summer, or close down the day camp. The camp had thirty children, in addition he was giving seventeen private track lessons. That was quite a bit of extra revenue for the club. He decided to test his strength with a sizable lie.

"She's the sister of a classmate of mine at St. Luke's, sir," he said, showing more firmness than he felt.

"Really." The senior board member was taken aback. He had heard that St. Luke's was admitting a few. Part of the general leftist, New Deal trend that was ruining the country. Still, what St. Luke's had chosen could White Spring reject? Supposing this young man told the Rector? Many members of the club wanted to get children into St. Luke's. But nothing would happen to those applicants. And White Spring had standards. He was about to say, "No," when Dent suggested a compromise. That Helen could remain his guest if she restricted herself to the nurses' beach. That was a special strip of sand separated from the main beach by a low fence behind which nurses and children were segregated.

"After all, sir," Dent concluded, "they have Negroes there."

"Yes. They do, Dent. They do. A sister of one of your classmates at St. Luke's." The boardroom eyes grew hooded and crafty. "Ah, ah, is he at Yale with you now?"

"No, sir. Harvard."

"Oh, Harvard. I'm Harvard myself."

"Hasty Pudding, sir."

"Interesting."

"Then it's all right, sir?"

"Well yes, Dent. Yes. I think that's a compromise we can entertain. Quite reasonable. St. Luke's. The nurses' beach afternoons. I'm sure the board will understand. Though you realize I must consult them."

Dent was tremendously upset by the incident, and not sure he shouldn't have quit. To his surprise Helen was less angry than himself.

"Where have you been in this world, George? Your world particularly. It happens all the time."

"It does?"

"What do you think those stories coming out of Germany are? Science fiction?"

"I never connected them with people I know."

"Benjamin's told me about you and he at St. Luke's. You must have known then."

"No, I didn't. I just thought: 'What's happening to him I don't want to happen to me.' I never knew." He paused, trying to feel his way for an instant inside Benjamin's life pattern; inside Helen's. "I never knew. If I had I'd have acted sooner. —What a dumb coward I am."

Helen was cooking spaghetti and hot dogs on the little two-burner Pyrofax stove in the "shack-shack." She was not much of a cook. She turned from the stove, ran to where he stood in the center of the room, threw her arms around him. He could smell the slightly burned cooking on her. Bean juice from the spatula she still held smeared her bare shoulder.

"George, for all your 'yes sirs,' you're so damn brave."

"Me?"

She pulled back frightened of her own intensity. "There's hope for you, George. In my arms, of course, there's hope."

"I would like that."

"Would you? I would. Oh, how I would. I love you."

"I love you."

From then on they thought and talked seriously about marriage, money, and the draft.

Money: his and Helen's first battle. What would they live on if he was an artist? How could he go to art school? He tested his father to see if art school was included in the graduate education his father had said he would pay for. He received a detailed, specific, four-page hand-written "no."

Helen had refused to face his concern. "The Wollenbergs will lend you money for art school."

"Helen, you can't borrow from strangers."

"They aren't strangers."

"I don't know when I could pay them back."

"They wouldn't care. —And if they ever buy one of your pictures you're set. Everyone will buy them. He's famous as an original collector."

He never could make her see the difference between what was

done and what was not done. Indeed, she taunted him for being stuck in the mud.

"Listen, Dent, listen, I'll show it to you again, on my fingers. My family gives me a thousand a year. You can teach camp in the summer. I'll work. That'll give us maybe three or four thousand a year. We've both got cars. We'll sell one and bank the money for that rainy day you're always looking forward to. —I'll bet you after a few months your old man kicks in anyway."

"And if that's how we're living, Helen, five years from now?"

"Five years! Who can see past a year? —Dent, we're better off than most people. Trust what we've got. If you really want to paint and marry me, we can do it."

"It's not that easy."

And his stomach would fill with molten lead in the heat of her silence. If Helen worked while he just painted that made him a failure as a man, unable to compete in the world, unable to send his children to good schools. When he tried to explain, she got angry.

But his fears were true. His father used to say, "It's the twentieth reunion separates the doers from the failures." If he was still painting in a garret twenty years from now he'd be unable to face himself or anybody else.

Also he had to admit that now and then Helen set his teeth on edge. She would suddenly move out of focus for him, become a slightly crazy, irresponsible girl, whose ordinary features were distorted in length to the point of ugliness. Perhaps she was just a tough outsider, trying to work changes in him.

He was infected, in those days, by large splotches of the double standard. Helen knew more about sex than he did. She must have learned that somewhere. How would she behave after they were married, if he were drafted? Sometimes when she had him so close to the edge of sexual explosion he had no idea what was happening she would tie a short length of string about his balls to totally control his movements. This was fantastically exciting.

Blake talked about the "lineaments of gratified desire." But should his wife be so far ahead of her husband?

Back at Yale his friends applied their pressure. They were painfully frank and man-to-man. "Dent, I'm sure she's a great lay. But don't get yourself tied up with that wild woman. She'll drag you down to some hole in Greenwich Village and we'll never see you again."

To confirm his fears his painting went sour. Hard as he tried, his canvases came out stiff, academic, lifeless. He had painted better stuff in school five years before. At the same time he saw no job in the world around him he wanted. To go to graduate school, to get a Ph.D. in history and teach—the alternative he'd been toying with—meant four more years in the world of books and he was sick of that already. Besides, he would have to re-study Latin, a language he hated.

He was about to graduate, to become fledged for some purpose, but what purpose he could not discern. He felt like a pioneer scout captured by Indians and condemned to death by being bound between two bent saplings that were then released. He would be flung into the world from college, torn in two. And no matter how he decided, his number, so far passed over, might come up in the lottery of the draft; and his whole life change.

Desperate, he saw an answer. He could put off the decision by volunteering into the Army. Get his year of military service over with first, then decide. He convinced his father and told Helen.

"I've figured out what I'm going to do. Volunteer into the Army. Get my year over with. Then go to art school. My allowance goes on while I'm in the Army. I can save it and we can get married."

"That's crazy."

"Helen, it's not. It's accepting the future."

"Congress may abolish the draft."

"But we don't know that. This way we're set. If you love me, you can wait."

"No."

"I'm not wild about the answer. But it's for the best."

"You're running away."

Spouting patriotism, he fled into the Army. Six months later Pearl Harbor made him appear heroic and far-sighted.

eight

"I don't know, I don't know." Dent paced back and forth in his Fifth Avenue apartment late one October night, in a private huddle with Sam Kleinman and Adrian Dell, head of the Citizens for Dent. "I'd like to run another poll, especially with Bannon killing us; but with money so tight, we need that dough for TV spots."

"There's no chance CBS will poll for us in the name of news?"

"None, Adrian," answered Dent. "A week ago I thought I had them persuaded. But not now."

"Dent," Sam was emphatic, "nobody ever researched his way to success; repeat, never. Use the dough to hit 'em between the eyes. Which brings up that little memo from your Washington friend."

"Later, Sam. Let's solve this first. You don't want to poll under any circumstances, right?"

"Right."

"You do want to, Adrian?"

"I need to know where to put my people."

"The ad agency wants to poll. God, if we only had more dough." Dent paused an instant wondering if he could tap Sarah's father again; but he owed Mr. Frost too much already. They were going to wind up this campaign deep in the hole as it was. "We won't poll."

"Dent, suppose . . . ," Dell began.

"Let's drop it, Adrian, we've spent too much time on it already. Now this information from the Air Force colonel, Catenberry. I hadn't intended to use it. I don't like it. But this election is too close."

"If you just hadn't endorsed Bannon."

Sam shot an annoyed look at Dell. He had told him not to bring that up, though Adrian, out hustling for volunteers, was being hurt most by Dent's convention move.

Dent felt his temper begin to rise. "We'd still be in trouble," he said tightly.

"We shouldn't use this information, Dent. Even if it's true." Adrian continued. "It's out of keeping with your character and your campaign."

"The only thing out of keeping with the character of the candidate is to lose," said Sam. "But maybe the voters of this district would prefer a man who has the chutzpah to cheat on his taxes."

"Woodbridge didn't cheat on his taxes, Sam," said Adrian. "He had a client that . . ."

"I know," Sam interrupted, "but will the pure in heart and the lower orders understand? The tax experts the Republicans have already."

"I'm a tax expert." Adrian smiled. "They don't have me."

"What would your Presidential candidate do with this one, George?" Sam asked.

Dent took a deep breath and blew it out slowly, letting his shoulders sag. He was as tired as he had ever been. "You mean Kennedy?"

"Yes."

"He'd slip the information to a friend to use for him."

"At least you're honest about him," said Adrian.

"Okay, who do we slip it to?"

"I don't want to use it, Sam."

"Perish the thought. It is out of keeping with your character. I shall descend to the gutter and find some lowlife who pants with rage at the idea of a candidate for Congress cheating on his taxes and is so infuriated that he bellows it to the press through a megaphone.—Have you any suggestions who?"

"Don't be funny, Sam." Dell was annoyed. "We can't use this anywhere. It's McCarthyism; and it stinks."

"Adrian, you're overlookin' the big advantage of bein' a reform candidate. You can smear people because everybody knows you're too high-minded to do it."

"Count the Citizens out."

Sam and Dent shot each other a covert look. One of their constant headaches was the refusal of Citizens' groups to take orders.

"The fact Woodbridge took this action with his client's taxes doesn't bother you, Adrian?" asked Dent.

"Dent, it's the sort of mistake anyone can get trapped into. I'm sure the client lied to him. That's why the Government kept quiet and didn't prosecute."

"The voters should at least learn how Woodbridge reacts to pressure."

"That's a lousy argument, Congressman."

Dent hunched his shoulders forward, and massaged the little finger of his right hand. "I think you're probably right Adrian. Besides, information as hot as this is probably being peddled around town elsewhere. Some reporter will break the story anyway."

Dent could tell from the way that Kleinman deliberately didn't look at him, that Sam had caught his meaning. He was going to have to use the information against Woodbridge; but there was no point in hurting Adrian's effectiveness by letting him know.

A week and a half later Dent bitterly wished he'd listened to Adrian. The information against Woodbridge had backfired. Catenberry hadn't gotten it quite straight; Woodbridge's denial was hard, indignant, and detailed; the *Herald Tribune* ran an editorial against smear campaigns, and the Fair Campaign Practices Committee made pious clucking noises. Woodbridge then used the incident to pressure Dent into a TV debate which Dent had been trying to avoid, since he was ahead and had the bigger name.

As it turned out, the TV debates backfired against Woodbridge, who showed up at the first one wearing a vest. Sam was exultant as he peered at that garment before air time.

"No man with a vest is going to Congress from this district. He might just as well have put on a top hat. He's killed himself."

"You're wearing a vest, Sam."

"On me it's a reminder of my spectacular rise from the gutter to affluence and friendship with the great. On him it's aristocratic hauteur. Call him 'Your Excellency' when ya ask a question."

Once they went on the air and Woodbridge started to talk, Dent realized he had him. Woodbridge had a passion for accuracy and logic which led him to make every answer so complicated he seemed to be ducking the question. He talked in such detail about his probity as a taxpayer, that even Dent, who believed him to be honest, began to have doubts. When one of the TV reporters asked about housing, Woodbridge's comprehensive answer made him sound like a pompous accountant. Dent gave a quick, sincere answer from his black book which made it seem as if he spent every waking hour battling slums. The studio audience applauded.

Fortunately, in the grind of the daily campaign Timothy Bannon was most of the time mercifully out of sight, waging a narrow-gauged battle that kept him submerged, reaching for a few friendly hands under the surface of some Bronx backwater. But Dent was continually plagued by his move to make Bannon's nomination unanimous. Just when he thought the issue was dead, a trotting scandal broke that was large enough to involve Bannon and the attacks began again.

Nor had the endorsement helped him with the organization as much as he'd hoped.

"Dent," Calahan was on the phone, "we need some help from you raising money at these next two dinners."

"Jim, I told you in Albany Bannon was going to give the party problems. You didn't believe me then. I've helped you all I can. I'm being slaughtered in my district because of Bannon."

"Dent, our figures show you're the only one of us spending big money on TV."

"And I've got less than ever before and I could use twice as much. I was thinking of coming to you for money. I'm being outspent twenty to one."

"Dent, believe me, I didn't want Bannon any more than you. That's why I asked you to help put Fratranelli over the top. Because when the boys want something you can only hold them off for so long. And it was the Bronx's turn. We need your help."

"No."

Friends, enemies, and neutrals kept telling Dent that he had never campaigned better. He himself was not conscious of this. He felt he was being repetitive, doing things by rote he'd done too often before to breathe life into now. Most days he felt tired, campaigned without joy; and this lack of return made him more conscious of his loss in so seldom being alone by himself, or with Dee, or with his children.

Coming into the final two weeks, the home stretch, his fatigue caused the bits and pieces of his drive to montage together. Dent on a pickup truck at a crossroads; Dent on the cocktail circuit; Dent at the TV studio; Dent outside the subway stop; Dent being interviewed; Dent talking; Dent listening; Dent running; Dent handshaking; Dent smiling.

The corner of 86th Street and Lexington Avenue was an express subway stop. There, in the long shadows of an early evening, he climbed onto the flat bed of his campaign truck. The wind blew soiled, old newspapers against its wheels. He turned to the small knot of people about the truck and to those beyond hurrying home; and began to speak. Like a runner drawing on his second wind, he felt a sudden surge of vitality. He was his brother's keeper and here were his brothers waiting for the word. So neither he nor the world were perfect. He still had a chance to move some of the blocks others could only stumble over and curse. He had delivered this little speech ten thousand times. Then let him deliver it one hundred thousand times.

"Fellow New Yorkers," he began.

On election day Dent's alarm pounded him awake at 7:00 a.m., after two hours' sleep. Between 3:00 and 4:30 that morning he had been appearing between platters on an all-night rock 'n roll program, reportedly much liked by the younger set in his district, white and black. He staggered for the bathroom, bumping into the bedroom wall.

Why, he wondered as the shower water hit him, do city people bother to vote? What brings them out from the locked boxes in which they cower, to exercise a bogus rite devised before the birth of Christ by a slave-owning Greek oligarchy to flummox the common people?

In a small town it was different. When Fred Hoxie defeated Minnie Bowes 57 to 53 for Alderman, the three or four close friends of Mrs. Bowes not recorded as voting would avoid her at the church bean supper. And Willie Funstable would decide not to call Fred's bluff at the Saturday night poker game, for fear of what his absence at the polls might have done to the assessment on his garage.

Of course, many of the urban herd did avoid the polls. Vote, and they feared they might be noted by authority, stuck for back taxes, obligated for jury duty, listed, involved with their neighbors. They could no more pull the voting lever than they could see the murder at their feet or perform with satisfaction the act of love. And yet the majority came. They defied the pollsters who told them all was predetermined; and entering a box smaller than his shower, pulled down the shape of their future.

The polls opened at 7:30. Dent's strategy called for him and Sarah to be among the very first to vote. With luck and an assist from Sarah's looks, he would be on the morning and afternoon TV shows. He had a little speech ready, urging everyone to vote. No politics—heaven forbid—just a little reminder that his name was George Dent. His mouth as he swilled the mouthwash was thick and gummy, his lips puckered; his stomach felt stuffed with straw, his eyes and hands ached.

Sarah was already at the dining-room table. He kissed her forehead.

"You look well in that suit, Sari-dari."

"Thank you, Daddy. I bought it for today. You'd better hurry."

"Yeah."

"Will the voting be light or heavy?"

"Light most places. Our district will run about average though."

"Why?"

"The educated vote out of duty; not conviction."

Sarah frowned at him. Sometimes Daddy was impossible. Here they had hardly talked to each other for a week; she asked a question to show how interested she was in politics, and he put her off with one of his smart-aleck answers. He ought to thank God for the educated. They elected him, from both parties. —At least he'd noticed her suit. Though he hadn't realized it was new. Did he think she thought so little of him that she'd be content to wear just any old dress on his election day? But then he was awfully tired.

"You look all done in, Daddy. Where are you going to rest? To that club in the Bahamas you went to last time?"

"I haven't planned yet. I'd rather hoped you'd come with me."

"You know I can't desert the children. I've hardly seen them this campaign."

"You've been a great help."

"I like to help you, love-dove."

"It would be nice to go together."

"Don't you think I want to?"

"I plan two weeks. Come for a week. You look so well in a tan and you need the rest as much as I do."

"I've really got to pull the house together and see the children."

"I'd like to stay in Washington with you. But the phone will ring, you know, I'll get no rest."

"You should go south and build up your strength. We'll get away later this winter to ski. And don't worry, if you lose, which you won't, I'll go with you."

No, he thought, you will not. If he lost he would have to paste the pieces of himself together, rearmor alone the tank hull of himself against the world. To do that patch job would be impossible with Sarah watching him and thinking "my husband is a loser."

Sam joined them on the voting line, even more overtly exhausted than Dent. His flesh seemed to be in the process of melting off his bones, his cigar smoke drifted down rather than up, his cigar itself drooped earthward, the jaw muscles lacking strength to hold it horizontal.

"Good morning, Congressman; Mrs. Dent. It's a lovely day for exercising the democratic ritual."

"You should have slept, Sam."

"Sleep! Already the problems have started. We have people who swear on the family Bible they'll show up as pollwatchers, and then don't turn up. Give me poor people who want to watch for pay. They'll be there. Not lousy idealists who volunteer for nothing, then fink out when they wake up feeling bad."

"Are we in rough shape?"

"No. I had some extra teams ready to go."

"Well, we'll be dead or heroes in a few hours."

"Don't count on it. There might be a tie."

A couple of photographers and two TV crews arrived, grousing about the hour. Dent, on camera, reminded everyone of their patriotic duty to vote; then entered the booth himself, swinging the curtain closed with a professional slam.

There was his name.

George S. Dent. Congress.

All through his district people would be looking at his name and deciding. He would have liked to remain in the polling booth himself, just looking at it awhile. But if he lingered, watchers would think he was splitting the ticket. He made a snap decision to vote for neither Bannon nor the Republican, and flipped the other Democratic levers down.

"Did you vote for Bannon, Mr. Congressman?" the press wanted to know as he came out.

"Well, I'm not sure I can answer that question so close to a polling place." He laughed. The press all joined in the laughter and walked away satisfied. The campaign was certainly over.

Though not quite over. There still remained the job of getting every last voter who might decide for him to the polls. That was the job of his organization, his people, his money; all those independent clubs he had organized; devoted to getting girls married, men laid, and George Dent to Washington. This was their day. All he could do was move from polling place to polling place, from club to club, exhorting, encouraging, checking. By 7:00 p.m. even that was over. Though the polls did not close till 10:00 he could no longer affect the outcome. He went home to a hot bath and allowed himself, while in the tub, a tall bourbon and soda, his first drink in two weeks.

He and Sarah ate alone in their apartment, lamb chops and fried eggplant. That's what they'd eaten together before his first primary. Now she always made it as part of their ritual. Though he liked the food he was so tired he just pecked at it. Then he and Sarah went down to the hotel suite that served as his campaign headquarters.

The outer rooms were already jammed with people. Dent looked at the giant pictures of himself grinning from the walls. Damn, no Bannon pictures. When the TV cameras photographed this room that would be a slap in the face of all the regulars. Jean Aaron was going to have to get two Bannon pictures up and see they stayed up. He looked for her as he smiled and shook the hands of well-wishers who pressed round himself and Sarah, glad to see that most of them were young. The polls would close in ten minutes.

He opened the door of his private office, greeted Sam, who by now had turned the color of his cigar smoke. Inside were two

TV sets; one tuned to NBC, the other to CBS. Dent wondered idly which of the rival electronic brains would make the biggest blooper. He sat down on the couch opposite the TV sets and felt in his side pockets for the few notes he'd made. Right pocket, if he won; left pocket, if he lost.

"George," Sarah was smiling at him, "I'm going out to see if any friends have arrived."

"Do that, darling. And if there's anyone I should meet, bring them back." He slumped down, watching the two bright squares of TV light.

He remembered his first election night in '54, people cheering, reaching out to touch him even before his victory was certain, thumping him on the back; Sarah at his side. He'd had the feeling a new life was beginning. The memory of that night nourished him still, strong and pungent. He wished he felt some of that elation now.

He found he was at one of the TV sets, fiddling with its dials. He saw himself for an instant in double image and laughed at where he was. Before battle he always gave his crew simple chores to do: check the turret mechanism, ready rounds, machine-gun belts, the routine acting as a soothing drug against fear. So now he adjusted the TV set. Well, another way to get through the present was to plan for the future. Where the hell was he going to relax after this campaign?

Last time he had gone to the Shell Beach Club in the Bahamas. But he had been the only person there alone, everyone else either surrounded by children, honeymooning, or in the center of some middle-aged affair. He felt too lonely to really enjoy himself. But if he picked one of the bigger hotels in Nassau he would find too many singles, the joint jumping too much; he would never get the rest he needed. He wanted someplace between, which meant he would have to risk some new place alone. If he had someone with him, a girl, he wouldn't mind trying a new place.

But he had a girl. His mind shied violently from the suggestion. He must be too tired to think rationally. To go someplace with Dee would require plans, contingency plans, cover plans, avenues of retreat. It would be fun: talk, swim, paint, fuck. And was it so dangerous when everyone knew he always went off by himself after a campaign? He'd really pressed Sarah to go; that was a perfect cover. He and Dee could both just turn up at the same place. Red Donner would know some quiet spot that was safe.

By the side of the couch sat a phone. He inspected it closely. It was a direct outside line not going through his switchboard. If Sarah came in, he could be phoning Chelsea East for some late figures. Would Dee want to come? They hadn't seen each other for such a length of time. He would have to find out. He looked round the office. Everyone was busy either watching TV or on phones of their own. From time to time they shot him a glance; but everyone in the room knew him well enough to leave him alone, unless he asked for company, until his future was determined. He dialed the familiar number.

"Hi, Dee."

"George." Her voice rose in surprise. "Where are you?"

"In my headquarters, waiting for the returns to start. Until we know what happens, I get left pretty much to myself. What are you doing?"

"Just sitting here watching television. Nobody thinks the Democrats will do well."

"We won't. Dee, would you like to go south with me? I'm going someplace I can swim and paint for about ten days."

"What!"

"Unless I lose. Then I want to be alone."

"Of course."

She paused. He said nothing.

"Where are you going?" she asked.

"I don't know yet. I'll decide tomorrow."

"And you want me. Why?"

"Because I do. Do you want to come?"

"I'd love to."

"Great. I'll call you tomorrow."

He won by 56.2 per cent of the vote. Just enough to keep his Senate chances slightly alive; but not enough to rocket them off the ground. He was up two whole percentage points from two years previous, when Eisenhower had been at the top of the GOP ticket. But he was just a mere whisper ahead of his 55.7 per cent of four years ago. So he'd gone up while Bannon crawled at the head of his party up the ass of disaster. He hadn't helped himself enough.

The TV cameras were ready for his victory statement. Smiling, confident, he let himself be propelled through the enthusiastic jam of celebrators to the platform beneath the lights.

Chance assures that some serpent enters every Eden as soon as coincidentally possible. Their second day in the sun, Dent dove off the side of their dinghy, slipped on his bad leg, and wrenched his back. He spent the next two days full of codeine either in their beach bungalow or on a towel in the sand, while Dee kneaded contracting muscles. On the third day, as his back began to recover and he could at least dog paddle about the warm water, Dee had an overdose of sun and boiled crab.

They had cooked the crabs themselves in an aluminum pot on their cabin's two-burner Pyrofax stove. The night was moonlit, starry, and windless and their cabin stank of rotting fish, an aroma they learned too late accompanied the boiling of crab. Two in the morning found Dent awake on his bed, exhausted after three pain-filled nights, while Dee retched and gasped. Where would he find a doctor on the island, he wondered. And if Dee was seriously poisoned there would be publicity.

Dee called to him from behind the closed bathroom door. "Dent, there's no water."

"I love you," he said.

He pulled on trousers and a shirt and stumbled into the moonlight toward the hotel. A sleepy porter told him water being scarce was shut off by law from 2:00 a.m. till seven.

He shuffled back to the cabin; explained the situation to Dee, who didn't want to hear; and retrieved the ill-smelling cookpot from in back of the cabin. Three potfuls of water from the ocean fifty yards away filled the toilet enough so it would flush. If Dee flushed every five minutes, which he figured as conservative, that meant thirty-six potfuls an hour. He increased his speed, tripped on a palm root and fell forward, spilling the pot and wrenching his back again.

He lay on the sand, bitten by small bugs, thinking of the postal card he'd written Sarah, telling her he was getting a great rest. Then he rolled over and staggered back to the ocean for another pot of water.

It was late that afternoon before he and Dee could stagger the short distance from their cabin to the beach.

"Dent, look at us. Two cripples who can't step over a piece of seaweed. And anyone spying on us probably thinks, 'That lucky pair. They're so exhausted by fucking they can hardly move.' "

They touched each other and wailed.

By the next day his back had returned to almost normal. Dee enjoyed a steak, and started teasing him about bringing his paints.

"When did you think you were going to fit that in, Dent? Twenty minutes every afternoon?"

"I guess painting is the last thing you want to think about."

"You're right."

He knew what Dee was saying. It's annoying to have amateurs around toying part time with what to you is the daily grind. He felt the same way about people who thought they were in politics because every four years they collected a few signatures on a petition.

"I'm going to take the dinghy," he said, "and go out to the reef and snorkel. Do you want to come?"

"I'll just stay here and tan. Be careful."

He rowed out to the coral reef and anchored the dinghy in the shallow, clear water on the landward side. Then adjusting mask, snorkel and flippers, slid into the water. He planned to swim through a passage in the reef and explore the far side, the deep ocean side. He had never swum there. Pushing through the schools of brilliant little fish in the shoal water, he breast-stroked through the coral pass.

He reached the ocean side and suddenly the sea world changed. The calm, blue, color-filled waters vanished; he hung now above darkness, hugeness, black spaces sliced by enormous shadows. He was terrified. Forcing his courage back into his muscles, he gulped a deep breath through his snorkel, kicked up his legs, and dove down. Around him surged the colors of nightmare: blind purples and deep blacks. The little corals and friendly ferns that waved in the sunlight of the shallow side were gone. Here rose gigantic mountains and great trees, erect, jagged, solid, with hostile thick spaces in between. At his own level the fish that swam round him were the size of his limbs, while in the further deep maneuvered greater lozenges of solid dark.

He became conscious of a new sound, one he'd never heard before. It surged and hung around him in the water, rising from far below on the ocean floor where no light fell. The sound had great power, yet rang with little rose-red chimes, summoning bells with high, silver notes. These sea bells begged him to swim down further and explore. "Come and see us in beauty down here." Drawn by the bells, he swam deeper. He knew as he did so that though part of the sound was outside him, part was also inside, caused by the pressure on his ears and the strain against his lungs.

The bells grew more intense.

With a wrench he thrust upward. His breath holding miraculously, he finally broke the surface. He floated, gasping.

For his pride he took another short dive on the deep side, then turned and swam back carefully through the reef's opening to the bright pleasant warmth of the shallows. He did not want to face those sounds another time, ever. He would not even think about them again.

The cabin he and Dee shared was a room-and-a-half concrete blockhouse, mass designed to fit at any angle, into any tropic resort, in any world. Green shutters, blue walls, Formica table, two-burner Pyrofax stove, closet covered by guest-proof light-green curtain, three canvas-and-steel chairs, a plastic dresser, an imitation mahogany counter. Instant, total, hideous, nowhere.

To this cement box Dent and Dee returned a day later to make lunch, drink some wine, and nap through the heat. Dent, picking at his salad, looked up at Dee sprawled on a chair reading, in bikini pants and shirt. As he watched, Dee began to alter. First he noticed that she seemed to glow, as if her skin were lit from inside by a soft red fire from hardwood coals. At the same time her eyes grew bigger and darker. Next her face, so changeable with her moods as to be often unrecognizable, began to go smooth and lengthen to a true oval. Not the sexually demanding madonna of the Munch portraits she sometimes became; but a linearly perfect shape, exquisitely shaded and molded.

While he watched her, she closed her book, got up, and went over to the twin beds she had pushed together and tied with the string he always carried for such emergencies. As she walked her edges rippled and gleamed. Her beauty slackened his jaw. She lay down and rolled over on her side to smile at him and he just managed to smile back.

I've fallen in love, he thought. I didn't mean to; but I have. And Dee is never going to look the same to me again. This change could make me vulnerable. He got out of his chair and went outside to sit on the sand with his back against a palm.

To be safe he must fix exactly where he was: married to Sarah, a Congressman, with two children he loved. He was in love with Dee; but that must not upset the rhythm of his life. As a lawyer, he told himself, you've seen too many people mess up in situations like this. That must not happen to you. You love Sarah. Think what you owe her.

Sarah and he had met again at the ski lodge the weekend after their first encounter on the slope. One of his friends held Sarah's fiancé in some discussion at the bar, while he and Sarah went up to his room and necked. Two weekends later he came down to New York to see her. The weekend in between, when he'd told Sarah he had to study, he'd been with Helen Freid.

Helen and he had had a ball the summer before traveling

through France and Scandinavia on a motorcycle; then they had had a major fight in Oslo, and come home separately. Now they were together again, still talking marriage; but Dent knew he was consciously stalling. Helen thought law school pettifogging and didn't want him to be a lawyer. Their old argument about law or painting dragged on. Meanwhile Helen had other guys, as she had while he was away during the war; and he, radaring around for something to site, had other girls.

He had taken Sarah to dinner to the Canard Flambé, a restaurant his mother and father used to take him to. His own favorite restaurants where he and Helen ate he had not considered grand enough for this first Sarah date.

They went back to the studio he still held onto on Smith Street, from which he had carefully removed all traces of Helen. In the taxi Sarah had been talkative, excited, while they both ran their fingers up the insides of each other's arms. Climbing the four flights of stairs he watched her lithe legs flashing between layers of petticoats (crinolines were in fashion that year) and trembled so with anticipation he had trouble fitting his key into the lock. Once inside the door they turned to each other. She kissed him hard, raking the back of his neck with her nails. They pulled apart and he removed her coat, then his own green trench coat and suit jacket.

"You should have a better-looking coat for evening," Sarah said.

"Why?"

"So people won't think you're a truck driver."

"People I know don't make judgments on coats. Besides, I know some great truck drivers."

"What about people who meet you for the first time?"

"If they're going to judge by coats, I don't want to know them."

"You might be humble enough to consider their point of view."

He kissed her to stop the silly argument, maneuvered her toward his couch, and pulled her down beside him. They necked seriously for a while, their tongues working over each other's mouths and ears. After a while he yanked off his tie and opened his shirt.

"What do you think you're doing?" Sarah asked. He didn't bother to answer that. Already stiff with excitement, he kissed on.

Working his hands around her back he pulled her zipper down. Her body twisted away from him and a barrage of "no's" began. He paid no attention. This was the American game. The girls said, "No, no, no," to propitiate some ancient tribal god called "niceness." The wise man closed his ears. Girls that didn't want to be made didn't kiss back this hard.

Moving by plan, he flanked the no, no, no line, paused briefly, then pulled dress, slip strap, and bra strap off her right shoulder. Her right breast was revealed with its thin tapered middle and busting tip. (Years later at a Democratic convention in Chicago, while greedily kissing the incredible breasts belonging to one of Red Donner's "Florida Welcomes You" girls, he had dislocated his jaw at the start of the act of love, and had to go through the routine able only to grunt. But that traumatic and hilarious experience lay well in the future.)

He kissed her breast tenderly and skillfully; but instead of softening, Sarah stiffened and squirmed, while her "no's" became a torrent. Perhaps he should have recognized her resistance as something more than the good-girl game; but by now he was too excited to have been stopped by anything less than kicks, screams, and blows.

"If you squirm so, I'm going to tear your dress."

"You won't. You won't dare."

"I will."

He kissed her some more. She relaxed and kissed back. They ended on the floor. He got the top of her dress off. She stiffened again. Again he quieted her. Then he picked her up and half carried, half steered her to bed. He took off his shirt.

"You don't mind my scars?" His line washed over her without any reaction.

"If you won't make me, I'll take off my dress."

"Don't be silly," he said.

"I'm going home!" she screamed, bounding up.

"All right, I promise." Shit, if a lie was part of the game, he'd play the game. "I promise," he said again. He shucked off his clothes quickly and leaped into bed. Sarah took off everything but a half slip and hung her clothes in his closet with care. (Months later when he told her how provocative she was then, reaching up naked in the light, she'd been horrified.)

Clothes arranged, she hurtled into his bed as if ski jumping and burrowed under the covers. They grabbed each other and held. After he got the half slip off it was just a question of time.

When the fucking had finally come, it was violent. He had to use his full weight and strength to impose his movments over her own. But she appeared to like sex, and they had made love three or four times. Sometime in the night he had tried to maneuver her into another position besides the basic one with himself on top. But she had been so clumsy he'd abandoned the attempt. She was wild and strong enough on the bottom so he didn't miss the variation. He could teach her the other positions later. (He'd been wrong there. She'd never really mastered them.)

In the end they fell asleep, tangled together. He had wakened around 4:00 a.m., wanting to make love again. They had. Right afterward Sarah had insisted on leaving.

"What will my roommate think, if I'm out all night?"

"You're too old to have a roommate."

"She's a nice girl."

"She'll think you've been out making love."

"Why are you so horrid to me when I love you?"

What could he say to that? —At least she knew her own mind.

He helped her on with her clothes and thought once again: what a beautiful body; this could be fun. Also he'd thought, have I got her naval lawyer beat. —Three weekend meetings later she told him her engagement was off.

In between were nights with Helen.

"Why do you see me, George?" Helen asked.

"I love you."

"I can't believe that any more."

A more honest answer would have been that he kept seeing her because she was wonderful in bed and he didn't want to curb that part of his life; so he played her along, though not much else continued to work between them. However, that answer, which would have lost Helen, would still have been only partially true. Some days he felt that a second George Dent existed, whose law-school grades weren't very good, who was bored by most of his courses, and who could have a lifetime of excitement with Helen.

"What do you want, George," Helen asked, "to bury yourself in some big firm and make money?"

"That's not a bad idea."

"Money for what?"

"Don't talk like a sophomore."

Sarah, on the other hand, was concerned by his bad grades.

"With those marks, George, you shouldn't see me next weekend, you should stay in Cambridge and study."

"There's more to life than law-school grades, Sarah."

"For someone as bright as you are these grades are wrong. Look what you've accomplished already. You can do better. Much better."

He broke a date with Helen to study.

"George, do you want to be a lawyer?"

"I've told you, Helen, some days 'yes' and some days 'no.' "

"I hope you don't. What ever happens to us, George, I hope you don't."

A few weeks later he was explaining some point of law to Helen.

"You're pushing me out, George."

"I don't think so."

"You are."

All he could think of was that old Army saw: one girl is too few and two girls are too many.

Sarah introduced him to her parents. He introduced Sarah to

his parents. "She's a better girl than you deserve, George," his father said. And he hadn't decided anything yet.

"George, I'm so tense with you in bed," Sarah told him several times. "I'll be more relaxed after we're married."

"Uhhhu."

"You don't think I'd let you leave me, do you, George?"

Sarah was of his world, his friends, the law, his father's house. His law-school classmates were envious of him. And painting? He couldn't rely on that; that could go sour. And Helen? So in the end he committed himself to Sarah.

Looking back now he realized he hadn't recalled Helen so completely in years. He slammed his hand down so hard against the trunk of the palm tree he bruised it on the bark. That was dumb, he thought.

He got up and brushed the sand off his trunks, grinning. All right, he'd fallen in love; he certainly wasn't going to waste more time out here thinking about the past. He still had five days. And no more boiled crab.

Jim Dent knew he could open the front door now, every time. He could push down the smooth catch and get the door to swing with his quick, strong tug. Front door had given him more trouble than any other door in the house.

When he was just learning locks, bathroom door had tried to kill him. He shivered remembering, then smiled at how little he'd been. The key knob hadn't wanted to turn for the longest time. And he'd been told not to lock it; so he had to get out himself. He thought he might starve. Starve was awful. You ended up the word he didn't want to think about: dead. And before that word you looked like the pictures in Pop's book about the places where they starved people. Pop liked the book because he said people forgot too easy. When Pop was away he'd looked at that book once. He was still frightened, he wouldn't forget easy.

My, he hadn't seen Pop for a long time. He was watching out the window for a cab to stop. Then he'd run downstairs and open the door for Pop so he wouldn't get wet in the rain and would know how much he'd been missed. Maybe he could even tell Pop about the wolves.

Jane waited for Dad too; but with deliberate circumspection. She was older and had homework. Then she had her room to tidy and her animals to put to bed. If they went to bed in the wrong order or out of place they fussed; giraffe in particular was a fussbudget. If Dad loved her he would come up and hug her when he came home.

From time to time she did look out the window to see if Dad's taxi had come. But she pretended one of her animals wanted to see how dark it was outside. Then if Dad came home and forgot her it would be the animal who was sorry. She knew this was not really true; that she would be the one that suffered. But playing it was the animal that wanted to look, made any hurt that might come less sharp.

Sarah had lighted the fire, which burned smoky and small. She never could get the fire to burn as well as George. He said it was because she poked it too much. That just plain was not true. Daddy poked the fire as much as she did.

She reached in with the poker and harshly shoved the logs around. The flame lessened, the smoke increased. As she stepped back, the garish colors of the Beckman over the mantel assaulted her for the hundred thousandth time. Why did George insist on having that picture so prominently displayed? He couldn't like that wanton, nude woman. Still it was by a famous artist; and it had been given to them by Mr. Wollenberg, who was a connoisseur and important in the district. Guests commented on it.

She heard a rush of small feet leaping down stairs and Jim's voice exploding: "It's Pop, Pop, Pop!" He really shouldn't open the front door without his bathrobe.

Dent had brought a stuffed barracuda for Jim, a treasure chest that played music when you opened the lid for Jane, and small calypso drums for both of them.

"Drums, Daddy, is that wise?" asked Sarah, after he kissed her over the heads of the children.

"I don't know. Here, these are for you; and this." He had stopped in the airport florist and bought a great bunch of gladioli. These he handed her along with a small beautifully crafted silver rabbit.

"Oh, Daddy, they're lovely and the rabbit's cute." Sarah went out to put her flowers in a vase of water. Jane opened and shut her treasure chest trying to make absolutely certain what turned the music on and off. Jim hugged his drum and fish and pressed against his father, describing what he was building in school. Dent opened his arms to carry them both upstairs. Jim snuggled into them. Jane gave him her lion to carry instead of herself.

"Lion likes to be carried better than me. He's young."

"But I'm sure he likes to be carried by you best. So you carry him and I'll carry you. Then he'll be happy."

"All right."

Dent smiled to himself as he carried his children upstairs. How different the chemistry of them both since birth, one a hugger, the other a doubter.

He got his children upstairs. They came down again while he had his martini and bounced around him with excitement going in to sit with him and Sarah at dinner. He looked down the dark length of the mahogany table, over the candles, to Sarah at the far end. He told her how much he'd missed her. She described the trials of life without him. They laughed together at Washington gossip. He blew her a kiss. She giggled.

"Did you have a good vacation, Daddy?" asked Sarah.

"Only fair. I didn't meet anybody really sympatico; and I put my back out diving and had a couple of painful days; but the weather was lovely.—I got a good rest."

"Did you paint any pictures?"

"No."

"You made such a fuss about packing your paints."

"I discovered I didn't want to work that hard. I guess I was more tired than I thought."

"You should paint, Daddy, as a hobby. I just read an article about Churchill. He finds it the most restful thing he can do."

He remembered Dee describing her agonies over painting and his own over *"Birches over Ice."* Now the act of art had become for him merely something to do when he grew too old to swim or play tennis. You made your bed, George, now lie in it; his mother used to say. Fortunately, he liked his bed: this home, his children.

"You've given me a lovely return," he said with a smile as they finished dinner. "Delicious duck."

"Congressman Wilson sent them."

"There's a friend."

"But his wife is tacky." Sarah rang her little silver bell to have the maid clear the table.

"Well, Sarah, it's interesting you should mention Churchill's painting, because I decided on vacation to have the little shed at the back of our garden here fixed up as a studio, so I can paint some in my spare time."

"Show me what you want and I'll get it done for you."

"You're great."

Later in bed her welcome was flaccidly dutiful.

Happy as Jim was to have Pop home, in the dark the wolves still came for him. Their time was after his lights were out before, terrified, he drifted into sleep. First the wolf-shadows thickened just outside his window. He'd pretend the shapes weren't really wolf-shadows, just branches or leaves. No wolves, he'd tell himself, no wolves. But he knew any moment the first wolf would begin to flatten itself incredibly thin, like an earthworm when you squashed it to stick on a fish hook; and squeeze, nose first, underneath his window screen and into his room. Already brown-bear, who slept beside him on his pillow and was alive during the day, was turning into a terrified little toy. When brown-bear did that the wolves had come.

They were here.

They grew huge and dark inside his room. He breathed through open mouth, huddled in bed, waiting. As on all nights, they did not attack immediately; but moved about the corners of his room to growl, watch him, plan their meal. They circled closer. He tried to cry out; but could not, the noise might make them leap. His only hope was to lie still, small, not move. Then the wolves might think him too tiny to make a good crunchy.

It did no good to tell the wolves he was a good boy. They didn't care. If he'd have been bad they would have smelled that and killed him quicker. But being good was no help. And he had to watch the wolves every instant; because if he took his eyes off them or even blinked, when he looked again a wolf might be right over him with its jaw open, ready to chew him into the red blackness of its throat. To suddenly see a wolf that close would kill him. He lay in terror-filled dark alone, begging, "Please, no. Please, no."

Next afternoon, driving back from school with that day's mother, he thought about whether to tell Pop. The trouble was that if he told Pop and Pop didn't understand, the wolves would learn and know he was alone without big friends. Then perhaps it was bad to see wolves and he'd get punished. But Pop would not punish him, though he might say, "Don't be silly." He couldn't tell Mom. Mom just didn't know. In the old days Pop would have known; but in closer times he'd been away so much.

Pop came home while Jim was eating supper. Jim raced through his peaches and went into the living room to size up the situation. Pop and Mom were talking about the day.

"Hullo, Jim," said Pop.

"Hullo, Pop." Jim walked around the room looking over the man on whom his hopes lay. Dent thought his son looked like some old judge in beach pajamas debating a case with himself. He gave Jim a shy smile, the inner one he sometimes gave himself when something pleased him.

"How was school today?"

"Fine."

"How's Billy Johnson?"

"He's still my friend." Jim realized he had to go forward; risk the chance of help. "Pop, were you ever afraid of wolves?"

Dent caught the forced note of unconcern behind the question. Wolves. Wolves? He wrenched his mind from the forthcoming opening of Congress to try and burrow into Jim's world.

"On the television?"

"No." His son shook his head and seemed to withdraw.

"I used to be afraid of the ones that came into my room at night."

"That's them!" Jim rocketed across the room to leap into his father's lap.

"You'll give him nightmares, Daddy," said Sarah.

Dent put his arm around his son. "I used to be so frightened," he could remember now clearly enough to have the fear start to shrivel his crotch, "that I didn't dare hide under the covers. Because if a wolf got his snout in the top I'd be trapped."

Jim curled into him with a sigh.

"The same ones, Pop."

"We can fix them."

Jim relaxed. Tonight, he thought, will be all right. Pop put him down and took him by the hand, and they went upstairs together, into Pop and Mom's bedroom for a "little think."

Pop sat on the big double bed and Jim climbed up beside him.

"Now, Jim, we have to do two things. First we have to take care of those wolves. Then we have to figure out where they come from." Jim nodded soberly: that made sense. Pop disappeared into his closet and come out with his enormous shotgun.

"These wolves," his father was very serious, "are afraid of real guns. So I'll cock this one so you get two shots. And we'll lean the gun against the head of your bed so you can grab it, if the wolves get close. But I don't think you'll have to use it. Because when the wolves see this antiwolf gun, they'll probably stay outside—way outside."

Dent placed the gun on the bed, and tried to think of more magic. He had asked for a light in his room: first from his nurse, then from his mother, finally his father. Request denied. Fear, he was told, was something you conquered.

"Run once, George," said his father, "and you'll keep running all your life."

"Just a little light, Daddy."

"There are no wolves. They are in your mind. Just keep telling yourself that."

His father obviously did not know about wolves. So he had lain in the dark each night for a year or longer; and waited to be eaten.

"I tell you, Jim, here's my old Army sweater that kept me safe during the war. You take this sweater and sleep with it beside you. It has something in it that protects you."

He handed the sweater to Jim, who hugged it and smelled it.

"I like this sweater," said Jim.

Together they walked into Jim's bedroom, Jim leading, clutching the sweater. Dent tucked Jim and the sweater in, switched on a night light, and placed the gun by the head of the bed.

"Here, where the wolves can see it plain."

"Good."

Dent sat down on the edge of Jim's bed. "Jim, now that we've got them scared of us, we can talk about where they come from. At night the things we're afraid of inside come out of us and we see them, just as in the old days people used to see dragons." He paused. Jim was watching him gravely, not shying away from his words. "I don't know what you're afraid of, Jim. Maybe of dying."

"Pop, don't say that word."

Dent kissed his son. "That's all right." His own wolves had returned to his son; was some mysterious chemistry of fear inherited? "What we've done will stop those wolves. Are they going to be surprised tonight, when you're here ready for them!"

"Wow!" said Jim, almost looking forward to seeing the first wolf.

"And if they do come, Jim, you yell! And I'll come up and really fix them. I hate them. But I don't think they'll dare."

They kissed good night. Dent shut the door.

The next morning at breakfast Jim was bright with good news.

"You were right, Pop. A wolf looked in the window and I reached out and just touched the gun and he went away."

"I thought so. You get a good night's sleep?"

"Yes."

"We'd better leave the gun there for a few more nights though, Jim. To make sure the wolves know how strong we are."

"A good idea." Singing to himself, Jim went off to school with his sister.

Sarah attacked Dent's decision.

"You'll weaken him," she said, "telling him fibs like that."

"How?"

"He should conquer his fears himself."

"He has conquered them himself. Don't you want to give him any help?"

"I don't want him to grow weak by being spoiled."

"Look, Sarah, it took me at least a year to get over being frightened of wolves. With my help Jim will get over it in a week. That's what being a parent is about."

"Could you be more helpful before you go to work for once, and make up your mind what you want for dinner?"

His eggs, dry and fluffy, stuck going down his throat.

nine

"Hi-ya, George."

"Press the flesh, Pete."

"Greetings Bill."

"Morning, Mr. Chairman."

In a flurry of back-slaps, chest punches, handshakes, smiles and gossip the Eighty-fifth Congress was beginning.

"Dent, buddy, hear you had a tough one in New York."

"We behaved like Republicans, Pat. I remember you were worried."

"That was before the Republicans sent John Foster Dulles into my district."

"Did you pay them to do that?"

"Nope, their kindness. What happened to Sol Alpert?"

"Got too close to the Teamoes."

Red Donner wandered by with two new members of the Florida delegation in tow, introducing them both as a combination of Lincoln, Machiavelli, Casanova, Robert E. Lee, and Diogenes. However, he dropped behind them as he walked away to whisper to Dent, "That tall son-of-a-bitch is tied up with Dade County gambling; made it bullshitting the old folks. Don't trust him."

Dent saw the chairman of the Armed Services Committee and wandered over to pay his respects.

"Hullo there, young fella," said the chairman. "You going to make more trouble this Congress?"

"Nobody could make trouble for you, sir. You know too much."

"When people give out information without telling me, that's trouble."

"You've got a safe district."

The chairman shot Dent a shrewd glance. If Dent had grabbed all those headlines and had started the missile hassle last term because he was in trouble in his district and needed the publicity, that wasn't good but it was permissible. Just another damn pushy Yankee shootin' off his face. But if Dent acted out of conviction and wanted to change things, then he was going to have to be stomped on.

"We don't want to do anything on the Committee that weakens the country, Dent. You just remember that."

"Yes sir."

Wup-'em was leaning against the wall with a group of Westerners. They all pounded each other.

"Thanks for the duck again, Wup-'em. Say, I just heard you beat that rodeo singer better than two to one."

"Crooning never beat honest effort, son."

"Was the chairman still frosty with you over the missile deal?"

"Nope. Just thanked me for the duck."

"You politician."

"Good year for duck."

Dent took his seat and half listened while the formalities limped along. Here he was again, he thought glumly, and look at the killers ahead this session: federal aid to education, nuclear test ban, draft extension, raising the debt ceiling, labor legislation, trade to Communist countries; every one of them, no matter how he voted, would make him enemies. He was going to have to do a lot of listening and careful research, two things he hated.

As he sat, Dent pushed his palms on both sides of his butt against the bench, squirming to find a more comfortable position. Damn, he thought, my tail must be changing shape; the benches of the House had never seemed this uncomfortable before, their cushions were harder then a metallic tank seat. His good leg was starting to fall asleep. He shifted himself so he was seated sideways and felt somewhat better. Perhaps he'd always sat in this position before and just not noticed it; but he didn't think so.

Two and a half months later Dent sat, in the same uncomfortable position, while the House grumbled, groped and fumbled its way through a series of votes on aid to Latin America. Ordinarily such a measure would have been perfunctory and brief, the minimum kernel of begrudged charity grandly dispersed several days before. But this was the first year of the Beard. Member after member felt the deep gut-relieving need to rise and let the home folks know that he had been on to Castro from the first and would have courageously popped him in the kisser had the Beard ever ventured among the sacred peanut groves of motherhood in the home district.

The vote might have stretched much longer but the Congressional leadership had cannily scheduled the Rivers and Harbors bill next. And much though the average Congressman loved to talk against Communism he loved to glut his own district with federal cash even more. For the greed of a Congressman is not the greed of a tern flashing silver and swift above a school of fish, or even the greed of a swine grunting in honest effort to shove his lard toward the trough. Congressmen lust like moles, burrowing in the dark to gorge themselves upon the seed and root of what they publicly claim to protect.

Dent, along with quite a few other urban Congressmen, would draw no benefits from the rivers and harbors bill. So he sat now in the chamber ready to deal. If a member needed his vote for a pet project—to widen a river, dam a sea, deepen a channel, or fill some obscure swamp so that a chosen crony might erect a trap-door factory in the wilderness—Dent would pledge his vote in return for a favorable vote on his cities bill.

At present "Steelhead" Trout was explaining to him the absolute need "fuhnationaldeefence" to deepen some obscure estuary in the interior of Georgia. Dent, mind wandering, listened politely. Steelhead had made it clear he wouldn't support the cities bill.

"Hey, Dent?" Steelhead interrupted his monologue. "You're meant to be one of the thinkers of this here House. What do you think of this Castro shit?"

"With some of the bastards we've been supporting in Latin America, we're lucky to have gotten off so lightly."

Steelhead looked shocked. Damn, thought Dent, why did I let him trap me? An honest answer has no place on the floor of Congress. One or two unconscious slips like that could kill his Senate chances deader than they were. And after he got to the Senate he'd have to be careful. Make his gimmick some safe issue like consumer protection and flash his white mane before the TV cameras while waving a jar of rancid salad oil to fix his name in the minds of housewives. That would be fun. He gave Steelhead a big laugh and punched him in the chest to show he'd been kidding and wandered out of the chamber.

In the New House Office Building he managed to trap Congressman Pete Liskowsky in his office.

"Jesus, Dent, the cities bill doesn't have a prayer of passing."

"I know that."

"The leaders are against it. I got things I want from them. You know that."

"I do. I've got the same problem."

"Then why vote for it?"

"Look Pete. Nobody thinks this bill is going to get fifty votes, right? Well, we're going to get over ninety. Maybe one hundred. Then the leadership is going to look. And the press is going to look. And maybe next year we'll get something for the cities. — And your district and mine. We'll be strong enough they'll have to deal."

"One hundred isn't enough."

"Pete, I'm talking to you because you're one of the few people strong enough to stand up to the leadership. You know you have to educate people sometimes for a few years before you can get a measure through. And frighten them a little too. One hundred will frighten them. I know you're for this bill. And I know unfortunately the good Lord made you the kind of guy that likes to vote his conscience now and again."

"Shit, Dent, you didn't go along with me on the whisky-labeling bill."

"Come on, that was a payoff to the Indiana distillers. —This one helps all of us live in cities."

"Goddamn it, you son-of-a-bitch, I wish you hadn't found me. But yeah, yeah, I'm with ya."

Dent reached out and grabbed Liskowsky by the hand.

"Great, Pete, thanks. And those two new guys in your delegation, Frankenthall and Hirst, they listen to you."

"What do you want, an arm and a leg? Okay, okay. Hirst listens anyway. I'll talk to them."

They slapped each other on the back and separated.

Dent pulled five clipped-together file cards from his jacket pocket and checked off three more names. One hundred and four promised votes. He broke into a vast smile; jammed the cards into his pocket; and slapped his fist into his palm. He would have leaped into the air if there hadn't been so many people around. He was going to win. Get so many votes people would have to notice. Not this year, but before he was quit with Congress, there would be a Department of Urban Affairs; and the cities would have more clout than the goddamn farmers.

The next day in his office Mayor Zeigler reached him on the phone from Rochester.

"Good to hear your voice, Frank. What can I do to help you out up there on the urban firing line?"

"From the papers you don't appear to have been asleep yourself."

"Talk's easy. But unless Eisenhower kicks us in the ass, which he won't, this Congress won't accomplish much. We're all too busy maneuvering for 1960."

"Dent, I won't beat around the bush, that brings up why I'm

calling. You know I'm totally for your cities bill. But I'm also for a friend of mine called George Dent for Senator. That bill is killing you up here. They see it as something only for New York City. I've had two efforts to get you to speak in Buffalo blocked."

"Jesus."

"It's bad."

"My wife had a letter from her father about the same thing."

"Mr. Frost knows his upstate."

"God, Frank, this urban-affairs bill is one of the few good things I've ever done. Buffalo should love me."

There was a pause in the phone conversation. Dent felt his stomach fall away from him. If they wouldn't vote for him because of his cities bill, if the missile investigation backfired, what was left to him but his fake smile, smearing opponents, and waving rancid salad oil?

"Well, I don't know, Frank." He continued, "I don't see how I can drop the bill. I've been lobbying for it for the past three months. I'll do my best. —Thanks for your call."

A Saturday in early spring. Dent came out of the shed at the back of his Georgetown garden where he had been painting and watched Jane climb on the swing in the yard. The two hours of painting he had planned to allow himself had stretched into three. Now he intended to rush downtown and get a haircut. For some reason he'd had trouble getting his hair cut recently; he kept forgetting appointments, or putting them off.

"Hi, Dad."

"Hi, Jane," he went over to the swing and began to push her.

"What have you been doing all morning?" his daughter asked.

"Painting."

"Oh."

He swung his daughter some more. "Remember how scared you used to get when I pushed you up high?"

"That was fun. —Would you like to see my paintings?"

"I'd love to." His haircut could wait some more. "Do you have any here?"

"I just happen to have brought some home."

"To show to Lion, I suppose."

"Yes." His daughter laughed.

"And you just happened to be swinging here when I came out."

His daughter gave him a guileless smile. "Now isn't that a coincidence," she said.

"Yeah, Jane, or a plot." He helped her off the swing and they started up to her room together.

One thing he had done right, he thought, he had given Jim and Jane the happy childhood he had not known. They in turn would have a future he had not known. Perhaps Jane would paint, like Dee. Whatever they did, both his children would lead a life full of joy. And their joy and success would nourish him.

He stopped so abruptly on the stairs that he almost pulled Jane, whose hand he was holding, over backward. Suddenly he had seen where he was. He was in his father's house building his father's prison for himself with his own hands.

"I have always wanted you, George," his father would begin, following up with some request. And he, Dent, would stand there thinking: then why don't you do it yourself? Or, when older: why should I follow your advice when your advice has not worked for you? Now here he was, convinced he was going to lead his children into a promised land he could not find for himself. He was the caricature of the bad officer: "Don't do as I do, men, do as I say." But he was worse. He was planning to draw off from his children part of their life to fill his need. Perhaps he was already trying to keep them young to fulfill some fake dream he had of ideal childhood.

He restarted up the stairs. "I'm sorry, Jane," he said, "I just thought of something I forgot. Nothing to do with now."

"Red," said Wup-'em to Florida's Donner, in the House gym, "I'm worried about our boy Dent."

"He sure is in a bind most of the time. Never even got time for handball."

"What do you hear about him for Senator from New York?"

"Nothing good."

"I hear bad."

"Yeah. They ain't going to give it to him; and he hasn't got the muscle to take it."

"Exactly what Ah hear," said Wup-'em.

"Must be a disappointment. —Wup-'em, did you ever ask yourself why we're Dent's friends?"

" 'Cause he likes us. But you're right. That's a hell of a reason to make friends in this town."

"Sure, he could be up there hobnobbing with the leadership, or the National Committee, or the Senators, or anybody else who can help him. But who does he stop by and jaw with? Us. Maybe he doesn't want the kind of advice would get him the Senate."

"Red, old hoss, you're not dumb."

"But I'm shifty."

"You ever want to run for the Senate?"

"Takes a lot of work."

"Ah was offered a big passel of dough if Ah ran, with no strings attached. Just wires; copper wires."

"What the hell are we doin' in Congress, Wup-'em?"

"You're fuckin' your ears off; and Ah'm gettin' rich. Would you care to invest a big dollar on the outcome of our contest?"

"Spot me three points and I'll make it two dollars."

"Why you loudmouth tinhorn, you're on."

"I like Dent."

"Damn straight."

"What's he doin' in Congress?"

"Now you're gettin' to my worry."

"George, do you know how much you've changed?" The June morning was deliciously cool and the sunlight made soft clear patterns on the ceiling of Dee's studio.

"Have I? I can't measure from inside."

Propped up in bed on one elbow, Dee traced circular patterns across his stomach.

"There's one change. You used to be certain about everything. That was rather wonderful too—in its way."

Dent shivered beneath the drag of her nails.

"Are the changes bad?"

"They're changes." She paused. "Don't you know?"

"No. I've felt a shifting. I've been looking at my life. But I've no conclusions."

Much of the time when he claimed he was painting in his shed, he actually was probing into himself: his childhood, his parents, his school, the war, his dreams, Helen, Dee, Sarah, sex, painting. Since he wasn't going to get the Senate, at least now, he faced some major choices. Should he come out for Kennedy, gamble the Senator would be elected, and try and land a top job in the Defense Department? Or would he rather remain in Congress? Where did he want to be five years from now? He didn't get much painting done.

"Give me a for instance of change," he asked.

"My dearest Congressman, for one you always used to have to rush somewhere in the morning."

He smiled; that was a problem with changes: they weren't gains, they were swaps. This one gave him more joy but less campaign time.

"And your 'click-click' smile," Dee continued. "I don't see that so much."

"Glad to give it to you." He fixed his best political smile on her, teeth, sincerity, the works.

"George, stop. I hate it."

"Well, I'll tell you one thing that's changed; my neck's gotten bigger. I had to buy a whole new bunch of shirts with larger collars."

"Maybe you need more room. At some periods of my life certain clothes have been much too tight; and my weight hadn't changed. I've one dress that always binds across my upper back unless I'm happy."

Dent grunted. He didn't believe that. New shirts reflected the growth of his neck, a physical change he could understand, like a paunch from eating or a muscle from exercise. The same diameter of neck should not suddenly require more space around it.

How much of a difference in himself had been caused by Dee, he wondered? He'd been careful with her since he realized he'd fallen in love. Yet years ago he'd promised himself he'd never consider painting again. And here he was not just seeing Dee, but spending time painting. What combination of Dent and Dee had caused that? He suddenly grew upset he wasn't in his New York office answering mail.

"You mean a great deal to me, Dent."

"And you to me."

"With summer coming we can see more of each other. —I hate this hiding."

"Yeah."

"It gets to my work."

"I'm sure."

Everywhere he looked were problems.

Two nights later he and Sarah were at a theater opening and Dent was completely enjoying himself. Waiting for the curtain to rise three alluring girls had come over and introduced themselves as having been part of "Broadway for Dent" in his last campaign. He thanked them and told them to keep taking an interest in the issues because he needed help all the time. They asked for his autograph and whether he was for Stevenson or Kennedy. He signed and ducked. To his happy surprise, they were for Kennedy.

"Don't charm the girls too much, Daddy," said Sarah as the three left. Nothing like getting attention from others to make Sarah a contented wife, he thought. He looked about at the women in the first-night audience. Here money was certainly the plumage of the successful male. But since no fashion permitted a man to weave his tuxedo out of thousand-dollar bills, the winners purchased suitable women on which to hang their gains. And Sarah could parade with the best of them.

Coming out of the theater afterward, he was interviewed on CBS radio as to what he thought of the musical. He hadn't thought much of the show, but got off an energetic platitude about the musical as an indigenous American art form. No other member of the New York delegation, he thought happily, would get interviewed or asked for their autograph at a New York opening. This sort of spontaneous press exposure piled up votes.

At the opening-night party, Dent and Sarah sat at a forward table round the dance floor of the St. Regis roof, rented by the producer for that evening. Sarah, in a silver-blue, sarilike ball gown, threw off sparks of charm and graciousness. They danced over the floor with the ease and rhythm of long partnership. Several times as he held her he could feel her hugging back.

The cast arrived; the show, while not a smash, would be successful; the party grew lively; a switch of dancing partners left Dent at the table alone, content to watch, conscious he was being watched, a celebrity himself. Suddenly the dancers on the floor before him divided into two species: "the warm" and "the cold." Once he became conscious of the division, he saw that it ran everywhere through the room like a great serpent or some lunatic Balkan border, past watchers as well as dancers, sometimes even splitting couples, placing everyone on one side or the other.

The clothes of the "cold" were more striking, usually in brighter colors and more elaborate weaves; but they hid more of the body. The clothes of the "warm" were simpler, less varied in color, though what color they had was of higher hue. Between the bodies of the "cold" and the fabric of their dress or jacket there seemed a thin layer of air. While the "warm" possessed their clothes as flesh. The skin of the "cold" appeared middle register with a hint of yellow; while the skin of the "warm" was either bleach-white, or contained pigments of brown.

Many of the "cold" were skillful dancers, elaborate, professional; a few of the "warm" were not; but the "warm" were inside the music, and threw off excitement. The legs of the "cold" never ventured far from the perpendicular. But the legs of the "warm" particularly the women, flickered in all directions, a series of sensuous tubes, arcing against their hips, shattering the line of their backs and the rectangle of their bodies. Both the "cold" and the "warm" were up for the party. The "cold" were predominantly on display, while the "warm" were both on display and enjoying themselves; and far more sexually promising.

Dent felt frozen as a mother-drowned child. He sat among the "cold." He had not been born here. He had not always lived here. At some point in his life he had chosen to forsake the "warm" and join this side.

As he eyed the dance floor, the music stopped briefly. Looking across the room at Sarah's self-contained perfection, Dent noticed a young actress who was staring, devouring every inch of his wife. The body of the girl flowed out of her eyes, emptied her, hollowed her; she was transported, possessed, by jealousy. Not a hidden, gnawing jealousy; but a driving envy. Spread any lie, suck any body, sell any principle; but get where Sarah was. The actress's body hardened to a black shaft. The music started up. When the girl unscrewed her eyes from Sarah and began to move, her first few steps were jerky and catatonic.

He had watched the young girl dance, noted her among the "warm" and envied her. Maybe all that was happening to him was that far away fields looked greener as he hurdled forty. There was no division in the room, merely a split in himself. Why should he envy anybody? He had what most men wanted.

"Are you happy?" he asked Sarah, taxiing home from the party.

"Yes, love-dove, I had a wonderful time."

"So did I."

Later in their apartment, sipping a weak bourbon, he rubbed his knuckles and asked, "Sarah, where do you see us five years from now?"

"In what way, Daddy?"

"Well, everyone has goals. What are yours?"

Why did George always ask this type of question late at night? she wondered. Naturally everyone had goals. But there was nothing to be gained by sitting around and analyzing them. "I want to be with you and love you. And love my babies and keep them happy."

"Ummm. I guess I was thinking more about me. Where do you see me?"

"Sometimes, Daddy, you're impossible."

"I'm not going to get the Senate nomination."

"If at first you don't succeed."

"But the next try is six years away."

"Remember Robert Bruce and the spider."

Christ, he was caged in by homilies.

"Sarah, my problem is this. Some of the things I most believe in, that I want to fight for, make my chances for the Senate uncertain—ever."

"Didn't you have a good time at the party?"

He reached out for his drink and couldn't find it. He knew he'd put it on the table beside his chair. He turned to look at the table. There was his glass. But the table was well below the level of the chair arm. He had reached directly sideways and passed over the tumbler. Yet this was his favorite chair. He had reached for his drink a hundred thousand times from this position and always found the glass in his palm.

"I had a fine time, Sarah. I was just wondering."

"Is it the Kennedy-Stevenson problem?"

"In part, perhaps."

"You do want the Senate, don't you, Daddy?"

"Yes." He realized as he said the single syllable that a true answer to her question would have to be long, complicated, and full of hedges.

"Then you'll get it. No good thing comes easy."

That was the sort of advice his father would have given him.

"I'm going to bed," he said.

"You're on your high horse this evening."

"No I'm not." He entered the blue chintz world of their bedroom alone and shut the door.

That he had been among the "cold" at the party scared him. He was tearing himself in two, he realized, in a great many ways. There had been that flash of insight going upstairs with Jane, his dissatisfaction with his work, the slender amount of time he was devoting to politics, his shortness of temper recently with Sarah, his daydreaming about the past, his painting. Above all he was in love with one woman and living with another. That was stupid. He was having enough trouble in his life without that. If he was going to work through the next few years he was going to have to drop Dee. He froze at the thought.

That's being a coward Dent. That's running. He hated to think of himself as a coward.

The odor of the past came to him so strongly that he sniffed. The smell of fire, oil and grease burning, and the sickening fumes of charred hair and human flesh.

He reached down to tug at his gunner, McQuade.

He'd been fighting the lead weight at the top of his head, trying to keep it balanced, a weight that always arrived on the third day of too little sleep, when merely to keep awake became a major part of his war. Once his neck muscles broke discipline and allowed the weight to slump his head forward, he would be through. Asleep before he knew he'd blacked out. Out of control for a few disturbed, dream-filled seconds before the motion of his tank jerked him awake to battle sleep some more.

His world shrank with tiredness. The steel turret contracted. His microphone cord entangled him, the turret swivel pinched him, the hatch cover pressed down on his head. His seat stuck. Cold metal projections everywhere caught him: breech block, grenade rack, radio edge. Just to control his personal world sapped his energy; to stay warm, to move inside his many layers of clothes. He became a wool cocoon in a steel case, trying to peer a few seconds into the hostile future through eyes that burned as if continually full of smoke.

He heard the great gong of noise, and light flashed behind his eyes. Silence. No engine. In one of his instants of dozing a shell had hit his tank.

He was struggling through the turret as the second round entered, ringing and shaking him like the clapper in a bell.

I've had it.

The tank thrust out tentacles to hold him. Iron teeth that tore at his overstuffed edges. The headset cord garroted his neck. A turret lock grabbed his waist, the periscope snared his left shoe. Then he was out. Crumpled on the ground. Gasping, he automatically picked his body up to drag himself into a run before the tank exploded.

He came out of fear, out of sleep. What had happened? From where? How badly was his tank hurt? Other tanks? What should he do?

He was angry. Furiously angry at everyone in the world. Mostly at himself. What the fuck was going on that he was running? He'd left his map in the tank. Shit. Smoke came from the engine compartment. The tank would burn. And he had two bottles of cognac behind the radio. Christ, his sleeping bag was on fire. At least he'd saved that from the last tank. One, two, three men and he made four. That was right. They were all out. But even as he counted he knew why he was counting; to avoid a truth. He counted again to hide from knowledge. One, two, three, and he made four. But that wasn't right. He should make five.

Who was left?

McQuade must have gotten himself hit, that idiot fuck-up. Why didn't someone go back and help him out? Not me, I have to fight the company. He paused. Hoping for the excuse to work inside him. Knowing that McQuade was not a fuck-up; but a great gunner. Waiting for someone else to start for the burning tank.

He ran back to the tank. The side of the tank rose before him, a wall taller than any dream. Tracer was going by. He could hear the bullets crack but not too close. He grabbed hold of the deck and climbed up. With all this smoke I'm nothing but a fucking target. Cautious, he raised himself to look into the turret. McQuade stared back at him, eyes open, twisted against the gun.

Dead.

Unconscious.

He must be dead.

But is he?

Dent stretched into the turret and grabbed McQuade. He could move him but not lift him. Again the turret caught at his extra layers of clothes. I'll be trapped. He could smell the oil smoke, thick, domestic. The multicolored noses of the shells soon to explode from heat blazed at him.

Get out.

Lift McQuade.

He jerked further into the tank and was slammed hard in the face. His goddamn field glasses. He still had them on. They were dangling from his neck downward into the turret. If those break they'll make me pay for them. He dropped McQuade and reached for his glasses. His mitten got in the way. His mittens were fastened to string which ran through his combat jacket so he wouldn't lose them, as he always did when he was tired. He batted the mitten aside. Grabbed the glasses. Put the strap in his mouth. Reached back for McQuade. His helmet fell off his head and onto the turret floor. He saw his map case; let go of McQuade; threw out his map case.

Go.

Get McQuade.

The gasoline is going.

Go.

He tugged at McQuade with both hands. A machine-gun belt twisted round the gunner's waist, lashing them both to the turret. Again he let go of McQuade and fought the belt. An instant of flame snaked along the turret floor. His forty-five caught on the turret edge. More flame.

Go.

Stay.

He's dead.

The heat tore at him now like a madman's scream.

Stay.

Go.

He went.

Was McQuade dead? Probably. At least as the flame crawled

out the turret top he was spared the high endless scream of a man burning alive. But then he wasn't close enough to hear. On the way over to the next tank to get on the radio, regain some control of his war, he stopped by a dead somebody, not one of his, and grabbed the guy's helmet. It was much too small.

He'd run.

Sometimes he had just had to run.

Joyce Farad had trouble remembering things she wanted to, so things she didn't want to remember she genuinely forgot. Two nights before, when she realized she would soon have to tell Colonel Catenberry she was pregnant, she found she didn't truthfully know if she had taken her nail scissors and cut a small hole in the center of her old diaphragm, or just dreamed she had. As she explained her condition to Frank her eyes were full of surprised tears.

"I don't know how it happened, Frank; honestly I don't. I'm always so careful."

"Yeah. And I always check you out first."

He did that too. The brutal man. She felt him do it. How ugly of him not to trust her.

"Yes. So you see I don't know why it happened to us."

"To you, hon," he corrected.

"Oh, I love you so, Frank." She was sitting naked in his lap and threw her arms about him, squeezing hard. "And this makes me love you even more. Don't you love me?"

"Yeah; sure, hon." Keep 'em happy till you worked out a plan. He looked at her neutrally the way he looked at a target before selecting rockets, napalm, or fifty caliber.

"They say the thing's effective ninety-eight per cent of the time. I guess this is one of the times." Joyce giggled. "Perhaps it happened because you're so strong."

Catenberry looked at her. She wasn't that stupid. Her obvious lie made him more suspicious.

"You got any friends, hon, can fix you up with an abortion?"

"That's it, Frank. That's what I'm trying to tell you. I can't have an abortion."

"Shit you can't."

"No. We've been so careful that when I began missing—you know, missing my period," she was very shy about mentioning bodily functions, "I thought I was just nervous or something." She dropped her eyes and snuggled her breasts against him, and began to finger his crotch.

Nothing shows, he thought. What a great figure.

"So, I didn't see a doctor," Joyce went on, "until this month. It's been four months, Frank. That's what the doctor says. That's too late."

"I can remember you having the rag on two months ago."

"No, Frank. You can't."

He could. What he remembered, he remembered. He was being lied to. This was a put-up job. Was she really pregnant? He'd have her pee in a bottle and take it round to some lab himself. But he was sure she was. She'd be that thorough. But four months? No. He could knock the hell out of her right now and get the truth; but that would make her more difficult to handle later. He'd save beating her up till it would do some good.

First, he had to make it absolutely clear to her she didn't get marriage out of him this way. Then, bullshit her along, tell her that if she did what he said and got rid of the kid he might get a divorce and marry her. Like hell he would. But that would be the carrot. And the stick? He'd find a stick. And wallop her good. She was messing with his career.

"Here's what you're going to do, hon," he said.

At 9:30 at night Dent's Washington office was deserted. Dent sat at Joyce Farad's desk, typing slowly.

Dear Dee:

There are times when all a man can do is break off the action. The truth is I love you deeply and profoundly. What fills my days is the thought of when we will be together next. With you I see all sorts of things about myself and the world that I did not see before. I am changing.

But I am also myself. I have a contract: to Sarah, to the voters, and especially to my children. I cannot be with you and fulfill that contract. If I loved you less, if you were less wonderful, if I were different, then I could. But none of these things is so. To do my work I am going to have to get on with my life the way it is.

I know you are worried, that something inside yourself always causes your affairs to turn out badly. To bring pain to people. I want to assure you that just isn't true here. I am doing this to myself. You are a wonderful and loving person. Your very strength makes it impossible for me to see you and lead my present life.

This is not easy for me. Even as I write I feel your body, hear your laugh, see you concentrated before your easel. But I have no choice. I must re-establish the order of my life, which is not without its own joys, though it lacks the greatest joy I have ever known, yourself.

I love you, Dee. I wish you well. If you ever are in need, call me.

Yours always,
George

He walked down the marble corridor of the House Office Building, the lead in his stomach sagging his gut toward his knees. How constricted the corridor ceilings were with their overbright neon lights. Had he hit the right note? Probably not. But there was no lie in the letter. Well, only one. His son Jim was the greatest joy he had ever known—yes, and Jane. But Dee came right after them.

He looked at the mail chute opening. The heavy brass was gummy with stuck polish. He put the envelope in, checking first to make sure his doubts about sending it had not led him to forget the stamp.

Dee first read Dent's letter standing at her mail box in the paint-peeled front hall of her walkup. She always told herself to wait and read her letters comfortably after she walked upstairs. But she never did. Now she stuffed the quickly read letter along with her other mail into the top of her grocery bag and labored through the heat up the four flights of scuffed stairs.

It's come, she thought, I thought it might; but I feel awful. Still, damn it, it's a relief. But why would he never talk about us? He'd just hunch into himself and pretend things were fine.

She stowed the milk in the ice box and put the rest of the groceries away, deliberately putting off studying the letter. Then, draping her legs over her chair arm, she turned to it again.

How like George the letter was, so much hidden behind it. Like a stage magician saying look here while what was important went on someplace else. This letter was both a revelation and a barrier. Just as she could be talking to Dent, getting closer to him, and then suddenly hit a blank wall. Blam. She shook her head. At those times Dent's eyes didn't seem like ordinary eyes, but the lenses for another set of eyes deep in his skull from which a frightened animal peered. He pretended love but he gave chivalry.

She felt her anger beginning to rise at the way Dent had walked out just when he wanted to, with no thought for her. How like a man. But then the other way was just as bad, with the person dragging her down until she'd have to end it herself.

She got up and walked around. Her anger ebbed and depression began. She braced herself against its flood. Here I am again, alone, cold, at the mercy of the telephone for dates, friendship, sex. Why can't I grab a man and hold him? Maybe I could take George away from his Sarah, if I played my cards right; but at what cost to myself? And after I have him what do I do? Put him in a mahogany box with a glass top and cotton wool at the bottom for my friends to ooh and ah over?

Look around this place, she thought. Not even a decent easy

chair. Where are the fine fabrics I'd love to have for curtains? Silk linings that make you feel when you run your fingers down them that you're on the safe side of the world. Instead I have two avocado plants I raised myself; and one of them is sick. I have plenty of paintings, all my own work, for dealers to make money off when I'm dead. I'd burn every one of these canvases for a man and children. —No I wouldn't. At least I have Turkey. I must call him tonight.

And women envy me my "freedom." Freedom to grow old alone, to sleep single, to masturbate, to rub my own back when I'm tired. To fetch my own electric pad when I have cramps. Cook my own soup, when I'm down with flu. Prepare great meals for myself and then not be able to eat a quarter of them. Fight off idiots who think a single woman must be desperate for any bed-partner. Oh, I can make it now. But ten years from now? And no children. Finally she began to cry.

ten

The physical shock from the amputation of Dee caught Dent unprepared. His body limped. He felt cold all the time. Between himself and the world a gray curtain lowered like a membrane, filtering out color and light, so that he moved through a gruel-like monotony.

He had no appetite or stomach for food. Duck, hamburger, pancakes, everything tasted like stale boarding-school meat loaf. The sight of food caused his stomach to bloat before he had eaten a mouthful, while the edges of his mouth were drawn down by nausea. He awoke hung over without alcoholic cause. Life's simplest actions—signing a letter, answering the phone, talking to Sam, going for a swim—could only be started and completed after consciously mustering his energy. He kept a vigilant watch on his temper, especially with Sarah.

Also he had forgotten there was a withdrawal problem with sex as there is with dope. He ached to get well laid; not just grudgingly taken care of once or twice a week. Any piece of fluff that swung by him quite literally made him salivate. He was continually prodded and shaken awake by erotic dreams. During the day when he should have been working he'd catch himself idly dreaming of performing gigantic sexual feats. He was afflicted by "Irish toothache" in his left testicle, which swelled to twice its normal size, became hot to the touch, and made him wince in agony when his pants leg pressed against it.

He knew the short-term answer was to find someone and get laid hard. But all that would mean was that he would have to begin the withdrawal process over again. You came out cold turkey or not at all.

He flew down to Easthampton to vacation with his family for the month of August. Standing at the airport to meet him, his children looked out of an advertisement, tanned and blond in the summer drizzle. He let Sarah drive so he could listen to Jim and Jane bubbling over with excitement.

At one point Sarah looked hard at him and said, "You don't look well, Daddy."

"It's been a tough session."

"I hear you're still shooting your face off."

"Goddamn it, what does that mean?"

"Don't swear in front of the children."

"Don't talk nonsense you know nothing about." He guessed she was referring to some of his efforts to organize for Kennedy in New York State. She still wanted him to remain neutral between Kennedy and Stevenson.

Three days later at the Country Club, Dent was batting tennis balls softly and accurately at his children, who peered at him, their serious faces half hidden by rackets, across the net, their small bodies crouched at the service line. Jane waited tensely, rooted to the spot. Jim's excitement kept him bouncing off the ground.

"It's great of you to play with us, Dad," said Jane.

"I like to," said Dent gently.

He batted balls back and forth with them for about half an hour more and then excused himself, saying he wanted to go and watch Mummy play. In point of fact he felt so edgy he was unable to stay in any one place for very long.

He walked off between the rows of tennis courts filled either with politely perspiring females or contesting children. How white and scrubbed everyone looked, how proper, to use one of Sarah's favorite words. Even teen-agers trying to look raunchy, and rebellious, carried their squalor with an artificial air, wearing dirty shirts with unfrayed, button-down collars.

He certainly didn't want his own children to grow up to be like any of these, or like the adults, most of whom he couldn't hold five minutes' conversation with; and the women were sexless. Yet he vacationed here. He must be crazy. There should be some other place they could go.

He paused at the edge of the court where Sarah was playing ladies' doubles. She certainly had an aggressive forehand. The ladies were communicating with each other in country-club language.

"Are you ready?"

"How's Frank's adenoids?"

"Nice shot."

"Behaving nicely."

"Oh, good try."

"Is Pamela's new man nice?"

"Balls please."

"Ooooph!"

"I think so."

"Just out."

"Nice try."

"Dinner, Friday, seven-thirty."

"What's the score?"

Sarah, who was ahead, knew the score.

He wandered back to his children, wanting to play with them again. But they were now engaged with friends their age in some form of game he couldn't understand, which seemed less tennis than a pecking-order argument. As he moved on he heard Jim say, "If my sister says it's in, it's in. You want this racket up your mush?"

That's right Jim, Dent smiled to himself, stick with the clan. The family that fights together stays together. Listlessly he wandered over to another set of courts and hunching his shoulders forward sat down on the grass with his back against the backstop wires.

Suddenly the people and the courts around him seemed unreal, merely abstract blobs of white, positioning and repositioning themselves according to some trigonometric rule, the whole pattern held together by the green stripes of lawn running between the gray squares of courts. The tennis balls even left little powder-white arcs in their flight. How Dee would enjoy this vision, he thought, and went numb.

He felt a hand grip his shoulder and with surprise looked up to see his son, Jim, smiling down at him. For an instant he was puzzled why the hand on his shoulder should feel both familiar and strange. Then he recognized the pressure. Jim was returning the same grip he used to reassure his son when he was troubled.

"Pop, is something wrong?"

"Nothing, Jim. Or rather, it's something like your wolves. Even I get them sometimes."

"I love you."

"Oh Jim."

They kissed each other.

Dent had believed that having done the right thing he would forget Dee in a few months and that his present life would become more bearable. Well, he thought, Time the great healer must be at work someplace; but from inside the process the change was not noticeable. One night, for example, he'd awakened around 1:30, unable to sleep, and decided to go downstairs, make himself a drink, and read. His first shock came as he began to slide noiselessly off the bed so as not to wake Sarah. His feet didn't hit the floor. For an instant he thought he must be in a dream; but he was awake. He slid further off the bed than he usually did and his feet finally touched the carpet.

Going into the living room he couldn't find the light-switch. He had found that particular switch thousands of times in the dark. Now he carefully felt up and down the right-hand side of the door jamb and found nothing. On a whim he tried the left-hand side of the door, knowing firmly the switch could not be there. After a few gropes he felt it. The incident was trivial, but the pattern repeated itself at other times, making him a stranger in his own house.

He always seemed to have to be doing something, running from place to place. Sarah had him on a schedule worse than a boys' camp. He needed time to himself. If he could charter a sailboat for a couple of weeks and sail off alone, then he could begin his serious cure.

Then he had an even better idea, he could take Jim. The two men would cruise together; Sarah couldn't horn in on that. It would be a bit unfair to Jane; but he would make it up to her some other time. He had promised Jim that when he was grown they would go sailing together. Jim was old enough now. They didn't have to sail far each day, merely be alone on the water together. Just thinking about it made him feel better.

Three nights later, his plans laid in secret, Dent followed Sarah into the living room after dinner. He was about to cast himself into his favorite easy chair, when he remembered that Sarah had one justifiable complaint—that he broke the bottoms out of chairs by sitting down in them too violently. So using the arms, he lowered himself in them cautiously, picking up Brownie points. From the next room where his children sat came the sounds of televised gunfire.

He looked at Sarah and wished he could just tell her, not have to negotiate with her. She was pondering a book. The Easthampton Garden Club was on a great-books kick and Sarah was dutifully wading through two books a month. The session was on *The Way of All Flesh*. What secret sins forced her to do penance with that Victorian dullness now? Or had the good ladies been led up the garden path, like generations of schoolboys, by the title?

"Sari-dari?" he began, feeling guilty about going off with Jim.

She reached onto the lamp table beside her, picked up a green band with a gold tassel on it, inserted that at her page for a bookmark, closed the book, and said, "Yes, Daddy."

"Well, Sarah, you know I'd really hoped to get a shot at the Senate seat. Now when I . . ."

"I told you what would happen," Sarah broke in, "but you went right ahead shooting your face off too much."

He pulled back from that argument.

"Well it was quite a blow to me, and I've had a problem adjusting. I thought I should go away by myself for about two weeks. So I've chartered a small sailboat just this side of Cape Cod from Pete Hackensack, you remember him?" Sarah had stiffened and now peered at him intently. She had to Dent the air of one recording the words of a weakling for judgment. "For a week from today. I was just going off by myself. Then I thought: Why not take Jim? I've promised Jim a sailing trip when he got older. Why wait? I may never have as good a chance."

Sarah leaned toward him, a little blond dart of angry purpose. She was really quite beautiful with the electric light catching her hair.

"Love-dove, if you would just spend those two weeks working on politics instead of running away, you might get the nomination."

"Not true. There's a time when added work does no good. I could study mathematics from now till doomsday and still not be an Einstein."

"You don't want me with you?"

"Would I be sitting in this room, instead of down in Washington or in New York, if I didn't want you? But I also want some time by myself. And to be with Jim would be even more fun."

"Jim's too young."

"Sarah, he's eight now. And a strong and responsible eight. I'm not sailing across the ocean."

"Jane might like to go too."

"We'll all go next time."

Sarah looked at her husband hard. Why was he pushing her off to galavant around by himself on a sailboat instead of work? He must be ill. The idea suddenly struck her that maybe he didn't intend to be by himself, that wanting Jim was a fake; that he expected her to say no so he could go off with some girl. Dirty men.

"Take Jim if you want. Go ahead, take him. But it's your responsibility if anything happens."

"Great, Sarah, great. You're very understanding. I'll go tell Jim." He saw her start slowly in her chair. She'd been maneuvering in some way and hadn't expected his answer. Well, he'd won. He got up to go into the next room and tell Jim. Sarah was quite capable of looking him in the eye tomorrow morning and saying, "I never said any such thing"; and losing her temper to prove it. But she would not go back on her word to the children.

The boat trip went even better than Dent had hoped. First he and Jim were blessed by fair weather. Then Jim turned out to really like working on the boat. By the time they had been at sea three days Dent had established a routine inside which they both relaxed. Jim got up first, scrambled from his bunk, put on his swimming trunks, and climbed up the companionway.

"What's the weather like?" Pop asked.

"Another sunny day."

"Are we lucky."

"Are we lucky," Jim repeated. And the knowledge that "we" meant Pop and himself, no one else, no girls or other grownups, and that the luck fell on them equally, regardless of size, because they were men together, made him giggle with delight.

Jim was not really sure he liked to swim so early in the morning, the water hit him so cold. But Pop liked it; and it did make you feel good. He sat down on the warm deck and waited for Pop to come up and dive in, then he climbed over the life lines and jumped in himself. He was always a little frightened as he fell through the air. The deck was so high and he went so far down, down into the water, struggling and thrusting to come back up toward the light. He broke through to the surface and looked around with delight. There was Pop right beside him. He looked at Pop and dared a word that made Mummy mad.

"Shit, it's cold," he said.

Pop let out a great big laugh.

"It is, Jim, it is."

After breakfast Jim had his job to do. Untie the strips of canvas, four on the main and three on the jib, that went around the furled sails to keep them from flapping during the night. The seven strips were then put under the seat on the port side of the cockpit. After that he had to fasten the jib shackle onto the head of the jib. While he did this, Pop did the dishes and made everything secure in the cabin so things wouldn't spill if they heeled way over while sailing. Not that they would today, because there wasn't that much wind. But as Pop said, "At sea it's always wise to be ready."

Each morning as he sat astride the boom to better work at the knots on the canvas strips, he was flooded with happiness. The thought that his job waited for him kept him smiling through his milk and cornflakes. Not one of those jobs you pushed at kids to keep them out of the way while grownups did what needed to be done faster; he had real work.

In the cabin, Dent smiled. He carefully timed the work below each day so that Jim would have his moments on deck alone, lord of the boat, with his own responsibility. He remembered the agony of his wish to have his father share the grownup world with him. That wish had been denied. He would not make the same error with Jim.

Humming "From Greenland's Icy Mountains," he pushed back the bunks and slipped the canvas retaining straps over them. This sail was just what he needed. And Jim was a true help. He could use field glasses. He was great at finding buoys. In good weather like this he could hold the boat on course while Dent went below, adjusted the sails, lengthened the dinghy painter, or just relaxed a moment. And today already felt like another great day.

They weighed anchor and reached out across Buzzard's Bay, the soft blue sea gently slapping round them.

"She's a good ship," he said to Jim, slapping the warm teak decks of the boat. "They built 'em solid in Maine in the old days. She may not be as fast as some of the other boats we see. But come a blow, we'd be dry and safe while they'd have to run for home."

"And the man we got it—her," Jim corrected himself, "from, sure keeps her nice."

"Yes, he does."

Dent stretched himself out in the lush, warm sunlight of early September. The weather was more like August. "You want to be towed behind, Jim?"

Jim got up and put on his life jacket.

"Sure."

Dent threw a line over the stern, letting it stream out past the dinghy. Jim jumped over. Dent let the wind out of the mainsail so the boat slowed until Jim had grabbed hold of the knot at the end of the line. Then he speeded up again. He waved at Jim. Jim waved back. All systems A-okay.

They had practiced emergency procedures on the second day out. Dent threw a sponge overboard and showed Jim how the boat was jibed round to come back and pick up the sponge as the boat lost speed.

"We did that with our dinghies in sailing class, Pop."

"Good. It's an important thing to learn. And it works just the same with this big boat." He threw the sponge over again and had Jim jibe the boat round to pick it up. The weather was light, like today, and on the third try Jim, panting with excitement, got close enough to the sponge for Dent to reach way over the side and grab it.

"Good work, Jim," Dent shouted. "Good work."

He got to his feet and hugged his son.

"Now, Jim, here's the sponge. You just throw it overboard sometime when I'm sailing and see if I can get it."

"Okay."

About five minutes later Jim heaved over the sponge. Dent jibed around easily and retrieved it.

"Now I'll do it to you."

Dent held the sponge about three minutes, which he guessed was all Jim's excitement could take without giving him permanent St. Vitus's dance. Then he dropped the sponge over. Jim jibed about perfectly and Dent was able to easily retrieve the sponge.

"That's got it, Jim. You can do it. Now get the boat back on course toward that point, there. Right."

The boat steadied on course. Dent stood up, went below, and picked up an extra life jacket. He came back on deck. Jim held the boat easily on course.

"Okay, Jim, ready. Now pick me up."

Grabbing the life jacket, he leaped over the side.

As he broke back through the surface of the water and looked at the boat he knew he had gone too far. Frozen at the tiller, Jim's life-jacketed form gazed out at him, the face a stone mask of horror and surprise as an eight-year-old watched his father vanish forever. My God, thought Dent, he'll panic, and jump in after me. Can I possibly catch the boat as it comes into the wind? He felt fear boil up cold inside him, like dry ice dropped into a glass of water.

But even as he cursed himself he saw Jim slam the tiller to leeward hard, his whole body a line of desperate force. It wasn't the best emergency procedure in the world. Jim was so nervous he didn't gather enough speed on the downwind leg. But as he shot the boat into the wind Dent was able to swim to her side.

He hauled himself back on board.

"That's the way it's done, Jim. Now neither of us has to worry."

The smile on Jim's face cracked the horizon.

Each night they lay in their bunks, sometimes rocking gently, always hearing the water, and talked till they fell asleep. Most of Jim's questions were easy: Why does wood float? Who's the greatest quarterback? How do you tell the weather? But occasionally they tipped over the edge of knowledge into exploration. "How come there are so many stars?" "Why doesn't Billy McClay like me when I like him?" "What makes wars?" "Weren't you afraid in the war?" That question held the floor tonight.

"Sometimes, Jim, particularly at the beginning of a fight. When there was nothing to do but sit there and get shot at. Before I was doing anything."

"Why didn't you run?"

Dent was about to explain about social conditioning, small unit loyalty, childhood training, not letting your friends down, when he stopped. Those, even where true, were book answers.

"Well, Jim, I didn't run because of a fight I had with a toilet when I was much younger than you."

He heard his son's delighted gurgle. What had Blake said: "Truth can never be told so as to be understood, and not be believed"? He began the story, threading himself back into his past to keep a jump ahead of his words.

He could date the period of terror quite accurately because his new nurse had not yet come. She appeared with his baby sister, who showed up, entirely unexpectedly, when he was three. His battle had been just before that.

His fear was that when he flushed his toilet he would drown. No, worse than drown: be swept from the apartment; whirled away to some stinking blackness of rushing waters and filth; only to be allowed to drown at the dark end. And he had to flush several times every day because his nurse made him. He once tried crapping on the bathroom floor to escape; but that brought punishment.

Also he tried not to tinkle, the word by which the minor deed was known. That brought stomach-aches; and his nurse led him to the bathroom and watched to make sure he did it, just as if he was a baby. He could see no possible escape. He had to pull the shiny lever that stuck horizontally out from the right hand back side of the curved white pipe.

So he pulled the lever and raced to his bedroom, the room he was moved out of when his sister came. Gigantic door sills loomed up to trip him, pieces of furniture bumped him down, his feet tangled. He scrambled up into his bed to burrow beneath his pillow and wait in darkness for the roar to go away.

Twice as he ran for the bed he fell. Then he lay, eyes clenched, breath stopped, curled up on the floor waiting for the first foul wave to cascade over him.

But, and now came the incredible part, after about three weeks of hiding from each flush he realized that George Dent had to face that handle: the lever that held in check all the waters of America which, his father had explained, were kept penned high in the mountains in some huge place known as "reservoir," and flowed down through a tremendous pipe to here, his bathroom, and then to the ocean.

Breathing hard, he peered round the edge of his bathroom door and advanced upon the toilet. He put out his right hand and touched the lever. He could feel its chill go through him. He closed his hand about the lever with difficulty, because the cold made his fingers stiff. With a compulsive jerk he pulled. The noise of waters came; his courage broke and he turned and fled, sobbing, to scramble onto his bed, and hide as before. Twice more he tried and fled. Fortunately Nurse had never seen him running. The shame she would put him to if she caught him would be even worse than pulling the handle.

Miserable, and totally ashamed of himself, he resolved a few days later to try again and not run. He gripped the handle. He pulled. He stepped back. He stood there in agony, holding himself in place upon the bathroom floor. The water rose. The roaring grew, and swelled, and burst. It was all around him now, the pipes beneath the floor must be breaking. He covered his ears, closed his eyes and moaned. Then the noise subsided. There had been no flood.

Shaking, he approached again, touched the flushing lever, and pulled. Quickly he stepped backward. He still lacked courage to stand close. But this time he could keep his eyes open. The noise was less. He waited till the noise was gone with a final shisssh and gurgle. The rivers, oceans, and sewers were trapped beneath the handle again. He turned and walked away.

"And because I won that fight, Jim, I just knew, in some way, scared as I might get, I'd do all right in battle."

"Wow," said Jim deeply several times. Then he asked, "Where did the fears come from, Pop?"

"You're ahead of me, Jim. I don't understand."

"Remember my wolves? Those came from inside. Because I was afraid of . . . you know. What made that noisy toilet so bad?"

Dent stared at their cabin ceiling in amazement. All his years of living with that battle, nourishing himself with the story, and he had never asked the next glaring question. He had reacted out of proportion to the stimulus. How nice to be educated and use big words. I ran when there was no need. I know the fight was a victory over me; but why was the battle necessary?

"Jim, I don't know what made it so bad. And I think I'd better do some thinking and find out."

They sailed, splashed and talked their way through nine lazy days on Buzzard's Bay, Vineyard Sound, Nantucket Sound, until with two days to go they ended up on Nantucket Island. Now, at the end of the second week in September, the sheltering circle of the harbor, fringed by white houses and green lawns, was pleasantly deserted. The wind had been gusting hard as they came across the Sound, with cloud making up in the west. Entering the harbor Dent had been surprised not to see the red triangle of a small-craft warning flying from the Coast Guard flagpole. He had been premature. A few hours later, at 5:00 p.m., the little red triangle went up. Dent listened to the marine weather forecast: northwest winds twenty to thirty knots with rain, nothing alarming.

"We're going to have rain, Jim. We'll stay in port tomorrow. Let's get everything snug and cozy."

The rain and wind blustered through the next day, while they rode easily at anchor. In rainsuits they rowed themselves ashore, Jim proudly handling the oars while Dent sat in the stern. They sloshed through town and bought Coca-Cola, potato chips, a sweater for Sarah, and a mouse in a sailor suit for Jane.

Tomorrow the boat had to be back in Falmouth, on the Cape. And the day after he was a principal speaker at a big political dinner in New York; Sarah expected them. He studied his charts and listened to the marine weather forecasts. Same sort of weather as today: small-craft warnings, southwest winds twenty to thirty knots, rain. From Tennessee a major storm center was moving eastward out to sea. Already the weather was turning colder. The cold front must be starting to pass through Nantucket now, the winds might well drop tomorrow. And if they didn't, in this boat they could reef and handle twenty to thirty knots easily.

Still, to sail singlehanded in such a wind is an effort and Dent made his preparations meticulously. For Jim, for all his willingness, would be too little to be much help. He checked the rigging, reef points, sheets; he figured alternate courses and wrote headings on the chart; he put covers over the portholes and made everything extra secure below; finally he got the dinghy on deck and firmly lashed.

"We'll get wet tomorrow, Jim. And it won't be too pleasant. But it will be a short sail. The wind is just right for us. And then we'll be home."

Early the next morning, 6:30 a.m., he hoisted the reefed mainsail, decided against carrying the jib, and with the engine slowly turning over stuck the boat's nose out of the harbor. The wind seemed harder than the forecast. But he decided against spending the day in port, since only the red triangle signifying small craft warnings flew from the Coast Guard station. He was probably overestimating the wind in the first shock of it.

Dent adjusted his life jacket, shut off the engine, checked the compass course, and settled his rainsuited form against the tiller. The rain whipped past in droves of ice-pick points. The boat heeled over and slammed into the steep seas. He could see only about twenty or thirty yards. Jim sat with his back to the rain huddled in rainsuit and life jacket in the forward, starboard corner of the cockpit. Dent smiled at his son to reassure him; and Jim smiled back. He hoped Jim wouldn't get too cold.

Half an hour after Dent left Nantucket the red small craft warning triangle was lowered; and the red square of a whole gale run up the mast. If Dent had been a more slipshod sailor, less organized, and not got under way so early, he would have seen the change in flags and learned that during the night the storm center over Tennessee had become diffuse. A secondary system had developed at the mouth of the Chesapeake. This new storm had not moved eastward as the weather bureau had predicted, when Dent listened at 10:00 p.m., before going to bed. Instead it was tracking rapidly north-northeast up the coast. Already the winds around him were over thirty knots. In an hour they would be fifty to sixty knots with higher gusts. But secure in the ignorance of careful preparation, Dent had set sail.

"When you asked me what sailing would be like, I told you wet, cold, rainy and miserable," Dent yelled at Jim. "Here it is. We're lucky this waited till our last day."

Jim smiled back. "It's fun," he yelled; and turned to test the rain battering against his face. He had never felt rain so strong before and wanted to try its hardness.

Dent watched Jim peer to windward. It is fun, he thought, if everything goes well. But your old man isn't all that great a sailor. And suppose I miss Bell Seven off Tuckernuck Bank and we have to hunt for the lightship and take a new departure from there, then it could be a long, cold, hard day. Jim shouldn't get seasick though, they'd been in rough weather before and he'd shown no sign, this late in the trip he was probably used to the motion.

Without the jib the boat had quite a weather helm. Dent had foreseen that and rigged a line to help him hold the tiller to windward. Now he got the line adjusted to please him; but still the tiller was a strain. There'll be one tired Dent tonight, he thought. He looked at Jim bracing his legs against the roll of the ship. Two tired Dents, he corrected himself.

He began to feel depressed. Either the wind was much harder than he'd expected, or the lack of visibility, the wet and cold, were beginning to get to him. He could not even see Great Point light. Should he have gone down to the second set of reef points? He'd never be able to reef out here alone. Well, maybe he could.

With the rope Jim could hold the tiller. No Jim couldn't. Perhaps he should have stayed in the harbor.

A curl of wave slopped over the boat's side and drenched the cockpit. Jim looked up at him, worried. Dent smiled.

"That's nothing, Jim. We've got the big board keeps water out of the cabin. Want to stream the log?"

Jim pursed his lips and nodded. How huge the cockpit grew in this weather. He shivered a little, not so much from cold as from the thought of what might happen if all the outside waves came in here. Another wave splashed in, bigger this time. But the water ran out through the little drain holes in the cockpit floor. Whoever had put those holes in the boat had had a good idea. And Pop said our boat was built well. They'd be all right. He headed for the twirler log in its wooden box.

"Why do we need this?" he yelled.

"Somewhere out in that rain, Jim, is a bell buoy. I'm steering for it. But the wind might blow me to one side or the other. I need to know how fast I'm going, so I know when to start to look for it."

Hanging on, Jim scrambled down to the lee side. It was frightening here so close to the water. How loud it was. He opened the box quickly and handed the twirler to Dad. Dad threw it over the stern. The line ran out quickly and Jim looked at the gauge in the box.

"Now, Jim."

"Five and a half," he shouted. Boy it was important to read. Suppose he hadn't known.

"Good," said Pop. "We're really making time."

Right on the nose, forty minutes later, Dent saw the bell. It was about twenty yards to port. Only twenty yards off in four and a half miles, he exulted.

"There's the bell, right on the nail, Jim," he yelled.

Jim raised himself into the rain and looked. There it was; a bell buoy coming at them. Through all the waves and rain they'd been pointed in the right direction. His father could really sail.

Finding the bell warmed Dent. The wind was rising, he felt sure, the note in the rigging was higher. The spray was no longer being blown off the tops of the waves; but was being flattened against the sea in long streaks. He'd forgotten what force of wind that meant. More serious, the wind was changing direction: backing to north. He had to keep hauling in the sail to hold course. If the wind kept shifting to northwest or north, they would have to tack into it. The trip would become infinitely longer, wetter, rougher. To say nothing of his added problem of navigation as he had to zigzag toward Falmouth Harbor against the wind.

Straining, he pulled the tiller toward him; rounded the bell; set the boat on a new course: 305 degrees for the Mid-Channel Whistle. At this speed, by noon they'd be safe in Falmouth.

Now the constant pressure of the wind almost held the lee rail under. A squall hit blind out of the rain. The boat went over dangerously fast. Dent pushed hard at the tiller to bring her head to the wind. Forgot he had the tiller tied. Quickly eased off the line. Shoved. The pressure on the sails eased. The boat righted. He should have put in the second reef. Hell, already he was getting tired, he should have stayed in port.

Should he spin around and run back for Nantucket? No. Better to head for the lee of the Cape. He didn't want to run before such wind. Last night he'd planned what to do if this happened. Even laid out the compass headings for Cross Rip Lightship and Hyannis Harbor. He pulled the chart out from under the cushion. Instantly it was soaked and the wind almost shredded it in his hands. Seventeen degrees; almost due north; even if the wind went northwest, he could make that. When you planned ahead you had it made. Another gust started to bury the lee rail. He smiled at Jim and eased up. The wind was still shifting toward the north. He'd keep on this course as far as Criss Rip Nun, then make his decision: Falmouth or Hyannis.

Ten minutes later he knew he could not reach Cross Rip Nun.

Jim had abandoned the seat and was huddled on the floor of the cockpit, smiling now and then from under his hood to reassure himself. He hoped the boat was all right. He watched Pop strain against the tiller. If he was just a little bigger he could go back there and give Pop a rest. A great wave slammed in the cockpit and broke over him. He couldn't see Pop and started to slide across the cockpit floor. I'm drowning, he thought. Then the wave went away and there was Pop smiling and shaking his head.

"Better get up on the seat and hang on," Pop yelled. Jim did, though it was colder on the seat.

By now the boat was making but little headway through the water. The sails cracked like snapped branches as Dent held the boat into the wind to keep from flooding the cockpit. Every third or fourth wave broke over the windward side, rolled back along the length of the boat, and slammed into the cockpit. The enormous pressure of wind and water began to push Dent down. The slam of the boat against the short, steep seas was teeth-shattering. He felt the back of his hands begin to chill and numb with fright. If the sail shredded the boat's small motor could never drive her through these seas. As the wind shifted toward north it pushed him always leeward toward Hawes and Tuckernuck Reefs, Muskeget Rock, Bass Ledge, Tom's and Shovelfull Shoals, graveyard of ships since the Pilgrims. He had to risk the following seas, spin her and turn back. Then if something horrible happened, they would at least drift aground on Nantucket and break up there with a chance of reaching land. Not founder on the reefs and drown.

But a following sea could put a lot of water in the cockpit. He should get Jim tied in first. He could use the swimming line; tie Jim to a stanchion with that. Jim could get the line out from the lazarette for him. If only the boom didn't catch in a wave and the mast crack as the boat turned.

"Jim, come here!"

Jim stood up against the force of the weather. How small he looked. "Get me the . . ."

The boat slammed down into a wall of ocean. The waters divided an instant, then reformed to hurtle back along the deck. The bulk of the cabin broke their main force; but still they almost dragged Dent's feet from beneath him. Jim slammed up against him.

"Is this a gale, Dad?"

"Yes, Jim." He had to yell to make himself heard. "We have to go back. And I want to tie you to the boat with a life line. Get me the swimming line."

"Okay."

Jim bent down to raise the starboard seat. The sails filled; the boat picked up speed; and slammed into another slope of water. There was a crack and a jarring thud up forward. Dent instinctively left the tiller and lunged to the front of the cockpit to look. The ship lurched sideways, lifted up, then slid fast down, almost throwing him. Again the splintering thud shook the boat. One of the blocks to which the dinghy was lashed had pulled loose from the deck; and the dinghy, now only fastened at one end, was surging and battering at the cabin roof. If the roof stove in they would founder.

He slammed the boat into the wind.

"Jim! Try and keep her in the wind." In the impossible situation issue the impossible order.

He climbed forward against the force of water to cut the dinghy loose. Quick, he ordered himself, before the boat gets away from Jim. And for God's sake don't get your arm mashed beneath the dinghy. He clawed for his knife beneath his rainsuit; grabbed it; and began to slash at the lines that held the dinghy. Another wave hit. He ducked and grabbed for the cabin top. The wave passed. He came up gasping and looked back. Jim was doing great. He inched forward and began to work on the last two ropes.

The boat heeled way over. Into the wind, Jim, his body yelled, into the wind. He felt her start to come up. Saw Jim's small body strain the tiller. A harder puff started the boat over again. The stern of the dinghy began to slide leeward and its bow leaped round at him. He jerked back out of the way. A new wave catching the boat far on its side rolled along the length of her. The water tore at Dent. He grabbed a stanchion and hung on as the wave tumbled him about like clothes in a dryer. The water swept aft. That boat staggered upright. He slashed the last of the dinghy tie-downs; freed the dinghy; looked aft.

No Jim.

A great slash of steel ripped his stomach open and disembowelled him.

He saw a small flash of orange life jacket astern in the water. Another wave swept the boat; and Dent floundered and plunged with it back into the cockpit. He knew the drill. Jibe the boat around; get downwind of the overboard man; pick him up. They'd played it as a game. But today, in this sea, with this wind, the dinghy loose on deck, the boat would never stand the jibe; never be able to beat back toward Jim against the sea.

The boat and Jim were drifting in the same direction, Jim getting closer. Dent let out the main sheet. The freed sail cracked back and forth like an exploding tank. He grabbed the swimming rope, threw a bowline round the stanchion, a half hitch around himself; and jumped into the sea.

As the boat had heeled on its side, down, down, down, Jim had been pushing, body and arms, against the tiller. He felt his feet begin to slip from beneath him. He stopped pushing and just hung on. Then the water hit. He had always thought the inside of water would be dark; but this was white and singing. The water grabbed him. He gripped the tiller. The water was bigger than he and stronger. It held him and twisted. He opened his mouth in terror to scream: "Pop," and the water rushed in. Now the water did turn black. He tried to break it apart but it got darker. Then the thin line of light that divided him from the dark faded. The eternal wolf night came.

Dent's first feeling on hitting the water was relief. The sea caressed him and was warm and peaceful after the cold madness of the boat. He could rest now. Then as the water came into his rainsuit and the spray choked him, came panic. Would his life jacket support him? It did. He began to kick and claw through the sea upwind to where Jim should be. The rainsuit and wet clothes flapped around, exhausting him.

He battered his way upwind, unable to see more than a few feet through the spray. No Jim. He looked for the boat to get his bearings. She seemed already an eternity away. Not a boat; merely an alien shape on the sea. He'd be at the end of his rope soon.

"Jim!" he yelled. "Jim!" The wind drove his voice back inside his throat. With luck he'd see Jim on a wave. Without luck he wouldn't.

The orange of Jim was almost beside him. I can get there; I'm going to win, he exulted. The waves shoved him back. Where was Jim? Don't look. Swim. Swim. He grabbed his son.

"Jim! Jim!" Oh God, he can't be drowned. Not yet. Not yet. There hasn't been time.

With one hand holding Jim, he could not drag himself back to the ship. The ship seemed to be drifting downwind faster now. The line jerked and tugged at him. He tried to work his arm through the front of Jim's life jacket so he could pull with both hands. But Jim's life jacket was too tight.

His elation had gone. He trembled now with cold, despair, exhaustion. He must tie the rope to Jim. Work his way back to the ship with two hands. Then pull Jim in. The tossing ship, jerking at the rope around his waist kept pulling them both under. Float with your mouth above water, Jim, damn it. Help yourself.

He grabbed the cords of Jim's life jacket between his teeth; and with buckling, rubber fingers worked at the jammed half hitch around his waist. He realized he was moving frighteningly slowly. He got the rope undone from himself; and had an instant of fear that it would be torn from his grasp. Struggling, he worked the rope around Jim and secured it with two half hitches. Gasping, he turned his head over his shoulder out of the wind to breathe. The sheet of spray blown along the top of the water was almost as solid as the ocean itself. If he had trouble breathing, how could Jim breathe? He dragged himself like a mass of sodden seaweed back to the ship.

He could not get back on board. The waves would bring him and the boat together at terrifying speed, threatening to crack him open against the hull. Twice he got a hand on one of the stanchions only to be battered against the hull and wrenched away. Once the hull descended on him, smashing his shoulder and forcing him under. He thought for a terrifying instant he had lost the rope. Why hadn't he been born stronger? He was weak; too weak to save his son. He tried to relax against the rope and gather strength; but merely to hold on was an effort.

A wave lifted him above and alongside the ship for an instant. He let go the rope; grabbed a stanchion with both hands; and, convulsing like a beached fish, flung himself inboard. The next wave tore at him as the boat lurched away. But his grip held and one flabby leg was inside the boat. He wrenched the rest of himself over the side. He lay on deck now, gasping, holding on.

I've won, he thought. I've won. His breath came in great heaving tears like an exhausted miler's. "I'm coming, Jim," he choked.

He lurched to the stern of the boat. Bits of shredded sail were all about the cockpit. The boom had fallen to the deck, fortunately pinning both the loose dinghy and itself to the boat in a snarl of torn sail, life lines and sheets and halyards. Otherwise it would have become a huge battering ram to tear the hull apart.

Braced against the weaving sides of the cockpit he grabbed the bitter end of Jim's line and hauled. He gasped at the dead way Jim lay in the water. Drowned people lay that way. Still there should be time. He'd practiced artificial respiration since he was a little bigger than Jim in camp. He looked over his left shoulder to judge an interval between waves; picked his time; braced his body against the ship's side; and dragged the water-soaked limpness of his son on board.

Waves and rain had filled the cockpit with water. The boat slipped and heaved. He would have to go below to work on Jim. He wrenched and tugged at the cabin door, jammed shut by the fallen boom. He could not put Jim down for fear a wave would slam him against the cockpit side; break something. The door gave as a wave hit. Dent tripped backward, went under the water, slammed his head. He blacked out for an instant, falling on the shoulder that had been smashed by the ship's side, and pain shot through him. Simple actions were almost impossible. He rested his weight on the cabin edge to lower his son down the ladder. The boat pitched; the door swung closed on his hand, mashing his fingers.

He got Jim below, bouncing him cruelly, but speed was all-important. He cut the line and life jacket off his son. Slammed closed the cabin door. He scarcely noticed the mess about him; cans had burst out of their drawers and rolled on the floor, along with broken Coke bottles, spilled sugar, a soggy gum of pancake flour. Already there was too much water on the cabin floor to rest Jim there. Lurching, his right arm almost useless, he raised his son onto the starboard bunk. Then as best he could he perched himself astride him and began the ritual of artificial respiration.

Arms rigid in front of him he pressed down against Jim's back. Raised himself up. Down he pressed; up he raised; again and again and again. "In goes the good air," he said as he raised up. "Out goes the bad," as he pressed down. The words providing the rhythm to which he must move to restore life.

He had to continually readjust himself on the bunk as the ship tossed him about. His hopes shrank to a dull, cold whisper: "Jim. Jim. Jim." A life of tamped tears splurged from him. He shook so he could hardly continue pumping.

"In goes the good air. Out comes the bad."

He had killed his son. Somewhere in that sea and turned-to-water air Jim's lungs had failed for too long.

"In goes the good air. Out comes the bad." He pressed down and raised up. The book said never give up. Never. I will never make the same mistake again. Never.

"In goes the good air. Out comes the bad."

Dent's body continued to pump up and down reflexively, a phonograph needle stuck in a groove. And the ship, unguided, pitched and fell in the waves.

Then Dent gave out. A great choking seized him; he shook so violently he could hardly breathe, let alone pump on Jim. Small half cries dragged from his throat. Through his numb pain he could no longer see Jim at the ends of his hands.

"Jim, Jim, why have you died? It's me. Live. Damn you, live. —Live. Live." He collapsed over the body of his son and rolled to the cabin floor.

He was drowning in an ocean of blackness. He tried to fight his way up, up through the nightmare waters, but they pressed him back. Above the pit in which he was drowning, gray forms peered. He knew he should not shout to them or water would flood into him. He was choking now. Gasping, he slipped out of dream to the nightmare of reality. There was no light. He was lying, doubled up, in sloshing water. Outside was the constant shriek of wind and pounding of sea. I can't be here. He felt on the starboard berth for Jim's body. There was no body. Hope flared like a struck match. His son would be sitting up. "Jim, Jim," he called weakly, foolishly feeling against the back of the bunk. Nothing.

On his knees, each breath an ache—he must have smashed a rib—he groped with his good arm through the wet dark of the cabin floor. The boat tossed and threw him about the small space. In his pain he kept blacking out. He told himself.

"I will not find him. I will not find him. I will not."

He kept groping. The slimy cabin was alive. Alive. His arm hit a dead wet weight. He felt about it in the dark.

"Jim. Jim." Now there was no place to hide. He tried to shove the soggy body of his son onto the bunk. In the pitching dark the limp weight kept slipping from him. He kept worrying that he'd hurt Jim, trying to raise him, forgetting he was dead. Finally he got the body on the bunk and drew himself up beside it. He passed out again, alive because he was not cold enough or battered enough to die.

The ship slammed and pounded in the gale. Stripped of the driving power of her sail she hove to under the pressure of the wind and force of water against her hull. Other sleeker ships might have turned stern to, heeled over, turned turtle, broached sideways. She rode bow a quarter into the sea, slowly making way backward toward the shoals. The seas broke over her but did not swamp her, the waves pounded her but did not start her. Well crafted, she held.

The very force of the gale helped her, piling waves and water on top of reefs that would have been exposed and fatal in a lesser storm. Twice as Dent lay unconscious her keel grated against the sand of Bass Ledge. Each time the seas lifted her off again before her ribs cracked. Then she was beyond the reefs, out of Nantucket Sound, in the open Atlantic, gale-tossed and drifting.

Once in the ocean her motion and rhythm began to change profoundly. The larger and more powerful, but less steep and numerous, waves of the ocean produced long intervals of violent downward rush with a heavy check and twist at the end that seemed about to submarine the whole boat. This downward slide was followed by a corklike upward bob, then a brief period of almost calm climbing, before the boat bobsledded down the next wave.

Hours later, Dent, mostly unconscious and with his brief moments of wakefulness distorted by pain, recognized the change, realized they were in the Atlantic.

He was tangled with something. Jim. He should tell Jim what had happened. He looked at his son in the gloom beside him. His limbs were twisted at angles that the tension of life would not permit muscle and sinew to assume. He raised himself over the body and looked at Jim's face. His Jim, grin gone out, color turned to clay-dust white.

He grabbed the soggy body to him and rocked it back and forth, sobbing, until he finally collapsed on the bunk.

When a Congressman is missing that's news. And when the missing Congressman is already slightly famous, comes from New York City, is married to a beautiful woman whose father owns a newspaper chain, that's big news. And when he had an eight-year-old son with him, that's big news plus human interest, which is banner-head stuff. And when banner-head news breaks, from a trapped dog, to a star's divorce, to an astronaut's triumph, America snaps to attention.

As the winds increased to full gale the friends whom Dent and Jim had visited in Nantucket became worried. They telephoned the Falmouth boatyard. When Dent had not shown up there by nightfall, they called Sarah and the Coast Guard. Sarah called her father. The story broke.

The Navy admiral in charge of the Eastern Sea Frontier, the Coast Guard admiral in charge of Air Sea Rescue, and the Air Force general in charge of the Eastern Air Defense Command all realized that to find the Congressman and his boy, dead or alive, would bring kudos to their services and probably a promotion for themselves. Plans were made to converge ships and planes on Nantucket Sound and its surrounding reefs, and even the ocean beyond. But they remained largely plans. Through the next day and night and into the second day the gale held command.

In Washington, Colonel Catenberry read the news stories and instantly saw himself in them. To find Dent was just the break he needed. With Congress in recess, there was little activity in his section. He picked up the phone and called his boss, General Batenberg, Vice Chief of the Air Staff.

General Batenberg was telling dirty jokes to a WAF major. She was a hot number, his mistress, whom he'd illegally promoted up from corporal. His enemies knew he'd done this and had let him know they knew. So he was in a painful position of being a powerful man without power, hung by his own balls.

"General, you seen them stories about the missing Congressman?" asked Catenberry over the phone. "George Dent, the one that's shipwrecked with his son?"

"Yeah, Frank, I have."

"I thought you should know the Navy's already sayin' they're the ones going to find him; because they're the only ones know how to operate over water."

"Annapolis bastards. I'd like to punch them in the teeth."

His simple strategy having put his boss in the proper frame of mind, Catenberry continued.

"I was thinking, General, with your permission, maybe I could go up there and jazz our boys up some."

"Okay, Frank, go up there and smear the Navy's face in this one."

Two hours and forty-seven minutes later, whining in through the gale-driven rains, ceiling one hundred feet, visibility two tenths of a mile, Catenberry slapped his T-33 jet trainer onto the runway of Otis Air Force Base at Cape Cod. No plane had landed or taken off from the base in three days. Catenberry looked contemptuously at the Base's interceptors parked on the runway waiting better weather to begin their search. The interceptor boys always were chicken, he thought.

He strode into the briefing room. He was not the senior officer present, there were a major general and two brigadiers. But he was from Washington, he spoke for the Vice Chief, and he had flown in while they had come in by car; they deferred.

The Base weather and intelligence officers gave Catenberry a briefing on where Dent's boat might be found. The evidence indicated it had probably broken up on the reefs between Martha's Vineyard and Nantucket. However, the Coast Guard had had a cutter along the inner edge of the reefs and one of their planes had made two passes over them and seen nothing.

"There's always a chance," the briefing officer concluded, "that the boat might have passed safely over the reefs and be drifting out in the open ocean." Yeah, it might have, thought Catenberry. But the place to begin to look is the reefs; play the percentages. Another officer handed him a description of the boat.

Catenberry stood up. He was about to ask for volunteers to search the reefs with him when the phone rang. A captain picked it up.

"It's some airline pilot. Says he's got a theory where Dent may be."

"I can't be bothered with any civilian now," snapped the general.

"What's his name and airline?" asked Catenberry, more to establish his presence in the room than from any desire to learn.

"McTurk," said the captain.

"McTurk!" Catenberry's bark snapped all eyes on him. "Christ, don't you know anything but how to finger your cock?" He moved decisively toward the phone. "If that's Arthur McTurk, he practically taught Lindbergh how to fly." He grabbed the phone. "Arthur McTurk?"

"Yes." Turkey answered over the line.

"This is Frank Catenberry. We met at the Harmon Trophy a couple of years ago."

"I remember."

"I just flew in from Washington to lead the search. They've been sitting on their ass up here. But we're movin' now. What's your theory?"

Briefly McTurk explained that he was a friend of Dent. That he had fished the waters a lot and knew the area. He had called the boat's owner and learned she was of shallow draft and would heave to under hull conditions. That led him to believe that the boat had cleared the reefs intact and was now drifting in the open ocean. The place to search was the ocean to the southeast. "And search that area first," added McTurk, "because if that's where the boat is, Dent and his boy could still be alive."

Catenberry's gut alarm went off. Not just find a corpse but rescue a living guy. Be a general in a month, maybe even a ceremony at the White House.

"Goddamn, Arthur, that's the best theory we've heard. We'll search the hell out of that area." He replaced the phone and turned to the officers in the room.

"Okay. We're going to find this Congressman and find him alive. Who's coming with me?"

Three fliers stepped forward. Catenberry looked at them and swore. Only three volunteers out of more than thirty men. What was his Air Force coming to?

"You guys must shit blind when some girl touches your prick," he hurled at the rest and pivoted from the room.

Out over the ocean between the heavy layer of cloud—Catenberry could not see his wing tips as he flew—and the whipped fists of water above the wave tops, was some one hundred and fifty feet of rain-filled open space. Into this tube, at two hundred miles per hour, Catenberry inserted his aircraft. He came down through the blackness from twenty thousand feet toward the opening that might or might not be there with no change of expression or pulse rate. He knew his aircraft, the procedure, the chances. He eased the throttle, mushing down slower now, eyes split between the altimeter and the gray box around him. The bottom of the box opened beneath him, then closed immediately as solid ocean. He had threaded the needle. He radioed the other three pilots he was down. Two of them made it behind him, though it took one of them two sweat-filled tries.

(The third never made it. Alone in his blind box on his second try down he suddenly felt the ocean dead ahead. His plane seemed to twist and roll in the air. Fear grabbed him. He shot his plane up, full power, to finally reach sunshine and sight. On his radio he mumbled something about altimeter failure. Catenberry's "Chicken-shit, pansy," crackled back in his earphones from somewhere in the deathly gray miles below. The pilot headed back toward Otis. There the ceiling was still only 100 feet and on his second pass at the field his once broken nerve failed again. He fled west to finally find a clear field in southern Ohio. That night he developed a blinding headache. Two days later when he saw his wife—he had to come back by commercial airliner; his headache would not let him fly—he found he was finished in other ways.)

Spitted above the spray, Catenberry jetted through the gale, cutting a thin two-mile-wide rectangle of vision, two hundred miles long. At the end of each two hundred miles he did a perfect hundred-and-eighty-degree turn and rethreaded himself in the tube two miles further south to search again. If Dent was there, he'd find him. He saw two destroyers (also looking for Dent), two passenger liners, and three freighters, but no small sailboat. He returned to base three times, refueled, resumed his search. By dark he had not spotted Dent. But no one else had either. For tomorrow the weather was forecast to improve: the ceiling lifting to perhaps five hundred feet, the visibility to four miles.

Catenberry had a steak and a couple of drinks at the Officers' Club; persuaded the wife of one of the pilots to go to bed with him; took her to his quarters; fucked her twice; got her back to the club and her husband; and went to sleep. At 4:30 a.m. he was in his single-seater jet, feeling great. At dawn he was descending through the gray again to cut his rectangles once more in the compressed space between cloud and sea.

At 10:57 a.m. the bulletin went out over the AP wire that Congressman Dent's boat had been sighted by Colonel Franklin P. Catenberry of the Air Staff, war hero and personal friend of the Congressman. He was guiding the Navy to the scene. Then followed a brief biography of the colonel with a picture on the photo wire. Catenberry had given the biography and picture to the Base Public Relations Officer, to use if he found Dent.

Some four hours later Chief Bo's'n's Mate Sorley, of the destroyer Poseidon, managed to leap aboard the battered hulk of the sailboat. Prying open the cabin door, he found the unconscious Dent twined about the stiffened body of his son.

eleven

"This will make him Senator."

"Sam!"

Sam Kleinman and Jean Aaron sat in Dent's New York office, cutting and filing newspaper clippings. Page after page of pictures: Dent carried down the destroyer gangplank on a stretcher, the wreck from the air, Dent in the hospital, the sewn canvas bag containing Jim beside a smiling insert of Jim alive.

"Leaps overboard. Battles gale for son," Sam quoted. "He can't lose."

"You cold bastard."

"I burn with human compassion; but I know the lousy voters of this state. Look at this, in the Buffalo *Morning Post,* the heart of enemy territory: two front-page pictures, Jim, and Dent in uniform gettin' decorated; and inside on the jump another picture of him floating through the air, a pole-vaulter yet. Did you know about that, Jean?"

"Yes."

"I tell you, I've lived with him night and day for almost five years and I know less about him than some guys I've met in a bar for five minutes. Hah, the Rochester *Times,* hopes this won't take the brightest young light in the state out of politics. Does Ambassador Kleinman sound better to you than Chief Justice Kleinman? —How close was he to the boy, Jean?"

"Close, very close." She had no knowledge of this; but her George Dent was perfect in all things and his child part hers, a portion of the late-night fantasies she wove to knit them both together.

"He didn't even carry pictures of his wife and children in his wallet till I told him he had to. You never know with the goyim."

"They were very close," Jean repeated.

"They could be too close."

"Sarah will be a great comfort to him," said Jean. "They'll have another son soon."

"Yeah," said Sam, numb at the thought of what would happen inside him if the phone rang with the news that Sam Junior was dead.

For Dent the funeral ceremony in a Park Avenue church was public torture. Ribs taped, left shoulder imprisoned in plaster, he sat in the front row feeling the eyes of friends and political acquaintances upon his back judging, condemning, boring in to try and steal from him a grief and agony which were all he had left. Afterward there was a reception at which he smiled and shook hands. "You have to have a reception, Daddy," Sarah had said. "People want to pay their respects to my son." Matchelder, Calahan, district leaders, even briefly the Mayor and Governor, milled through a beflowered room. He was left a stranger at the funeral of his own son.

The burial was private. Dent had been in the small country graveyard only twice before, when he was very little and Grandfather and Grandmother Dent had died within a year of each other. In the family plot the oldest stone beneath the oaks read: "Hezekiah Dent, 1640–1692. Man of God."

I can't be standing here for Jim, he thought over and over. No one had told the gravediggers they were opening the ground to receive a child's coffin. Jim's little box looked ridiculous and lost in the huge hole. When, at Jim's age, he'd watched his grandfather buried, he'd thought the tombstones looked like giants' toes growing out of the ground.

Inside his right pocket his hand clutched the small blue teddy bear, "Small Bear," that Jim had taken on the boat so "Bear could share the trip." Suddenly he jerked his hand from his pocket and flung the small bear into the open grave.

"Daddy," blurted Sarah.

"Gracious," gulped his mother.

"I shall go to him, but he shall not return to me," said the minister.

"James F. Dent. 1951–1959. Having been made perfect in a short time" said the stone.

He turned and, taking Sarah by the arm, started through the lovely fall afternoon toward the rented car. Sarah took Jane by the hand. A chauffeur closed the door. The three of them were alone.

Sarah had accused him of unforgivable stupidity in setting sail from Nantucket with such a wind. Dent, having checked with the weather bureau over the unforecast arrival of the gale, could defend himself against her charge. Far from being stupid he had trusted his careful preparations above his instinct.

The charge he leveled against himself was far more serious. Those seas had been too big to risk with a small boy and he had kept on because it was easier. He didn't want to be late. He didn't want to make Sarah mad. He was to make a speech that might help his Senate chances. He had killed his son for his ease, repeating his war pattern—killed Jim as he had killed Costa.

He had neither forgotten nor forgiven himself for that past decision. He remembered his body had hurt then as it hurt now. He sat, crumpled against the side of his tank turret, coughing too hard to sleep. Beside him his gunner, McQuade, and his loader were both out cold. He felt hot and burning and his teeth chattered with fever. He eased the hatch of his tank up a bit and snow hit him on the face. How many of his tanks would start tomorrow? Christ, if only his musette bag hadn't burned with his grippe pills in it. If he went to the doctor for pills, Doc, who was new, would probably order him to the rear.

He coughed again, his head exploding into white streaks of pain.

From the direction of his second platoon a machine gun fired, its sound muffled by snow and wind. The gun shot off a few bursts, then stopped. He waited in the dark a few seconds to see if the field phone slung inside his tank would ring. It didn't. He eased his forehead against the turret steel to cool the ache. That worked for a few seconds, then he began to shiver again and pain slammed back. He wrapped his scarf around his head and slumped into the small space between radio and grenade racks, beaten and limp like an old wino.

Who should he make his headquarters platoon sergeant? He'd jabbed at that problem all yesterday, fighting the answer he'd known he must make ever since he'd learned his old sergeant had been badly injured when his truck had skidded off an icy road.

The uninitiated American, plucked from his breakfast table and placed in Dent's headquarters platoon, would give himself less than twenty-four hours to live, as he quivered through the first day. Actually, headquarters platoon was a haven. Unless some chance shell fell on the man, or the enemy broke through, or he took a wrong turn and got ambushed, headquarters platoon sergeant was going to live out the war. Which of his sergeants most deserved to live? Obviously Sergeants Vorlock and Costa. However, Vorlock, being senior, was in for a battlefield commission. That left Costa, but Costa was one of the few head-raisers he had remaining.

Dent judged the worth of his tank commanders by a standard as harsh and implacable as an Old Testament Prophet's—though he allowed any man some bad days; he had them himself; he was measured against the same rule. —When the fire fight began, all commanders ducked for an instant into the safety of their turrets. Then some yanked their hatches closed and watched the battle through periscopes. They were useless. Others brought their heads slowly up and began to fight. The speed with which the head rose measured the man.

Dent, bringing his own head back up after his reflexive jerk into safety, eyes tight closed, shoulders hunched, would find up with him certain others, his head-raisers, vulnerable human shapes disfiguring the clean angles of the steel tank turrets. Time after time he saw the same heads: men he relied on, who took risks without order.

He remembered Costa one time at Salzdorf in the Siegfried Line. Dent, just promoted to Company Commander, had been jogging through the town's rubble trying to find the best place to position the two tanks left in his first platoon. Christ! there was a lot of stuff coming in that day. Lieutenant Wells, the Infantry Company Commander, was standing on a stone wall peering into his field glasses. Wells takes a lot of chances for an old soldier, thought Dent.

"Dent. Lieutenant Dent." Dent heard the crack in Wells's voice and recognized a soldier pushed beyond all limits. "I can't reach my second platoon."

Dent could see Wells's radio operator shifting from place to place behind the wall, talking into his microphone, listening, shaking his head. Dent clambered over the cold stones, he was not yet wearing gloves, and climbed up beside Wells.

He didn't need glasses. His company had been ordered back and his old second platoon, Costa's, also down to two tanks from five, was pulling out of the orchard they had held all day, swiveling backass toward town. No infantry ran alongside them or rode on their hulls.

Shit, thought Dent, but that Wells runs a good company. He tells his doughs to go out and stay. They don't get no order to retreat. So they stay, even when the tanks pull out. They'll get murdered.

"I'll go get 'em," he said.

He jumped off the wall, scuttled over the rubble to his tank, clambered up on the front, yelled directions at his driver, then heaved himself into the turret. The tank bucked forward with its peculiar recoil and snap as he settled inside. The field between town and woods was broken by lines of cabbages, drainage ditches, mine craters, shell holes, and the ruts of two days' tank battle. His tank heaved and lurched. This was not his tank, that had been shot from beneath him yesterday; but already it was home. Crouched on his seat, he braced himself against the turret wall, plugged in his earphones. McQuade leaned toward him. Dent pointed at the armor-piercing ammunition. Bobbing and weaving like two shadow boxers in their isolation of slam and noise, the two looked at each other, then turned back to the great truths in their lives. McQuade to his ready rounds, solenoids, sight-picture, trigger switch. Dent to his map and radio.

As he pressed his mike switch to talk, his own earphones erupted.

"Charlie six, Charlie two-seven, over," Costa called him.

"Charlie six," he answered.

"Charlie two-seven. Should our little friends come home with us? Over."

"Charlie six. They should. Over."

"Charlie two-seven. Will get them. Over."

"Charlie six. Roger. Out."

Unbidden, Costa had started back. Dent stopped his tank and jackknifed out of the turret to watch him. Goddamn, he thought, this war is hotting up. Strings of gray and black beads hung above the orchard. Costa was out of his tank running toward the woods in the bent, ground-hugging crouch of a man under fire. A line of gray puffs marched toward Dent's tank. Mortars.

"Driver, move right."

Here came the doughs. They swung out of the woods and disappeared into a ditch. Two guys being carried and some walking wounded. "Hurry up, Costa," Dent yelled from inside, "get 'em on your tank and hurry up." —He ordered McQuade to fire four rounds at the next town. The tank shook, the smell of powder floated round him. He shook free of the noise. The fire wouldn't do any good, but it would give the doughs the feeling the tanks were with them. Here came Costa now, leading two more doughs. Roll it, Costa! Roll it!

He ordered his driver to head back into town.

"I hear Costa went back and picked up some doughs," said Colonel Boyden, his battalion commander. They were in the root cellar of a crumbled farm, a gasoline lamp hissing from the ceiling. Outside came the crack of sporadic shelling.

"Yes, sir."

"The infantry want to give him something."

"If they don't, we should."

"They'll do it. I want to give their man Vance a Silver Star."

"That the big red-headed sergeant carries a tommy gun?" Lieutenant Doyle asked through a mouthful of beans.

"Yes."

"He moves," said Doyle, who had had three tanks shot from beneath him that day.

"With soldiers like them," said Boyden, itching the top of his scalp with both hands as he always did when tired, "we can't lose."

They lost Vance and Doyle the next day.

And you and Costa are still alive, Dent thought. He's done enough. His luck can't last.

But he couldn't give Costa the headquarters platoon; not now. After he was out of this Ardennes battle he'd get him something in the rear someplace. But he'd lost so many men his company didn't move the way it used to. He had to keep the few head-raisers he had left. Between coughs Dent felt his headache pulsing, deterring real sleep.

Sergeant Fellows of third platoon, not much of a fighter, got headquarters platoon and the gift of life. Costa burned (alive?) at Hamgenbruch, while Dent had watched.

"Charlie six, Cobra six, what's that smoke? Over," Boyden asked him on the radio.

"Charlie six. That smoke is Costa."

In that grave was Jim.

Dent had been brought up to believe, and in fact did believe, that hard work was the great cure for everything, excepting perhaps double hernia. He knew he should throw himself into politics; invitations to speak flooded on him, Matchelder asked to introduce him to a few moneyed friends; the association of upstate Mayors wanted to be associated with his cities bill; Calahan made a special trip to Washington to pledge his loyalty. The phones rang, the letters came, the people called. Jim had gained him a clear shot at the Senate. All he had to do was hustle. Instead he schemed and plotted to get two hours each day alone in his shed to paint.

From 8:30 to 10:30 in the morning, after he had taken Jane to school, but before he had to go to the Hill, he painted. He knew he was doing what he had promised himself he would never do again, taking time out from his life to paint; yet the moments in the shed were the only ones that eased him. At least here he could think uninterruptedly about Jim, Dee, the war, the aircrash, the Senate, Sarah, Congress. Elsewhere he had to turn himself on and off for others.

What he wanted to do was paint Jim, get him down "warts and all," a boy who caught colds, got poison ivy, had temper tantrums; not some dream out of an old *Saturday Evening Post* cover. But each portrait he started began to turn into an ideal boy he could hardly recognize as his son.

So he abandoned the idea of Jim's portrait and began a series of paintings that were extensions of the caricatures he'd been doing over the past years, vicious compositions of venal Senators trading the public interest with vacant faces. One of the paintings of two Senators talking politics with eyes like Nevada pit bosses pleased him so he repeated the theme three times, turning the Senate chamber into a neon honkeytonk, with slot machines for desks, crap tables beneath the flag, and groups of Senators either shilling or being taken, gambling their birthright for a mess of verbiage. The paintings were in tempera, hard and bright.

He kept telling himself it was wrong to spend so much time painting; but he found it so hard to do his political work. Instead of just yelling to his secretaries as he used to that he wanted to call so-and-so, and so-and-so, and so-and-so, he had to laboriously make a list, hand the list to one of his secretaries, and get her to prod him to make the calls. Often when he was free to take a call, he'd find himself refusing to take it; he just didn't have the energy. Dictating letters made his face itch. He didn't want to see anyone except a few old friends such as Wup-'em and Red.

Was he, he asked himself, developing an "Uncle Schuyler" complex, something he used to fear right after the war? Uncle Schuyler, his father's brother, had had a profound effect on Dent's life. Five years younger than his father, Schuyler Dent had abandoned a successful law practice to enter the ministry. Only he never quite entered. He took courses, he was always taking courses. He left his wife and children and met outstanding men of faith who liked him and spent months with him in discourse and prayer to bring him to ordination. But at the last moment Schuyler always developed doubts that God could possibly have summoned as His representative on earth such a miserable sinner as himself. Terrified at not being able to perform God's mission properly, Uncle Schuyler would flee: sometimes into alcohol, sometimes to Paris, sometimes into a little room to fast for his sins to the point of serious illness.

Whatever the form of his flight, Dent's father would remark to the family breakfast table: "Schuyler has done it again." They would all sigh, knowing Father would be often absent and irritable as he tried to track down his younger brother; a process that took time, for in his bouts of abject unworthiness Uncle Schuyler could be elusive.

At moments during the search when he was home, Dent's father would point out to his wife, Dent, and Dent's sister the hideous fate of those who abandoned work.

"And work is not easy to find in these days."

That stuck with four-year-old George Dent. He could see work, a small dark bag that gave out little puffs of white when you poked it, lying lost by the side of the road in the bushes—perhaps in the bramble-bushes along the road in front of their house—while men went about with sticks poking for it. Clearly to be a good work-finder was an important thing to be when he grew up. No one would use that tone about him that came into his mother's voice when she talked of Uncle Schuyler: "And he used to be such a good lawyer."

But how could you tell a silly, grown-up work-loser from a good work-finder? Uncle Schuyler, when he came to visit, looked just like any other grownup, indeed better than most. He not only was always willing to play ball but had a good throw. He was excellent at finding worms. He would even go out while it was raining to the manure pile and dig for them. He said he didn't mind the manure smell. "It's the odor of God at work, making things grow." Dent hadn't been so certain about that; but Uncle Schuyler could sure find worms—though he wasn't so hot at putting them on the hook, always pricking himself. But above all Uncle Schuyler deviated from the normal grownup pattern in that instead of making Dent small and himself big, he seemed to be trying to make them both the same size.

Dent felt closer to his uncle than to his father. Yet this man was a work-loser who sometimes had to be "put away," just as he, Dent, was sometimes locked in a closet by his mother when he'd been bad. And finally there was Uncle Schuyler's "sorry end." Concerned over both politics and religion, Schuyler had come to believe that Adolph Hitler was really the archangel Lucifer returned to earth to punish mankind for its sins. He walked around in burlap bags with ashes on his head to show he was ready to accept God's judgment any time Hitler got ready to mete it out. He had to be "put away" for good. Inside the asylum he went on a prolonged fast and died while Dent was at Officer Candidate School at Fort Knox.

"And he was such a fine lawyer," said Mother.

"He should never have left work," said Father.

"It was the Depression, I think," said Mother.

"No," said Father, closing the door on his brother, the work-loser, forever. "It was himself."

To help lose his dread of Uncle Schuyler's disease, Dent decided to get the names of several New York galleries, write them; and see if they would send someone down to look at his pictures. That way he could get some objective evaluation of the worth of the time he spent painting. He wrote several of his campaign contributors who were in the art world for names of galleries, omitting Wollenberg because he didn't want to reveal himself so early to such a close friend. He wished he could consult Dee; but he was afraid of opening even the briefest contact with her.

To have more work to show the galleries he began spending almost four hours a day in his studio, for the first time missing votes on the floor. After all he was so strong politically now he didn't have to worry about a perfect attendance record. He pushed hard on his satiric paintings of Congress; which he judged the most salable part of his work. His colleagues might not like them, but that was their lookout.

He started a series of five paintings called *A Bill's Passage,* showing the hazards of getting a bill through Congress. He had a great time with the final canvas, where crowds of voters held their noses while the bill was ushered onto a Roman-type balcony before them by the Leaders of both Houses. —Jim, he felt, would have laughed at the picture.

He knew these satiric canvases were not "art," the pictures that jumped off the walls and hit you. He could, he told himself, try pictures like that later, if these succeeded. Right now it was important to see if he could paint at all, produce anything the public would accept. Otherwise, he should take himself in hand and drive for the Senate.

One of the galleries he wrote was politely not interested, another suggested he bring or ship some canvases to New York for evaluation. Two others were willing to make appointments to see his pictures in Washington. He checked Sarah's calendar to find when she'd be out and made dates for both of them.

The first gallery sent a smooth, slender man who was obviously impressed with Dent's work. Dent could see his fixed smile relax into honest appreciation as he looked around Dent's studio.

"Yes, Mr. Congressman, I think this is going to make us some money. Quite a bit of money. You have a great future as a Congressman and artist."

"Thank you."

The man also advised Dent to paint small.

"Just remember, Mr. Congressman, it's pictures that sell, and two small paintings sell for more than twice as much as one medium picture and take a lot less than half the time to do. What we want is an early exhibition, while you have name value. The more canvases the better and the small ones come faster. Besides, not to be critical, hahaha, but to be commercially honest, in some of the larger canvases your touch has a tendency to dissipate."

The next gallery sent two representatives, a jovial, plump fag called James Jamers, who continually wrung his hands; and a statuesque blonde called Kate. Thank God he'd made certain Sarah was out committeeing, and he didn't have to explain this Juno in his shed.

Jamers and the blonde were a professional combination, the man, full of sincerity and charm, talked about Art, and admired Dent's talent and brushwork which, he said, reminded him of Eakins. The blonde opened a notebook and talked money.

On the nine pictures he had ready, she put prices ranging from four hundred and fifty to two thousand dollars. To Dent she seemed to be doing it mostly by whimsy; though she gave off an air of confidence.

"Why," he asked, "is the third of the *Bill's Passage* paintings two hundred dollars more expensive than the rest?"

"We sell a great many pictures, Mr. Congressman, and we learn to appreciate what the public will pay."

"I guess I don't know much about the pricing of paintings."

"You already know a great deal more than most artists," said Kate with a man-melting smile. "You know enough to let us do it for you. And you paint what you can do best. You are going to make us, and yourself, money." She smiled again. Dent smiled back—no point in double-guessing the experts. The whole process was more crass and commercial than he'd visualized; but then he was a stranger in the art world, lacking standards of comparison.

"Do you do abstracts, Mr. Dent?" asked Jamers.

"Not for a long time." In point of fact he didn't like abstracts and didn't paint them.

"Oh, I feel you have a technique and passion most suited to violent abstracts."

Kate was more specific. "There is a certain section of the public, Mr. Dent, now buying abstracts for prestige reasons. You have a name. You will, we hope, be in our gallery. They will buy your name from us, for a reasonable price if it is attached to an abstract. Not if it's on a picture they might find disturbingly real. Supposing you tried some abstracts on, say, *The Violent City.*"

"You have a point. I suppose it would be wisest if I kept the abstracts small."

"You understand art, Mr. Dent. You are going to be very successful."

"Call me George."

"George."

The two left.

He started to be happy, until he remembered Jim and felt miserable.

Still, he reminded himself, he'd only been painting part time for six months and already he had a commitment from a top Madison Avenue gallery, something many painters didn't get in a lifetime. Undoubtedly in part they were doing it because of his name; but what was wrong with that? Cranach had been a mayor, Reubens an ambassador and secret agent, Cellini had got commissions because he was such a good artillery captain. If he had a successful show, several successful shows, Sarah would accept the loss of the Senate after a time; and he certainly would be happier.

Now he had to tell Sarah. He looked at her calendar for the coming week. The best time to hit her with a major decision like this was after lunch. Mornings were bad because he hated to fight over breakfast. After dinner was the absolute worst, because Sarah took the battle to bed, and rose thirsty for blood the next morning, when he, frankly scared of fights that went on for more than a day, was willing to compromise and forget. He needed a lunch, a female business lunch in which Sarah played an important part.

In the coming week Sarah had a lunch on Wednesday, Thursday, and Friday, an embarrassment of riches. Wednesday: the Washington Committee for Better Housing. Thursday: the Education Committee of the League of Women Voters. Friday: the Smith Club of Washington. Which would leave Sarah in the best frame of mind? Not Better Housing, she was just a member of that and she was an officer of the other two. She was vice president of the Smith Club, but she always returned from those lunches full of sociological comparison; who was in which place on the racetrack of life. That left the Education Committee of the League of Women Voters, of which Sarah was secretary. She would return from lunch feeling useful and refreshed. Even better, she had a hairdresser's appointment before lunch.

He laid the groundwork casually, announcing at breakfast that he would be home early on Thursday to work on a speech. He was all set when Sarah came through the front door.

"Hi, Sarah."

"How's your speech coming, Daddy?"

"I'm all through, luckily. How'd your lunch go?"

"Very well."

"Sarah . . ."

"Love-dove, do you know how many children there are in the District of Columbia who never read beyond third-grade level?"

"Around seven per cent."

"How'd you know that?" —Wrong move, he thought. He should have guessed low and let her tell him.

"Heard it someplace."

"It's shocking. Absolutely shocking."

"I agree. . . . Sarah—"

"What are you going to do about it?"

"Me?" He hadn't said anything about painting and already he felt guilty.

"You." Sarah jumped into his pause. "It's something you should be concerned about, love-dove. Even though they don't vote in New York."

"Sarah, there's something I need to talk about." His wife sat down, took off her gloves, crossed her legs, and arranged her skirt in her professional listening attitude.

"Ever since Jim's death," he began, "I've found myself enjoying politics less and less. At the same time, as you know, I've been painting a lot. I wrote several galleries and they've been down to look at my pictures. They liked them. I've signed up with one of them to have a show. What I'm going to do, Sarah, at least for a while, is not run for the Senate, continue in Congress, and paint in my spare time."

"What?" Sarah stiffened.

"You know all my life I've thought about painting as well as Congress. It seems I can do both. —It'll mean more time with you and Jane."

Pause.

"You're joking."

"No."

"Not want the Senate."

"Sarah, what sort of job is it they give you as a consolation prize for killing your son?"

"Daddy! —Jim wanted you to be Senator."

"I doubt that."

"I know what my son wanted. Not a father who quits."

"I'm not quitting."

"You are."

"I'm going to stay in Congress and paint."

"That's ridiculous. When are you going to do your duty by me and give me another child?"

He had hoped the argument would not reach this ground because here he felt defenseless. Sarah had started talking about another child the week of the funeral. She'd begun fondling him, necking him, seducing him more than she had in years. But he wanted no more commitments now. His present life seemed like a nightmare tank turret, full of projections and demands that squeezed in to trap him. Sarah had sprung Jane on him before he was ready. He'd thought they'd planned to go round the world that year, he'd even arranged his law practice so he could get six months off. Jane came instead.

"Sarah, I've told you, I'm not ready to have another child."

"You're not ready. Brother, is that rich." She started toward him furious and he thought she might hit him as she sometimes did, but instead she swerved and collapsed on the couch crying, "Daddy, Daddy, you are so mean to your little Sari-dari. I miss my Jim so. I remember holding him for the first time he sneezed. The first time he sneezed. I thought he was going to blow away."

He went over to Sarah and patted her head nervously.

"Do your duty by me," she sobbed. "I want another child."

He'd be damned if he'd buy that bargain, be permitted to paint in return for a child. "Sarah, that's not the issue now."

"It's always what you want in this house. You want. You want." She flipped over to furious again. The whole taut line of her body challenged him: breasts up, thighs open, lips wet. Sex wove its own erotic lines through all their battles. "You don't want a child. You don't want the Senate. You want to paint. You wanted to sail with Jim. You. You. You. My father told me you were no good and a quitter. He was right."

"Sarah, this isn't getting anywhere."

"You're yellow."

He turned to leave the room and let Sarah cool off in private. He could safely turn his back on her because her sense of domestic order was so strong she never threw anything.

"Come back here," she yelled. "Don't start something and not finish it."

He continued through the door.

"You run out on me to paint, brother; and some day you won't find me here."

God knows, that would be pleasant, he thought. How could she scream and demand a child at the same time? Was Sarah so violent because they had so seldom had sex these past years? Her energy boomeranging to explode somewhere else? "Where the fuckin's right, the complexion's clear and the mind sweet," said Red Donner, the Freud of Congress.

Sarah had not simmered down by dinner. He took it for about fifteen minutes, until she accused him of not having jumped off the boat to rescue Jim at all. Then he left to eat and spend the night at his club. People would talk; but he'd already thought up an excuse: a possible diagnosis of mumps in the house.

About the lavishly decorated Officers' Club ballroom at Andrews Air Force Base the guests grouped themselves decoratively by rank and status. They had been through the receiving line to meet and congratulate the new brigadier general, whose stars had been personally pinned on by the Chairman of the House Armed Services Committee. Now the guests sipped gin and tonics, mint juleps and bourbon and branch, and carefully gossiped where it would do them the most good, while stiff-backed sergeants circulated among them filling glasses.

An alert group of interservice mixers clustered around the senior White House staffer present. A larger mass of upwardly mobile ass-kissers nodded at the wisdom of the new Vice Chief. A group of gallants and left-outs conversed with the wives. A hatch of comers continued to swarm around Brigadier General Catenberry, who rumor said was going places. Another clutch, ordered to do so by Catenberry, mixed it up with the Congressmen and Senators present.

Off in a corner a specially planted nucleus leaked to the press statistics on the cost and failure of the new Navy jet fighter that would produce instant apoplexy in all Admirals reading their morning newspapers. To one side a few visionaries watched alertly for the Chief of Staff to make his appearance so they could be the first to take his cap. Last, a nondescript but eager number escorted the two Madison Avenue executives retained by the Air Force to improve its image.

"Don't make us look so intellectual everybody thinks we're pansies," the Chief of Staff had instructed the escorts. "But we don't want the public thinkin' all we kin do is drop bombs, see."

The senior of the two executives being so escorted was J. Herbert Cary, who had once introduced Dent at a luncheon. Beside Herb was his badge of status, the Edam blonde, the gorgeous model whose face and figure appeared above the slogan: "Blondes have more fun. Get more. Get Edam. Edam blonde rinse." (Edam was "made" spelled backward which provided the year's big yuck along that crack of American culture, Madison Avenue.) Every red-blooded adman coveted the Edam blonde, but Herb, who provided her with the billings, owned her.

Catenberry eyed the party, taking everything in, planning his next move. He saw George Dent moving early toward the door to leave. That guy is really out of it, he thought, and made no move to say good-by to the man he had once rescued. —After all, they had been photographed together in the receiving line.

Still roving, his eye fixed on the Edam blonde across twenty feet of chatter. Bored by Herb's continued litany of what a privilege it was to serve the Air Force, she looked up and saw General Catenberry. They smiled. They both felt their smiles coming, realized they had time to suppress them; but let them happen. With total certainty they recognized each other: two survivors who understood every smell, twig, and movement in the killing ground, who knew the name of the game was winner take all and had no doubt who would win. Slowly they took in the details of each other's perfections and then turned away. They both knew they belonged together, would miss not having screwed each other; but both realized business came first.

Catenberry had long ago forced Joyce into the abortion by

threatening to spread the word the child was George Dent's. Now he had fixed her up with a handsome major, as dumb as she was, who was set to marry her. He'd force his own wife into a Mexican divorce by the end of the month. He was secretly meeting with Jane Rogers, a carefully reared, twenty-seven-year-old, washed-out brunette who taught school, and was the only daughter of Senator Rogers, Vice Chairman of the Armed Services Committee.

He really had Jane pantin' for it, he thought, while he put her off out of respect for her "soul." Shit, when he made his play Tuesday night she'd jump into bed with her legs open, all juiced up, convinced she'd seduced him. If parents wanted to raise their children so fucked up they stayed virgins and didn't know the score, good. That made it easier for poor boys from Oklahoma who didn't mind eating a little shit on the way up.

He began to maneuver toward the corner of the club where Senator Rogers and his daughter were standing. What an easy target, he thought. And after I marry her I'll get her pregnant fast, because kids keep a woman out of trouble. And even with all the Senator's dough, I'm going to bring my kids up hungry, so they know the rules. Send them to Harvard or some place like that, but keep them mean. Hell, with what I'll be givin' them they could end up President. The new Vice Chief was a missile man too. I've been a little slow gettin' off the ground—he tensed—but I'm in the pattern and flyin' now. Get my second star within a year.

With each decision he made Dent expected his problems to lessen; instead, both at his desk in the House and alone in his shed, his anxieties grew. It became an effort even to make appointments for lunch and handball with his friends. As he headed toward the dining room or House gymnasium, the feeling would permeate him that he ought to be somewhere else, that something important was about to happen and he was wasting his time. He knew this was ridiculous; he had to eat, keep in shape, and he liked to see his friends but his fears remained.

Also he had trouble deciding how to vote. Simple issues on which he was absolutely certain where he stood, such as statehood for Hawaii, required that he consciously will himself to go to the floor. He would catch himself loitering as he walked through the tunnels from his office toward the chamber, grabbing a few moments alone underground to think about painting or to daydream.

While painting he was plagued by his inability to sketch. He knew that to improve his canvases, to expand as an artist, he should get out of his shed and sketch a certain number of hours each week, and that before starting a new canvas he should make drawings and experimental studies. But the thought of taking time away from work on the actual canvas unnerved him; so though he knew he was not working correctly, he rushed from picture to picture.

The few times he did force himself to take time off and sketch were disastrous. He would wander the streets and parks of Washington looking for a subject, knowing he was passing by things he ought to attempt, but unable to decide which one. Finally, face itching, he would order himself to pause; open his sketchbook and begin.

He felt strange sitting on a doorstep or in the front seat of his car. He must look odd. He ought to be in his shed at work on the pictures that were going to bring him recognition and money. He'd promised the gallery canvases, and he was falling behind. So he would hurry through the sketch, make a few superficial lines, and return to his shed to attack his canvas with all his energy. But underneath his inability to experiment lay like a cancerous lump in his chest—a growth which a patient in his fright refuses to admit he can feel, but to which his fingers keep returning, hoping to prove nothing is there.

While he was in his shed his concentration was continually shattered by erotic fantasies. As he stood painting, his prick would begin to stiffen. If you're going to be an artist, he would tell himself, live like an artist; have lots and lots of models. The outline of one, never fully seen, would drift about his studio: a slender, feisty girl who loved him, stroked him, did fantastic sex with him. As he was painting her, she would break her pose and come over to slowly fondle his prick to the edge of explosion. It was impossible to paint with this great swollen grenade between his legs.

He stood, he moved around, he sat, he adjusted his pants, he yelled, "Stop this adolescent shit" at himself; but nothing helped, the need remained. The temptation to masturbate was overpowering; but he'd been that route when he was young. If he played with himself he'd really waste time. Besides, someone might barge in. So he hung on in agony, accomplishing nothing.

In bed he and Sarah fought.

As he lay on his back, she poked him in the ribs with two extended fingers.

"Daddy, are you awake?"

"Yes."

"Then do your duty; give me another child."

"Sarah, we're not ready."

"Weakling." She dug her nails into his shoulder and sides as she tugged and pushed.

"Sarah, we've been through this before. I'm not going to change now."

"Get out of my bed."

"Let's talk about this tomorrow."

"Get out."

"It's our bed."

"I paid for it."

"That's nonsense."

"You're not fit to lie in it. Get out."

He was tired, and there was no point in fighting. Ashamed of his cowardice, he got up and went to the guest room. There he failed to make up the bed properly and slept poorly. Early in the morning he woke radiant and warm. He had dreamed he was sick with, of all things, chicken pox; and Jim had come into his room with milk and crackers to talk to him so he wouldn't be lonely. And here he was in a strange bed not sleeping with his wife. He had no need of nightmares; his reality was worse.

Three nights later Sarah came to bed in a new nightgown: dark green, lacy, not her style at all. She lay on the bed in a caricature of seduction, then began to kiss and caress him, only a little too hard. He responded and fondled her back, his excitement rising.

"Come on. Come inside me." But each time he tried to caress her between her legs she twisted away. "You've got nothing on," he said.

"You lie."

"Sarah, you're not wearing your diaphragm. I just felt."

"You're a horrible, filthy, dirty liar." She began to hit him.

"Goddamn it, stop."

"Liar. Liar. Filthy liar."

"Sarah, stop it!"

"Get out of my bed." She drew up her feet and kicked out hard at his bad leg. The kick caught him by surprise and tumbled him from the bed in pain. He hit the floor and exploded in anger. She kicked, struck and tore at him as he fought back into bed.

"Coward. Coward." Her voice was low and enraged. "Get out!"

For the first time in the marriage he hit her; hard; fist closed; on the temple. As he had guessed, she stopped fighting immediately and began to cry.

"You hurt me. You hurt me."

"Roll over and keep quiet." He lay beside her, enraged at what she'd done, and miserable because he'd hit her. Her sobbing went on, a quiet sobbing designed to be heard. What she hadn't been able to force from him by sex and battle she sure as hell wasn't going to get with tears.

"Sarah, calm down. We both need sleep."

"I is so sorry I hit you, Daddy. Forgive little Sari-dari, please."

"I forgive you, Sarah, now go to sleep." He rubbed her head briefly as he used to Jim's. But forgive her? That was like forgiving the Germans; you tried because it was the right thing to do, but it never thoroughly happened.

Still on the surface his life continued to glitter. He was George Dent, the envied young Congressman with the beautiful wife, whose life had recently been touched by tragedy, providing him with public sympathy and the common touch; and making him a definite possibility for the Senate. Several weeks later he and Sarah went to dinner at the home of the Israeli chargé d'affaires. David, their host, was brilliant, young, and Dent believed him to be a friend, though the diplomat did make his cultivation of rising young American politicians a little obvious. Dent had wondered whether he should accept the invitation when it came. If, having decided against the Senate, he wasn't sailing under false colors.

After dinner the women had left the table and the men were having cigars, brandy, and Washington gossip. Suddenly with an almost audible gasp, Dent found he had turned deaf. Around the table people's mouths moved but no sound reached him. He realized he had not heard anything for some time. He had been concentrating on the new painting he would start tomorrow, concerned that his work was becoming repetitious, and had not noticed the onset of silence.

Desperately he concentrated to listen. Nothing came through whatever aural barrier had suddenly sprung up around him. He was terrified. What if he was asked a question? He couldn't remember what they'd been talking about when he'd last been listening. Frantically he watched the speakers' lips for some clue. Nothing.

It was not that all sound was absent. He was surrounded by sound. But the ordinary noises—coffee-cup clink, conversation, chair scrape—were gone. His deafness was not silence but the drowning out of the usual bustle by some inner theme of his own. He pretended briefly he did not recognize his personal noise. But he knew. He was encased within the bell chimes he had heard on the deep side of the Caribbean reef.

He sat consciously trying to appear normal, mouth closed,

breath regular, looking around the table, smiling, as in terror he cast about for ways out. He had witnessed, he remembered, such sudden deafness in others during combat. It did no good to shout or yell at such men. The afflicted stood there, slackly frightened, not hearing. He checked his face with his hand. Sooner or later most of his men recovered. They merely needed to quit the noise of tank combat for a while.

Something in this room must be getting to him. Hoping he was not breaking up some major story, he pushed his chair back from the table; and rising carefully, headed for the bathroom.

Inside the bathroom he locked the door, took off his dinner jacket, undid his bow tie and collar, turned on the cold-water tap, and splashed cold water over his face. He could not hear the water running into the basin. Easy, Dent, easy, he coached himself. Control your fright. Don't force yourself to listen. Just try and relax. Your hearing will return. This sort of nonsense doesn't happen to you. He laughed at that self-deception. To whom was this happening, then?

He slipped off his suspenders, lowered his tuxedo pants, and closing the door to the toilet sat down to try and relax. He breathed out a sigh as his water passed from him and at the same instant realized he was hearing his urine splash in the bowl. He leaned over and tapped his knuckles against the side of the bathroom. He could hear that too. Trembling, he dressed himself and went gratefully back to the Washington conversation.

He was going to have to devise a cover story to get himself off the hook should he ever go deaf again. Perhaps something about an old war injury. And surely with the decision made about painting and the Senate, with Jim's death receding, and another summer recess coming up, his life would improve.

twelve

With twelve more of the promised canvases completed, six satiric studies of Congress and six abstracts of New York City, Dent called the gallery to say he hoped he was ready. Kate and James Jamers returned to Washington and exited from his studio shed all smiles and talk of money. The date for opening his show was set, April 24, a month and four days away.

"Perhaps you can provide us with two or three more abstracts by then, George."

"I'll see."

Triumphant, he told Sarah about the gallery's reaction and the definite date.

"You know, Sarah, being a painter is much like any other job. If you go in there and do it, it gets done. If you don't, it doesn't."

"I can believe that, Daddy."

An exhibition on Madison Avenue, something to which she could point with pride before her father and her friends, mollified Sarah. She produced their master Christmas-card list of six thousand names and broke it down into those who should be invited to the opening, those who should receive the special announcement plus literature, and those who should receive merely the routine announcement. She checked with friends in New York and spent several afternoons on the phone with the gallery running over lists of names.

"I hope you know what you're doing, love-dove," she said. "From when first I knew you, you've always gone chasing after things."

"Like you, Sari-dari."

"Seriously. It wasn't so long ago, you were desperate for the Senate. And before you became a Congressman you wanted to teach law. And before that, in case you've forgotten, you wanted to specialize in trial work. And before that . . . You lack a sense of true purpose, Daddy."

"Do I? Maybe."

Sarah smiled at him. Glad all was calm again, he smiled back. There was no point in arguing, though he was certain her charge was untrue. He had a sense of purpose; was cursed with one. He was just never certain how to recognize "true" purpose. If Purpose were to walk up the front steps now and ring the door bell, would he welcome Purpose into the house for a drink as a long-lost friend; or inform him sternly that they didn't need any?

Two weeks before the exhibit Dent moved his easel and paints up to their apartment in New York. He rolled back the rug in one corner of the living room, installed some flood lights, made a drive at turning out the final canvases. This represented, he knew, a scandalous neglect of his Congressional duties; but right now the objective was to exhibit not legislate. —If only Jim could help him judge this new life.

The night before his opening he took Sarah to dinner.

"We might just as well treat ourselves to Twenty One, Sari-dari. Enjoy this windfall while it lasts."

"Nice, Daddy. Truthfully, I never thought you'd do so well so fast."

"Well, we haven't made it. But we're farther on than many painters get in a lifetime."

"You're more able than most painters, love-dove."

"Yeah, but can I paint as well?"

"If you can't, you won't just keep stubbornly on, will you?"

"No, Sarah, I won't. I'm not going to starve in a garret to prove some abstract point."

"Good." She snuggled up to him in the cab.

So much depends on this exhibit, he thought. Just as everything used to ride on the outcome of an election. If it just went well, his life would be back on the tracks, Sarah would be happy, perhaps they could have another child.

The next morning he went to the gallery early to see his pictures by himself. He looked from one to another of them in shock. They weren't his any more. Framed, in these professional surroundings, they looked washed out, their lines and spaces weak and contrived. His face itched at the thought of the ridicule he'd take. He was exposing himself before he was ready. The only sane course was to call off the exhibit. Why had the gallery led him on? Was this a macabre joke to humiliate George Dent and make him realize he'd pissed away his substance when he threw over his Senate chances to paint? To paint? He wasn't even close to painting.

"Kate, do you people know what you're doing?"

"Quite a shock, isn't it? Don't worry. It happens to everyone. How about lunch, George? We can't have a glum artist."

They had lunch. Kate was full of gossip, warmth, and promise. He was full of martinis. He turned a deaf ear on his cries of self-doubt. Maybe he was an artist after all.

He and Sarah arrived at the gallery an hour after opening time, Dent dreading to go, fearful that everyone would either stay away or come to laugh. But already the gallery was pleasantly full. Kate turbined forward to meet them and introduce Dent to "one or two important people who've come early to actually look at the pictures." She was wearing a short red dress with vents about the waist.

"Who's that?" hissed Sarah.

"She's the appraiser. Pretty fat, isn't she?" Dent knew by now that Sarah always reacted with hostility to big women.

"Disgusting. See she keeps her hands off you."

Someone else greeted them and Sarah turned on her best public charm. Dent watched the man light up; in this world too he was lucky enough to have such a wife on his side. Professional smile on, he moved off to meet Kate's important people, as usual not getting their names. Here he was at another party, he thought, only this one was about his pictures. He'd soon know how good they were, if they would sell. Art was like politics after all. You learned your future, who you were, from the public and the press.

A blast of sound funneled out of an inner room in the gallery. A black hard-rock group had started up. Cute girls in see-through plastic dresses circulated through the crowd passing out drinks. The gallery was certainly doing its best to make sure no one looked at his pictures.

By now the three rooms were jammed. A ravishing girl with blond hair and black slacks wanted to know if he would do her portrait. Damn right. She gave him a card. A group of immaculate young men congratulated him on the social perception of his pictures. A bearded black told him they were ball-less fakes. A critic told him they were priced too high. Another expert told him they were priced too low. He saw Kate stick a red star on three of them: two satires and one abstract. Maybe his pictures were better than he thought.

He greeted Sam Kleinman and his wife; the Wollenbergs; Jean Aaron; Francis Matchelder and wife; Mayor Zeigler, a pleasant surprise; four members of the New York delegation ("Jesus, Dent, you live like this all the time?"), Wup-'em and Alice Wilson; an ecstatic Red Donner; quite a few summer friends of Sarah's; two other good friends from Congress; his mother and father.

"A very impressive opening, George."

"Thank you, sir."

"Who are all these people, George?" asked his mother.

"I don't know."

"You don't know?"

"I've never been in this world before."

"Oh."

"Are you staying in town for dinner?" he asked his parents.

"We had an early dinner."

"Oh. Well, I've got to keep circulating." He wandered off.

Later he saw Sarah's father, Timothy Middendorf Frost, in the center of the room surrounded by clear space. Sarah was at his left; on his other side, just to the rear of his right rump, hovered the inevitable flunkey, notebook in hand. Dent wormed his way toward them.

"So you're getting out of the race, huh," boomed Mr. Frost across eight watchful knots of people.

"Just running on two tracks at once, sir."

"Nonsense! Nogoodevercameofthat. —Who's paying for all this?" He dismissed the opening and all those in it with one sweep of his arm.

"The gallery."

"Damn good promotion. Edwards, take a note." The camp follower eddied out from behind Mr. Frost and flipped open his notebook like an obsequious waiter. —Dent knew that each of Mr. Frost's papers had an editor whose sole job was to follow through and answer "the Chief's" notes.—Mr. Frost paused. "Try sexy girls as newsboys in Rochester.—Edwards."

"Sir."

"Find out where the gallery gets its girls."

"Yes sir." Edwards shut his notebook and moved off.

"Wherethehellareyagoin'?" Frost yelled.

"To find out, sir, where . . ."

"Not now, you idiot. Later. I may have another note." Edwards oozed back behind Mr. Frost's rump. Frost swung on Dent. Dent braced. "All these paintings yours?"

"Well, I can't see them all for the people, but they were when the show started."

Sarah and Edwards laughed politely; Frost roared on.

"Don't like what I see. Can't understand those color blotches. And those others: disrespectful of the government. Don't want to bite the hand that feeds you. Now a cartoon, see, that just hits one thing that's wrong. Some crook. Or phony-baloney issue. But these pictures attack the system."

"Parts of the system are wrong, though, Father."

"You like these pictures?" Mr. Frost fired broadside at his daughter.

"Yes." Five-foot-two of angry blond jaw.

"You gotta loyal wife, Dent. Bestthingamancouldhave." Mr. Frost looked at his watch; yelled "Time" at the flunkey; kissed his daughter; ha-ha'd at Dent; and left.

"Thank you, loyal wife," said Dent.

"I couldn't have him treat you like that in public, Daddy. But he's right, you know."

"No, I don't know. I'll just go find out how much longer we're expected to stay." He drifted off.

Then he saw Dee. When the gallery had asked him for his personal list of opening night guests he had included her name, a little bit fearful at such a public disclosure. Now, checking carefully to make certain Sarah was occupied, he worked his way toward her. She had on a large black hat and brilliant scarlet mouth; he recognized her on-display look. She seemed older than he remembered, just as beautiful, only drawn in finer lines.

"Hullo, George, wild opening."

"Hi, Dee, that's a great hat."

"Glad you like it. So you're really going to be one of us?"

"I'll know soon."

"Know soon? Oh, you mean when the reviews come out. Yes, that's one way of knowing."

"I'd like to see you and talk about the pictures." Had he asked too much? "Could I give you a call?"

"I'd like that. I'll come and look at the pictures some time when I can see them."

"I'll see you."

He moved off. How long a contact seemed too long, how short a contact seemed suspicious? There should be a manual on that. Maybe the CIA had one.

He noticed that two more of his pictures had red stars. He should have been elated, instead he was depressed. He felt as he did when as a small boy he snuck out of bed to peer downstairs at a grown-up dinner party. The room was full of laughing, talking people whose meanings he would never grow up enough to understand.

The reviews killed him. He was a fellow member of the liberal establishment, so the critics did not amputate publicly; and most of them had some praise for his color sense and technique. But they left no doubt that they thought his satiric paintings were cartoons rather than art; and the kindest thing said about his abstracts were "derivative" by both the *Tribune* and the *Times*. Nobody was going to walk off in the street and buy a Dent unless they were lured by the snob value of owning a painting by a Congressman.

You are a freak, he thought, and the gallery has given you a freak show. And the worst part is, you knew this all along but hid from seeing it.

If he could have thought up some polite way to cancel his lunch with Wollenberg he would have, for he particularly dreaded what Benjamin, who knew art, would say.

After their conversation all too obviously had skirted the central question through most of lunch, Dent finally asked.

"What did you think of my show, Benjamin?"

"What did you think of it, George?"

"Well, I wasn't satisfied." That was safe.

"What I would enjoy seeing, George, are some of your failures."

Dent looked puzzled.

"The pictures," Wollenberg continued, "where you tried and missed. The exhibition was so pat, George, so rote. I've known you for a long time. I know you to be thoughtful, concerned, rather unique. I know you've just lost a son. I saw none of that in any painting."

"I've a few . . ." He checked himself in the middle of saying, I've a few of those canvases around; because he hadn't. Art was meant to be truer than politics and here was artist Dent about to lie to an old friend to whom politician Dent had always told the truth? "I've tried a few times; but gotten nowhere. And the effort took so damn long."

"I can believe it. —You didn't expect it would be easy, did you, George?"

"No."

"And truthfully I did not like those abstracts. Did you feel anything while you did them?"

"The gallery told me they'd sell."

"They are not worthy of you, George."

Dent almost hit him.

"You sound like my father."

Mr. Wollenberg looked unhappy and embarrassed. He pushed on.

"You have a lot of rich friends, George, who don't know much about art. So does Sarah. You also have talent. I have no doubt you can become a financially successful painter. Is that what you want?"

"I don't know."

That was a lie. He knew. But he did not want to hear the next logical question. If you do know, why don't you do something about it. —And tomorrow he had to get through a lunch with Dee.

That lunch danced around even more unasked questions.

"Tell me what you thought of my pictures, Dee. I've wanted to hear." His words came out tight and high, though he'd rehearsed them over and over to make his voice sound natural.

He looked at Dee across the restaurant table, afraid she could read behind his glance and so learn that he saw her as his only real lever into the world of painting. That he was terrified of his need for her and therefore of the possibility of losing her.

"I was surprised by how much you'd painted, George. How fast and hard you work. But it's not my type of painting, so it's hard for me to say. Oh, hell, I might just as well put my foot in. I didn't like it. But maybe I'm jealous."

He felt a cold mist dampen his arms and legs.

"What didn't you like?"

"Don't you know?"

"Because I didn't try anything big?"

"Maybe. Maybe. —God, George, those abstracts. Of all the things you are not, it's abstract. You didn't paint them to find out what abstracts were about, did you?"

He was silent.

"The gallery told you they'd sell; and you thought up some sloshes that said 'city' and used your skill to get them down. I know you; and I couldn't tell which was the first or last picture painted.

"That little sketch you did of your jacket and socks in my apartment; I went and dug that out. I got more power from it than from anything in the exhibit. You paint as if you were still a Congressman."

"I am still a Congressman; but I feel there's been a tremendous change inside me."

"I don't see it." She paused. "Why did you write me that letter, George?"

"As I said in it, I was tearing myself in two."

"You could have simply told me."

He couldn't answer that he felt safer handling unpleasant personal decisions by letter. To say so was to admit cowardice.

"Why are you seeing me, now?" she asked.

He had to lie about that too. "I admire you, your work, what you are; I want to have you as a friend."

She looked at him. He felt he was staring into a gun muzzle. Held powerless in the sight reticule. He looked away.

"How do you change your style?" he mumbled.

"What?"

"How do you change your style?"

"That's an impossible question. I just hammer and hammer away, with my stomach all tied up in knots. Believe me, it's not talent or inspiration makes a painter out of me. It's fear."

"Your stomach knots?" He was completely surprised.

"For weeks, George, weeks."

"I thought you'd be beyond that."

"Beyond! —I doubt Picasso's beyond that."

"I get terrified my work won't be any good, Dee. And I just

start painting, and painting, and painting, anything to ease the ache in my stomach." Easy, Dent, he cautioned himself, too much self-revelation and you'll lose her.

"You mustn't do that, George. You mustn't."

He saw fear actually rise off the tablecloth of the posh restaurant. It clung to the silverware and eddied round the glasses, a gray mass. It was all very well to say he must not. But how did he stop? How did he keep from running in this battle?

"I get up in the morning, George," Dee continued, "and try to paint. Then I go to bed at night and don't sleep. I get up next morning feeling like a pig; and try again. It's the only way I know. Says the old mother witch."

"You're wonderful."

"Maybe we can be friends, George. I don't know."

After lunch he walked the few blocks to his gallery. Nothing came off the walls to help him. Here and there he'd see a line that he might have executed differently; but as for the next step, the new message, the real changing—these he could not find. He had started to paint again to bring himself ease and joy and ended with a blank.

On the street corner outside the gallery was a glass phone booth. On impulse he stepped in and dialed.

His mother was at home.

"Is that you, George? How are you? How are your pictures selling?"

"Fine, Mother. How are you?"

"I'm having some trouble with the new cook; but otherwise things are all right. I told you, didn't I, that Annie, who was with us for years, recently . . ."

"Mother," Dent interrupted. When his mother got started on her trials with her domestic staff a filibustering Southern Senator could but raise his hat in envy. "I called to ask whether we still had any of my old paintings in the attic?"

"Your old what?"

"Paintings. Pictures I painted. Right before and after the war."

"I don't know, George, we might have. We had a big house-cleaning about six years ago; or was it seven. But I don't recall seeing any pictures going out. But then I don't recall not. —How many paintings have you sold?"

"I don't know. But the gallery seems happy."

"They do. Good. That is good news."

"Mother, I'm going to rent a car, right now, and come out to Greenwich. If I may?"

"You're coming out now? But I've already done my shopping for today. I'm not sure there's enough food in the house to feed you tonight."

"Mother, I have to get back to town anyway." That was a lie but he'd explode at the family dinner table. "I'll just take about an hour to look at the pictures."

He always forgot, till he walked in the front door, the magic smell of his father's house. The well-polished wood, the stainless plaster, the rich blend of tended lawn and clean linens, a perfumed essence of ordered comfort. The smell was particularly strong in the attic where he and his sister had played. Outside was today's alienated April; inside Keatsian autumn.

In a corner of the old attic nursery, stacked behind a sheet-covered doll house, he found his pictures, carefully labeled, wrapped and tied with a string. He recognized his own clumsy knots and lettering: "George Dent. Important. Please Save." And the names of the paintings. But only six canvases. Two from before the war and four from the years with Helen. And a notebook of watercolors done in the hospital that he'd forgotten all about.

He remembered many more canvases than that. Where were the others? All those paintings from the shack-shack, from Yale, from school, such as *Birches over Ice*. He looked about for a knife or something else sharp to cut the string and, finding nothing, was forced to wrestle with the jammed knots.

Deliberately not looking, he got the six canvases lined up against the nursery wall. He walked into the center of the room, then slowly turned to face this part of a past he thought he'd rejected.

Oh God. Oh, no, he thought. I'm nowhere. I'm dead.

Two of the pictures were awful, one from college, the other done shortly after the war pretentious, tricky fakes. It turned his stomach that he could have shown them with pride or found them fit to save. But the other four. He had been with it then, pushing himself against the world, open, and vulnerable. The excitement from the canvases surged across the years to prick his skin.

A pulse of green doubt dribbled down the left side of his self-portrait. What a risk to paint that way, he thought. I must get back there—I must.

He'd totally forgotten that self-portrait. How could he, when he had planned a whole series of himself at various stages of life, like Munch, Beckman, or Rembrandt? —Munch, Beckman, Rembrandt, he had believed himself limitless in those days.

And there was Helen's portrait. Warm, pensive, not how he remembered her, either. He walked over to squat in front of her portrait. Damn, that was one fine nude. He'd made the curve of her ass jump right off the wall with a strong stroke of the palette knife. Looking closely he could see where he'd scraped it out and put it back, scraped and replaced again. Then, suddenly—part lover and part surgeon—he'd cut right where the line belonged.

He looked at the two paintings, the best of his postwar period, and a dark memory crept back. He had lived with terror then. Faced it every day. Not just the vague anxieties he sometimes felt now as he began to paint; but the black, before-battle fear: He wasn't going to make it; today his best would fall short. Why some days his doubts had hung so heavy from his arm his brush moved jerkily across the canvas.

Now that he remembered the terror he recognized it as big brother of his present doubts, his inability to sketch, his running from easy canvas to easy canvas with no attempt at risk in between. He had not chosen law school over painting or Sarah over Helen; he had run from this fear. And this was the world he had elected to push back into, the life he had secretly wanted for Jim.

His face began to itch and his anxiety escalated to nausea. It might be too late for him to change his style; to be anything more than a glorified cartoonist with a sense of color. He should drive for the Senate. Suddenly he wanted to escape from the attic. Jim used to play here when they visited his parents. He would bind up the paintings, make some excuse to his mother, and leave.

He'd take the pictures home with him. No, they might not be safe there. Not safe in my own house? He hung on, debating what to do with the paintings, while his terror grew. Suppose Sarah took a knife to them? Suppose his mother went on an orgy of spring cleaning and threw them out? He sucked in his breath hard against the clamped teeth of his jaw. He'd leave them here for a month, tell his mother not to touch them, find a safe place for them, then return and pick them up.

While rewrapping the paintings he realized suddenly that when he thought of himself as a painter he thought of himself as a failure. But when he saw himself as anything else, he saw himself as successful. He started college certain he'd garner a gentleman's *cum laude;* he entered the Army feeling he'd be a good soldier; went into battle nervous but still believing he'd hack it; he thought he'd win a few as a pole vaulter; make money as a lawyer; was convinced he was a good Congressman; would make a better than average Senator.

Why did he feel that way about his painting? He studied the question and found no answer.

He had a choice. He could feel the physical weight of it, perched on his shoulder like a predatory bird. Yet strangely, now that he saw it, he realized he was choiceless, the decision already irrationally welded closed. He had to take the risk, accept the terror, commit himself even this late to do nothing but paint; to find what size artist he was.

For three days he put off making his choice definite, then he took five actions that locked him in. He told Sarah, he went to New York and told Sam. He wrote to his father, he called and explained to Dee; and finally scheduled a press conference to announce his retirement from Congress.

Sarah was all battle, tears, and baby-talk, declaiming words such as "quitter," "yellow," "drifter," and "coward." She had known he would end here when he decided not to run for the Senate. Jim's death had made him sick. He should see a doctor. Fortunately her father was traveling in Europe, telling the makers and shakers abroad how to shape up, and seeing in every windtossed poppy the excellence of the American rose, so that further explosion was deferred.

Sam was harder; he disagreed violently with Dent's decision, and he had been right about so much in the past.

"Dent, painters are all over where I come from. Every schlemiel who can't break loose from Mama. Guys without chutzpah; all wrapped up in their own gut. They don't even know who's President, much less the name of their Congressman. You like to spin the dime, to get up in front of people and win. Sock 'em between the eyes. You don't want to be second, ever. Now you're putting yourself last."

What could he say?

"Is it because of your son's death?" Sam continued. "You just don't want to be out there in public. Believe me; keep working."

"Sam, if Jim hadn't drowned, it's true I might never have done this. But that's not the full reason."

"At least wait till after the next campaign."

"Sam, I'm thirty-nine years old, I can't wait. Look, what I'm concerned about is you and Jean and the others in the organization. We've got to find a candidate that can win and keep you all together."

"Congressman, that candidate is you."

So they went round and round again.

The press was kind. The death of his son, his Senate chances, his liberal record, Sarah's money, had made him a celebrity and his final performance drew a good turnout with easy questions. After the conference several friends among the reporters came up to wish him well.

"Off the record, Dent," one of them asked, "how do you feel about this choice?"

"Foolish."

His father responded to Dent's careful letter with one of his own.

Dear George:

I read your letter with mounting misgivings. Having tried unsuccessfully several times to arrange a lunch to talk things over, I am dictating this letter. To be blunt: I find your decision ridiculous. You have recently had a grievous loss. In that, as you know, you have my profoundest sympathy. But that is no reason to throw over the hard-won accomplishments of a life.

You are, as you well know, an excellent Congressman. I have every confidence that sometime in the future you will make a first-rate Senator. But patience, unfortunately, has never been your long suit. I had hoped that by now you would have mastered your former need to shift continually from pasture to pasture. It appears not. I feel that I myself am not without blame in this matter. Had I insisted while you were in college that you pursue a definite discipline such as engineering or architecture, you might have had less trouble later settling down.

But all that is water over the dam. What is important now is that in the shock of your grief you must not disrupt your life. Draw on Sarah for strength, she is a strong woman, and weather this crisis. Do not, I beg you, like the base Indian, throw away the pearl of your past achievement.

As for painting, that is a profession that requires years of strenuous apprenticeship, as does engineering, before one can even begin to scale the foothills, let alone the heights. Had you truly wanted to be a painter you should have buckled down to that long ago. Now it is too late. And no vision through rose-colored glasses can change this fact. You cannot begin now and expect to achieve anything satisfactory. Further, think of the effect this decision is bound to have on Sarah, who so loyally has campaigned beside you.

Life is a contract. The good man acquires certain commitments along the road that he is expected to fulfill. Do not, for your own sake, try and escape from them into some dream. For no matter how alluring that dream may appear today it will prove no substitute for reality. I am sorry to be so blunt but I have learned from painful experience that honesty clears the air.

As your mother has written Sarah, we are planning a trip soon to see all three of you. I shall have my secretary confirm the exact date.

My best as always. I am certain that on mature reflection you will recognize your present position for what it is, one you can accept with pride; and continue in Congress.

Yours,
Father

Dent carefully read his father's letter through twice, then took it home to file in his personal file beyond the eyes of his office staff. As usual everything his father said was frighteningly true. Only he had considered those truths and found others, invisible to his father, and more important.

Red and Wup-'em were at a table in the House restaurant grabbing a quick bite between constituents.

"You're lucky, Wup-'em. My people are so worked up about Hawaii becoming a state it's driving me up four walls. Every Florida Chamber of Commerce is beatin' me to death to vote 'No.' "

"How are you goin' to vote?"

" 'No.' It's going to pass anyway. And I might just as well make my people happy by showing a little domestic greed. But I'm letting them twist my arm first, so they'll be grateful when I change my mind."

"Never agree with your friends, Red. They'll vote for you anyway."

"Wildcat, you planning to argue with Dent?"

"Nope."

"Oh."

"I wouldn't know what to say, Red. When he told me, I told

him I wished he'd stay. But conceited as I am, I didn't exactly expect that to change the course of history. Shute, I don't know anything about being an artist. Fact it sounds like a good deal to me, drawing naked girls, travelin', thinkin'. One of the best lieutenants I had was an artist; good little old boy; got himself killed.

"Now if Dent wanted to be something crazy, like a sheep farmer, I could sure as hell tell him he don't remind me none of a sheep farmer and to straighten up and stay here. But he ain't talkin' about sheep farmin'. Maybe I even like what he's doin'. He's got it made; but he's sayin' he wants something different. I'll miss him."

"I don't agree, Wup-'em. We got lots of painters in Florida and they aren't like old Dent at all. He likes to eat on time. He's organized. He don't do all his thinkin' with his gut. He's got a good life here, chance of a better one. I don't understand it. Besides he looks tense. You think he's all right?"

"No, Red, I think he's all shook to hell, like you would be if you decided to get married. If you want to talk to him, Red, talk to him. When a man's makin' a big decision the last thing he needs is friends that don't level."

"Do you suppose there's something we don't know, Wup-'em? A girl? That he's in trouble?"

"Red, if we don't know, who does?"

Dent showed his best political finesse in setting up his successor. First he offered the job obsequiously and publicly to Frank Matchelder. This united the pure in heart behind him, and when the embarrassed Matchelder, with his eye on larger fields, refused the offer, Dent was able to get all his clubs united behind his actual first choice, Alan Fosberg, an energetic but disaffected young Wall Street lawyer, with enough dough to make him independent.

The more important work, his new resolve to paint seriously and in depth, got nowhere. He started on a self-portrait and produced a caricature. He knew he was painting himself as he thought he should be, not as he was. But even knowing, he couldn't break through the stereotype. He was still tormented by erotic fantasies, he still rushed when he sketched.

Gradually he found it harder and harder to start the day's painting. Since he knew his work would go badly, why should he begin? He sat in his studio shed listlessly, letting fantasies surge through him in which he became an idolized artist, or a distinguished Senator, or did a picture of Jim that came to life. After four hours of this, with nothing accomplished, he would drag himself downtown to the Capitol.

A month later, while trying to sketch in Rock Creek Park, he experienced a return of deafness. Not the same total loss as at the Israeli Embassy, when he heard the summoning bells. This time he saw sounds as colors. The next few times he tried to sketch the symptom recurred.

Instead of a honk, a little black flood would spill out of an automobile horn, roll across the road, then evaporate quickly like spilled lighter fluid. Little bursts of red scattered beneath the feet of running children; jack-hammers sent out fists of purple; cheeky blue bubbled out of manholes: greens and yellows from arguing women's mouths would bat at each other with fake Punch and Judy blows. The trolley two blocks away from his Georgetown house ran on a golden thread. The colors were incredibly fine and pure and beautiful, much more so than natural colors, with the intense hues of dreams.

However, the sum of the experience filled him with terror, for he never knew when the sound-to-color transfer would begin or end. As the weeks progressed, it seemed to arrive more often and last longer. He decided a major part of his problem was living in Washington. All about him people were engaged with the process of power, drawing visibly ahead of him; while he tried desperately to start a new career. The studio shed at the back of his garden was too close to his old life, too near Sarah. He needed a new place, one in which he had never done anything but paint.

In both his Georgetown garden and at the bottom of his lawn in Easthampton grew a small, common weed: the senecious fern.

This weed was native to the entire globe. It never grew big, so gardeners tolerated it provided it kept out of the way: tiny, weak, ugly, a nuisance. Yet in Uganda, on the upper slopes of Mount Karisimbi, the senecious fern sprouted twenty feet high, produced gorgeous orange-red flowers over a foot long, and ruthlessly choked out any other plant life. There the days were hot, close to or over a hundred degrees; and the nights cold, just below freezing, and the fern flourished. So there must be a somewhere for him.

"Sarah," he said, "I've reached another decision." He knew he was battering at his wife, like giving tired troops a fresh order to move out; but he had been putting off telling her for two weeks, trying to find a better moment. Now he detailed the reasons he needed a studio in New York.

"You want to move?" she asked incredulous.

"Well, you know, we've always claimed we live in New York."

"I thought you loved this house."

"I do."

"George, I won't move."

"I could commute on weekends, like I've done in the summer."

"That's ridiculous."

"True."

Sarah's jaw set in the familiar hard line. "There you go again, always what you want. Why can't you paint out back? I had the shed fixed up."

"Sarah, it's quite frightening to paint, and it's doubly frightening with all my old friends around here in Washington who remind me of my choice."

"You're a coward. I told you you were yellow."

"For God's sake, Sarah, how can I talk to you?"

"When are you going to give me another child?"

They were off on that again. Pretty soon she'd shift to the fact that Jim's death had unhinged him and he ought to see a doctor. That he had no intention of doing. It would mean that he would have to waste a great deal of the time and energy that he should spend painting and curing himself, inventing rational lies to keep the doctor happy. This would increase his nonpainting time and make the symptoms worse. Psychiatrists were like voters, they had a set of prejudices and they waited for candidate or patient to mouth something that corresponded to those prejudices. The stupid candidate or patient tried to press his ideas on doctor or voter. The wise conformed and won. —He smiled at the insight.

"What are you laughing at?"

"A thought." He mustn't let those smiles show.

"Listen to me!"

Dent looked hard at his wife: blond hair, handsome face, the pert nose; and bare black dress. They were going out. The dress said: sexy, warm, vibrant woman. That wasn't Sarah.

His wife had a public and a private image just as he had a public and a private image, he thought. Believing himself unique he had missed that simple truth. He was turning from a public to a private man. The public Dent had lived well with the public Sarah. Could the private Dent fit the private Sarah? —No —The "no" hung there, terrifying and simple.

He climbed out of the New York subway already depressed. The neighborhood into which he emerged was disjointed, loud, crumbling, lying between Sixth Avenue and the Hudson, an area he thought he knew and liked. He had several studio listings in his pocket from the newspaper real estate pages and as he walked, he looked at the bulletin boards of neighborhood drug stores. The pickings were slim. He paused, trying to figure out the best way to one of the places advertised, too embarrassed to ask.

The day had turned dishwater gray, more like February than early June. He had been hunting unsuccessfully for a studio for two weeks. He wished he'd worn his raincoat, but he felt it looked too expensive for an artist. Two panhandlers lurched toward him from a doorway, though they had left other pedestrians alone. Children surged at him in threatening play.

In the crumbling entrance of the tenement, a small slip of spattered paper stuck with tape above the mailbox said: "Studio for Rent." But which button was the studio? How did one find the super? He backed out the door feeling conspicuous and lost. Two stoops down a group of teen-agers bantered. He walked over to them. They gave him hard silence.

"Do you know where I could find the super to that building?"

"Super . . . Super . . . Super?" They shook their heads with veiled eyes.

"I want to see about renting the studio that's advertised."

"Nah, you don't want it," said a guy.

"It's rented already," said a girl.

"It is?"

"Maybe." Hard and flat.

"You don't know where the super is?"

"That's what we said. You think we're liars or somethin'?"

"I'd like to see that studio." The boys began to whistle and the girls to giggle.

He felt an intolerable itch creep up both sides of his face. He backed off down the street, rubbing his skin hard with both hands. The itch transferred off his face onto his hands, his arms; and ran down his back. He wriggled to squash it against his suit. He'd have to scratch that studio.

At the start of the next week of looking he called Dee, forcing himself to do so, because he hated to admit that he wasn't self-sufficient.

"Dee, I'm having a godawful time looking for a studio."

"Take your time, George," her voice came gaily over the wire. Ridiculous, he thought, to have worried so about calling her. "When I was younger I could work anywhere. Now the place and all its resonances are of great importance to me. And don't get a basement, George, they're too easily robbed."

"Do you know any place?"

"Not that I'd recommend. But I'll ask around. Why don't you get an uptown studio? You've got the money."

"Then I'd paint uptown pictures."

"Not necessarily."

"I think I would."

"You might be right. Space can be tricky. But take your time, George."

Another week of looking. He saw more places that were awful, many neutral, some almost right. One of these last represented the type of compromise that as a Congressman he would have quickly taken. But he held back. If his analysis had been correct, he needed as perfect a place as possible in which to risk failure and push himself toward better painting. He didn't want lagging doubts that again he had rushed too fast and compromised, lurking as shadows in the corners of his work area.

However, as time wore on, his lengthening search began to breed its own fears. Was this another decision he was walking around rather than making? He knew no test or opinion poll that would answer such a question.

He dragged from bed one morning in their Fifth Avenue apartment and made coffee and toast. He felt fagged out, as if recovering from a bout of flu, too listless to even squeeze orange juice or cook himself eggs and bacon.

After breakfast he opened his closet door to select a tie. Could he search for a studio better with or without a tie?

No tie, he thought, was more his present character. But supposing he met some political friends; or picture buyers; or wanted to lunch in some ties only place? And why should he change his character to be an artist? George Dent wore neckties. But did George Dent wear neckties? Or just George Dent the Congressman?

His hand froze over the tie rack, as with horror he recognized the pause: The same flash of impotent terror that accompanied a decision to sketch, make unpleasant phone calls, even find time for a haircut. All his life he had been reflexively putting on or not putting on neckties. He didn't wear a necktie to swim, play tennis, or go sailing. "Sailing" blasted apart his train of thought and he gasped, pushing his mind back to the reconsideration of neckties. He wore a necktie to the office, and to political rallies, but not to labor picnics. When he campaigned in the summer he showed his good-guy image by taking off his jacket, however, he left on his tie to stress his organization cool, rolling up his sleeves to show he meant business.

Suppose today he put on a tie, but left off his jacket and rolled up his sleeves. But it was another cold day. He should leave off his tie. Most of the people in buildings he'd looked at don't wear ties; he didn't usually wear a tie to paint. But he wasn't painting; he was looking for a studio; he needed a good-tenant image.

He could flip a coin. But after the flip the decision would still be there, merely at one remove; he would still have to decide whether to abide by the flip or not. He could wear a tie today and not tomorrow, and so test which worked best. But he might see the dream studio today and miss it because of the wrong choice now. He'd wear a tie; reach out his hand and blindly grab one. Arm muscles knotted, his hand trembled before the rack. There were the different colored neckties. He willed his hand to move and select one for him. His hand would not move.

His breath came into him a choking gasp, like being slammed against a tank side. The fear lodged like a fetus in his stomach. Little black tracers danced about the room. He'd never frozen like this in combat.

He reached up his left hand to pull his right hand down; but before he could grab his wrist his right hand dropped to his side. He went over to the bed, sat down, and regained his breath. He'd have to wear a tie. He was too close to the edge to risk any outward signs of deviation. Suppose he ran into one of Sarah's friends who'd say, "I saw George Dent, tieless in Gaza at the mill with slaves." He'd give himself two more weeks looking for a studio, then compromise on the best one available.

Dee had given him the name of a real estate agent sympathetic to artists; and Dent started the next day with her three addresses. The first was too dark. As he approached the second he saw its entrance was next a liquor store. That meant drunks in the hall and an extra possibilty of robbery. But at least the sign said where he could find the super in the next block; and though the super was out, his wife gave Dent the key. He'd been wise to wear a tie today.

He opened the front door and realized as he started up the stairwell that the building must be one of the few in each block that were four feet wider than the average. Also there was a strong smell of disinfectant, several open doors from which suspicious eyes watched him, and the walls were clean. Since the studio was at the top floor, the stairs would help keep him in shape: he unlocked the door and stepped slowly into the space beyond.

Like coming up after a long dive, he gulped in the space, the extra four feet of width. Not that the room was perfect; he would have been suspicious of that. Along the inner wall the plaster was flaking off like sunburned skin, while on the outer the brick badly needed painting. But the light poured into the room from three skylights; the whole space was vast and uncluttered, and the windows at both ends were flanked by wooden shutters.

In back, at the courtyard end, the room widened into the space occupied in front by fire stairs and landing. He saw the bare branches of a plane tree through the back windows. That would mean soft green light in summer. A tiny fireplace was set into the far brick wall. That wall was not straight but had a quaint jog that must be caused by the furnace flue or fireplaces on the floors below. In the front of the room was a small boxlike stall for toilet and bathtub; alongside that an ancient but immaculate gas range with oven, and a double sink. Above the stove and sinks hung three metal cabinets in a drunkenly zigzag line. Dent laughed. Who could have so botched a carpentry job? Or had a group of friends put up that reeling triptych on some drunken moving night?

He sat down on the center of the floor and laughed. He remembered all the tests he'd been going to make: borings of the plaster, investigations of the houses on both sides, inspection of the window frames. To hell with those; he fit here.

The next week he moved in sparsely. The space was too precious to clutter; and he wasn't sure how much actual living he would do in the studio. He needed a bed—after all, girls existed.

More important—he smiled at his protestant guile—there might well be nights he would not want to break the continuity of his work. He needed a bureau, boards to make shelves along one wall, and some good cooking utensils. Hot chow kept the combat soldier in condition. He'd forgotten how much he enjoyed looking after himself.

The bed was a particular find: king size, heavy brass rods rearing out of all four corners with a brass rail along the sides. It had been rebuilt to take a plywood center and foam rubber mattress. He paid too much, but he was only a week away now from getting to work in his own place. He put up the shelves, bought a bureau and three chairs, moved his easel and painting materials up from Washington, got a phone installed; and made his first phone call, the electronic baptism of his new address.

"Dee, come see what I've got for space and I'll take you out to dinner."

She came, dramatically delighted at the proportions of his studio. "It's marvelous, George. Light and free. I'm a bit envious. Don't clutter it up too fast."

"I won't."

They had a good dinner and went back to Dee's studio. He took off his jacket and tie and began to kiss her. She kissed him once, then backed away.

"George, I don't want to go to bed with you. I thought about this all day. I don't want us to start up again. I don't see where we'd go. To be honest, where I'd go. All those snatching bits of time to see you were bad for my work. That sounds like pressure to leave Sarah, I know. Believe me, it's not. I don't think we'd work right now. We didn't say much to each other tonight."

"I think we would. We're like gears, like two cogwheels. Just because we don't mesh perfectly sometimes, you don't throw the machine away."

He started toward her, trying to pretend this was the woman's game, but underneath afraid her "no" was final.

"I mean it, George. And I'd like to try and keep the friendship. That's such a trite thing to say, but I would."

He stopped, frightened. He could think up a great many arguments; but as fast as he thought them up he knew the answer. He needed Dee too much to risk the friendship.

"All right," he said, "I'll make us one drink and go."

"It's best, George. And I'll talk to my friends and get you into our life class."

Later, as he walked downstairs, the noise of her police lock thudding home behind him slammed into him like the whispers of a gang of boys at school plotting behind his back to beat him up.

He and Sarah continued their murderous series of skirmishes over his studio and having another child. He did manage to work her somewhat round to the studio by convincing her his painting would go so much better in New York that he would exhibit sooner and make money quicker.

For a time after he was established in his studio his painting came more easily. Then the whole dread cycle of anxiety and effort recommenced, with a new twist. Each time he finally did get started at his work, he felt an overwhelming urge to urinate. Recognizing his self-deception, he refused to permit himself the trip to the bathroom. That left him standing at his easel consciously constricting his bladder, not painting, just fighting the problem. After a couple of days of this tactic he switched maneuvers and hurried to the bathroom. That also failed. He'd lose the thrust of his concept in the time it took to walk across the studio floor and back.

After a few weeks of this, his problem shifted to eating lunch. That's where he was today. He stood before his easel, supposedly at work on an abstract nude, actually attending to the growls of hunger in his stomach. He looked over at the nude of Helen, which he'd hung on his studio wall. He still wasn't painting as strongly as he had back then. He might as well break off, go out and buy food, eat, and start up again.

In the supermarket he found only one check-out counter open. He was trapped, fuming, behind a long line of gossiping women with stacked carts. When he finally escaped from the market he was furious with himself over the wasted time, and also slightly afraid, because he hadn't been able to hear the check-out girl too well and little smoke rings of purple had puffed from the cash register each time it rang. Itches spattered across his face as he walked. Since his arms were too full of parcels for his hands to scratch them, he quieted them by rubbing his face with his shoulders. Pausing at the street corner, he waited for the light to change.

He stopped cold, flooded with terror. Suddenly the street had become foreign. He had no idea where he was. He might just as well be on some corner in Berlin. He groped desperately for a clue to his whereabouts and found he couldn't remember his studio address.

He commanded himself to think. But where the address of his studio should be, the knowledge of how to get there, was just a gray gap; an actual gap.

It wasn't that he had merely forgotten where he lived. He knew the address was there, it occupied space in his mind, like a page of a book, only there was no printing on that page, just a swirling fog. He could almost read his address through the fog, but not quite.

What if he never got home? He had no idea which way to walk on this suddenly unfamiliar street. He wanted to run; get anywhere away from here and find himself. But he commanded himself to stand steady, play the veteran tanker, show neither alarm nor panic. If he was found out, he could be in real trouble.

He moved off the edge of the sidewalk into a walkup's doorway. That got him out of people's way and he would no longer be so noticeable. He looked up and down the street searching for something recognizable to start the process of memory. Nothing. It was not that the street was totally alien. He knew he knew it. Parts of it were familiar, but distorted beyond recall, like the territory of a dream.

Did he have the address written down anywhere on him? He considered a moment. Yes, on his driver's license in his wallet.

You're thinking well, Captain, he reassured himself. He turned away from the street, taking his wallet cautiously from his pocket so no one would try and grab it. With his address, credit cards, and license stolen he'd be nowhere.

Hunching self-protectively he opened his wallet. A package dropped from under his arm onto the sidewalk. He bent down to pick it up, almost lost his wallet, and straightened up fast. Finally he got the package wedged between his legs and flipped through his wallet until he found his driver's license.

There it was, his name, and underneath were the numbers of his address. Them's numbers them are, he said to himself, giggling with renewed terror because the numbers had no meaning. He knew they were numbers; but the symbols before his eyes opened no previous connection into his brain. As he looked the numbers suddenly vanished and became Brueghel-like boys and girls juggling expanding-and-contracting oranges. Numbers had changed to pictures on him before but he'd pretended not to notice. Now these were more intense and continued on and on.

He almost panicked; almost sat down and started to cry; not just because of where he was; but because he might never get out. Never find his way home. At least he knew his name: George Dent. He said: "George Dent" over slowly several times to himself, holding on to that vital clue to his existence.

Again he studied the streets; and with a surge of hope, realized he could go up and look at a street sign. He left his doorway and headed for a lamp post. The figures on the street sign were definitely numbers; but they too had no meaning. They began to blur as he stared at them so he stopped. A bus went by, splashing a jet of red beneath its wheels. He almost leaped back.

If he kept walking, he decided, he wouldn't be so noticeable as standing still. But if he kept walking he might get farther and farther away from his place. He'd circle this block, just keep going round, turning left at every corner, till he recognized or thought of something. He'd been in tough places before. He could make it round the block. "Charlie six, move out." The instinctive use of his old tank call sign warmed him, even though he saw a red fox leap in the street as he said the number.

He strode out, deliberate and purposeful, to fool snoopers. The rhythm of walking felt soothing after just standing about. He made another grope for his address. Still just gray fog. Was there someplace close to his studio he could remember? Someplace he could ask the way to? —The Women's House of Detention. He could get located from there. He lived only three blocks away.

It would take courage to stop a stranger and ask the way to the Women's House of Detention, especially with a two-day growth of beard. He should have shaved this morning. He made another left turn and walked a bit more, gathering strength. Here came a knowledgeable-looking man.

"Pardon me, sir, could you tell me the way to the Women's House of Detention?"

"Three blocks straight ahead, Mac. On your left."

"Thanks."

Three blocks straight ahead. As if someone had just flashed on a light the street became familiar again. He lived right down there a block and a half. There was the sign over the liquor store.

How long does this war go on? he wondered back in the safety of his studio.

thirteen

Paint, he lashed at himself, paint. As on other days, self-exhortation produced nothing. Winter had come. No longer a Congressman, he was living practically full time in his studio. He felt out of place and alone in his Fifth Avenue apartment. Sarah chose to stay in Washington, refusing to move on what she called his whim.

He sat now on his floor, in the little jog, the odd corner in the wall of his studio catty-corner to the entrance door. He spent a great deal of time resting in that corner, legs drawn up, knees locked to his chest by the insides of his elbows, grasping his left wrist with his right hand. Sometimes he rocked back and forth; others, he snuggled his back against the bricks, which seemed strangely soft and familiar, like the metal insides of his tank turret before he went to sleep. He felt sheltered in the corner, more at ease, part of the weight lifted from his stomach, able to gather some strength to cope with the threats of his life, sketching, deafness, numbers, and the major ordeal of shopping.

In the supermarket all his problems fused. He was practically always deaf now when numbers were mentioned; the figures themselved disappeared, leaving only the fantastic pictures. This meant he could not figure the price of articles, hear the clerk tell him how much he owed, or read the total which exploded out of the cash register in little shoots of color. He lived in fear of being found out, cheated out of his change, having his money stolen.

Paint, he prodded himself again. He really had to get back to work because later that afternoon he had life class. He would have to start mustering the strength for class several hours in advance. Getting there on time might be tricky too, because often he could not read the numbers on his watch and had to guess at the time by the position of the hands. And where was his watch? Thank God the studio was small or he'd never find anything.

He rose, found his watch, and forced himself back to his easel. He was doing a picture of three zigzag fire escapes, in the foreground of which stood a woman with a baby in a stroller. He'd sketched it out, thought out how to juxtapose the round human shapes with the iron angles. Now he had to buckle down and finish the painting.

His work had finally begun to pick up momentum when suddenly the phone rang. In a rage he slammed his brush down, it bounced and fell to the floor in a splatter of blue. He leaped across the studio and grabbed the phone.

"Hullo."

Silence. He listened intently and heard the disengaged buzz of the phone. So he wasn't deaf. Someone had rung him and hung up. That had happened four times in the last two days; and each time he'd gotten to the phone after just a couple of rings. Who could be doing this to him?

Fear hit him and he headed for the corner. Perhaps he had invented the ring. If he could go deaf, see colors for sounds, he could invent a telephone ring. Continually summoned by the phone, he would never work again. The phone hated him anyway. Over it people demanded his time at dinners he didn't want to attend, pressured him to sit on boards in which he had no interest, badgered him to support causes he regarded as a joke, or in the name of friendship invited him to lunch; so that he had to face the ordeal of going uptown, of looking and sounding normal, of wasting time when he ought to be painting.

He would like to grab the hammer from beneath his kitchen sink and smash the phone. No, better, take the kitchen knife, rip the phone wires from his wall, cut them, sneak the phone from his studio and dump it into a garbage can. That wouldn't work; it would leave a hole in the wall and damaged wires which some snoop might see and report. Besides, the phone company probably had great machines whirring in secret that recognized immediately when someone cut wires or destroyed a phone.

Then the phone company sent its phone servants, huge, powerful men who hated people and loved phones. These phone servants would arrive suddenly at his door; break it down; and seeing the damaged phone cry, "Oh no, oh no, oh no, oh no," over and over like the busy signal. They would so fill his room with sound that he would go deaf and not be able to defend himself. Then they would handcuff him and bind up the injured phone, and sing to it, and sweetly oil it, and lay it in a box stuffed with lamb's wool—and call the police to come and put him away because phone murderers are mad.

To outwit the enemy he needed to control his temper and employ sneaky finesse. He wanted to be able to call out so he could talk to people like Wup-'em, Dee, Sarah, Jane. What he didn't need were incoming calls. He'd unscrew the base of the phone, take a wad of Kleenex and stuff the tissue between bell and clapper hard. That way he'd gag the phone. If it rang he'd know he'd made up the sound. He rocked in the corner feeling triumphant because he'd won again; and frightened because living was taking so much time away from painting.

Even with the phone not ringing, there were some appointments he could not break. His father wrote, saying that he had called several times, been unable to get him, and suggesting that he drop by and look at the studio. Probably his father wanted to make certain that he was not turning into Uncle Schuyler. If he went deaf in front of his father, he'd be in trouble. Fortunately there should be no reason to mention numbers. And he had never failed to hear his doorbell. He made a date. If only he had more to show his old man. To make him walk up five flights of stairs for the nothing he'd been painting was pointless.

When the doorbell rang he was ready; and instead of just pushing the buzzer to open the door, he went downstairs to walk up with his father Fortunately this was one of his good days.

"Good to see you, Father, you're looking well."

"Had a good summer. Good to see you too, George. It's been some time."

"A lot's been going on."

"I'm sure."

They started up the stairs together, his father, mustache trimmed and eyes bright, disdaining the banister. They halted at the second landing, and Dent stiffened to fend off the coming objection to building and neighborhood.

"Nice building this, George, well constructed and maintained. Built around 1889, a period of sound construction. In a neighborhood that's coming up, too. There aren't many such areas left in the city, I'm afraid. —In spite of your work in Congress."

"You're right, Father."

"You realize this house has an extra four feet?" Dent nodded. "You always had a fine eye for physical detail. I'd hoped it would carry into the family business. But. Upward and onward."

The winter sunlight flooded into the studio. Dent took his father's coat. His father sat down on the bed and looked around.

"Properly monastic, except for the bed. Seems like a good place to work, George. An excellent place."

"Would you like a cup of coffee, Father, or tea?"

His father rose and began to pace, looking at the canvases. "I had a studio once, in Paris, on the Rue de Lille. Do you know it?"

"Sure, runs into the Rue du Bac." Dent was totally surprised. "You had a studio?"

"It is not part of my life I advertise. The family sent me abroad to study foreign building construction. There was a young lady involved—from a good family." His father's eyes focused on him hard. "That's not your problem, George?"

"I'm a bit old for that, sir."

"I hope so. I was not cut out to be an artist. I don't believe any Dent is. But I could be wrong. I have been in the past. —How do you feel your work is going?"

"As you can see, slowly."

"That's not surprising, you've just started." His father had by now examined all his new canvases. "I didn't like your exhibition too much, George. Flashy, but no solid work."

Was his father being hostile or just fixing the point with his customary engineer's precision?

"As you said, I'm just starting." His father took another turn before the abstract nudes and the linear alley scenes which Dent had been working on.

"Composition's getting stronger in the street series, George."

"Thank you."

"Do you enjoy doing these nudes?"

"No."

"Why do them then? Abstraction does not appear to me to be one of your strong points."

"I was having trouble with nudes. I thought that by shifting to abstraction I might be able to break down whatever barrier was between me and the canvas."

"That's an adequate reason. I withdraw my criticism, though not the observation. I have found when people go wrong in my business the problem is usually between the eye and the mind, not between the mind and the drafting table."

His father suddenly seemed quite close. Would he answer a personal question or shut himself off.

"Have you been happy in your work, Father?"

"By and large, George."

"What were your best years?"

"Some time ago, I'm afraid. What I've done for the past twenty years is pretty routine. I'm not an engineer any more, I'm a salesman. I know the board chairmen because I built their buildings when they were hot-shot vice presidents in the twenties and thirties. Oh, I still do work; good work. But most of it's done by others in the firm." His father paused, then the lips came hard together. The plunge into communication would now end. "Fortunately I'm a good organizer. You are too, George. That's why I'm worried about you as an artist. I hope this time you've made the right choice. And you'll stick with it."

"I've given myself seven years."

"Aren't you sure yet what you want to do?" A note of testiness came into his father's voice. "And for God's sake, take care of Sarah. We are all very fond of her."

"So am I, sir."

"Good luck." His father extended his hand.

"You won't take some coffee?"

"No, thank you."

"I'll walk downstairs with you."

"That's not necessary."

"I'd like to."

They were back in their father-son minuet again. Quite possibly the dance had begun back when he was very small. If he had become an architect, would they now be sitting in a shared office, gassing back and forth about accomplishments and swindles, buildings and eccentricities, going out to lunch together?

Oh Jim. Jim!

But if he had become an architect he would have been different. If-questions were meaningless. His father and he circled each other, not like fighters—there was too little contact for that—but like anthropologist and artifact trying to puzzle out the logic or purpose hidden at the core of the other.

"Good-by George."

"Good-by, Father."

They turned their backs on each other.

Weekends he went to Washington to see Jane and Sarah. His best work of the week always seemed to start just as it was time to leave for the airport. But once, when he had painted on, nothing had happened, and Sarah was furious at him for missing his plane. Though he hated to leave the safety of his studio for Washington almost as much as he hated to shop, he'd discovered a way by which he could negotiate such voyages even on his bad days. This method which had begun mostly as a game, had gradually hardened into a saving ritual.

When he had to leave his studio under pressure, he became a tank. One day, while terrified in the supermarket, already deaf, and not yet at the checkout counter, he remembered that in his last war there had been relative safety inside his armored hull. To place such steel around himself now he pretended to be a tank. Tanks knew where they were going, were solid, steady and dependable, couldn't be hustled by hostile clerks or upset by sudden bursts of color in the street. Tanks crushed the opposition.

He might look a little funny as he went down the street going "Zzzzzrrruuummm, zzzrrruuummm, zzzrrruuummm," pulling now on the left-track lever, now on the right to maneuver through the crowd. But he was careful only to "zzzrrruuummm" quietly, as if sneaking up for a night attack. He got great satisfaction from completing a difficult maneuver as a tank, such as down-shifting before entering subway stairs, or pivoting sideways through a revolving door. To get the mail out of his box and unlock his front door were tricky too, because he had to take his hands off the track levers and firing solenoids to handle his keys.

He had a few bad moments today as he maneuvered up the stairs of the air shuttle. Could the plane take the weight of the tank? But they got off the ground okay; and the rest of the trip was easy: "Piece of cake," as Costa used to say. He didn't stop being a tank until he had paid off the cab and was almost inside the front door of his Georgetown house, because he remembered how Jim would rush to meet him as he went up the stairs and he needed armor against that.

Jane was out spending the night with a special friend. Why did Sarah let that happen on his precious weekends? He and Sarah had dinner alone.

"I've called you several times," she said, glaring at him over the candles. "You don't spend much time in our apartment."

"I've told you, Sarah, it's easier to get work if I spend the night in the studio. Just get up and walk to the canvas."

"I've got to see the studio."

"Any time, Sarah, love to have you." He shoveled in a little more food. He'd be happier if he had a girl in his studio, he thought.

"It's ridiculous having the apartment when you live in that studio."

"Sarah, we found a school for Jane and you still decided to live in Washington."

"I like Washington."

"So do I."

"Then why in God's name don't you live here?"

He kept quiet. He was down several hundred thousand Brownie points this evening already because when he'd come in from New York he'd tried to take Sarah to bed. He should have known better. They were due at cocktails with friends of hers and she didn't want to be late.

"Stop, Daddy. Don't you know where we're going?"

"The Potters. Sure I know."

"Then act like it. They're prompt people. They contributed to all your campaigns. And they bought one of your pictures. A large picture."

What prick would argue with such a social obligation? —He ate in silence. There was a great deal of silence around him lately.

"You don't have to come home at all," Sarah continued. She was probably a little drunk, he thought. "Jane and I see you so seldom we are learning to do quite well without you." He let that one ricochet out the dining room window, too. "Say something!"

"What's there to say?"

Loud, dead silence.

"Good lamb," he said.

"It's not lamb. It's veal. —With all these sacrifices Jane and I are making," Sarah pressed on, "how's your work coming?"

"Badly." She'd asked him that three times already tonight.

"Good God! When are you going to have another exhibition?"

"I just had one, remember."

"Eight months ago. I believe an exhibition a year is proper."

"Every month, if I was turning out stuff. I'm not."

"Why not?"

"I have no idea."

"Brother, that's a stupid answer. What do I tell my friends when they ask me what you're doing? When they can see another exhibit?"

"What do I tell myself?"

"I'd like to know!"

He kept quiet and chewed some more, taking a sip of wine to wash down the paste in his mouth. Courage, men, he thought, we'll be in Berlin this time next year. Those of us who are alive.

In the next four months he turned out a few canvases that satisfied him and somewhat increased his ability to function in a world without numbers. He was proud of the way he handled this problem. He'd like to see the average Joe standing inside his tank at the supermarket counter trying to subtract a chorus line of champagne bottles dancing on match-stick legs with cloche hats tilted left on their cork heads, while the clerk, who was probably stealing from him, yelled a third picture in which a rhinoceros with a pink lei on its horn charged round and round.

To ease the situation inside stores he laid in, one good day, a two-hundred-dollar supply of ten dollar bills. A bag full of groceries from the supermarket never went over ten dollars, so he could hand over a ten and stand glaring at the clerk as if he actually could understand the total on the cash register. That would stop them from stealing. Then, groceries in hand, the old tank could maneuver through the door of the supermarket and back to the safety of his studio, secret still safe.

Also he gleaned a fascinating piece of intelligence about the number world. Numbers produced two types of pictures. A few digits, the repeaters, gave off the same image every time. However, the vast majority of numbers were wild, vicious and shifty, always appearing differently, so that unless he had thought of the number himself he had no idea what it was.

The only four numbers that repeated were: One, Three, Seven, and Twelve. One he avoided thinking about. One was a great vaporous black cloud with fingers on it like a giant squid that oozed and expanded. He felt he had met One somewhere before and almost been killed.

Three appeared as three monkeys, either scampering along the top of a pointed picket fence holding hands like children's paper cutouts, or else squatting on the same fence in a hear no evil, see no evil, speak no evil position. Only these three monkeys were reversed: they saw no good, heard no good, spoke no good.

He spent most time thinking about Seven, old lucky Seven, his most fascinating and friendly repeater. Seven spiraled down on him, a giant white die with orange number spots, rolling and twisting out of a brilliant blue mist. The die would finally come to rest just short of him, as he knew it would; there was mystery but no menace in Seven, with the four orange spots of number Four facing him. Then the surface of the die with its four dots would zoom in toward him, growing bigger and bigger, till the dots passed him by, immobile sentries, two to the left, two to the right; and he was inside the humming ivory white of the die, safe. —But how could he buy food, or even talk about the weather, from inside a die?

Twelve came across rustic and puzzling: a little four- or five-year-old girl who stood in a green field and chucked herself under the chin with a buttercup. She had fat red cheeks and dimples, her white smock was hemmed with tiny red strawberries, and the tickle of the big yellow buttercup both made her smile and cast a soft yellow shadow on the bottom of her chin. He knew her name was the "Dutch Cleanser Girl" though that was preposterous because the Dutch Cleanser can had a little Dutch boy on it. The girl was either someone alive he'd met, or seen in a painting. But each time he pressed in toward knowledge of just who she was, her picture began to fade out and his anxieties flamed up.

There was one mutant number, son-of-a-bitch Four, usually wild but sometimes a repeater. He never knew where he stood with Four. When it decided to be a repeater it started out as a rolling die that came to rest showing Four, just like Seven; so that for a few moments he'd truly believe he was dealing with old lucky Seven. But then tricky bastard Four stayed where it was, bouncing a little like a dormant jumping bean, and the face did not move in toward him. Eventually a new picture would start to materialize between the orange spots. He hated Four for trying to fool him; and, worse, break up his friendship with Seven.

Beyond Twelve he was certain all the numbers were wild, though he had yet to explore beyond Twenty. By Eighteen and Nineteen the pictures became so complicated that he spent a great deal of time just watching each fantastic image; and he had more important work than exploring numberland for numbers that might repeat. When you've seen one big number, Dent, you've seen them all, he used to mumble to himself, now it's time to paint.

He understood that the repeaters, and perhaps even the wild numbers, were, like dreams, trying to tell him something; only they were trying to grab him by the throat and shake the truth into him while he was awake. He in turn tried to attack the repeating numbers, force the truth out of them, who they were and what they meant. —He never did this with One, because One, stronger than himself, terrified him. —He tried the direct assault of analysis, he tried the flank attack of free association, and he tried to lure the repeaters into ambush by thinking secretly about them while pretending to do something else.

One day sitting in the corner he pretended to think about a new series of self-portraits that would start from when he was little. Not from one (there came the evil blot as he thought of it); that was silly, he was too little for a portrait; he'd start with three. The three monkeys scampered along the fence and the middle one winked at him evilly. What was I like at three? he wondered. Then he heard his mother's voice say through the deafness produced by Three's intensity: "A little monkey."

A great rush of air burst from him and he danced out of the corner hugging himself. He'd solved his first repeater; the first solid bit of progress since he'd moved into the studio. He had the same elation as after his first tank attack. He knew there'd be more battles and greater danger; he might not make it; but already he'd done more than most men.

After a little time off for self-congratulation and a drink, he considered the implication of the three monkeys. The monkeys were evil, therefore at three he saw himself as evil. The self-portrait he had been pretending to plan when the truth of Three burst over him should not be George Dent as a smiling, imaginative, well-brought-up boy; but Dent, an already debauched and corrupt swindler of men. That was a ridiculous picture of a child of three, but the truth of the monkeys remained.

He started toward the girl and stopped. That group is too tight to break up, he thought, so he stood still, shaking the ice back and forth in his highball glass with intense concentration. You should have pushed on, he told himself, that's why you came to this opening, to get a girl. All she can do is say no; all you can do is go deaf. Start up, driver. He used to meet a thousand people a night and love it. Girls flocked around him as a Congressman. That had nothing to do with now. He stood at the edge of the group and listened, smile soldered on.

"Hi, I'm George Dent." Not Congressman George Dent any more. There must be a better opening. I'm George Dent the fink-out painter. As he'd foreseen, he got nowhere with that group.

He withdrew and started toward another clutch. Got nowhere there either. Christ, he thought, is everybody a twosome but me? I got married so I wouldn't have to do this. You're really happier alone, he argued with himself, go back to your studio, Dent.

Get the smile on. Check the ammunition racks. Move out.

"I'm George Dent. Are you in the art racket, or, God forbid, do you just like openings?"

"A free meal's a free meal, even a stuffed egg." She licked egg off her fingers as she spoke. "Sometimes I think I'll turn into a stuffed egg." She giggled. She had a fat ass. Dent disliked gigglers and fat asses.

"With my luck, I'd turn into a can of baked beans."

"You broke too?"

"Well, truthfully, I'm eating pretty well right now. I had a show at the Richardfield a few months ago that sold quite well."

"An art show?"

"Yes."

"How about that!"

He pushed the conversation forward with a few more commonplaces, ending with "I often wonder if a man gets the same sort of crowd at his funeral he gets at his openings."

"Hey, that's not nice. —Do you suppose they have cold cuts someplace?"

"I'll tell you what. This place is getting me down. I'll take you out and buy you dinner."

She looked at him. He shifted his eyes, feeling the old fear that people could see through them into his mind.

"You don't even know my name," she said.

"You could tell me."

"Alice Frank." He instantly forgot it, and stood looking at her, searching for the sounds that had just passed through him. "What's your sign?" she asked.

Congressman Dent knew that answer. Certain women wouldn't vote for you unless they knew your sign. "Gemini."

"Mine's Pisces; but I get on fine with Geminis. —I should stay here a bit longer. But. I'll get my coat. As long as you're not a Scorpio."

"Oh, no." He shoved with her through the crowded room, eyeing each group they pushed past with hostile fear, expecting some male to greet what's her name and grab his catch.

At the restaurant, the one to which he'd taken Dee the first time they went to bed, he fished for her first name.

"What do your friends call you?"

"Alice." He got it that time. She was an unemployed actress. He heard at length, when he bothered to listen, her views on acting. "I need to liberate myself. To learn to be. It's hard, really hard. But I'm learning with this powerful teacher I have. You should meet my teacher, George. You should. Such talent."

She discovered he'd been in Congress and oohed admiration. Her views on politics were instant ignorant sweetness, by contrast with instant ignorant viciousness: the disease of the thoughtless right rather than the thoughtless left.

"Stevenson sends me. He really sends me. Do you think he's going to be the next President?"

"No."

"I'm sure you're wrong. He sends everybody. All my friends. My teacher says he's certain to make it this time. —If we all work. How did you vote on war?"

"I led the fight against war."

"I'm so glad. I wouldn't like anyone who was for war. Do you know why some people are for war?" She was off again. From time to time Dent nodded. "You're so wise," she'd say after every nod.

If he ever ran for public office again, he'd have a TV program on which he didn't say a word, just sat and listened to the public, looked the tube in the eye, and now and again smiled and nodded. He'd drive his opponents up a wall. No position to attack, just total competence communicated. He switched what-was-her-name—oh yes, Alice—back on.

"Do you know why men have learned to fly, but not to control their anger? It's because—my teacher says this—it's because they spend more on one than they do on the other. Now isn't that a thought?"

Dent nodded again. He guessed you could call that a thought. It stretched the meaning of the word quite a bit. But in the interests of sexual harmony he'd go along with it.

After dinner she took a green mint frappe because she liked the color.

"That's the artist in you," said Dent. "Your love of color and harmony." He was following the Red Donner strategy: "Don't tell 'em they've got a beautiful body. Tell 'em they got a beautiful soul."

"I never thought of that, but you're right. You're so wise."

"Come back to my studio and I'll mix you a drink of a fascinating amber color."

She giggled. He paid the check.

She was amazed at the neatness of his studio. "You keep it this way all by yourself?"

"You can't work in a messy place."

"My place, you should see it. I've got to learn to pick it up. No man wants a messy person."

"Maybe you should keep it a mess as an excuse: to provide a reason for men not to want you."

"You've never been to a shrink?"

"No." They'd been through the psychiatry bit.

"You must think a lot. Wow."

He took her in his arms and kissed her. She had smeary lipstick. After a few wiggles and giggles, she kissed back.

He made her a stinger. He'd bought the white crème de menthe that afternoon, just in case. He drew the two canvas chairs together and they necked some more, the chair arms getting in his way. She wasn't fat, really, just not very slim, and a bit soft.

"We can't sit kissing here. This is silly." He pulled her up and headed her toward the bed.

"I don't know."

He hit her with the wounds bit.

After all his trouble she really didn't know what to do in bed; and kept right on talking almost until he was inside. After that he had the suspicion she wasn't reacting from desire but from the way she'd been taught in acting class. "Pant, one two, pant one two, groan, one two, deeper now, groan, one two, I'm liberated, say it, feel it, groan." She moved up and down much too fast, as if there was some electric contact in her tail that shot it up off the mattress each time it settled back. He came too soon, with little pleasure.

She stopped immediately and asked, "Wasn't that wonderful for you?"

"Oh yes."

She nuzzled him a bit. Then, a little later: "Don't let me go to sleep here, George. I have to go home."

He argued; she insisted. There was nothing he could do but get dressed.

Chivalry and the realities of the New York jungle required that he escort her home. A taxi was almost impossible to find. The next afternoon he developed a mammoth cold.

A few weeks later as he was coming downstairs to get his mail after a good morning's work, so good he didn't even need his tank, he was stopped on the first-floor landing by an old woman.

He'd seen her before, sitting in her doorway looking out at the stairs. She was part of a large Italian family that filled the house with the smell of their delicious cooking.

"Mister. Mister."

"Yes."

"You was a Congressman?"

Where had she learned that? "Yes."

"Aaah. Please, I have trouble with the Department."

"The Welfare Department?" This was going to take time from his painting.

"Aaaah. Who else?" She shook her head and Dent watching her felt the age-old resignation of "we," the eaten, toward "they," who feast.

"What happened?"

It was hard to figure out what happened. It seemed the old woman, Mrs. Marsalla, had collected money for the children of her cousin, "a no-good woman" who had run off and left them. The Welfare Department claimed that Mrs. Marsalla had passed the children off as hers to draw extra money. Far from continuing the payments, the government insisted Mrs. Marsalla should pay a large sum back. At the end Mrs. Marsalla was in tears.

"Maybe they right. The supervise she say to me: 'Watsa old tramp like you here for to bother me olla time.' Me. Maybe I do something wrong. Something I don't understand. You think I deserve?"

"I do not think you deserve."

How many times had he sat in his office and heard the same story? The system worked so callously, so bureaucratically, was so nearly impossible to reform. To provide welfare money efficiently, with decency, to protect the recipients from abuse and still satisfy the demands of the taxpayers who provided the money was a fascinating and complex problem. Once he had been one of the few people who made a try at understanding and solving such problems. Now here was Mrs. Marsalla before him, one victim of the endless battle.

She rubbed the back of her black woolen sleeve across her face to dry her tears. Suddenly she changed right before his eyes, so completely that he instinctively shook his head to clear his vision. She ceased to be a symbol, part of a problem; and became uniquely Mrs. Marsalla, herself alone, clearly outlined.

Arriving from Italy full of hope, watching the years scrape by, her dreams wring out, but still maintaining the heritage of loyalty, of work, of family, of cooking. Now she was old, and broken, and worthy; her tragedy was individual, and private. Hers alone. No other would ever be quite like it.

There were real people coming to see me all those years, he thought, and I saw only problems, abstractions.

He was as bad as those liberals he'd mocked. Well, maybe not quite, he reassured himself; at least he'd tried to make changes, not just help himself to good feelings. But he'd lost his sense of the individual.

No wonder I can't paint, he thought in terror.

"Did they give you a number, Mrs. Marsalla?"

"Yes. I got inside. Better you wait here. I'm sorry. The place not fixed up."

"I understand. It's early in the day."

"Yes, early." She smiled at him, dignity restored. "You come for cup of coffee some afternoon, when the men at home."

"I'd like that."

Already, by asking for her number he'd lost part of her. But as she came out the door, triumphant at having found the paper so quickly, he got all of her back again.

"It's a help?" she asked as he took the paper. On it were her name and a group of pictures that must be her claim number. If, later in his studio he could decipher the number, he'd phone his friend, Dan Falko, of the Sixteenth, South, who'd be glad to handle it. If not he'd go to the photostat place around the corner and photostat the claim and mail that to Falko.

"Just what I need. Let me keep it while I make a phone call to the right person. I'll give it back tomorrow afternoon, okay?"

"Thank you so much, sir."

"I like to help a neighbor."

Back in his studio he took out all his canvases, the ones the gallery hadn't been able to sell, the ten months of work since his exhibit, and lined them up against his studio wall. Seen now, they were contrived, and weak. He had forgotten what he knew when he painted the nude of Helen, forgotten that feeling and thought had to fuse. Each moment and person were both unique and part of a process; individual and complete, yet also the locus of the most complex abstractions of their times.

He stared at his recent paintings. He had hung these fakes on his walls to show people, grown excited when he painted them, felt he was making progress. How he had fooled himself.

He had to rid himself of these pictures. They crowded his studio, poisoned the air. His stomach knotted as he looked at them because each picture screamed that he'd never make it. He'd break the damn canvases up and burn them. He'd keep one of the Senate and one of the fire escapes to show himself where he'd been; but burn the rest.

He knew his minuscule fireplace, about the size of five *Britannica* volumes, worked, because he'd built a couple of fires out of milk cartons and old crates for Dee and himself. (In his Georgetown house a fire had burned every winter night, while Jim and Jane, fresh from their bath, played before it or watched TV.) The image halted him in the middle of his studio. In tears he went to the garbage and pulled out two milk cartons. He put the cartons in the fireplace as kindling and began to break apart his paintings.

With the help of a liberal splash of turpentine he got the milk cartons blazing and pushed in the first canvas. The picture caught with a pleasant whoosh. Relief flooded him as he pushed in the second canvas. The third picture was still wet and the stretcher jammed. He smeared quite a bit of paint on himself as he ripped the canvas off the frame. His face began to itch; and he rubbed his hands over his face to break the torture. He broke two beaverboard paintings against the end of his bed and wedged them in too.

He'd fed the fire too fast, he realized. The draft in its tiny chimney had failed and thick smoke began to roll into the room. He kicked at the fire to get it to draw better. Instead, one of the half-burned canvases spilled from the fireplace and fell smoking onto the floor.

He picked up the canvas by what he thought was its unlighted end and burned his fingers. He broke a stretcher in two and using the broken ends as tongs managed to work the canvas back into the fire. His studio was now chokingly full of smoke. Coughing, he decided to open a window to help the draft. His chimney hardly seemed to be drawing at all. In the movies the old masterpieces always went up with a roar and a crackle; but his canvases just smoked.

What was needed was a healthy shot of turpentine on the whole mess to get it to burn. He picked up the bottle and poured a couple of good slugs over the fire. Nothing happened. He gave the works another heavy slosh. The flame roared up the stream of turpentine and exploded into the bottle in his hand. With a yell he pitched the bottle into the raging fire. The bottle split with a crash and the whole mess flared out into the room.

Bits of ash, flaming canvas and beaverboard floated in the air. Fiery turpentine dripped from the fireplace onto his wooden floor. Dent stomped on the flames with his shoes. That didn't put it out and he raced to his bathroom, dunked a towel in the toilet and running back slopped the towel on his smoldering floorboards.

His doorbell went off.

Who the hell was that at a time like this? He gave his door buzzer a vicious jab, feeling he had to answer in case someone had seen the smoke and thought him in trouble. Perhaps it was Mrs. Marsalla. Or Avon calling.

A spasm of pain shot through his right foot. He looked down and saw his right shoe was smoking. He wrenched off his shoe and held it under the tap. Then hostilely flung open his studio door.

"Sarah!"

"George! What's this smoke?"

"Smoke?" He was unable to think up a convincing lie. He'd been out of politics too long. "Some old canvases." He looked over at his fire. The floor seemed to have stopped burning, and flames were finally roaring nicely up the chimney.

"Who's that?" yelled Sarah. Dent whirled around, thinking for an instant someone had snuck into his studio. Then he saw Sarah pointing in the classic pose of the female scenting a bird in the bed at the nude of Helen.

"Oh, her. You remember her."

"I do not."

"I mean the picture. It was hanging in my studio when we first met."

"It was not."

"Yes, it was."

"No, it wasn't."

He pushed away the smoke between them. "Sarah, it was. It was one of my favorites." Sarah stiffened more. "It's dated. Go over and look at it."

Sarah started to say something but choked on the smoke.

"Raise your hands over your head," he said.

"What are you burning?"

"Canvases. Old canvases. The last ten months of my work. I couldn't stand them." He'd rather not have answered. Sarah would find some way to use that truth to hurt him. "Did you tell me you were coming? I don't remember."

"What?"

"Which what?" He never could follow Sarah's mental shorthand.

"You're mad!" Sarah yelled. "You've painted your face. One shoe on. Burning canvases. On my money."

The room was filling up with smoke again. A man could get lung cancer here, he thought. He gave Sarah a big encouraging smile to try and head off a fight he didn't want now, when he wasn't ready, when he wanted to think about Mrs. Marsalla, and get rid of his canvases.

"You look sick," she said.

He smiled again.

"George."

George was himself. Now if she'd slipped and called him Tom, Dick, or Harry, he'd be ahead.

"George, I can't live like this."

Nature doesn't imitate art, he thought, it imitates summer reruns of TV soap operas.

"I never see you," Sarah surged on. "Jane never sees you. You won't settle down. Give me another child. Look at you. This place. Her." (That was Helen.) "That bed.—George we can't love you when you're like this."

"I love you, Sarah. But I have to find out if I can paint." The inadequate words sounded small and distant as they pushed themselves through the smoke.

"Find out!"

He moved forward to dust a piece of ash off the front of his wife's dress. Unfortunately he coughed as he did so, which gave the motion more force than he intended. Suddenly afraid that Sarah would interpret the gesture as feeling up her breast he drew back, having succeeded in merely grinding the ash into the fabric.

"What are you doing?" she exploded.

"Brushing some ash off you. —Listen to those sirens."

A wail of sirens, claxons, and general noise was rising from the street and drifting into his studio, half sound, half little streaks of blue color. Perhaps someone had seen the smoke coming from his studio window and turned in an alarm. He could be in trouble. He started toward his window.

"Listen to me," screamed Sarah.

"I can listen and look out the window at the same time."

"You're—you're feckless."

Where did Sarah get her Victorian words? Did she secretly sneak downstairs in the middle of night to brush up on her Tom Swift? He looked out the window. From both ends of the block fire equipment converged on his building and the one next door. Perhaps some burning canvas had blown up the chimney and started a roof fire.

"There's a fire, Sarah."

"It's your stinking canvases."

Dent raced over, picked the soaking towel off the floor and flung it in the bathtub. He had to get rid of the evidence. Thank God the fire had died a bit.

"Put your shoe on," hissed Sarah.

He'd forgotten about his shoe. He retrieved if from the sink and worked it, wet and soggy, onto his foot.

There was a heavy knock at his studio door.

"Firedepartment!" someone cried.

"Coming," he said; and threw open his door, beaming with the forced innocence of a liberal candidate smearing his opponent. Four large black raincoats, axes and fire extinguishers at the ready, surged into the room. They saw the minuscule Vesuvius in his fireplace and paused rigid, as if about to have their picture taken raising the flag on Iwo Jima.

"Dat your fire?"

"What ya burnin' Mac?"

"A few wood scraps and canvas. Chimney isn't drawing too well." He tried the smile again.

"Not drawin', Mac. The roof's on fire."

"I smell gas," said another.

"That's oil paint," he said.

Two more firemen entered the room. One joined the group before the fire. The other drifted over to ogle the nude of Helen. From within the huddle before the fire someone yelled, "Put it out, Joe!"

Two firemen unslung their extinguishers. There was a roar and clouds of CO_2 filled the studio. "Give her a couple of extra squirts, Joe." The firemen advanced on his fire, spreading bits of black soggy ash over his walls. Christ, how would he ever paint here again?

Sarah looked at him, shaking her head.

The fireman before the nude Helen raised his ax.

"Hey, stop that!" yelled Dent. The roar of CO_2 ended. The firemen pivoted toward him hostilely through the smoke. The one by the window lowered his ax reluctantly.

They are looking at you, Dent, he thought, and they see an artist, a schnook—the kind they hate. In a few moments they'll ax this place apart brick by brick to see if you've got a firebug hidden in the walls.

"What happened?" he asked, all guilty openness. "Spark light on the roof?"

"Yes, what did happen, Lieutenant?" Sarah moved forward in her best society manner. She smiled at the firemen and raised her right hand to fluff the back of her blond hair and lift her breasts. And the wonder of it is, thought Dent, she does it without knowing it.

"I guess a spark or something hit the roof, ma'am." Now the firemen were apologetic. "Was that all you were burning? Just scraps of wood? This smell."

"As my husband said, you probably smell the paint on the canvas." Her pronunciation of the word "paint" managed to convey the thick layer of excrement crawling with worms.

"Burning rubbish is illegal," said one of the firemen.

And your canvases are rubbish, he thought. You are caught. They probably have a special ordinance against burning rubbish of a semicombustible nature passed specifically to trap artists. This group would summon the lieutenant. The lieutenant the captain. The captain the battalion chief. The battalion chief the deputy area chief. They'd take him to headquarters.

"Certainly burning rubbish is illegal," said Sarah, treating the men kindly as if they were almost her equal. "Usually we start the fire with newspaper. Everyone does. But the city doesn't consider that illegal. Today we had no newspaper and we felt like a fire so we used some old canvas."

"A hell of a lot of it," said one of the firemen.

Sarah whirled on him. "It looks like a lot because you've made such a mess."

Easy Sarah, he thought, don't overdo it. But the firemen fell back before her.

"Yeah, I guess so." They began to move toward the door. "We'll tell the lieutenant. But we gotta make a report."

"Thank you. That's very good of you. You certainly got here fast." She shut the door behind them.

He opened his mouth to thank her for helping him out; but before he could speak she turned on him.

"You're mad. Plain mad. Not working. Painting. Starting fires. Driving Jane and me out. You're going to end up in jail, brother; yes, jail!"

He gazed at his wife through swirls of CO_2. She was alluring when angry.

"Sarah, we're not getting anywhere."

"All you do is play. Play on my money."

He let that lie. Sarah on money was impossible. He had tried to explain several months ago that, even counting his salary and office allowance, they had spent a great deal more of their own money when he was in Congress, or when he was a lawyer running for Congress, than now, when he painted. He'd gotten nowhere.

"George," she continued, "I was talking to my father yesterday. He's agreed to give you a chance. He needs someone to run his Washington office. Not write the news. The men can do that. But manage the office. Keep up the important contacts."

He felt a little boy, standing his ground when he knew he had no ground, just being obstinate, arguing when he knew he was wrong, because giving in was worse. He was probably about to lose Sarah. He would be left alone to battle through a divorce in a world where he was already failing in other ways. Fear flamed inside him. He could operate well in Washington; make Sarah happy; see Jane; be safe.

He looked down at his right hand and quite consciously went through the motion of squeezing it to depress the button of his tank microphone.

"No," he said.

Sarah stood and looked at him.

George, she wanted to say, don't you see how wrong you are? Jim's death has thrown you back into childhood. Act like an adult. Don't stand there shifting from foot to foot and not looking me in the eye. Fight. Grow up and be your old self. The man I loved. Who was worthy of my love. —I'm sorry I let you quit Congress. I should have stopped that. But we can start again. I love you. My father's offered you a good job. Take it. Look what you've done to yourself. To me. You've made me miserable, George. I cry a great deal at night.

But her anger at how Dent had betrayed her exploded, to trigger her for a kill.

"You're a failure. No friends left. You know that. A failure."

He was on the killing ground. He moved his tank to the flank and struck.

"Sarah," he said, surprised at how hard he cracked out her name, "I can't blame you and Jane for not waiting. I think you are right. I think it's best we end it and that I move out. We'll both be happier. —I'll come down to Washington and pick up some of my things."

He heard the rumble of the words as they moved away from him and wondered who had said them.

Sarah shook her head, jolted. He felt cold.

"That's what you want?" she said.

"I think you're right. It's best." He was ashamed for fighting dirty; but he had to survive.

"Brother, I've made you what you are. I'll take it all."

"Now, Sarah . . ."

"Don't now Sarah me, you filth. You're weak. Just plain weak."

But I'm winning, he thought. "I'll come down to Washington next weekend and get a few of my things."

"I'll not have you in my house."

"It's our house."

"I paid for it."

"We paid for it. And the lease is in my name."

"You bastard." She had never called him that before, he realized.

"Look, Sarah, for the sake of our only remaining child, let's not fight like children. I need my clothes and a few other things."

"What?"

"My extra paints in the shed. A few of my school books. The Beckman, Wollenberg left me. Small things like that. I'll drop you a note so you'll know in advance."

Just like his first combat. He'd planned what he'd do, but the action got away from him. Moments whizzed past him which he had to grab to survive—if this was survival: no son, no marriage, his paintings burning.

He opened the door for Sarah. "Thanks for being so understanding," he said to break up her next attack.

"I hate you."

She marched out.

Sarah and Jane were spending the weekend with Sarah's father in Syracuse when he arrived in Washington after a rough journey inside his tank. "So your daughter won't be forced to learn the type of coward you are," Sarah's note had stated.

He closed the front door behind him, and his love for his house grabbed at him, the cool odor of wood and stone, the smell of rich fabric and books, the light threading softly through the curtains, the solid hush of his ordered world.

He went to the library to take down Wollenberg's Beckman. In the corner of the library was Jim's tiny chair, the one his son used to draw up and climb on while he watched cartoons on television. The chair had been Dent's own when he was little, sitting in front of the fire and listening to his father read *Robinson Crusoe*. Had it also been his father's? Probably. This is the way the world breaks up, he thought. Chairs forgotten, libraries broken up, toys rusting.

He ran his hands over the small chair's much-re-covered back. Then bent down and smelled the cushions. No trace of Jim. The tears which he had heavy on his stomach vomited from his eyes. He fled to the bedroom, shut and locked the door, ashamed that the cook or someone coming to clean might see him cry and think him weak.

We are all refugees, he thought, sobbing on his and Sarah's bed for the last time. All refugees.

fourteen

He had assumed that when his painting started to improve, and he made progress toward handling numbers, the hostility of the world outside his studio would lessen. Yet he had done two portraits, one of Mrs. Marsalla and the other of her nephew, both of which he was certain were giant strides forward; and in the privacy of his studio he could see and write down more numbers; but his terror of the outside world, far from diminishing, had increased.

He had regained more control over numbers almost accidentally. One morning while gathering his energy to paint Mrs. Marsalla, he had been thinking about Jane, Sarah, the war, Dee, numbers; and watching a series of pictures in a flickery parade somewhere between the backs of his eyes and his brain. He would like to get the goddamn world of number pictures down on canvas, he thought, with all its annoyance, fascination and terror. And why did the repeaters repeat? Were they all numbers of special importance to him, as Three had been?

What other numbers, he wondered, not expecting any answer, define me? He heard: One, Seven, Nine. For an instant he saw the three numbers themselves clear of pictures, the first pure figures he had seen in several months.

He said: "One, Seven, Nine" out loud several times to himself. Suddenly he produced: "01824693." He saw that number too though pictures immediately pressed in to blot it out. He recognized 01824693 as his serial number as an officer in the Army; but what was One, Seven, Nine?

He got nowhere concentrating on One Seven Nine that day or the next, and succeeded only in driving the abstract numbers back into a series of menacing pictures in which even the friendship and stability of old lucky Seven was jeopardized.

On the third day he took time out from painting to try a flank attack, like the one which had worked with repeater Three. He stacked the Dent of One Seven Nine up against the Dent of 01824693. The two Dent-defining numbers had separate qualities. 01824693 shaved, wore long pants, worried, was serious, swore. One Seven Nine did none of these things. One Seven Nine got kissed, smelled his mother's perfume, had short pants, scraped its knees, and wore uncomfortable underwear that caught in the crotch. He hadn't worn underwear like that since?

He got it. Greenwich 179, their phone number when he was small. The first number George Dent had mastered. He put the number to one side to think about later and went back to some serious work on Mrs. Marsalla.

Over dinner that evening, as he celebrated by pan broiling a thin sirloin from the freezer, he gave himself over fully to his memories of One Seven Nine.

His mother had driven him downtown to the grocery store, then had to call home to find out something cook had forgotten.

"I'll work the phone. I'll work the phone."

"George, you don't know the number." His mother's hurry shredded the patience recommended in the latest psychology books and she picked up the phone off the store shelf herself and handed it to him. "The number is—"

"I know it! I know it!"

"Greenwich 179."

He flung the phone at his mother; lay down on the grocery floor; and screamed. His mother apologized to all the people in the store for her little boy's bad behavior; picked him up yelling, with people going tsk-tsk, spoiled brat, and took him straight home. That night he had to explain to his father why he had been bad. He knew there was no way to explain. His mother had shamed him. But that truth his father would never accept.

"I don't know, sir."

"You must know, George."

"I don't know."

"When you remember, you'll get your allowance again." After part of the summer his father restored his allowance anyway.

His real victory over 179 came several days later. He was visiting a friend for lunch, a rare treat that had almost been canceled because of his tantrum in the store. The friend could not believe that his pal, Dent, had knowledge of that grown-up mystery, the telephone.

So small he had to reach up and use two hands to lift it off the table, Dent had taken his friend's phone and called home. He wasn't sure he could do it. First you had to say: "Operator, Operator," several times till someone called "Operator" answered. Operator must live in a big house with a lot of wires, he guessed. Somebody said "Yes," through the thing against his ear. Was that Operator? A woman? If he did it wrong he'd be arrested.

"Greenwich 179." He forgot to say please. "Please."

"Thank you," said the voice in his ear. That must be Operator. She had a strange voice. Dent remembered the look of amazement on his friend's face as he gave his friend the phone so he could hear Dent's nurse inquiring what was wrong.

"Proved it! Proved it!"

After solving 1, 7, 9, he had a great deal of fun for a few weeks, and some terror, working on all the numbers that had defined him, bringing the pure numeral, itself, out from behind the pictures. Following Greenwich 1, 7, 9, came another series of phone numbers, Yale, New York, Washington, his many homes and offices since the war. And there were other numbers too, which seemed to hold importance for him but whose actual relationship to his life lurked just beyond his reach, even as the meaning of all the repeating numbers other than Three continued to elude him. He met, recognized, and mastered his Army serial numbers, his Social Security number, his street addresses, the addresses of his friends and their phone numbers, his radio call signs during the war: Dog two six as platoon leader, Dog six as company commander, Blue Seven as battalion executive. He found his safe-deposit box, his checking account, his Yale track numerals, his St. Luke's room, the number on the boat sail on the craft in which he and Jim had cruised. He, like every other American, was a mass of numbers. The hairs of his head, his length of days, all were numbered.

—Is this the face that launched a thousand ships? Sweet Helen, make me immortal with your phone number.

—I'm with a date, but I'd like to. RE2-7338.—

He grew so intrigued by numbers that he decided his next canvas should be the portrait of a man defined by numbers, an accountant. Fortunately, Dee's life class was using a strong male model; and he'd been able to force himself to attend the last three sessions. He could take his sketches and figure studies and transform them into a man at once defined and deformed, outlined and lost, with numbers all around his edges.

But all this progress held good only in his studio. Outside the world continued threatening. Sarah was in litigation with him over vast sums of money he could not possibly pay, refusing to let him see Jane because he was bohemian, unreliable, and neurotic. To shop was agony, his whole body itched as he entered a store. So he often went without adequate food. Inside a store or on the street he was still almost continually deaf; and the numbers were only pictures. He remained at the mercy of everyone; certain he was being despised, scorned and robbed.

Two weeks after he began *The Accountant,* which was giving him serious trouble, the real world struck out to decisively cripple him. He ran out of ten-dollar bills.

He still had lots of ones and fives and piles of silver that he had got as change for his tens at the stores. He could tell the difference between the bills by their pictures. To keep alive, he needed tens so he could lay down a bill and stand there waiting for his change as if he were normal. It's like being back in politics, he thought with a giggle, I'm defeated by lack of finances.

If he tried hard he could probably write himself a check for one hundred dollars and go up to his Fifth Avenue bank and get another bunch of tens that way. But for the old tank to take the subway or taxi into enemy territory would be dangerous. He might get lost. He would have to spend several days planning and gathering energy for such a trip and would get no work done. He doubted he could make the journey. The tank might throw a track, or get hit, and he'd have to abort the mission.

He considered his problem off and on for several days. There was a bank only five blocks away, a little farther than he usually tanked, but still his territory. A plan came to him whereby he could get that bank to transform his change, ones and fives into tens without their being able to cheat him. The plan was a bit mad, but that made no difference; mad plans work for mad men.

The next morning he took all the dollar bills and change he couldn't add and placed them in the right hand pocket of his jacket. That is all except one penny which he carefully secreted in the watch pocket of his pants. That penny was the stroke of genius by which Dent, the brilliant executive, would beat out Dent, the paralyzed artist nut. He looked at his watch to tell the time. It had stopped. He went to his silent phone to dial the time number. He couldn't remember it or read the numbers in the phone book. He had to gamble that in a little while it would be the right time for the bank to open. He knew it wasn't Saturday or Sunday. He'd been to life class two days ago and that was a Tuesday. He sat, terrified, waiting for H-hour.

He revved up his tank engine, testing it hard inside the studio because it would be a tough fight: along the streets to the bank, into the bank, dismount, skirmish up to the teller's window, hold, work the plan, regroup, remount, fight back home.

Perilously the old tank began to roll through his studio door, down the tenement stairs, with Dent, the combat-wise veteran, inching back the track levers, down-shifting to lowest gear, checking the tank's speed on the steep stair, so it wouldn't carom out into the street and turn over. Several times as he maneuvered around the landings he almost slipped a track over the edge. He didn't stop for the mail in his box because that would blunt the attack, deflect him from his objective.

He reached the bank safely, neatly maneuvered the tank through the revolving door and parked in a line before a teller's window. He was glad he had time to stand in line, dismount from his tank, remove his earphones, and shape himself up for the next phase of the operation. He was dressed all wrong for this battle. He was in overcoat, scarf, hat, and galoshes. Practically everyone else was in shirtsleeves, and tieless. It was possible that he was correct and everyone else was dressed wrong. But unlikely. To believe that would be paranoid.

His turn before the teller was next. Time to execute plan Able.

The clerk smiled at him. Nice clerk. Slowly Dent brought the change and the bills out of his right pocket and laid them on the counter. Very slowly. If he dropped something he might lose it in the sound-splash of color it made falling on the floor.

Halfway through taking out his change he said to the clerk, "I'm sorry I'm taking so long; I have arthritis." That too was part of the plan, to draw sympathy. Besides, Congressmen were always polite.

He felt he'd better explain to the people in line behind him why he was taking so long; after all, they might be voters. He turned to tell them; but they'd all left. He panicked. He must smell bad. Then he steadied himself; they were probably just impatient and had gone to other windows.

"Too bad they left," he said to the clerk. "They missed my nice explanation that I have arthritis." He hadn't planned to say that. The clerk didn't look so nice any more.

He got out all the change except the watch-pocket penny and smiled at the clerk. The clerk didn't smile back. Instead he said something Dent couldn't hear. No surprise there. He'd guessed he'd be so overwhelmed by battle noise at this moment he'd be deaf. Unless it was a number. Then he'd see pictures. He smiled again and said:

"I'd like it all in tens. —You'd better count it."

The clerk gave him a nasty look and started counting. He finished counting and said something. Dent saw a line of palm trees over yellow sand with candy-canes hanging from them. The clerk had told him how much he had, and he'd seen a picture, just as he'd planned.

Dent shook his head violently and said, "No."

The clerk glared and counted again. The clerk finished his recount and again opened his mouth. This time Dent saw a great blue python with its head in its mouth making a dancing circle before an orange water fountain.

"Wow, that's some number," he exclaimed involuntarily.

Easy, Dent, easy, or they'll lock you up, he warned himself. Don't lose it when you've got it; execute the plan. He pretended to search through his pockets for an instant; and then produced the penny as something he'd overlooked. He handed the penny to the clerk.

"That makes it correct," he said loudly. "And I'd like it in tens," he repeated.

The clerk looked down at a drawer. Dent had a moment's panic that he was going to push an alarm. But the clerk was counting out money. The penny had worked. He'd convinced the clerk he could count so accurately he'd even missed the penny.

Dent took the bills and some change from the clerk and stood looking at the man hard so that if the clerk was cheating him he'd become panicky and hand over the rest of the money. But the clerk just glared back. Dent stowed the money safely in an inside sponson: juicy ten-dollar bills, months of food.

As he moved away with a "zzzrrruuummm," pivoting his tracks easily on the bank's smooth marble floor, he noticed a large man staring at him. Dent checked quickly to make sure he wasn't "zzzrrruuummming" out loud; and in a panic saw the man turn to follow him from the bank. Perhaps he's seen you take up all that money, Dent thought, and has come to rob you; he certainly looks violent and powerful. How fortunate he'd already won the bank war. The tank could retreat now slowly toward the studio, not letting the enemy man know its terror.

The man moved closer to him, trying to get a flank position, pour in the killing fire. He started to increase his speed to pull away; but had to stop at the curb. A voice filtered through to Dent out of a humming, gray mist.

"Pardon me, sir, but I happened to notice you just now in the bank. You seemed to be in some trouble; but you looked so clean."

Clean? He looked at his hands on the track levers. They were gray.

"Do you need a friend?" the man went on. Dent didn't get the rest.

He wanted to shift into high and get going; but the passing cars checked him. He moved off in another direction. One block this way he could still get back to the tank coil. The man fell into place beside his right sponson.

"I am a very special person," the man said. "I keep my place in society. Would you like to see the Giants play this Sunday?" Dent tracked on. "We all touch girls sometimes, sir. That's nothing to be ashamed of."

A fag! He had to get away. He pulled visibly on the left track lever. Who cared who saw him. There was an opening in the crowd ahead. Bucking and jolting over the uneven ground he got through it.

"Look out." The man ran after him. "You crossed against the light, sir. Almost killed us both. Don't be afraid. I'm a friend. I like a man that's clean."

The man took him by the arm, gripping so powerfully he almost destroyed the tank. "Are you lost, sir? I can see you are a lover of football. Let me help you home."

"No." The word came out the tank cannon tiny, with great effort. What he had to do, Dent reasoned, was track right on by his door, then suddenly reverse into it and throw the man off. If the man attacked while his hand was off the firing solenoid and working his door key, he was in trouble.

"No," he said again, feeling a little black choke of sound pass up his throat like hot vomit. Had he made any noise?

Here was his door. The tank surged right on by it. Deception, a vital part of any attack.

"I've been in trouble too, sir. Let me help you."

The tank rolled through the menacing black smoke of his words.

"I'm going to have to call a policeman," the man's words burst closer, "If you won't let me help. And tell him you're sick."

Time to swivel and head for home. The man probably would call a policeman. Dent's hearing was going and the sound color transformation was blurring the street. He was almost beaten.

He felt tears of impotence begin and wiped them away quickly with the back of his hand. Never show fear before the troops. The man spoke to him again through purple roars. Dent heard the word "policeman" again; and "for your own good."

With infinite difficulty, the pull of gravity overwhelming against his suddenly shrunken self, he forced his tank to begin its turn. "Zzzzrrrruuuummmm." He pivoted on the left track and headed for home.

"You are sick, sir; stop those noises." He heard the man briefly, then all was battle roar, though the man's lips kept moving.

He doesn't know I'm a tank, I've that advantage, thought Dent.

He was before the door of his building now. He pivoted the tank, went into reverse, and reached for his key.

The man pushed through the door at the same moment as Dent, almost knocking him over. The jar and rasp of their clothes coming together set off rough sandpaper sheets of reddish-brown fire that raged about Dent in the corridor.

The man was inside. He was lost.

The man was talking again. Dent saw little opaque balloons, like those emitted by comic-strip characters, coming from his mouth. But the only word he heard was "gentleman."

What he had to do was get the man to go up the stairs in front of him. He couldn't let himself be grabbed in the engine compartment, that was the tank's soft end. He reversed again; backed the tank against the wall, smiled at the man; and bowed toward the stairs.

The man started upstairs. Dent down-shifted and started up after him in low gear, his tracks clanking. If the man pulled a knife on him he could at least run. Mrs. Marsalla's door was closed. But then a tank could never ask for help.

Now they were at the top landing, his own floor, and the man had grown enormous. From a great distance some sound squeaked out into his ears. "A studio. You are an artist. I knew it. Let me open the door for you."

Dent took out his keys again and slewed the tank sideways before his studio door. The key turned. Carefully he took it from the door and put it in his pocket.

Now.

With a roar he slammed the tank into first and swung the gun tube on the man, pressing the firing solenoid of his palm hard into the enemy face. The man staggered backward. Dent reversed through the studio door.

He grabbed the door and swung it to as the man started toward him. The man's hand and the studio door shifted to slow motion. Which would win? The door slammed shut in a burst of purple splashes, the police lock falling into place. Dent collapsed panting on his studio floor.

Later he sat coiled in his corner considering his present war. He'd won, made it to the bank and back with a horde of ten dollar bills; but he had also lost. His feeling of hopeless terror had increased. It might take several days before he could do any work on *The Accountant*. And going out to shop was certainly beyond him for some time, tank or no tank. Suppose Sarah barged in and found him this way, she'd get everything out of him she wanted.

He forced himself to face a question he'd been dodging for some time. Should he find a psychiatrist and get help? But as he asked the question he knew he had already answered it. All his life he had held the keep of himself against everyone. He was not going to admit someone else into that world, especially now that he was open and vulnerable, like a shell-less lobster, with a new self forming. If he got help from another person he felt he would be in part their creature; like taking money from a lobbyist, you might think that you could do it with impunity; but the hook remained.

Then he remembered his friends. He had to admit weakness, use them, or go under. He rocked in the corner a long time, gathering his courage, then after several false starts and two misdialings he finally got Dee.

She was at his door almost immediately.

"Why didn't you tell me before, George?"

"It's hard enough to tell you now."

"I knew there was something wrong. The way you looked in class. That's why I kept on asking you over for dinner. But you kept saying 'no.' "

"I was terrified of going deaf and being laughed at by you."

"Do you want me to stay through tonight?"

"No, no. I can make it through the night. I never had any trouble sleeping in combat. It's going outside; and writing letters; and phoning; and these damn numbers. And just when I'd begun to paint."

"I can believe that, George. This woman," she was standing before the portrait of Mrs. Marsalla, "that's the best work I've ever seen you do. I don't know about this man made of numbers."

"Thank you. You know, if you could get me some of Turkey's instrument charts and that book on blind flying he showed us last time we went out. I've got an idea for a portrait."

She took him shopping, chatting gaily at him so no one would know he was deaf, which he was most of the time. He should have thought of Dee earlier. She was better protection than a tank. Now he'd called her, it seemed so easy. They took his mail over to her studio and she made out checks to pay a great pile of his bills.

"You're lucky you're not in jail, George."

"Don't."

He risked the first drink he'd allowed himself since the day he burned his canvases and had the final fight with Sarah.

Dee walked him back to his studio.

"Why are you doing this for me?"

"You need me, George."

"I never did much for you."

"Perhaps I never asked."

They walked in silence a ways.

"What month is it?"

"July."

"July! No wonder I was dressed wrong at the bank. When we get home, would you make a long distance call to Wyoming for me? I don't think I could manage that. Not the first time."

It was an expensive phone call. He and Wup-'em talked a long while.

"Any time you want to visit, old hoss, any time. I'll fly East and get you. We got the best trout fishin' in the world."

"It's the air."

"Damn right. And keep callin' me. I'll always leave a number where I can be reached."

"Thank you, Wup-'em."

He called Wup-'em a lot. If he missed two days Wup-'em would telegraph. It was after a call to Wup-'em that he solved his second repeater, old lucky Seven. He was relaxed in his corner, watching the die of Seven roll down upon him time after time, and the four spots move past him, while he wondered what the repeater was trying to say about himself as a boy of Seven. Suddenly the sentence formed in his mind: "When I was seven I was twenty-five." What did that mean? He was at war when he was twenty-five. He and Wup-'em had just been talking about the war. Then with a cry he seized the end of the thread leading from the labyrinth.

When he was Blue Seven, battalion executive, right before he was hit, he had been twenty-five. And he used to say when a tank was shot from beneath him, or he got a bullet through the collar of his coat, or he had just ducked in time, "Four strikes and you're out. I haven't just had three strikes, I've had four."

He'd been lucky. He'd been hit twice but he'd lived. So here was lucky Seven coming up Four, with himself safe after four strikes. I'd never make it through life without luck, he thought, the rolling die of Seven. He felt elated at having solved another repeater; and called Dee to report his triumph.

He finished *The Accountant,* a failure of a painting. The only way he could finally get the human figure and the numbers to fuse was by optical tricks. There was no tension or resolution in the portrait; it remained merely an interesting intellectual exercise.

His anxieties about his work rekindled. Getting up in the morning, cooking, cleaning his brushes, drawing numbers to increase his control over them, sketching, everything was an effort. Earlier and earlier in the day he found himself compressed by fear, backed into his corner to rest and refuel.

Yet slowly, in spite of the pressures, by pacing himself and by making deliberately false starts to test himself, he began to produce a major picture: *The Instrument Pilot,* the face of a man created by the signs and symbols of the instrument flight charts and the gauges of an airplane's instrument panel. The basic flight instrument, the attitude indicator, gave cohesion to the center of the face, forming the nose and mouth. Round omni beacons off the charts made up the eyes, while delicate shadings and groupings of the omni radials, shadow boxes, low frequency homers, ILS corridors, and marker beacons outlined the face's contours. In the end he had a face both human, yet mechanical, the face of a man dedicated to a lifetime of checkpoints, speed, altitudes, gauges, frequencies, exactness; a man of risks and limits, a man he loved.

He had kept the picture covered while he worked on it. Completed, he sprung it on Dee.

"Dent, you've done it."

He took a deep breath. "I hoped it was good."

She gripped his arm, saying nothing.

"I missed in certain parts of it. I've got about a hundred new ideas. You know I've been outside without you a couple of times. Not to shop, just walking."

That afternoon in the supermarket he heard her all the time. He couldn't quite hear the checkout clerk or read the total on the cash register; but when Dee said, "It's nine eighty-two, George," she came through loud and clear.

Twelve blocks from his studio the government in all its glory and wisdom had torn down a block of badly needed lower-middle-income housing and was erecting a new Federal Office Building and Post Office. Work for the building trades, pensions for the union leaders, jobs for the party faithful; and as for the dispossessed members of the lower middle class, screw them; they were unorganized and voted Democratic anyway.

He and Dee had walked twice to the building site; and as *The Instrument Pilot* neared completion he discovered he could make it there and back by himself, though for the first time he went as a tank. The construction held a good deal of terror for him, not merely the loud sounds that would suddenly flame to color, but the situation itself reminded him he was powerless. While he sat there sketching he could see the padded work crews, the stealing, the union officials playing poker, the city inspectors getting payoffs. Some crook was making millions off this job and he could do nothing about it.

In the end he got so furious he was able to drop a note to Red Donner, who was on the Public Works Committee of the House.

"We know, Old Honesty," Red wrote back. "But that building is going up in New York City. I'm glad to hear there's actually a hole in the ground. Here in the Committee we'd heard they were paying off without even bothering to dig.

"How are you? And how are the girls? Is it true that painters have to double-lock the door to sleep alone? Drop by and see us. There're a few of us fool enough to miss you. You haven't missed a damn thing this session besides my winning at handball."

He held the letter in his hand thinking, I lived in that world and I miss it. But when I was there, I missed being here; only I didn't know it. Where I am now isn't everything I want either. If only I could combine both worlds.

His sketches of the construction site had produced his next painting idea: *The Surveyor*. Deliberately he kept the picture fluid, not wanting to set its form too soon and so lose some fragment of insight, or burst of energy. As he sketched he considered hosts of approaches to the idea, filling his drawing books with tractors, beam lines, men waving, hard hats, explosions, sight lines, transits, fills, excavations, blueprints, engineer boots, plane tables, eyepieces, poles, drills. These all jammed and squeezed together inside him creating such tension that he knew he would soon have to let them stream onto the canvas. Of course he might have tamped together too many bits and pieces; then the explosion would tear the painting apart. He had to balance size and energy against order, to control the conflict between these three.

Perhaps he'd do the face of the surveyor full front center, looking over his transit, with everything else small and reverse image as if seen through the transit eyepiece lined up like blueprints. Or he might elongate the surveyor, stick him askew in the upper right hand corner, while centering the picture's force lines on the pit, with the block as it was before, lower left; and at the bottom the mess the surveyor had created with his own order. Or he could put the top of the surveyor's hard hat and scope prick upright in the center, with wrecking balls, bulldozers, dynamite blasts, and rising beams all exploding out of the transit's sight lines toward the frame.

He sat on the side of the excavation, drawing fast now, enjoying his ability to distort the world through the merest change of line. He did a quick sketch attaching the surveyor's eye to his transit to make him the animal of precision, and he curled the men with measuring tapes like the spools into which their tapes reeled.

On the far side of the excavation, where the pit was propped up to prevent the surrounding tenements from sliding into the hole, an assistant engineer climbed the sides to steady a surveyor's stave with its red, white, and black stripes. Dent shifted position to draw him. The assistant wore Oxfords, not work boots, Dent realized, because he had to prove he was an engineer, not just a working stiff. The surveyor knew he was an engineer, so he wore work boots. Dent laughed, and gave the stave-holder a wing collar.

One day he got up feeling strong enough to probe at the mystery of number One: the dark cloud of terror with squidlike arms. He sensed, as an animal responds to its craving for salt, that somewhere within the almost recognizable black repeater was hidden a key to the anxiety that still burdened him. The solutions to Seven and Three had taught him he could not attack One directly, but had to sneak up from behind. "Grab 'em by the nose and kick 'em in the ass," they had quoted Patton at tank school.

But nowhere in the murky image of One could he find a nose to grab. And the number fought back; always lurking at the edge of his mind so he could not concentrate on his work. He might be trying to paint *The Surveyor,* shaping and reshaping, but his thoughts kept being drawn toward repeater One, like a child who is told to leave something alone, and tries to obey, but knows in the end it will reach out to touch.

As he got closer to the center of the number he noticed several times that his legs began to itch; not his face, as was usual, but his legs. They chafed as if sand were being constantly rubbed against them. The only time he could have had sand around his legs so unpleasantly was when he was very little indeed, smaller than monkey Three, and forced to wear leggings at the beach.

His escape from leggings was his earliest remembered victory.

Looking for an avenue into repeater One, he considered the legging revolt to draw himself back into the past. First he had to challenge the authority of his nurse. He had done this, since she never listened, by sitting down on the beach and starting to take off his leggings. He had been punished by being picked up by the ear, shamed before the friend he was playing with, and taken home early. After a few days he carried the battle to his mother. She ruled against him. He'd seen that coming. Mother backed the nurse the way he later backed his sergeants. He told his mother he wished to appeal to his father.

"I don't think that's wise, George. He may want you to wear ear muffs also."

"Yes, Mother."

His father, as befits the highest court, took the case under advisement.

"George, how many other boys your age wear leggings at the beach?"

"None, Daddy." He'd maneuvered to get asked that question.

"Are you telling me the truth?"

"Yes, sir."

"I'll look, you know."

He knew. "There are no other boys my age on our beach."

"We're not talking about the public beach."

"No, sir."

"Your mother and I will talk about it."

A dangerous answer.

Two nights later, having said his prayers, he lay on his back in bed, watching the crack of light beneath his door, waiting for his father and mother to come and kiss him good night. Tonight his father came in alone. His father's face bending down with the light behind looked like a gigantic clam shovel coming closer to swallow him.

"George." The prisoner at the bar will stand.

"Yes, Father."

"I looked at the Valley Brook Beach. You are right. Boys even smaller than you are not wearing leggings. Your mother says you will catch cold without them. But I feel we should leave them off and see what happens."

"Have you told nurse?"

He felt no joy of victory; merely the knowledge there would be some other fight tomorrow.

"I will tell her on my way down to dinner."

Nurse made him take two teaspoonfuls of cod liver oil before breakfast instead of one. "Now that we aren't wearing leggings we have to be more careful of colds." He threw up on nurse. That stopped that.

If he was still wearing leggings in the sand he would be playing where the breakwater at the end of their beach lost itself in the bushes above the high water. Here the breakwater was really just a small wall two or three stones high. Suddenly the terror of repeater One was all about him. On the far side of the breakwater he heard the crows. He could not see them, just as he had never been able to see them; but he could hear them going "squinch" on the sand as they stalked him. He knew the crows were gigantic, black, and powerful beyond comprehension. Their cawing had solid substance, he gasped, just like the sounds he saw as colors today. He would cower behind the breakwater waiting for the black cawing to flow over the wall, wrap around his huddled smallness, and trap him. Then he would be pinned down, netted in their cawing, while they rose slow over the wall with their pulsing necks and great orange beaks to eat him. His only chance was to crouch close to the breakwater, on one of the rock corners, so their cawing would flow over the rocks, missing him, and slowly soak into the sand.

When the cawing stopped it was even worse. For he knew then they had smelled him and were coming.

The black feelers of repeater One held the crow terror: the primordial dark.

Why, he wondered, had he been so powerless before the crows? The breakwater so necessary? He could have picked up a stone. He could have yelled. Fought them back with a stick.

Then the answer burst over him like an explosion: I gave the crows their strength. They were ordinary birds. I made them huge and powerful. I took the evil I believed in me, the lack of worth, and moved it across the breakwater to make my own terror. I could not stone the crows because they were part of me. We are one.

He saw the numeral One, straight and red like the number of the First Division insignia, blazing at him from the darkness. His terror began to ebb, and the blackness faded.

For a few days he hoped that having seen the truth of repeater One his world would decisively change, like Paul's on the road to Damascus. But his anxieties and their symptoms did not vanish.

Then he realized that the edge of madness was much like combat; and like combat almost impossible to describe to someone who had never been there. Because the unbelievable occurring every day became as monotonous as the nine-to-five life of any commuter. After a time death and terror seemed natural, the only world madman and soldier knew. A new recruit cowered in his hole. A reporter who had only visited the front was horrified; but proved his cool by using the old, exalted terms: slaughter, courage, carnage, fellowship, death, horror. While the veteran, for whom the battlefield was his natural habitat, made coffee because he was cold. The length of time, the inability to escape fear, were the vital core of the experience. Raw recruit and veteran lived on the same battlefield, subject to the same pressures; but the latter had learned to adjust and cope.

Dent painted on, gaining the techniques of survival. He had believed that "art" would be a privileged world for him, that when he switched professions his life would automatically improve. It had been a ridiculous belief. He had merely moved to a new place. He saw his past from a different angle: *Birches over Ice* loomed more important, his combat record less. To be an artist was no better than to be a Congressman or a plumber or pilot. The question was how the world fit round the man and the man around himself.

All his life when he had looked at himself in the mirror he had wondered who was the face looking back at him. That's why he'd been so fascinated by self-portraits, not knowing himself, he needed a record of where he'd been. The face in the mirror was a stranger. His next self-portrait would record someone he knew.

He finished *The Surveyor* and began work on the self-portrait, painting himself nude with the edges of his body dissolving into the background. While he was concentrating hard one morning, his doorbell interrupted him and he jumped. Two interruptions in a week, he thought, this place is getting to be like Times Square. He yanked open his door.

It was a telegram: "Decree ratified this morning. Sarah Frost Dent." —Always wrote a good telegram, Sarah did.

The delivery boy stood there.

"Any answer, sir?"

"No."

He felt nothing. An official announcement about how the world regarded his marriage did not touch himself and Sarah.

The day the war ended he had been in a wheelchair on Ward D-2, Officers, Major Surgery. He and his fellow patients had listened over the radio to the sounds of America yelling it up. For them the day was meaningless; their war was already over, their friends already dead. Just as his marriage was already over.

He had spent ten months of his life encased in thirty-two tons of steel trying to mutilate and kill other men before they killed him. He had spent ten years in marriage building a life for Sarah and the children with love, restraint, and joy. Now he had almost nothing. This telegram, like his honorable discharge, was a memento without meaning.

He finished the self-portrait. Another winter came. He began a second *Instrumental Pilot* bringing his new skill and self-awareness to the picture. He risked a trip to Washington to see Jane, ruining the meeting by trying to cram too much into too short a time. Back in New York, he finished the second *Instrument Pilot,* and started sketching for his next big project: a study of five figures outlined against a black background, titled : *Tanker's Last Supper*. The men faced front, strong and individual, outlined almost like icons; yet bent, distorted and huddled, lonely in the knowledge of what they shared; and behind them the black shape of fear, the bulk of a tank at night.

What he wanted in the picture was tension, and the crippling knowledge that the world was glued together backwards—as the Greeks had seen, as the Eddic bards had seen. Hector was dead, Tyr's hand eaten by the Wolf, Iphegenia sacrificed, Agamemnon stabbed, Costa burned alive, McQuade hit. Balder the Good murdered by mistletoe. Jim dead. Jim dead. Often he cried so hard at his easel he would have to go over and crouch in his corner, something he had not done for months.

He was lucky he thought he was painting well, because when Kate and the gallery owner came down to see his new work they gave him an emphatic "no."

"Not what we want at all, Mr. Dent. Remember, it's your abstracts and satires of Washington that sold."

"I'm afraid you're trying to be an artist," said Kate.

He called up Dee with the bad news.

"What can I do, Dee? I can take it for a little while. But I want to get my work seen and bought somehow."

"Use your friends."

He suddenly realized that except for Dee, some members of the art class, and a few models, no one had been in his studio for over a year.

He and Dee gave a dinner in his studio for another couple, friends of hers, and the Wollenbergs. He had a great deal of emotional trouble planning and preparing the dinner, because the ritual of giving a party caused so many memories of his past to surface and contrast with his dubious present life. However, when Dee asked him if he'd like her to do some of the shopping he was able to say no, he could do it himself, though he could only buy a few items each time he went out.

"George, you make a superb martini," said Mr. Wollenberg.

"That's what I was always afraid of, Benjamin. My epitaph—

'He was a nice guy and he made a good martini.' Portrait of a Yale man."

"There are two or three excellent pictures here, George, and some worth-while failures. Do you realize that?"

"I hope so; but I'm too close to tell."

"That *Tanker's Last Supper* is a strong and disturbing canvas. I could never own it. You understand why. —You know you'll have trouble selling these, George. They are not what people are buying, or museums."

"I know."

"Possibly *The Surveyor*. I have a friend buying for the Chicago Art Museum. Can I send him round?"

"Certainly."

"And my wife and I would like to buy the second *Instrument Pilot*."

"Benjamin, you don't have to."

"We've missed you, George."

Wollenberg's friend from the Chicago Art Museum came: young, bearded, intense.

"Benjamin told you you'd have trouble selling these canvases, didn't he?" the man asked. Dent had the buyer's name written down, but even with that aid he'd forgotten it.

"Yes," he said.

"I could never get this *Tanker's Last Supper* by my Trustees. Not modern. I'm not even sure myself. Was the war like that?"

"To me."

The man sat down and stared at the canvases for some time. Dent felt all the anxieties of election night.

"How much do you want for *The Surveyor?*" the man asked.

"Six thousand dollars." Wollenberg, Dee, and her friends had agreed on that as a fair price.

"Done."

He was elated but wise enough not to let the elation grow. It might be a long time before he sold another painting. But with a canvas in the Chicago Art Museum he'd at least be able to get a new gallery.

He walked down Fifth Avenue girl-watching. He spent so much time at it that he was even planning a canvas called *The Girl-Watcher*. He felt ridiculous, knowing he should be back in his studio working, but the afternoon was shot anyway. He'd had lunch uptown with three old lawyer friends who wanted to learn how he was making out, and were ready, he suspected, to offer him a job if he was willing to throw in the sponge. Not a good job, he'd strayed a bit too far off the reservation for that, but something to help old George out. His anger at their unconscious assumptions of superiority still rumbled inside him as he walked down the street.

He eyed the syncopated walk of a tall redhead on the sidewalk in front of him. How do I ever get a sidewalk to jive like that? The blast of an automobile horn hit him. He jumped. The light's red, you clown! What a way to go. Hit by a cab while watching girls. Dent, you're not going to live to grow up to be a filthy old man. He smiled, thinking how he used to have every second of his time budgeted.

Here came a pregnant girl: large, blonde, with good teeth well displayed, guided by an intense, tough man. Because he didn't see many pregnant girls on Fifth Avenue, he looked closely at the couple.

"Frank! Frank Catenberry."

"George Dent," Catenberry grabbed Dent by the hand.

I haven't seen Catenberry in years, Dent thought. No, just under two years.

"This is Jane, my wife," Catenberry continued. "You remember her, George, she was Senator Rogers's daughter. Hon"—Catenberry banked toward his wife—"George Dent was one of the first men in Congress to really understand about missiles. You've heard me talk about him. You remember, I was lucky enough to find him on that little boat."

"Yes," said Dent.

"Oh yes," said Jane.

"You look great, Frank, how's it going?"

"Just fine, George. As a matter of fact, we're celebrating."

"You're not a major general now."

"Ha ha, I've been that about two months. But we've just heard, Jane and I, that I've landed the Vice Chief of Air Mission, Vietnam slot. That's a lieutenant general's job. 'Course, I may mess it up."

"We're going to Bonwit's," said Mrs. Catenberry blissfully.

He's all smile and confidence, thought Dent, handling us both. Jane is going to stay behind as liaison with Daddy and the Senate. Frank will get back on leave to see the child born and perhaps a quick inspection trip two months later to get her pregnant again. In the meantime flying, another promotion, and those delicious Vietnamese girls. Dent, you got on the wrong escalator.

"You miss Congress, George?"

"Sometimes a great deal. But I don't miss what I had to put up with to stay there. And I enjoy painting." (Catenberry almost winced.) "How are Red and Wup-'em?"

"Mr. Donner and Mr. Wilson are just fine, George."

And they're Mr. Donner and Mr. Wilson, thought Dent.

"Good to see you, George, but we've got to take off. Tight schedule."

"Nice to see you, Jane. Tell you what, Frank, when you get to be Chief of Staff, I'll paint your portrait."

"You got yourself a deal. So long, George."

"So long, Frank."

Catenberry spun his wife and moved off. Watching him walk away Dent recognized his own old pace of controlled purpose. He did miss the power, the movement, the can-do of Congress. If only he could get his life more in balance.

Two months before, in early spring, he had spent a week with friends in Connecticut. He was considering a picture built around his childhood crows and he wanted to sketch the birds. The planned picture had never worked, though he did a couple of vicious small studies of crows pecking at carrion. That brief period in the country had triggered in him a need to get out of New York. He wanted to do landscapes, even though that might mean an additional period of exploration and experiment with nothing selling.

There were two problems. The first was money. How was he going to swing getting to the country, keeping the studio, paying his alimony, and also taking his daughter for his allotted month? Then there was the problem of where he should go. What sort of country did he belong in?

He was certain he didn't want to go abroad. His ecology was as American as Constable's had been English. Connecticut or Massachusetts, the two close, obvious choices, were too ordered, and would not fit him, and neither would the flat plains of the Midwest, for the same reason. Nor did he feel grand enough or stable enough for big mountains.

Thinking it over while working on *The Girl-Watcher,* he reached the conclusion that his country must be the abrupt, disturbed beginnings of the land: the badlands, the glacial moraines, the devil's clefts, the sea-rock ledges, the dead swamps. I'm outside what is already formed, he thought, outside the set order of beach, plain, mountain. I need to paint power, change, and violence! A bunch of mean foothills humping to make a mountain. A group of bagmen, my people, scheming to make a President.

The nearest hard-edged land was the Maine coast. He went to the library and got out picture books and guides to Maine. He brewed up fish-base glues and used poster paints to build up the brightness of blue tempera waves and harsh rock. He knew what he was doing: forcing himself out of New York, driving himself to travel, to accept the fresh risk and produce the promised landscapes. The physical background had been the weakest portion of *The Surveyor.*

He was reading the WPA guidebook about Maine and day dreaming when the doorbell went off. He pushed his buzzer and listened to some heavy-footed asshole who had to use the banister as he climbed up the stairs. Then the intruder's sprung rhythm registered.

"Wup-'em!"

"Hullo, old hoss." The grin peered up the stairs. "Glad to see you live high enough up to keep in shape."

"Christ, it's great to see you. Why didn't you phone me?"

"Why don't you answer your phone?"

"That's right. I shoved a paper clip in the bell yesterday. I've forgotten to take it out."

"Wish I could do that." Wup-'em entered the studio and looked around. "Wow!" He stared at *Tanker's Last Supper*. "That the way you paint, Dent?"

"When I'm painting well."

"That's the way it was. Not the way we remember it. Or how them shits that weren't there tell us."

"Thank you. Would you like it?"

"Shute, Dent. I never bought a picture in my life."

"No, I'll give it to you. You've just got to promise to hang it somewhere."

"Right in my office. Show 'em we got culture in Wyomin'." Wup-'em eddied about the rest of the studio. "You got something against crows?"

"At the time."

"Real farmer. —You sellin' much?"

"A little. One to a museum."

"Happy?"

"More days than before."

"I'm glad you're not paintin' that abstract stuff."

"Wup-'em, you know me. Was I ever abstract?—How about a beer?"

"Why not? Say, this is a comfortable chair." Wup-'em layered himself into a large wingback Dee had given him for Christmas. "Dent, boy, I'm glad to see you living so well. You ever miss us down there in the eye of the storm?"

"Very much. Some of the people in my old district too. It's lonely. It's also not as perfect as I thought it would be. What brings you up here?"

"The usual. Some defense contractor trying to explain why he sells an engine part to civilians for one thousand and to the Air Force for six thousand. —He even paints them the same."

"Nothing much changed, huh?"

"Gotten worse; but not changed." Wup-'em paused and looked at Dent, then at the pictures on the studio walls. Dent felt a sudden tension. "Old hoss, I got a proposition. You know Red Donner is on the Public Works Committee."

Dent nodded.

"Wyomin' is finally gettin' the six new post offices the East's been chiseling us out of for so long. I tell you, Dent, I was gettin' mad. They claim we don't need 'em because we don't have the people. Did they ever try drivin' fifty miles both ways through a blizzard in a pickup truck, because maybe today you'll hear from the kid in Vietnam? However, that battle's over. We got 'em. Now these post offices are going to have big murals on 'em, hell, in 'em for all I know, about life in Wyomin'. Three of the six are going to be painted by native Wyomin' artists. The best in the world, naturally."

"Naturally, Wup-'em, it's in the air."

"You should see the shit they paint. Now, the other three are to be painted by an artist of outstandin' national stature acceptable to the people of Wyomin'. That's what the Act of Congress says. And the people of Wyomin', havin' their head wedged, have chosen you."

"Wup-'em, I haven't got national stature."

"Are you insulting the voters of my state?"

"Never . . . but I . . ."

"Would you like the job?"

The square boxes of Wyoming post offices blazed around him, holding their own in the middle of the lonely American plains. They'd have walls, bare walls he could fill with shapes, forms, colors, and maybe even some crows by the world's greatest crow painter. The whole goddamn American shooting match with its infinite glory and total depression.

"I'd love it."

It was probably no crazier than the way Rembrandt got his

first commission. And his work would be there, and be seen. In a big space he had some strengths going for him that others didn't. If I can sharpen my inner vision, he thought, and get it all down: railroads, robber barons, Chinese laborers, Indians, pioneers, wolves, conservationists, cars, range wars, badlands, factories, and people, endless people shapes colliding across the grass.

"Good," said Wup-'em. "We got sixteen thousand dollars to do the three Post Offices. That okay?"

It wasn't much. There was a good two years' work there. But he could probably sell a few canvases locally.

"That's low for two years' work, Wup-'em. But thanks. It's a deal. Now, how about dinner. Bend my ear on the Bay of Pigs."

The first post office would not be built till late fall. He had all summer to work on landscapes and get ready for those walls. He bought a second-hand camper, found a cheap garage for it in the Bronx; and ripped out most of the insides to make a studio and a bed. He cut two holes in the roof and capped them with plexiglass bomber noses from a surplus store. All those wonderful bombers built and scrapped, he laughed, just to give me north light. Now I've got a mobile studio and a place to live. He hung the Beckman and the nude of Helen along the windowless wall. —Come on, Sarah, and remarry—I need the money. And what would she think about Jane sleeping in the camper? He could probably find a cabin for August somewhere in Maine.

On the side of the camper, just back of the truck door, he painted several swordfish and bass, reasoning that the police would stop a crazy artist in a camper and give him a hard time, but would wave to an enthusiastic fisherman and wish him luck. The fish looked so good he added a lush mermaid underneath.

On departure day, Dee cooked him a farewell breakfast.

"You're really going, Dent. Two years."

"Oh, I'll be back before that. Probably this fall, between Maine and Wyoming. That's why I'm keeping the studio. I need one home. The studio's it; all the old familiar cracks."

"George, do you think we'll get together again? I mean really together, in bed?"

"I don't know. I've wondered. We certainly meshed at one time. I'm not sure how I'm going to live."

He looked at Dee, her body, outlined beneath the shirt and skirt, that he could feel against himself, all her lonely female strength, and weakness. She was dyeing her hair a darker shade of red now, she'd had the mole beneath her right ear removed, and she had on a new pair of sneakers.

I've been looking inward too intensely, he thought. I do need people.

They walked from Dee's studio toward the subway. Just before the entrance he put down his suitcase and paint box and kissed her. Dee watched him walk toward the stairs: blue denim shirt, khaki pants, sports jacket with leather elbow patches.

Mark him well, Deirdre McTurk, she thought, there goes the man you could have married. Was I wise? Who's going to have me when I get old and wrinkled and puckered up from tension and living alone? Did he notice my new hair color? But two artists in one family. Two egos waltzing through two studios; edgy over who paints best. And pretty soon male artist has female artist sewing on his buttons, cleaning his brushes, and doing all the cooking. Is that such a bad life? I don't know; but it's not for me.

Would it have to be that way? If he came back would I want him? Not just the sex: but him, every day? —Look at this old blouse I'm wearing. I've got that blue silk one that fits me close and teases a bit. But I wore this, like some sloppy adolescent. You're a fool, Dee McTurk, a black Irish fool with no sense! Oh, he's waving.

Dent waved, then turned down into the subway. His eye caught the station sign: "West Fourth." For an instant a die rolled out of the sign toward him, showing four orange spots with a tiger face behind. Then it left. That was old son-of-a-bitch Four, part wild number, part repeater. How far away that battle was: like Jim, combat, Congress, the air crash, Helen, St. Lukes, Sarah, his father; and how close.

What a way to begin. To start west by going north on a subway to pick up a homemade studio that rode on a secondhand truck. I am here. On this platform. Among the stale stink, the twitching people, the spit on the concrete, the graffiti, the ugly ads, the noise, the threat.

The train roared in. Powerful, lean, cheap, alive, quick, glorious, New York, American.

Mine, he thought.

Mine.